In the world of international espionage
and global terror,
treachery is the name of the game.

P9-CCV-414

"A HIGHLY SUSPENSEFUL PAGE-TURNER."
Brian Garfield, author of *Death Wish*

ANDREW KAPLAN
SCORPION BETRAYAL

"Do this: Read the first two pages of *Scorpion Betrayal* right now. See what I mean? It just gets better from there. Kaplan has written one of the smartest, swiftest and most compelling spy novels I've read in years."

Harlan Coben, author of *Live Wire*

"Wow! *Scorpion Betrayal*, with two brilliantly unique protagonists, delivers more heart-thumping twists and turns, beliefs and betrayals, than *The Day of the Jackal* and *The Spy Who Came in from the Cold* rolled into one. *Scorpion Betrayal* breaks the mold. As a penetrating and fascinating look into the dark underbelly of those tightly-interwoven worlds—global terrorism and international espionage—it is almost a textbook example of how to write a great thriller that today's readers will love."

Katherine Neville, author of *The Eight* and *The Fire*

"Andrew Kaplan is back with a vengeance in this lightning-swift tale of espionage that opens with a shocking assassination in a Cairo café and then races through the capitals of Europe as Scorpion—a legendary ex-CIA now freelance spy—runs his quarry to ground before it's too late. The authenticity is palpable. I love this novel. Andrew Kaplan represents a gold standard in thriller writing."

David Morrell, author of *The Brotherhood of the Rose*

"Andrew Kaplan has a masterful grasp of the inner workings of intelligence agencies and their fight against terror that he weaves through this suspenseful tale of espionage."

Reza Kahlili, author of *A Time to Betray: The Astonishing Double Life of a CIA Agent Inside the Revolutionary Guards of Iran*

"The ending is both logical and refreshingly unexpected. It's a great read, filled with fabulous facts and frequent flashes that are surprising, but completely believable. I hate to use the cliché, but it's true: I couldn't put it down!"

Brian Garfield, author of *Death Wish* and *Hopscotch*

And resounding praise for Andrew Kaplan's previous novels

"Superb and original."

Nelson DeMille

"Pure dynamite. . . . Espionage laced with high-voltage Middle East adventure."

Washington Times

"Kaplan takes the thriller genre at its word, moving as fast as Ludlum but with ten times the eye for settings and crisp characterization."

Kirkus Reviews

"Kaplan, with the surehandedness of a pro, knows well the underbelly business of spycraft."

Gerald Browne, author of *Stone 588*

"In a word, *terrific*. . . . The pace is blistering, the atmosphere menacing and decadent, and author Andrew Kaplan is in marvelously smashing form."

New York Daily News

By Andrew Kaplan

ANDREW KAPLAN

SCORPION BETRAYAL

HARPER

An Imprint of HarperCollinsPublishers

HARPER

An Imprint of HarperCollins*Publishers*
10 East 53rd Street
New York, New York 10022-5299

Copyright © 2012 by Andrew Kaplan
ISBN 978-0-06-206458-5

First Harper premium printing: April 2012
First Harper special printing: October 2011

Visit Harper paperbacks on the World Wide Web at www.harpercollins.com

10 9 8 7 6 5 4 3 2 1

For Anne and Justin,
Who made it happen and made it better

SCORPION
BETRAYAL

CHAPTER ONE

Cairo, Egypt

He looks up from his coffee, careful not to make a move that would cause them to kill him. He has sensed a change, a faint electrical hum in the background sounds in the street, and at that moment the streetlights come on.

Normally, it is his favorite time of day. The evening hour after the Maghrib prayer, when the crowds spill out of the mosques and traffic on the al Kornish Road is a river of lights and all Cairo seems to catch its breath after the heat of the day. He is not alone. Sitting next to him at the outdoor table of the café is the Placeholder, a mustached Egyptian Secret Serviceman watching him, hand on his unbuttoned gun holster, though they had already frisked him twice for weapons. Three hard-faced Secret Servicemen watch from other tables. By their locations close to the street, he knows that within minutes they will be dead.

He sips the cardamom coffee, the Placeholder watching his every move. This is what he has lived for all these months. Everything magnified, almost too real: the electric blues and reds of scarves in the open-air shops of the Khan al Khalili, the smell of apple-tobacco smoke from the *shisha* hubble-bubbles of the older café patrons, the breathing of the Placeholder next to him. He looks away as a club-footed street vendor with a wicker tray hobbles around the corner and makes his way toward the café. The vendor squats on the cobblestones near the café, club foot twisted beneath him, and spreads his *farsha*: batteries, toothpaste, rubber shower shoes, the odds and ends of everyday life sold on every street corner in Cairo. He calculates the distance from the street vendor to the outer café tables with his eyes. It will be close, he thinks. Very close.

The Placeholder tenses beside him as a black Mercedes sedan approaches the café. He notices the Placeholder's mustache is trimmed more neatly on the left side of his face than the right. Left-handed; *haz wiheed*, bad luck for him, he thinks, as the Mercedes pulls up. An aide jumps out of the Mercedes and opens the door for a compact man in a dark suit.

There is a gasp as someone in the café recognizes General Budawi, head of the Mabahith Amn al-Dawla al Ulya, State Internal Security Intelligence, said to be the most feared man in Egypt. Whoever gasped had heard the rumors, the whispers at parties or in mosques frequented by government officials, of men and women screaming for months in underground cells. It was said that an imam of the Muslim Brotherhood clawed out his own eyes in madness after only a month in the cells of the Mabahith. He watches as Budawi makes his way between the tables and sits in the chair vacated by the Placeholder, who stands at his elbow. As soon as he sits, a waiter in a striped shirt appears as if out of thin air.

"*Shai*," the general orders, not bothering to look at the waiter. He takes in the man next to him. Slender, smooth-skinned, expensive white shirt and tan slacks, a gold Rolex on his wrist. Attractive to women, Budawi thinks, the type you run into at the pool at the Four Seasons on the West Bank of the Nile, surrounded by international models in bikinis while he does business on his cell phone.

"I know this café," Budawi says.

"They say it was a favorite of Mahfouz, the writer."

"They say that about every café in Cairo. If Mahfouz drank coffee in every café that claims him, his bladder would have exploded. You have something for me," Budawi says. It is not a question.

"A demonstration," he says, keeping his voice neutral, knowing it is being recorded somewhere, to make it more difficult to get a clean voiceprint over the noise of the café and the street. "Multiple demonstrations. Something they will not forget," he adds, starting the sequence he has practiced for weeks. He removes his left loafer and sock with the toes of his right foot, then with the toes of his left foot removes the right loafer and sock—and the scalpel taped with flesh-colored tape to the sole of his right foot.

"Where?" Budawi asks.

"*Lo samaht.*" Please. "We haven't discussed terms," he says. He has the scalpel between his toes and raises it to his right hand that he drops casually below the table.

"When?"

"Three weeks. Perhaps less." He has the scalpel in his hand, his heart racing.

"I'll need more than that."

"So will I," he says, his body tensing for the shock wave, ready to dive to the ground, thinking, *Dilwati! Don't wait!*

"Such as?"

"The two Brothers."

"Indeed?" The general puts an American cigarette to his lips, which the Placeholder leans over to light. "Those particular Muslim Brothers are assassins. Why should I release them?"

"The Americans and their allies will owe you a debt," he says, his hand tight on the scalpel.

Inshallah! Inshallah! God willing! Do it!

With a kind of relief, he sees the club-footed vendor turn to look at them, mouthing *Allahu akbar*. The general sees it too and starts to get up, the Placeholder reaching for his holster, but it is too late, the explosion deafening in the narrow street.

The shock wave, scorching hot and far more powerful than he had imagined, smashes them with incredible force, flinging them aside. Chairs, debris, fragments of metal and bits of human flesh and body parts fly past as he dives to the ground, burying the scalpel in the general's groin. The general screams once as he slices diagonally, cutting the femoral artery, bright spurts of blood instantly soaking the general's trousers.

Stunned, the general struggles to get up, but his strength is draining too quickly and he falls back, legs twitching feebly on the pavement. For an instant everything is silent, except for the thudding of dust and debris still raining down, and then the screams begin, though he can barely hear them, his ears ringing from the explosion.

He whirls to face the Placeholder, who is dazed and struggling to get his gun out of the holster. He kicks hard at the inside of the Placeholder's knee, and as the man starts to go down, slashes the scalpel across his throat in a single swipe. The Placeholder tries to speak, but only a bloody gurgle comes out as he topples over, his eyes not believing what has happened in just seconds as he falls to the ground.

Bending down beside the overturned table to retrieve his socks and shoes, he hears screams and the sound of people running. Straightening, he sees an elderly *shisha* smoker, face covered with soot and blood, staring at him with wide, stunned eyes. He nods at the smoker, gesturing, *Maashi*, everything is okay. He wipes his bloody hand on the general's jacket and stoops to put on his socks and shoes, slippery with blood. He knows he has only seconds before the police arrive as he wipes his hands again with the general's jacket and retrieves the Placeholder's gun from the ground.

Don't run, he tells himself, not looking at the *shisha* smoker as he makes his way to the street through the debris, the overturned tables and body parts. In the distance he hears the horns of police sirens and fire trucks blaring as they approach. He glances down at the *farsha* seller, but there is little left, only parts of his legs, scorched beyond recognition. He catches a glimpse of the first police sedan coming into the street as he ducks into the souk and turns down a narrow passageway he reconnoitered three days earlier. Inside the passageway, vendors and passersby have turned to stare in the direction of the blast and the sounds of the police sirens. He stops by a water vendor under an awning. The vendor looks at him wide-eyed, and he realizes there must be blood on his face and clothes.

"What has happened, *ya hader*?" the vendor asks.

"A terrorist attack. My hands, *shokran*," he says, holding his hands out. The vendor pours water over them and hands him a towel, which he uses to wipe some of the blood and dirt from his hands and face.

"You are hurt, *hader*?"

He shakes his head and washes again.

"*Ilhamdulilah*," the vendor says. Thanks to God. "Is it the Brotherhood?"

"Who can say?" he replies, handing the vendor twenty Egyptian pounds and keeping the towel.

"*Shokran, hader.* May Allah be with you," the vendor says.

"And you," he replies, already moving. He turns the corner into a narrow lane and enters a small men's clothing shop, light from the shop spilling into the street. The owner is of the Brotherhood and immediately motions him to the back, drawing a curtain to shield them from the street. He strips off his shirt and shoes, and the owner brings him a *gallabiya* and turban.

"How did it go?" the owner asks.

"Burn this," he says, handing him the bloody towel.

"Your blood?"

He shakes his head.

"Good," the owner says, and throws the bloody

towel into a metal bin. "The airports are closed. How will you get out of the city?"

He stares at the man. "Did I say I was leaving the city?"

"No, of course not," the owner stammers. "*Lo tismah*. Let me assist you with that," he says, coming over to help smooth the *gallabiya*.

He touches the back of the owner's head almost gently, then forces it down and slides the crook of his left arm under the man's neck, locking it at the wrist with his right hand in a guillotine choke hold, cutting off the flow of blood through the carotid artery to the brain. Pulling his left wrist up toward his shoulder with his right hand, he tightens the hold even more as the owner struggles, jerking and hitting him with his fists.

Within seconds the owner is unconscious. He holds on until certain the man is dead, then lets the body slump on the floor. Stepping over it, he moves to the mirror and arranges the turban. His forehead is smudged with dirt, but he leaves it that way, to look like a typical street porter or *farsha* seller, and slips the Rolex into his pocket. He pours lighter fluid from the cache of cigarettes behind the counter, which every shopkeeper in Egypt keeps for customers, over the bloody towel and then lights it. An acrid wet cloth smoke rises from the metal bin as he checks outside from the shop doorway. It is almost dark, the last traces of light barely visible, the humidity creating haloes around the lights dangling from the arched doorways of the souk.

* * *

Stepping outside the shop, he wove through the crowds of locals and tourists, a common street sight in his *gallabiya*, not drawing any attention. He stopped at a vegetable seller's stall, picked up an onion, tossed a fifty piastre coin to the seller and continued walking as he bit into the onion. The smell of it would dissuade people in the Metro from getting close to him, he thought, eating it quickly, his eyes tearing.

Hearing motion behind him, he moved to the side. Three policemen, riot guns at the ready, ran toward him. Heart pounding, he watched as they jogged past. As planned, he'd been almost invisible to them, an ordinary *arzuiya* day laborer who wanted no trouble with the authorities. He did not hurry, despite the fact that he had to get through quickly in case they shut the Metro down.

One of two Egyptian women in Western clothes and headscarves wrinkled her nose at the onion smell as he passed. Good, he thought as he crossed the avenue and joined the crowd headed toward the Metro station; she had seen him only as a smelly *arzuiya*.

He was now approaching the danger spot, the choke point. Spotlights had been set up, turning the area near the Metro entrance bright as a movie set. Three police riot vans blocked the street and dozens of helmeted riot police fanned out, forming a perimeter and scanning the crowds as they approached the Metro past the *farsha* sellers' tables on the sidewalk, the sellers calling, "Come and buy! Fresh juice! Come and look!" If he was going to be caught, it would be here, or later on, when he left Egypt. He had no illusions about what the Mukhabarat would do to him if he were captured. It was why he'd had to kill the store owner, whom he decided was either too curious or could not have withstood the torture cells.

He spotted one of the policemen, a young man, studying him as he approached the Metro stairs. But then the man's eyes moved on to a pretty young woman in a pink head scarf, who was being jostled and groped by a male office worker as she started down the stairs. The young policeman smiled and nudged the policeman next to him as the woman tried to move away in the crowd.

The subway platform was packed with commuters, the women moving toward the center, where the women-only cars would stop. Next to him, two men were talking about the attack at the café, and he felt a shiver of joy as they blamed it on the Israelis.

"What can you expect from the Israelis? They don't care who they kill," one of them said. "Women, children. It makes no difference."

"It's not just the Israelis. It's all the Jews. Have you read the *Protocols of Zion*? It opened my eyes. It's all documented," the other said, motioning him closer, their voices drowned by a rush of air and the sound of the train coming.

There was a surge on the platform as soon as the train stopped and the doors opened, men shoving to get out of the train against the rush of men pushing into the car. He squeezed in and checked the map. There were eight stops to Shobra, the working-class district where he had rented an apartment a week earlier. He glanced around. No one was looking at him. One or two office workers had sniffed and tried to move away from his onion smell, which was stronger than the omnipresent smell of sweat and cigarette smoke that permeated Cairo Metro trains.

At the next stop, riot police were deployed at intervals on the platform. He tensed as a policeman got on and began asking to see passengers' identity cards, the card every Egyptian carried, without which it was impossible to get services or shop in any of the state-run supermarkets. The policeman looked at each passenger's card one at a time and then at faces and hands.

As the policeman approached, he reached under the *gallabiya* and into his pants pocket, fingers touching the Placeholder's gun. He felt inside his wallet and retrieved the fake ID card supplied by the Brothers. It still looked too new for a poor *arzuiya* coming home from work, and he worried that it wouldn't hold up. He had tried to scuff and dirty it when he first got it, but it still looked fresh. With the policeman only a few passengers away, he cupped the fake ID in his left hand as his right closed on the Placeholder's gun. The policeman grabbed for a pole to keep from falling as the train pulled into the Road El-Farag station, then glanced at the remaining passengers as if suspicious of all of them. The doors opened and the policeman suddenly got off. He watched the policeman on the platform as more passengers got on. When the doors closed again, he realized he had stopped breathing.

At the last stop he exited the train and climbed the stairs. Night had fallen. The tables and trays of the *farsha* and food sellers clustered near the Metro exit were lit with kerosene lanterns. All at once, he was hungry. He bought a lamb shwarma grilled over coals and wrapped in *aysh* bread. As he ate, he tensed as an army jeep and a truck filled with soldiers passed. It was something rarely seen in this neighborhood.

"Have you heard of the bombing?" he asked the shwarma man.

"*Allahu akbar.* The government will find the killers," the man said.

"*Inshallah,*" he said. God willing.

He walked past apartment houses, their paint faded and cracked, laundry hanging from windows, and past a garbage-strewn lot where ragged boys played soccer by the light of a single streetlight. Was it his imagination or did the street seem emptier than usual? Just before he got to his building, he studied the street again, carefully. He saw no unmarked vans or cars with anyone sitting in them. No one loitering near one of the other buildings. No broken silhouettes on the rooflines, or street workers working late. Through some of the windows, he could see the glow of television sets.

Crossing to his building, he climbed the stairway. It smelled of poverty, *fuul*, and cigarettes. He opened his door and snapped into a shooter's position, ready to fire the Placeholder's gun, but the apartment was empty, the only light coming through the window from the streetlights outside. He went over and turned on the small TV.

The news announcer, a heavyset man with a slow, serious voice, reported that a number of suspects in the café bombing had already been rounded up.

General Budawi's photograph was displayed. According to a breathless reporter standing outside the Presidential Palace in Heliopolis, only Budawi, whose heroism and patriotism was esteemed by all, and a single aide were killed. In the meantime, air travelers could expect delays because of enhanced security following the attack.

The program then returned to a popular Egyptian soap opera, where the lead actress was suggestively approached by her doctor in his office while her husband was out of town on business with his attractive female assistant. On another channel, an attractive female TV newscaster in a head scarf said that authorities were looking for a foreigner suspected in the café bombing in the Khan al Khalili. He was described as being tall and fair-haired, she said. He shut the TV off.

They were downplaying the number of casualties and rounding up the usual suspects, he thought. Budawi's deputy was probably scrambling like crazy and under intense political pressure to pick up all the pieces. As for the description of him, it was of a generic foreigner. More important, they hadn't given the media a photograph. Budawi had probably assumed he would arrest him at the café and get all the photos he needed then. With any luck, all they had of him was a voiceprint. It was obvious they were watching the airports and looking for a foreigner matching his description heading north. That was what he had expected and planned for. Still, it wouldn't be easy. They would be watching every exit from Egypt.

He took a deep breath and wiped his forehead

with the sleeve of his *gallabiya*. He was still sweating. Next door, the neighbor's teenage son was playing Egyptian hip-hop music. The music echoed in the building and the empty street outside as he worked on bending and smudging the ID card and cleaning the gun and scalpel. He took a long shower, the water cool and rusty, and before he went to sleep he retaped the scalpel to the bottom of his foot.

He left the apartment shortly before dawn, the sky streaked with gold over the Nile. He took the East Delta bus from the Eltorgan bus station in the center of the city to the small port city of Hurghada some three hundred miles south on the Red Sea coast. Just before boarding the bus, he bought a live chicken at the open-air souk. The bus was stifling hot and when he glanced at a passenger's *Al Ahram*, the headline said only that the authorities were making progress in the bombing investigation.

At an army checkpoint ten kilometers outside Hurghada, two soldiers came on board and checked everyone's ID. They were looking for a foreigner; he could pass for a working-class Egyptian, he told himself, his heart pounding. His battered ID card and the chicken made them pay him little attention. They asked where he was going, and he said he was visiting his cousin in Hurghada. He hoped to work in a hotel there. The soldier shrugged and went on to the next passenger.

He traded the chicken for lunch in a worker's restaurant in Hurghada near the port and caught the ferry in the harbor to Sharm el Sheikh, the resort city at the southern tip of the Sinai peninsula. When the ferry landed, he went into a public bathroom stall and changed out of his *gallabiya* and turban into a "Rock for Africa" T-shirt, shorts, and sunglasses, more suited to the beach scene with its bikinis and Four Seasons and Starbucks cafés. At the beach at Naama Bay he connected with a pair of Danish backpackers. They went for drinks at the Camel, a rooftop bar where they were joined by a spectacular Swedish blonde who was, she said, a lingerie model in Sharm for the scuba diving "and the beautiful Arab men." She touched his forearm with her fingers and suggested they could see the sunset better from her room.

In the morning, he left her snoring on the bed and took the ferry to Aqaba in Jordan. There were army patrols by the ferry before he left Sharm el Sheikh, but they took one look at his backpack, sunburned face, and German passport and let him pass. By mid-afternoon he was sipping a Bloody Mary in the first class cabin of a Lufthansa flight from Amman to Frankfurt, leaving behind what was to become the most intensive manhunt in human history. Before it was over, it would nearly destroy the CIA and force everyone involved into the most terrible choice of their lives, including the American agent known only as Scorpion.

CHAPTER TWO

Karachi, Pakistan

The steel container hung high in the air as the gantry crane swung it over to a row of containers stacked four high on the dock. Two dockworkers shared a cigarette in its shadow, unconcerned as the container passed over their heads. They knew the standard twenty-foot TEU unit was at most fifteen tons, and that the big crane could easily handle three to four times that weight. The crane lowered the container neatly into the next position in the top row as though stacking Legos and swung back for another container.

Another man, clad like the dockworkers in an orange jumpsuit and hard hat, watched from the shadow of a tall reach-stacker machine. There was a scar over his right eye, and his gray eyes, unusual in this part of the world, focused not on the containers, but on the ship being unloaded. She was the *Bunga Seratai 6*, a mid-sized Malaysian-flagged container vessel bound next for Port Klang, south of Kuala Lumpur. Having berthed two hours earlier, the *Bunga Seratai 6* would leave before midnight, after unloading 370 containers and picking up 200 more.

That wasn't what bothered Scorpion as he watched, or why he'd waited more than an hour and still hadn't approached. Everything about the setup was wrong, last minute wrong. The RDV should've been in a safe house, like the one in the Korangi district. Instead he'd had to pick up an East Wharf stevedore's ID at the last minute from a drop in a pharmacy on 13th Street. There were only two possibilities: either it was a trap, in which case the network in Pakistan was blown and there was a good chance he was about to die. Or worse, something had gotten out of control and Langley was improvising, not what they were best at. Either way, the container ship was a potential red zone. For that matter, much of Karachi was a red zone. The city, one of the largest in the world and one of the biggest ports in South Asia, had become a haven for terrorists. They moved easily among the millions of Pushtuns and Taliban who had fled here from Pakistan's Northwest tribal regions and Afghanistan.

The heat was intense, the sun brilliant on the water in the harbor, and he had to squint against the glare. He sipped a can of Pakola orange soda, colored an alien green despite its name, as he quartered the ship, the dock, and the approaches to the gangway one last time. Everything appeared normal. The gantry crane was moving another container, gleaming in the hot sun, from the ship to the dock. Three loaders were working farther down the dock. The two dockworkers were walking toward their forklifts, the way clear except for a ship's crew member near the top of the gangway, resting a handheld scanner on the rail. No one was loitering or doing anything out of the ordinary.

Scorpion crumpled the can and tossed it in a trash bin. He walked across the wharf, climbed the gangway and stopped at the top to show his ID badge, which he had just gotten that morning. The crew member, a young Malay, checked his face against the photo on the ID, scanned the ID bar code, and let him aboard.

He opened a heavy outer door, closed it behind him, and instead of going down toward the hold as a dockworker might be expected to do, went up the stairs toward the crew deck. He studied a cross-section map of the ship posted near the compartment door, then went up another deck and entered the officers' and passenger deck quarters. At the last passenger cabin on the port side, he knocked twice and went in.

Bob Harris stood in a two-handed stance, pointing a Navy SEAL standard-issue SIG Sauer 9mm at his chest. He wore shorts and a T-shirt, one of the rare times Scorpion had ever seen him not in a suit.

"Put it away. You'll hurt yourself," he said.

"You're right. I haven't touched one of these since CST training." Harris nodded and put the gun down on the table in the small cabin.

Instead of sitting, Scorpion started checking the bulkheads and closet for bugs.

"It's clean," Harris said. "I had NSA Dubai sweep it twice, before and after I came on board last night."

Scorpion ignored him and continued checking the cabin, running his fingers along the edge of the windows and under all the ledges. Harris watched for a moment, then opened the small refrigerator under the TV counter, popped the tops on two Beck's and handed one to Scorpion. Then he turned on the MP3 player loud enough to drown out any possible eavesdropping with Bruce Springsteen.

The two men sat face-to-face, knees almost touching in the cramped quarters, and leaned close so they could whisper to each other. Harris tilted his bottle to Scorpion and swallowed. He's trying to do it by the book, Scorpion thought. Harris was the CIA's National Clandestine Service deputy director, and it had been years since he was in the field. For him to have flown halfway around the world to take a last minute meeting outside a safe house and try to act like an ops officer meant that all hell had broken loose.

"You've heard about the Budawi killing in Cairo?" Harris asked.

"There was something on the Pakistani TV. What about it?"

"Budawi was probably the most closely guarded man in Egypt, maybe one of the best guarded anywhere. His death has set off alarms in every capital in the world. The Egyptians locked up the entire country tighter than a gnat's asshole. They've sweated every informer they ever had—or will have at the rate they're going."

"And?"

"Nothing. Nada. They've come up empty. We've come up empty. MI-6, the BND, the Israelis . . ." Harris shrugged. "Nothing. Every intelligence service on earth's come up zero."

"Or so they say," Scorpion said carefully. The

last time he had worked with Harris was on the attempted coup in Arabia, and whatever there was between them, trust wasn't any part of it. The only time Harris ever told the truth, went the saying around Langley, was when he thought no one would believe him. "What's this about? You think the hitter's in Pakistan?"

"Listen," Harris said, touching an icon on his cell phone screen, then handed Scorpion a plug-in earpiece. "The second voice is General Budawi."

"A demonstration. Multiple demonstrations. Something they will not forget."

He heard a man speaking in an uninflected Fusha standard Arabic, not Egyptian or Iraqi or any particular country's accent. It was hard to hear. The bug wasn't close, and there was background noise and other indistinguishable conversations from the outdoor café and street sounds where the bombing had occurred.

"Where?" a second voice, Budawi's, said.

"Lo samaht." Please. *"We haven't discussed terms,"* the other man said, his neutral voice soft. He knew he was being recorded, Scorpion thought, and listened till the man said, *"The Americans and their allies will owe you a—"* The recording suddenly ended.

"Photos?" Scorpion said, looking up.

Harris shook his head. "It was a condition of the RDV. They wanted to hear what he had to say first."

"Really? Not even one? For the first time in history the Egyptian Mabahith kept their word?"

Harris grinned. "There was a partial the Mukhabarat retrieved from a piece of a cell phone chip. The phone itself was destroyed by the blast.

It shows part of a sleeve. For what it's worth, he was wearing a white shirt."

"What's the problem? Just go around the world looking for a man in a white shirt," Scorpion said. He and Harris had history, and he knew Harris hadn't come because he enjoyed Scorpion's company. "What do you want, Bob? We're a long way from Georgetown."

Harris motioned him closer. Their heads were almost touching.

"We think they were sending a message with the killing of Budawi. Not just that they can reach anyone they want. We think the threat is real. Something big. He said, 'a demonstration.' An odd word to use. He knew he was being recorded and he said it twice."

"How big?"

"We don't know. It could be anything. Planes into buildings. Assassinations. Kidnappings. Bombings. Poisoning the water supply. Killing all the kids in an elementary school like Russia. A new war in the Middle East. We don't know anything! We don't know who. We don't know where or when or how. For all we know, it could be disinformation. For the record, we don't think it is."

"Who's 'we'? The same geniuses who gave us Saddam's yellowcake in Africa?"

"Rabinowich in D.I. He said to tell you," Harris said.

Dave Rabinowich was a world-class mathematician from MIT, a Juilliard graduate violinist who had turned down a concert career and was hands-down the best intelligence analyst in the CIA. It was said that when he was bored, he would play mental chess games while simultaneously calculating prime numbers in his head. In fact, Scorpion had seen him do it once while at lunch at Clyde's in Georgetown. Rabinowich was also the odd man out who never bowed to pressure from the top or softened his dissents. His reports were precise, methodical, exhaustively researched, and rarely if ever wrong. If Dave was sending him the message personally, the threat was real.

Now he understood why Harris had flown halfway around the world to see him when he could've heard the same thing from any operations officer, and why they didn't wait to set up a safe house: to make sure he got the message. This wasn't a job for the CIA. This was coming from higher up. At a minimum, from the the Director of National Intelligence, who oversaw all U.S. intelligence agencies.

"He mentioned 'the Americans and their allies'," Harris said. "That puts us in the line of fire, only we don't have a clue, except that the messenger they sent is as good as it gets and is probably long gone from Egypt, and we don't have any idea who he is or who he represents, or how he got out of Egypt either."

"Multiple simultaneous attacks. You thinking al-Qaida?"

Harris shook his head. His hair was peppered with touches of gray, but at that moment he almost looked like the fair-haired graduate he'd once been. "Like a more sophisticated Brad Pitt," a female analyst had once said, dreamily looking at an old photo, to which a male colleague had replied, "Yeah, with the social instincts of Hannibal Lector."

"That's what the NSC thinks," Harris replied. "So does Homeland Security and the DCIA." He motioned Scorpion close again. "Rabinowich thinks Hezbollah."

"Hezbollah and the Muslim Brothers? Those are strange bedfellows."

"That's certainly the conventional wisdom," Harris said mildly, as if he were the Saint Francis of the CIA instead of its dirtiest infighter.

"But Rabinowich doesn't buy it. Why not?"

"Two things: One—the notation on Budawi's computer for the RDV at the café read, 'The Palestinian.' Just that. 'The Palestinian.' Nothing else in the Mabahith's files. Whatever else Budawi knew, he took with him when he died. Two—little ripples in the net. An NSA COMINT intercept here, a bit of MASINT from the DIA there, the odd BND rumor from an underworld informer not considered particularly reliable. No leads. Nothing definite. Nothing you can put your hands on. Not even odds and ends. What Rabinowich calls 'subtexture.' He says it's his word, that he invented it. He's actually filed a copyright application."

"So why kill Budawi?"

Harris shrugged. "Maybe as a gesture from Hezbollah to the Brothers. A bowl of figs to seal the deal."

"Or as you said, to send a message."

"But to whom? The Egyptians, the Israelis, or us?"

"The other Arab regimes. Letting them know there's a new player in the game."

"Interesting, that's what Rabinowich said," Harris said.

"I thought you didn't like Rabinowich."

Harris grimaced. "I don't. He's not a team player. Neither are you."

"No, I'm not," Scorpion said. Now it was out in the open between them. "What do you want, Bob?"

"You're a smart boy. You tell me," Harris said, leaning back, his arms folded across his chest.

"Rabinowich is right. And if he is, it's your ass on the line, which doesn't bother me in the least. Not after Arabia."

"Except it's not about us, is it?" Harris said.

For a moment neither of them spoke. Scorpion took a sip of the beer and put the bottle down.

"Does Rabinowich think it's a Palestinian? What about Hamas?"

"We don't know. The consensus is, probably not. It's probably a cover name to throw us off. Truth is, we have nothing. A voice. That's it."

"And that bothers you more than anything else, doesn't it?" Scorpion paused. From somewhere in the ship there was a clang of steel banging against steel, a container, hitting the side of the hatch. It was like an omen, he thought. Things go wrong. He had been lucky for a long time, but you couldn't be lucky forever. Something inside him tightened, telling him not to do it. He watched Harris take a sip of beer, pretending they were colleagues instead of men who hated each other's guts. Harris hadn't wanted to come all this way. He did it because he had no choice. Scorpion took a deep breath. "What's the mission?" he asked.

"This is a Special Access Critical operation. We're coordinating with NSA, DIA, FBI, State, and every foreign intelligence service in the world, including the ones that according to Congress we're not supposed to talk to. I'm personally running it. Foley's coordinating for Langley. Anderson for the FBI. General Massey for the Defense Intelligence Agency. Security will be tightened in every major U.S. city and every capital in the world. We've already launched the most massive worldwide manhunt anybody's ever heard of. Every agency and DOD department is running 24/7 shifts to handle all the data streaming in."

"All this because of Budawi? This is bullshit. What aren't you telling me?"

"Nothing," Harris said, inspecting his nails. If it were possible for someone as deceitful as Harris to reveal true emotion, Scorpion would have said that he was running scared.

"I'm not a virgin, Bob. I don't need foreplay. What is it?"

Harris shook his head. "Need to know." Scorpion knew that the deputy director was within his rights to withhold information. The rule was "no excess baggage." You only told a field agent what he absolutely needed to know. Except he was getting a bad feeling about this one. He stared at the cabin porthole, the Arabian Sea a distant blue beyond the breakwater while Springsteen went dancing in the dark. Neither man spoke.

"You've got plenty of firepower on this. What's the problem?" Scorpion asked finally.

"It won't work. I have a feeling about this Palestinian. He's good. Too good and absolutely ruthless. No matter what we do, he'll find a way. That's where you come in. I want you on your own, running your own operation, completely separate from everything and anyone else in the Agency. You'll have unlimited access to anything we have anytime you want it. Spend as much money as you have to. If you want, I'll give you the Chairman of the Joint Chiefs' private cell number. Call out the goddamn Marines. You have one job. Stop the Palestinian. However you have to do it. No questions asked."

"It'll get dirty. You know what we're dealing with."

"Whatever it takes."

Scorpion waited. He picked up the Beck's but didn't drink. The only sounds besides Springsteen were those of the port machinery and someone on the dock shouting in Urdu. As an independent agent, for Scorpion there was always the matter of payment. Finally, Harris said it.

"Double the usual fee plus a triple bonus when the Palestinian is—" He hesitated. "—no longer an issue. The first half'll be in the Luxembourg account in an hour."

Christ, they were scared shitless, Scorpion thought. Harris didn't even bat an eye at so much money. What the hell was this?

"Hezbollah means Lebanon. I don't trust Beirut station," Scorpion said, putting down the beer.

"Rabinowich agrees. Keep it separate. Do it any way you like. There's a backpack with a dozen passports, credit cards, money, contacts, some gear, the usual. Get it at the drop on 13th Street." Then Harris told him the website they'd be using and the emergency password and countersign, what Scorpion's old mentor, Koenig, used to call the pilot eject button. "Anything else?" he asked.

Scorpion stood up. "I have a plane to catch."

"You have two weeks; probably less," Harris said.

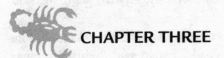

CHAPTER THREE

Beirut, Lebanon

Fouad was sitting by the window over a café au lait at an inside table at the Café de Paris. He was pretending to read a copy of *Spécial* magazine, a sexy Lebanese actress in a low-cut dress on the cover, as Scorpion entered the café. It was the signal that he was clean. If there had been any opposition, any one of the dozen different Lebanese factions opposed to his group, the March 14 Druze, the magazine would have been lying closed on the table.

Scorpion sat down across from Fouad and looked around. The café, with its orange awnings and multicolored chairs, was a Rue Hamra institution, and most of the clientele, he noted, was older. Gray-haired men who still wore suit jackets and *en vogue* women of a "certain age" who had kept their shapes. They looked like they dated from the nineties, when the café had been a hotbed of politicians, journalists, and spies.

"*Salaam aleikem,*" Fouad said, limply shaking Scorpion's hand, passing a small plug-in flash drive as he did so.

"*Wa aleikem es-salaam.* This place is still here," Scorpion said. "*Un café turc, s'il vous plaît,*" he said to the waiter.

"The students all hang out at Starbucks now. The old Lebanon is dead," Fouad said, lighting a cigarette. He spoke a Druze-style Arabic distinguished by the *qaf,* the guttural *k* sound. "The photo is on the flash drive," he whispered, leaning closer and opening his cell phone to show Scorpion the image of a man in Western clothes and a checkered kaffiyeh draped around his neck, talking on a cell phone on an apartment balcony.

"Salim?" Scorpion said.

Fouad nodded. "It's him."

"How do I know it's him? Man on a balcony with a long distance lens. Could be anybody."

"You know Choueifat?"

"Druze village. East of the airport," Scorpion said.

"Hezbollah came at night. They took four boys. One of them was my brother's son, Badi. Before they killed him, they cut out his eyes. This is Salim," Fouad said, tapping the cell phone. "How many will you need?" He stopped and they waited until the waiter served Scorpion the thick coffee and left.

"Depends. Does he ever leave?"

"Sometimes." Fouad looked around. "He has a woman in Ashrafieh."

"How do you know?"

"She is one of us." Scorpion raised his eyebrows and didn't say anything. "Her mother was Druze," Fouad explained.

"And he trusts her enough to visit her?"

"You should see her. Dark-haired, dark-eyed . . ."

Fouad tried to find the words, his hands in front of him as if to touch something exquisite. "A beauty."

"Where's the apartment?"

"On Baroudi, near Shari' Abdel Wahab. You know it?"

"Near the football stadium? That's an expensive neighborhood," Scorpion said. "How does she afford it?"

Fouad shifted uncomfortably. "She is a singer. A patriot," he said.

"She's yours?"

Fouad nodded. "This will end it for her?" he asked.

"We'll try to make it appear that she's a victim too," Scorpion said. "Maybe they won't kill her. What floor is her apartment on?"

"The eighth. The building has ten floors."

"How many men does he come with?"

"Seven usually. Two SUVs. Four in one and three with him in the second. All with AK-47s."

"Do any of them come into the apartment with him?"

Fouad shook his head. "He leaves two to guard outside the apartment door, the rest downstairs or outside."

"I'll call and let you know after I check it out," Scorpion said. "Probably need just the two of us plus two with a car for the getaway. But no one knows who the target is or what it's for or where they're going till the last second. Understood?"

"Of course. Only the two of us?"

"The fewer, the better." He could see Fouad was worried. "It'll be enough. Security's a bigger concern than firepower."

Fouad leaned forward and put out the glowing tip of the cigarette by slowly crushing it between his fingers. "We will kill him?"

Scorpion didn't answer.

"He has to be killed," Fouad said. "The price is agreed?"

"Sixty M-16s, ten M203 grenade launchers, and two M-240B machine guns. A thousand dollars U.S. for each of your men, ten thousand for you," Scorpion whispered in his ear as he stood up. "And no one touches him. He must be taken alive and unharmed or I pay nothing."

"*Maashi. Mafi mushkila.*"

He's lying, saying okay, Scorpion thought. He'd have to deal with it when the time came. "*Inshallah, Ma'a salaama,*" he said, touching Fouad on the shoulder as he left.

"*Alla ysalmak, habibi,*" Fouad said, not looking up.

Outside, Scorpion caught a *Service* taxi that he shared with two women, one in a head scarf, and a male student, heading toward the Corniche. He stopped the *Service* on Kuwait Street, crossed the busy street and jumped into a taxi heading the other way, toward downtown, making sure no one was suddenly reversing directions with him. He got out on Fakheddine, waited till the taxi left, then walked into a Japanese restaurant and out the back door. From there, Scorpion walked several blocks down a side street to the high-rise apartment building on Omar Daouk where he had rented a furnished flat earlier that morning. He nodded to the *portier* and took the elevator to the apartment. As soon as he got in, he went to the window and scanned the street below from behind the curtain, but there was nothing. Just ordinary street traffic. Beyond the street, he could see the side of the Ramada Hotel, and beyond that the Mediterranean, blue all the way to the horizon.

He went to the table, turned on his laptop computer, transferred the image on the plug-in drive from Fouad into the computer and opened it with Photoshop. The man in the photo was Salim Kassem, Nazrullah's deputy secretary and a member of the *al-majlis Al-Markazis*, the Hezbollah Central Council. It wasn't his face Scorpion was interested in, but his cell phone. He enlarged the photo almost to the point of seeing individual pixels, till he was sure he knew the exact Nokia model Kassem used. Using an RSA token disguised as a functioning credit card, Scorpion logged into the website of the International Corn Association, which promoted American corn exports that Harris was using as cover for the operation. The randomly generated code number plus a password enabled Scorpion to initiate a Virtual Private Network with a special port on the site that used an advanced DTLS protocol. This created a highly secure network tunnel that was far more difficult to hack than the standard SSL used by most so-called secure websites, such as banks. Once he was connected, he made the arrangements he wanted.

Only then did he unpack his suitcase and methodically check his equipment, one piece at a time, including a 9mm Beretta pistol with a sound suppressor. From this point on he would be carrying a gun everywhere he went.

Leaving the apartment, he took a *Service* to Ashrafieh. He stopped in a real estate office and pocketed a few business cards from an agent who tried to interest him in a condo in the Gammayzeh district. "*Pas maintenant,*" not now, he told the agent, using French as part of his cover ID, then caught a taxi that let him off on Baroudi, two blocks from the target. He studied the street and the building as he walked past and then completely around it. In the lobby, he slipped the *portier* one of the real estate cards and thirty thousand lira, told him he had a client who was interested and to keep it to himself. After taking the elevator to the top floor, he walked down the stairs to the eighth floor and checked the corridor to determine how he wanted to handle it when he returned.

Finally, Scorpion went back outside and called Fouad. He spent the rest of the day changing taxis and making further preparations.

Near sunset the next day Scorpion got the call from Fouad. He was seated at a café on the Corniche near Pigeon Rocks. The line of palm trees along the Corniche rustled in the breeze. A slim young woman in a miniskirt was walking arm in arm with a girlfriend in a black *hijab* scarf and skintight designer jeans, the two of them laughing, the sun turning the sea a fiery reddish gold and at that moment, Beirut was the most seductive place on earth. The waiter was talking with the bartender about Lebanon's upcoming soccer match against Jordan in the Asian Cup, and on the TV behind the bar an Egyptian female singer was crooning about love.

It was good to hear Arabic again, Scorpion thought. It had been too long and he'd missed it; missed its musicality and expressiveness, and even more, a sense of his strange interrupted childhood in the desert of Arabia after his oilman father had been killed. It brought back the world of the Bedouin and Sheikh Zaid, who had been more of a father to him than his own father, whom he'd barely known, and the extraordinary nights of his boyhood when the stars filled the desert sky from horizon to horizon. He remembered how it was near the end, when it was all about oil and money and the Bedu way was gone, and when he went to America to go to Harvard, Sheikh Zaid telling him, "You have to find out who you are, my *dhimmi*."

He was thinking about all that, and about dropping out of Harvard and going to war in Afghanistan and later the Delta Force—because in a way it was like going home—when his cell phone rang. He listened for a moment, said *"D'accord,"* and snapped the phone shut.

Scorpion slung his backpack over his shoulder and walked along the Corniche, the waves lapping at the shore as he went over it again in his mind. They had gotten lucky. An informant working in a garage in South Beirut spotted Kassem's car being moved and called Fouad. That meant they would try soon, but there were multiple trouble spots. For one thing, there might be gunfire, and no guarantee that a stray—or not so stray—bullet would not get Kassem. Unless Kassem was unharmed, Scorpion knew his plan wouldn't work. Also, the woman had to leave the balcony door unlocked or they might have to smash it in, alerting Kassem and the guards outside the door and precipitating a gunfight. And even if it all went as planned, keeping Kassem alive was a problem, since Fouad had a powerful motive to kill him. Plus, there was the matter of getting away, because Hezbollah, with informants everywhere in Lebanon, would be after them within the hour, probably a lot less. And he had to do it all in such a way that neither Kassem, who was perhaps the shrewdest mind in Hezbollah, nor anyone on the Central Council, would suspect his real plan.

In a way, what he was doing was the opposite of normal intelligence gathering, where you ran embedded assets who would turn over everything they could to an operations officer. Normal spycraft was like spreading a net across a river and taking in and analyzing everything till you got the fish you were after. Here, he was forcing the issue because there was a clock ticking and no way of knowing when it would go off, and he had to do it in such a way that the intelligence was absolutely real—so much so that the enemy didn't suspect they were helping him, he thought as he waved down a taxi and headed downtown to the RDV location.

An hour later they waited in the restaurant for Fouad to come back from the telephone by the bar. The waiter had told them there was a call for "Hamid." No more cell phone calls for the woman, Scorpion had told Fouad. After this, Hezbollah would analyze every call she had made. Scorpion watched the street and the headlights of the cars outside through the reflection of the interior of the restaurant in the window. Fouad came walking back to the table, and by the look on his face Scorpion knew they were on. She had called, alerting them Kassem was on his way.

"*Yalla!*" Fouad said. Let's go. They headed out to the SUV.

Scorpion and Fouad left the two Druze gunmen parked in an underground parking garage around the corner, their lights and engine off and close enough to hear any gunfire, while the two of them made their way around to the rear entrance by the garbage bin. Scorpion picked the lock and they climbed the stairs, pausing at any sound until they were out on the roof. They unpacked their gear and night vision goggles and set up their equipment. He cautioned Fouad again against making a sound or letting himself be seen from below or from another building, then left him crouching below the line of the roof as he went back inside and down the stairs to the landing above the woman's apartment. The only sound he made was while cutting the wires to the light on the landing, putting it in shadow, and the barely audible metallic whisper as he screwed the silencer onto his gun.

Scorpion waited, sweating in the darkness. Somewhere, he heard the sound of a television. It came from an apartment where someone was watching a popular reality TV show to find the next Lebanese singing star. When his cell phone vibrated, it startled him so much he almost dropped it, and at that moment he heard the elevator coming. He pressed into the shadow of the wall to make himself as small as possible. The elevator door opened and he heard men moving quietly. He sensed one of them approaching, just beyond his line of sight, probably peering up into the darkness of the landing. It could end here, he thought, aiming the gun.

Then he heard a voice that had to be Kassem's: "I won't be more than an hour," a knock on the door, and the woman letting him in, saying "*Haayil, habibi*. Can you stay?"

At the sound of the door closing, Scorpion glanced at his watch. He would wait twelve minutes. He wanted them occupied in bed.

One of the guards coughed and shuffled his feet. One of them murmured something about the TV show and the other chuckled. Scorpion crept downstairs, one stair at a time. He was almost in their line of sight. He checked his watch; it was time. He pulled on his ski mask and pressed the Send button on his cell phone to let Fouad know. One of the guards said something but he couldn't catch it. He tried to control the sound of his breathing. *Yalla beena*, he thought. The first move had to be Fouad coming down the rappelling line and in from the balcony.

Suddenly, they were shouting in the apartment and a woman screamed. Scorpion stepped into the line of sight in shooting position. One of the Hezbollah guards was pounding on the door, the second was aiming his AK-47. He shot them both in the head before either could turn around. He moved toward the apartment door, the shouting louder inside, and had just reached the door when it opened. Kassem, stark naked except for his undershirt, started to run out then stopped, stunned as Scorpion put the muzzle of the silencer against his forehead and motioned him back into the apartment.

"Kes emmak!" Kassem spat at him, not moving.

Scorpion smashed him in the face with the gun, knocking him back and putting him into a choke hold as Fouad, also in a ski mask, tied Kassem's wrists behind him with plastic zip-tie handcuffs.

"Be polite," Scorpion said in Arabic before kneeing Kassem in the groin. He and Fouad heaved Kassem onto the dining room table on his back. Scorpion hit Kassem hard in the mouth with the gun, knocking out some of his teeth. Kassem lay there, moaning softly, blood bubbling out of his mouth. Scorpion grabbed a dish towel and used it to blindfold him. The woman, clad only in black panties, stared wide-eyed at them.

"Take care of her. Make it look real," Scorpion whispered to Fouad as he bound Kassem's feet with another plastic zip-tie. The woman screamed as Fouad grabbed her by her hair and began slapping her hard, shouting *"Eskoot!"* for her to shut up. He slammed her against the wall, knocking her down, then dragged her to the bedroom and tied and gagged her.

Scorpion opened the apartment door, checked the corridor to the elevator and listened. The TV show in the other apartment was still on. Either they had heard nothing or, more likely, didn't want to get involved. There was no sound of the elevator moving or anyone coming up the stairs. They had a few minutes, he thought as he pulled the bodies of the two guards and their AK-47s into the apartment. He locked the door from the inside and joined Fouad, who had already started to question Kassem.

"Where is the Palestinian? The one who killed the Egyptian general Budawi? Tell us!" hissed Fouad in Arabic.

"*Kul khara!*" Kassem cursed, the words muffled by the spray of blood that came flying out of his mouth.

"Tell us!" Fouad said, grabbing a small saucepan from the stove and smashing it down on Kassem's groin. Kassem moaned. "The Palestinian. Where is he?"

"*Kis em ick!*" Go do something obscene with your mother, Kassem cried out as Fouad hit him again.

Fouad put the saucepan back on the stove, turned the flame on, and went back to questioning Kassem, while Scorpion worked on the reason why he'd planned this in the first place. He found Kassem's cell phone in his pants pocket, crumpled on the floor in the bedroom, and examined it for any scratches or noticeable smudges. There was a single small scratch on the outside casing, and a nicked corner. He pulled an identical model from his pocket, made a tiny scratch and nicked the corner with a Swiss pocketknife to mimic the first phone and smudged the screen with his sleeve. Using a port-to-port connector, he copied the memory from Kassem's cell phone into his phone, then took the SIM from Kassem's cell and put it into the new phone. Checking the new phone to make sure all Kassem's contacts and messages were there, he put the new phone back in Kassem's pants pocket.

It had an NSA-supplied computer chip and DSP

processor inside. Any call Kassem made on it would be relayed via satellite to NSA headquarters at Fort Meade, Maryland, the "Black Building," so-called because of the color of the outside window glass, and from there to Scorpion's cell phone.

Scorpion turned off the dresser lamp he'd been using and went over to the woman, lying bound and gagged on the bed. Her face was swollen and bruised from where Fouad had hit her. She stared up at him, a man in a ski mask, and whatever was in her dark eyes, he couldn't read it. He put his finger to his lips and removed her gag.

"If you want to live, you need to come with us," he whispered.

She looked at him with her dark eyes but didn't answer.

"I don't think you should stay," he said. "I can give you asylum in America, but you have to come right now."

She shook her head, her long dark hair a mane on the pillow, the movement making him aware of her superb, nearly naked body. "This is my country," she said softly.

"They'll have to suspect you. Once I leave this room, no one can protect you."

"Ana fahim." I understand. She smiled wistfully, wincing as she did, and despite the swelling and bruises, he could see how attractive she was. "I don't want to go anywhere. Let Hezbollah and the Syrians leave."

Scorpion heard a terrible muffled high-pitched squeal in the next room, almost like an animal's. He replaced her gag and hurried into the dining area.

Fouad was grinding the red-hot saucepan onto Kassem's privates. Scorpion pulled him away, then put a choke hold on Kassem, cutting off the carotid artery and rendering him unconscious.

"We have to go. Did he say anything?"

"He said it wasn't the Central Committee. He didn't know the 'Palestinian'. He said Cairo was the work of the Al-Muqawama al-Islamiyya."

"The Islamic Resistance? Who are they?"

"A secret cell within Hezbollah. More radical than Nasrullah. We've heard only whispers. No one knows anything about it, or if they do, no one speaks. Do we kill him now?" Fouad asked, taking out his gun.

Scorpion saw Kassem starting to stir. Whatever he did, he would have to do it quickly.

"He has to escape," he whispered into Fouad's ear. "That was the plan."

Fouad shook his head. "You don't understand Lebanon," he said, and pointed his gun at Kassem.

As Fouad started to squeeze the trigger, Scorpion reached over and, with a Krav Maga maneuver, twisted the gun away from Fouad and fired it at him three times, killing him instantly. From another apartment he heard a scream, and then gunshots from below. Kassem's men had heard the shots and were no doubt already on their way.

Scorpion ran into the bedroom, untied the woman and pulled her with him back into the next room. He grabbed one of the AK-47s from the floor, fired it at Fouad's body, opened the balcony door, stepped out and fired the gun at it from outside, shattering the glass, then ran back in and handed the AK-47 to the woman. Lights were going on in apartments in buildings all around, and he could hear shouting and gunshots and dogs barking. He only had seconds.

"You freed yourself and killed him," he said, indicating Fouad. "You saved Kassem. I ran away. Understand?"

"I understand," she said, pushing him. "Go with Allah."

"Stay away from the door. They'll come in shooting," he said as he grabbed the backpack.

Running out to the balcony, he hooked up to Fouad's rappelling line from the roof and leaped over the rail as the apartment door was shredded with AK-47 fire, shots ripping into the apartment wall. He rappelled wildly down the side of the building, not daring to take a second to look up. The instant his feet touched the concrete of the alleyway, he detached from the line and ran into the shadows.

Behind him, Scorpion heard the sound of bullets pinging off the concrete. As he ran he pulled off his ski mask, stuffed it into the backpack, and pressed his cell phone to alert the Druze getaway drivers. He raced down the alley to the side street. Just as he got to the sidewalk, the SUV screeched to a stop. He jumped in and they sped into the darkness.

"Where's Fouad?" one of the Druze asked in Arabic.

Scorpion shook his head. "Keep driving," he said. "I'll tell you where to stop."

The two Druze gunmen drove around to make sure they weren't followed and dropped him off on Avenue Clemenceau. He waited till they drove away, cautioning them to say nothing and not to go home. Once Hezbollah discovered Fouad's identity, there would be retaliations against the Druze. He was walking the few blocks to the apartment on Omar Daouk, the streets still active with pedestrians and traffic despite the late hour, the streetlights spaced like lonely sentinels in the darkness, when Kassem's call came.

"You shouldn't have called," a voice said. Scorpion's cell phone screen showed the phone number of a Dr. Samir Abadi in Damascus, Syria.

"They wanted to know about the Palestinian," he heard Kassem say, his voice sounding surprisingly normal, despite the pain he had to be in.

"And?"

"I told them nothing." There was a pause. "They know of Al-Muqawama."

The phone in Damascus clicked off.

Scorpion took the elevator to the apartment and within minutes had uploaded the contents of Kassem's cell phone to Rabinowich via the Corn Association website from his laptop. He cleared out anything in the apartment that might identify him, wiping down whatever he'd touched with antiseptic wipes. At the bus station near the port, he caught a night *Service* taxi to Damascus that he shared with a Syrian businessman who had come to Beirut to see his dentist and a Shi'ite woman who was going to visit her sister. They drove through the city and up the winding mountain roads in the darkness to the Syrian border.

Scorpion hadn't wanted to do this at night, but Hezbollah would already be mobilizing, and he knew it would be harder to cross the border if he waited till morning. As it was, there was a chance of Hezbollah gunmen stopping them anywhere in the Bekaa Valley or in one of the Shi'ite villages in the mountains. As for the border, the Syrians would soon be alerted. His best chance was to get through before they were all over the border station. The *Service* stopped at the border and they were ordered out of the taxi. He handed the Lebanese border officer a French passport and a press pass that identified him as Adrien Leveque, a journalist from *Le Figaro*.

News about the killing was on a television on the wall behind the officer. A reporter standing outside the building on Baroudi Street said that two bodies had been found in the apartment, a man and the nude body of a woman. There was no mention on the TV of the two gunmen Scorpion had killed or Hezbollah. The police assumed the female body was the woman who had rented the apartment, but identification would take time because she'd been badly tortured and mutilated before she died. The reporter said police were focusing on the sex angle, with speculation about a sadomasochistic game between two lovers that had gotten out of control.

The officer looked at Scorpion's passport and press pass photos, then at him and typed something into the computer.

"*Êtes-vous écrit une histoire sur la Syrie?*" the officer asked.

"*Sur l'effet de la crise financière sur le commerce libanais et syriens,*" Scorpion said. He was concerned that they were doing a computer check. The credentials from the CIA were supposed to be rock solid, so it wasn't that, and *Le Figaro* often featured financial stories, such as the one on the financial crisis he claimed he was covering. That usually made people less interested, which was why he had chosen it. The officer glanced at the television screen behind him, then at Scorpion while they waited for the computer. Scorpion felt a bead of sweat slide down his back. Every second increased his danger. The Lebanese border police were staffed with Shi'a, often from either Amal or Hezbollah. And crossing the border into Syria didn't mean anything. They were on both sides of the border.

The officer checked the computer, then with a blank expression handed him back his passport. It was the time of night that had made him suspicious, Scorpion thought. But he'd had no choice. Sooner or later someone would remember seeing someone who looked like him with Fouad. The police wouldn't put him together with Fouad and the woman, but Hezbollah might.

He went outside and got back into the *Service*. They'd tortured her before they killed her. *This is my country*, she had said. The mission had barely started and already he had casualties.

They stopped at the Syrian border station and went through the procedure again, then got back in the *Service* and drove on. The only light came from the headlights of the *Service* carving into the darkness of the road.

They arrived in Damascus before midnight, dropped off at the main bus station in Soumaria. Although it was late, there were still a few vendors selling roasted meat kabobs over glowing charcoal braziers and a line of taxis waiting at a stand. Scorpion took a taxi to Le Meridian, the type of hotel a French journalist would stay at. As he handed his luggage and backpack to the hotel porter, he spotted two men he had seen standing near the taxi stand at the bus station, one with a mustache in a white shirt and blue pants, the second in a dark patterned shirt, both with bulges for holsters under their shirts. He was being followed.

CHAPTER FOUR

Utrecht, Netherlands

The Palestinian heard the call of the muezzin echo from the mosque loudspeaker out over the rain-slick street. He stood in the Moroccan grocery store across the way, watching the worshippers—men still in their work clothes and a few women in black *hijab* head scarves—enter the mosque. The store smelled of couscous and fresh *khobz* bread and spices: cinnamon, cumin, mint, ginger, and green coriander leaves for *tagines*. He would not enter the mosque. It was sure to have been infiltrated by AIVD informers even before Cairo, and now the Dutch were under even greater pressure from the Americans and the other European intelligence services. He bought a sprig of mint leaves wrapped in paper and stood outside the store. There was nothing about him to attract attention, just a man under an awning, taking shelter from the rain.

A woman in a *hijab* and a small boy walked toward him on their way to the mosque.

"*Salaam aleikem*," he said.

"*Aleikem es-salaam*," the woman said, still walking.

"Do you know the imam? Imam Mohammad So-lilah?" the Palestinian asked in Fusha Arabic.

"I know him," the boy said, turning back. "He comes to our class sometimes."

"Could you give him this?" he said, handing the boy the package of mint leaves. He added, "This is for you," handing the boy a two euro coin. The boy took the coin and looked at his mother.

"You are a friend of the imam?" she asked, looking at him for the first time. He was taller than average, close to six feet, with smooth, even features and skin that had recently spent time in the sun. He looked exceptionally fit, with a lean athletic build, and although he was smiling at her and the boy, there was something in his brown eyes that made her uneasy. She took the boy's hand and pulled him closer to her.

"*Aywa*, an old friend. Mint for his tea. And this for you." If he handed her a twenty euro note and mussed the boy's wet hair with his hand. "You'd better go in or you'll drown."

She hesitated to take the money, but Kanale-neiland was a poor immigrant neighborhood, and after a moment she put the money in her pocket.

"Should I tell him anything?" the boy asked.

"*La*, nothing, *ma'a salama*," the Palestinian said, and opening his umbrella, walked away in the rain.

She watched him for a moment, then holding tightly to the boy's hand, crossed the street and went into the mosque.

The Palestinian walked to a corner kiosk, where

he bought a German newspaper, the *Frankfurter Allgemeine*, then he went into a small cafeteria that appeared to be frequented mainly by Moroccans. There did not appear to be much mixing between them and the many Turks in the area.

He sat down with a tray of chicken and rice and read the newspaper while he ate. From time to time he glanced up from his paper and through the cafeteria window at the darkening street, the lights from storefronts and streetlights reflected in puddles and wet sidewalks. No one paid any attention to him. This was a rough Muslim neighborhood and they were used to people with no work and time on their hands.

He was still jet-lagging from Mexico, in his mind seeing hawks riding the thermals in the sky over the desert east of Mexicali, shacks along the road, and César, the vicious little coyote in an Angels baseball cap waving his pistola in that tunnel under the border to the U.S., saying, "No more *mierde, cabrón.* Show me what's in your pack." Then the surprised look on César's face a second later with a bullet hole in his forehead.

Once he was on the U.S. side in Calexico, it was so easy. All he had to do was go into a Kinko's and FedEx a box containing the pack to the office of the fictional chemical company he had set up months earlier in the industrial Sunset Park section of Brooklyn in New York, after which he just crossed back into Mexico through the border station, no questions asked.

The waiter, a young Moroccan in a soiled apron,

came over, and the Palestinian ordered a cup of tea. The waiter put the paper slip for the bill under the saucer and whispered in Arabic, "Ask for Saïd."

The Palestinian saw a local telephone number handwritten on the slip. He memorized it, then spilled some tea on the slip till it nearly dissolved, and rolling it into a tiny ball, dropped it into his pocket. He asked if he could use the cafeteria phone, explaining that his cell phone battery was low, and they pointed him to a public phone near the toilet in back. Calling the number, he said he wanted to speak to Saïd, and a man on the other end said "Prins Claus Brug" and hung up.

The Palestinian went out into the rain and walked along Churchillaan Street toward the Prince Claus Bridge over the canal. As he walked, he checked his reflection in rain-streaked store windows to make sure he wasn't followed. He walked past apartment houses, satellite TV dishes sprouting like mushrooms on the sides of the buildings, graffiti from Turkish and Moroccan gangs painted on alley walls. This wasn't the guidebook's Utrecht, with its clean streets, world-class university, medieval Dom Tower dominating the skyline, and the tree-lined Oudegracht Canal, with its charming cafés and restaurants along the water. This was Muslim Europe, the heart of the struggle. It wasn't just the Americans. The Europeans too would be punished, he thought. A more terrible punishment than they could imagine.

Near the corner, a group of tough-looking young Moroccan men were crowded under an awning, smoking cigarettes and what smelled like hashish. They watched him, saying nothing as he walked past, his posture utterly still even as he moved, something about that stillness precluding them from challenging him. He walked along the path beside the canal, raindrops making circles in the dark water, the ripples shattering the reflections of the streetlights. As he walked, he flicked the tiny ball of paper he had spilled the tea on into the canal.

Just as the Palestinian went up onto the bridge, a BMW sedan pulled up beside him. Two Arab men got out, hands in their raincoat pockets. "Get into the car," one of them said in Arabic.

He got in the backseat, sandwiched between them. The car drove across the bridge, suddenly spun around on the other side and headed back onto the bridge going the other way.

"*Lo tismah*, we have to do this," the first Arab apologized, putting a blindfold on the Palestinian. He sat quietly, letting them do it, swaying as the car made turns, changing directions so they couldn't be followed and so he couldn't find his way again.

After what seemed a long time but might have been less than half an hour, the car stopped and they led him out, knocked twice on a door and took him inside a building. The first Arab took off his blindfold. They were standing in the vestibule of an old-fashioned apartment building near a dimly lit staircase. He smelled damp rotting wood and water and thought they might be in an older part of the city, near the Oudegracht Canal.

"I leave you here. Go to the third floor. The

apartment on your left," the first Arab said, opening the door and going back outside. The Palestinian glanced around the vestibule and looked up the staircase. There were no obvious hiding places for anyone who might be waiting for him. He went up the stairs, knocked on the door and went inside.

The apartment was dark and sparsely furnished. A blanket hung over the only window, the only light coming from a candle on a wooden table. It was likely a temporary meeting place, only used this one time, he thought. The old man, in a round white *taqiyah* cap and *gallabiya*, sat behind the table with a glass of mint tea, and even in the dim light the Palestinian could see he was blind.

"*Salaam aleikem, Imam,*" he said.

"*Wa aleikem es-salaam,*" the old man said, gesturing for him to sit. "You will have *shai atai.*" It was not a question. The old man's hands trembled as they found the battered metal teapot and poured the mint tea into the glass, adding lump after lump of sugar and stirring it with the spoon from his glass. The two men sipped their tea in silence.

"There is a *hadith* of the Prophet, *rasul sallahu alayhi wassalam,* peace be upon him, who instructed us that there is no faith for one who has no trust, and no religion for one who does not fulfill his promises. You do not need to tell me why it was necessary to kill the shopkeeper in Cairo," the old man said, holding up his hand. "I know it was necessary or you would not have done it. You need not make explanations to me, now or ever."

"It was necessary."

"It is of no consequence," the old man said, waving his hand as if brushing away a fly. "But are you ready for what is next?" he said, looking at him with his sightless eyes.

"I understand your meaning of the *hadith*. The warning has been delivered. We must fulfill our promise," the Palestinian said.

"We shall teach the unbelievers a lesson they will not forget. Are your preparations ready?" the old man asked, the glass trembling in his hand.

"Phase one in America is complete."

"How was it?"

"It went well. I entered California from Mexico, then shipped the parcel to New York. The Americans do not monitor internal package shipments."

"I thought they had improved their security."

"There are tens of millions of packages every day. It would be impossible. After, I went back to Mexico. There was only one casualty. A narco, a drug runner. He showed too much interest in my backpack. From the moment I hired him, I knew I would have to kill him. It was inevitable."

"You did as you should. The Americans will learn fear. It will be their new home. What of phase two?"

There is still much to do, but *inshallah*, we will be ready," the Palestinian said.

"And the main target?"

"That will be the greatest difficulty. They will tighten security. There will be checkpoints everywhere. Getting close will be almost impossible."

"Is it impossible?" the old man whispered, his voice quavering.

"*Inshallah*, God willing, anything is possible. What is most important is that there is no photo of me. No one knows who I am," the Palestinian said.

"No one," the old man agreed. "You are invisible to them, but you will end the war against Islam in America and Europe."

"*Inshallah*, God willing, all will be completed."

"It is well. How you accomplish this, you will decide. Whatever you need will be supplied. Whatever orders you issue to our people will be obeyed without question. If you need to spend more, no matter how much, the money is at your disposal. If you need to enforce discipline, you must do as you see fit. And may the blessing of Allah be upon you."

The Palestinian sipped the sweet mint tea and didn't say anything. He watched the specks of mint in the glass swirl in the candlelight.

"You go to Russia next?" the old man asked.

"Not yet. There are things I must do. Then Russia."

"Trust no one there. They are godless creatures, the Russians. For them is reserved a special place in *jahannam* . . ." The old man hesitated. "You have not asked about what is most important of all. I appreciate your discretion, but you should speak. We shall not meet again."

The Palestinian stared at the old man's blind eyes.

"You know what I want," he said. "How is she?"

"She is well."

"Swear it. Swear she is well."

"It is not permissible to swear. But I assure you, she is well," the old man said. "Here," holding out an envelope. His hand was shaking, the skin spotted with age and waxy yellow, almost translucent, the veins clearly visible in the candlelight. "Here is your contact information. Memorize then burn it."

The Palestinian took it and stood up.

"*Ma'a salaama. Inshallah*, we will meet in the world to come, in Jannatu al-Khuld," he said.

"*Alla ysalmak*, my Brother," the old man said, looking up with his blind eyes. "As of this moment, you are the most important man in the world."

CHAPTER FIVE

Damascus, Syria

They were caught in a traffic jam on Choukry Kouwalty Avenue, the air shimmering from the heat rising from the pack of honking cars, yellow Star taxis and *Service* minibuses barely moving in the hot sun.

The taxi driver shrugged. "*Ma'alesh.* Damascus traffic is always shit."

"*Mafi mushkila,*" Scorpion said. Not a problem. He glanced out the side window. In the distance beyond the buildings, he could see the brown slopes of Jabal Qassioun, the mountain looming over the city. In this most ancient of cities, it was said to be the mountain where Cain killed Abel.

He wasn't concerned about the traffic; his errand wasn't essential. He was on his way to 17 of April Square to interview the director of the Syrian Central Bank for *Le Figaro.* He had set up the interview because, as Koenig used to drill into them over and over, "Cover isn't a false identity; cover is who you are." The director was probably waiting for him in his office now, but Scorpion's real interest was in the two cars—one a white Toyota SUV with four men in it three cars behind them, the other a blue Renault Megane a few cars ahead—that were tailing him. It was a standard front and back tail, and he'd recognized one of the men in the Renault as the man with the mustache and white shirt who followed him to his hotel last night. He had to find out who they were, his mental clock clicking down the precious seconds, wasting time dealing with tails while the Palestinian, who was likely no Palestinian, moved step by step closer to his target.

The taxi inched forward, the driver's worry beads dangling from the rearview mirror swaying as they moved toward the cause of the jam, the crossroads where Choukry Kouwalty intersected with three main streets. Ahead, beyond the intersection, loomed the stone tower and wall of the Damascus Citadel at the entrance to the Old City. In the twelfth century the citadel had been the headquarters of Saladin, revered by Muslims as the leader who liberated Arab lands from the Crusaders. Scorpion thought about trying to lose the tail there, then glanced back at the white SUV in the rear window and made up his mind.

"Turn right on Al-Jabry," he told the driver.

"The bank is the other way," the driver said, turning his head for a second.

"I've changed my mind. Go right as fast as you can. I'll tell you where to stop. *Yalla!* Go now, quickly! *Dilwati!*"

"*Dilwati, inshallah,*" the driver said, hitting the horn and swerving in front of another taxi, squeezing by with not an inch to spare and up on the curb, barely missing a pedestrian. They turned right onto Al-Jabry Boulevard, the traffic easing as they moved away from the intersection. Behind them, Scorpion saw that the Renault was too far into the crossroads over toward Port Said Street to follow, its way to the right jammed. But the SUV behind them was blaring its horn, and one of the men in it was leaning out of the window, shouting and holding up a badge, ordering traffic out of their way and pointing to the right toward Al-Jabry.

Now he knew who they were, his mind racing. Plainclothes authorities, probably GSD, the Idarat al-Amn al-'Amm. The Syrian General Security Directorate. It was worse than Hezbollah. He had to get away. If they arrested him, it would take weeks, if ever, for him to get out of Syria, and by then, whatever the Palestinian was planning, it would be too late. He also had to find out if the Syrians were involved, and he had to do it now. But first he needed to escape the tail. It would've been easier if he were driving, remembering Koenig once saying, "Breaking a tail requires a very good driver to behave like a complete maniac."

Ahead, he saw the General Post Office, a square gray concrete building hung with red, white, and black Syrian flag banners and two-story posters of the Syrian president. Waiting till the last second, Scorpion told the driver to make a sharp right turn and step on it. "Now! Now! *Dilwati!*" he shouted.

The driver swerved, barely missing an oncoming car full of wide-eyed Syrian men. "Now where you want?" he demanded. "Crazy guy. Can't decide," he muttered to himself, shaking his head.

"I'll give you an extra five thousand pounds if you can get me to the Cham City Center Mall in less than five minutes," Scorpion said.

"For five thousand, *habibi*, I'll get you to Amman," the driver replied, speeding up and honking on his horn as he knifed between two cars to his right. Through the rear window, Scorpion could see that the white SUV had been cut off by a bus while trying to make the turn.

"Turn here," he ordered.

"It's faster straight," the driver said.

"Turn here, then go the way you know."

The driver made a fast sudden turn and accelerated down the street, bystanders raising their fists and screaming at him. Within minutes they pulled up in front of a big modern shopping mall.

"*Maashi*? It's okay?" the driver asked.

"*Zein al-hamdulillah*," Scorpion said. Fine, thanks to Allah. He shoved money at the driver and got out, and just spotted the white SUV coming around out of the corner of his eye as he raced into the mall.

When trying to break a tail, he remembered Koenig saying, it was essential to change the image. He ran into a men's clothing store, grabbed a different color shirt and changed into it. He handed the money to the clerk and went out another exit, where he caught another taxi just as two women with their children were getting out. He told the driver to take him to al-Azmeh. On the way, he called the director of the Syrian Central Bank on his cell phone, apologized for missing the interview because of the traffic jam, and rescheduled the interview. *Inshallah*, they would do the interview *bukra*—tomorrow—

which in the Middle East, as they both knew, could mean anytime from tomorrow to when hell freezes over.

He assumed it was the GSD that was after him, as they drove past shops and buildings draped with more Syrian flags and posters of the president along al-Ithad Street. He had to find out how deep in this the GSD was. If Damascus was running the Palestinian through Dr. Abadi, that would change the equation and he just might need the Pentagon and the U.S. Marines after all. He decided it couldn't wait, he had to find out now, while the Syrians were still off balance and trying to figure out who he was and what was going on.

The problem was, how to penetrate the innermost circles of Syrian intelligence? Normal tradecraft procedure was to ID a Joe inside the GSD and turn him. But that could take months. He didn't have the time. Worse, this was their country. They would pick him up the second they could. He would have to do something more drastic. He remembered somebody asking Koenig about how you could be sure you were getting good intelligence, and Koenig said, "If you need clean water, you have to go to where the water is." It gave him an idea.

Spotting an Internet café, Scorpion told the driver to pull over. He went inside, paid for a computer stall against the wall, got online, and in a couple of minutes found the address of the Ministry of Interior, headquarters of the GSD. He went back outside and after checking the street for tails caught another taxi.

At a juice bar on a side street off al-Marje, as the

locals called Martyrs Square, he was propositioned by a long-haired teenage shoeshine boy turned pimp.

"You want *farfourd*?" the boy said, using the Arabic slang word for very young girls. "Iraqi girls. Very nice. Moroccan. Albanian. How old you want? Twelve? Thirteen? Very clean. Beautiful girls. They'll make you feel good."

"I need a hotel room close by, where no one asks questions," Scorpion told him.

"Come," the boy said, picking up his shoe-shine box and leading him down the street. "What else you need?" he asked, looking back over his shoulder.

"Rohypnol, the date rape drug."

"Listen, boss. With these girls, believe me, you don't need it." The boy grinned.

"I want Rohypnol and I'll give you ten thousand pounds for you to forget you ever saw me."

"Mafi mushkila," the boy said. No problems.

The boy stopped at a tobacco stand and came back with a plastic vial with tiny white pills that he handed to Scorpion. They walked on, turned a corner and went into a small hotel with a narrow doorway. The lobby smelled of insect repellent and stale cigarettes. An old man in a crocheted skullcap behind the desk nodded at the boy. He was toothless and had one eye with a drooping lid, suggesting he'd had a stroke. Scorpion told him he wanted the room for the night.

"We charge by the hour," the old man said. The boy sniggered.

"I'll pay five thousand pounds for the night," Scorpion said.

"You have your *bataqa shaksia* identification card? It is required by the police."

"No. No ID card and no questions," Scorpion said, looking at him with cold gray eyes.

"Six thousand," the old man said, his good eye blinking rapidly.

Scorpion handed him the money, then took the boy aside and gave him five thousand pounds. The boy looked at the money in his hand.

"You said ten thousand," he said.

"The other five will be in the room. Get rope and a tube of glue and bring it to the room."

"Sure, boss. *Mafi mushkila*," the boy said. "Anything else?"

Scorpion pulled the boy close. "Don't come back after you bring the rope and glue. Forget you ever saw me," he whispered into his ear.

He waited till the boy left, then went up, checked the room, bare but for the bed and a dresser, left the money on the dresser and went out. He took a taxi, bought an *al Baath* newspaper and sat at a sidewalk table outside a small hummus restaurant across the street from the Ministry of Interior office building.

At noon, employees began to come out of the ministry for lunch. Scorpion waited, glancing up from behind his newspaper. It was logical that ministry employees would eat at the inexpensive restaurant so convenient to their office. A man in a white shirt and tie came over and sat at a nearby table. They were close enough in height and build, Scorpion decided. He got up and on his way to the bathroom nearly tripped a waiter, then caught the man to prevent him from falling. During the distraction, he slipped three pills into the ministry man's juice drink.

A few minutes later, after Scorpion went to the bathroom and returned to his table, the ministry man was showing signs of the drug. He staggered to his feet, reached for the table to steady himself and knocked over his glass, sending broken glass and juice flying. The man swayed, staring stupidly at the broken glass as the waiter hurried over.

Scorpion stood up. "I'm a doctor," he said. "This man is sick."

"I don't feel so good," the man said, his eyes bloodshot and nearly closed.

"He needs to go to the hospital. I'll take him," Scorpion said. "Come help me get him to a taxi," he told the waiter, who waved down a taxi.

"*Ilhamdulilah*. You are a good man, Doctor," the waiter said, helping Scorpion get the man into the taxi.

Scorpion told the driver the address of the hotel and tried to keep the man upright and awake in the taxi. By the time they got to the hotel, his eyes were rolling in his head and it was all Scorpion could do to get him out of the taxi. He half carried the man into the hotel.

The old man came from behind the desk and helped him get the ministry man to the room. When he was sprawling on the bed, the old man smiling knowingly at Scorpion, as if to indicate he now understood why he'd wanted to keep his homosexual rendezvous secret. Scorpion winked at the old man and gave him an additional thousand, locking the door behind him. He went through the man's pockets and took out his wallet.

"I don't feel so good. Need to call my office," the man moaned. He looked like he was about to throw up, and tried to get up. Scorpion pushed him back down on the bed, took the rope and tied him up hand and foot, shoving a towel into his mouth as a gag. By then the man was out cold. He'd been right, Scorpion thought, finding the GSD ID card in the wallet. He memorized, then put it into his own wallet and went out. He would now be Fawzi al-Diyala, deputy supervisor for Ar Raqqah Province.

Within minutes Scorpion was back at the Internet café, where he printed out his own photo, scanned from his French passport, cut it to size and pasted it with the glue over the ministry man's photo on the ID card. After taking a taxi back to the ministry, he used the ID to get past the security guards and into the building.

He took the elevator to the third floor and walked until he found an empty cubicle. The computer's Web browser took him to the GSD internal home page. He checked the organization chart for the director's name, office number, and telephone extension, then glanced around and dialed the extension.

The director picked up the phone at the first ring.

"*Naam*, what is it?" he said.

"Fawzi al-Diyala told me to call," Scorpion said. "We have the man from the Cham Center. He's a CIA agent. You must come!"

"What the hell is this?"

"*Min fadlak*, it's urgent! You have to come at

once!" Scorpion said, then hung up. He went out to the elevators and took one to the top floor. The director's office was at the end of the corridor. Scorpion took out his gun, screwed on the silencer and walked in. As he had hoped, the office was empty. Najah al-Hafez had taken the bait and had gone down to Diyala's office.

Scorpion sat down in al-Hafez's chair behind the desk, put his gun on the desktop and began to go through the desk drawers. He found a button that he assumed was an alarm button under the desktop. In a top drawer he found a BlackBerry, and was about to pocket it when al-Hafez came back into the office.

"Who the hell are you? Get out of my office!" the director demanded.

"*Eskoot.* Close the door and sit down," Scorpion said in Arabic, picking up the gun and pointing it at al-Hafez's chest. When the man didn't move, he added: "I will kill you."

"*El khara dah?*" al-Hafez growled. What the hell is this?

Scorpion cocked the hammer of the gun. "Sit down. I almost never miss and I won't tell you again," he said.

Al-Hafez's eyes darted around his office as if looking for a way to escape, then at the gun. He sat down in a chair facing his desk.

"You'll never get out of this building alive," he said.

"Yes I will. You'll see to it. But first we have to talk."

"Who are you? Mossad? CIA? DGSE? You're

the one who came in on a French passport," he said. "But you're not French. American?"

Scorpion nodded and put the gun down on the desktop.

"*Maashi*, CIA," al-Hafez said, his eyes resting for a moment on the gun. "So tell me what you want. I'll tell you why you can't have it and I'll even let you try to give me one reason why I shouldn't have you interrogated and killed."

"The Budawi assassination in Cairo."

"You don't think we had anything to do with that?!" al-Hafez said, looking discomfited.

"Stranger things have happened."

"It makes no sense. What have we to gain?"

"So why are your men following me? You've been on me since the minute I arrived in Damascus."

"Of course we're on you. A French journalist shows up at the border late at night in a *Service* a short time after four people are murdered in Beirut; two that we know were Hezbollah, one a woman who must have had information because someone tortured her, and the last a Druze from the March 14 Brigade. We'd be derelict if we weren't curious. That was interesting enough. When you escaped surveillance, that made you more than interesting. Now the fact that within a short time you went from hunted to hunter into my very office makes you more than a person of interest—it makes you dangerous to the state."

"I had to find out who was after me. Normally, I would've been more discreet, but right now I'm in a bit of a hurry."

"*Min fadlak*, we were very impressed. What we don't know is why you are here."

"You know Salim Kassem, of the Hezbollah Central Council?"

Al-Hafez gestured to indicate that of course he knew him.

"The first call he made after he escaped in Beirut was to a Dr. Samir Abadi here in Damascus."

"How do you know that?"

Scorpion smiled.

"Americans and their technology. Amazing! Truly." Al-Hafez shook his head. "How can you be so smart and yet so stupid?"

"Do you know Dr. Abadi?"

"There are many doctors in Damascus."

"Don't play stupid. It insults both of us," Scorpion said.

"Why should I help you? How does that help Syria?"

"Because you don't want to be on the wrong side of what is about to happen. This isn't about the Golan or the Israelis or who killed Hariri. You're right about us. We can be stupid," Scorpion said, his fingers lightly resting on the gun on the desk.

"If you don't report in . . . of course there will be repercussions. You could've just called for an appointment," al-Hafez said.

"No, I couldn't."

"No, you couldn't," al-Hafez conceded. "We had nothing to do with Budawi. But you already know that or you wouldn't be here. We're not even sure it was Hezbollah."

"Just when we were almost talking," Scorpion

sighed. "Tell me about Al-Muqawama al-Islamiyya, the Islamic Resistance."

"A myth," al-Hafez said, shifting uneasily in his chair. "Aliases and half-baked groups consisting of two jihadis in ski masks and an imam who talks too much are more common in the Middle East than fake goods in the souks."

"You say it wasn't you, it wasn't Hezbollah, and the Islamic Resistance doesn't exist. There's only one problem. Budawi didn't kill himself. What do you know of the Palestinian?"

"Who?"

"Now you're overplaying your hand, Najah. A man code-named the 'Palestinian' killed Budawi."

Al-Hafez leaned forward. "Are you sure? How do you know that?"

Scorpion didn't answer. For a moment they just looked at each other, the only sound the hum of the air-conditioning and the faint sound of traffic from the street. The phone on the desk began to ring.

"Don't answer it," Scorpion said.

The director let it ring till it stopped, then said, "They'll be checking on me."

"No. You're too important to disturb," Scorpion said.

Al-Hafez shrugged. "You're sure about Cairo?"

Scorpion didn't answer. Al-Hafez glanced out his office window at a superb view of Damascus, looking toward the Old City. From it, Scorpion could see the citadel and the Umayyad Mosque, where both the head of John the Baptist, revered by both Christians and Muslims, and the body of Saladin were entombed. Looming over it all through the smog haze was the distant ridge of Jabal Qassioun.

"It seems we both have secrets," al-Hafez said finally. "May I smoke?"

Scorpion picked up the gun and gestured with it for al-Hafez to go ahead. Al-Hafez started to light a cigarette and asked, "How about *shai*? Shall I have some brought?"

Scorpion shook his head no. Al-Hafez lit the cigarette and exhaled.

"Of the Palestinian, I know only a little. Very little, and for that you have to shoot me," he said.

Scorpion fired the pistol, the bullet hitting the seat between al-Hafez's legs with a loud *thunk*. Al-Hafez stared at him, stunned, wide-eyed.

"The Palestinian," Scorpion said. He cocked the hammer, and al-Hafez flinched involuntarily at the click. "Is he really Palestinian?"

"I have no idea. There was a rumor that he fought the Israelis in Lebanon in July 2006."

"What's his name?"

"I don't know, and if I did, I would not say," al-Hafez said, raising his hand. It trembled, just slightly, and he was embarrassed by it. He took a deep breath. "Even if you shoot me, I can't tell you. I've probably told you too much already."

"How is it you don't know? You support Hezbollah, you and the Iranians."

"Against the Israelis, of course. And in Lebanon, where we have legitimate national interests. Lebanon was part of Syria for thousands of years, until the 1920s when the French came along and invented it as a country. But not against the Egyptians—or the Americans."

"Why not?"

"Because we're surrounded by countries allied to you, including the strongest army in the Middle East, the Israelis, right on our border. We are not so smart like you with satellites and gadgets, but also not so stupid. It's not in our interest, just as what happened to Budawi was not in our interest. And please, where is the BlackBerry that you took?" Scorpion placed the BlackBerry he'd found in al-Hafez's drawer on the desk.

"I can't let you walk out with that," al-Hafez said.

"You can't stop me. Unless . . ." Scorpion hesitated.

Al-Hafez nodded, accepting the implied offer. "We've heard rumors of a power struggle within Hezbollah," he said. "The Islamic Resistance is the action cell of a violent radical faction. That's why we weren't surprised when you showed up on our radar, and why I'm telling you now. There are whispers of something very big about to happen, but we don't know what and we are not involved. To prove it, in exchange for returning my BlackBerry and letting you walk out of here, I'll give you Dr. Abadi's address. Inside Islamic Resistance his nom de guerre is Abu Faraj." He got up, walked over to his desk and wrote the address on a piece of paper. He started to hand it to Scorpion, then stopped. "Where is my man, Fawzi al-Diyala?"

Scorpion told him the name of the hotel.

"Is he alive?"

"He's tied up and he'll have a filthy hangover and won't remember much, but otherwise he's unharmed."

Al-Hafez offered the slip of paper. "Call off your men. If anyone else follows me, I'll kill them," Scorpion said, putting the slip of paper in his pocket.

"It's in the al Mouhajarine district. Be warned. He's well protected," al-Hafez said.

"So were you."

"Extremely well protected."

"I'll keep that in mind," Scorpion said, leaving the BlackBerry on the desktop and getting up.

Al Hafez walked around and sat down behind his desk. Scorpion stuck the gun in his belt, pulled his shirt over it and headed for the door.

"By the way," he said, pausing at the door. "What's Abadi a doctor of?"

"He's a medical doctor."

"What's his specialty?"

"Infectious diseases. Why?"

"Just curious. Wait five minutes before you press the button under the desk, Najah," Scorpion said. Something al-Hafez had said was setting off alarm bells in his head, but he wasn't sure what.

"I want you out of my country, Monsieur Leveque," al-Hafez said, using Scorpion's cover identity, his eyes narrowing. "You have twenty-four hours. After that, *bi 'idni allah*, you will never leave Syria. Not even as a corpse."

The night goggles cast a greenish glow over the trees and the wall and the guardhouse outside the gated estate. Scorpion studied the layout from his rental car down the street. Dr. Abadi's compound was well protected, all right, he thought. In addition to the guardhouse by the gate and the razor wire atop the high concrete walls, he spotted a number of security cameras, wireless alarms, and motion detectors along the perimeter, and more no doubt were strategically located on the grounds and in the house. And he heard the barking of guard dogs from inside the walls.

He put the night goggles in his backpack. There wasn't any choice. He'd have to go in. The question was how. Al-Hafez had kept his word about the tails. He'd been free of them all day. He'd been given twenty-four hours because al-Hafez wanted to distance Syria and the GSD from whatever the Islamic Resistance was planning. As for him tackling Dr. Abadi's compound, for al-Hafez it was a no-lose situation. The Syrian GSD and Mukhabarat were tied to the traditional Hezbollah leadership. From al-Hafez's point of view, whether he killed Abadi or Abadi killed him, the director won.

Scorpion had spent the day making preparations. He'd rented a Renault Megane, a car they'd used to tail him, obviously popular with the GSD. At an Internet café, he'd posted what he learned from al-Hafez about the Islamic Resistance to the International Corn Association website. Enough to keep them scrambling and to keep Rabinowich happily digging through databases. In response to a cryptic coded post by Rabinowich, Scorpion indicated that so far as he could tell, al-Hafez was most likely telling the truth about no Syrian involvement in the Cairo bombing, but he would know more after tonight.

That afternoon, he had gone to a number of shops in Saida Zaynab, a slum district filled with refugees from Iraq where, for a price, you could buy anything or anyone. Later he'd mingled with the evening crowds in the lanes and shops blazing with light in the Souk al-Hamidiyeh, in the walled Old City next to the citadel, where he bought an inexpensive suit like the one his cover, Fawzi al-Diyala, would wear. He was prepared as he could be. If Abadi's men captured him and he had to get out, he was counting on the Houdini trick, the one that had enabled the magician to make his famous escapes. But there was no way to stop the dryness in his mouth or his heart rate from going up. He knew there was a good chance he'd end the night as a headless corpse floating in the Barada River.

He'd made his choice that afternoon. Basically, there were only two ways in.

He could sneak in, deal with the perimeter guards, and tranquilize the guard dogs with Diazepam. As for the alarms, a preliminary drive-by earlier in the day convinced him that for such a large compound, they were likely using wireless alarms. Trying to eliminate alarms individually meant getting to the alarms or the controller without setting off motion detectors and other sensors that were probably all over the place, and then required someone who knew what he was doing to disconnect them. The system was almost certainly multichannel, so that the instant you disconnected one, the other channel would set off the alarm. But all wireless devices were based on RF technology, and a better way would be to disable them all at the same time with an electromagnetic pulse. All that required was a powerful enough transmitter—say a 2.4 GHz transmitter with a miniparabolic dish—and something to create an electromagnetic interference wave. An iPod playing Bruce Springsteen would do.

But the problem with breaking in was you never knew what you would run into. Sooner or later there would be a confrontation with other guards, and gunfire and police to deal with. And all that so at best he could briefly interrogate Abadi under pressure where the value of information from torture was always suspect. Anything you got from such interrogations was always a mixture of lies and half-truths, and that's if you had time, and he had none.

The second way in was to make an appointment and try to talk himself in. As with what he had done with Kassem in Beirut, the real intelligence would come not from what was said, but how Abadi reacted afterward. Except they were not stupid, and his cover was thin, and if they started to question his cover, he might be the one screaming in a dark cellar trying to think of lies and half-truths they'd believe. From somewhere, a dog barked just once, and he realized his heart was pounding.

A car came down the street, its headlights carving the only light in the darkness except for a dim red glow from the interior of the guardhouse. As it passed, Scorpion started his rental car and drove it to the gate. A guard in olive-drab fatigues stepped out of the guardhouse. At the same instant, a second guard appeared on the other side of the car with a Chinese Type 95 assault rifle pointed at him. It looked brand new and very lethal.

"I have an appointment with Abu Faraj," Scorpion said in Arabic, using Abadi's cover name and showing the guard the GSD ID card that identified him as Fawzi al-Diyala. A bead of sweat trickled down his back. If al-Hafez had alerted Abadi, they would let him in and it would go bad very fast. The guard glanced at the card, then at his face, and nodded to the other guard.

"Ahlan wa sahlan," he said, pressing a button to open the gate and gesturing for him to drive in.

He drove around a circular driveway, a marble fountain splashing water in the middle of a lawn, and parked in front of the villa, bathed in white light from outside floodlights. As he got out of the Renault, he spotted a guard with a German shepherd patrolling beyond the floodlit area, and surveillance cameras on the side and roof of the villa. He walked up to the entrance, and three armed men appeared and asked him to take off his suit jacket. They checked the jacket and frisked him thoroughly, taking pistol from the holster at the small of his back. It was a Russian SR-1 Gyurza, standard issue for the Russian FSB and former allies like the Syrian GSD, which he had bought that afternoon in Saida Zaynab. When they were done, one of the guards took him inside and asked him to wait.

The foyer was marble and sleek, an interior designer's dream. After a moment the double door to a living room opened and a paunchy middle-aged man with a goatee and wearing glasses came out. In the gap of the door just before Dr. Abadi closed it behind him, Scorpion caught a glimpse of a well-dressed woman and a young girl watching a big screen TV. He was glad he hadn't come in shooting.

"*Min fadlak*, this way," Dr. Abadi said. He led Scorpion into a small office, the walls covered with books. The guard who had taken his gun waited outside the door. "Would you like some juice? Turkish coffee?" the doctor asked, sliding a folder on the desk into a drawer.

Scorpion looked at the books on the walls. They were on medicine, mostly infectious diseases, anthropology, and Islamic studies.

"You come from Najah al-Hafez?" Scorpion didn't answer. "So what does the Idarat al-Amn al-'Amm want at this hour?"

"Where's the Palestinian?" Scorpion said.

"There are millions of Palestinians under brutal Israeli occupation in the West Bank and Gaza," Dr. Abadi replied.

"Just the one," Scorpion said.

"Why is this of interest?"

"You know why! Do you take us for idiots? We're having to deal with the Egyptian Mukhabarat now!" Scorpion shouted, standing up. Behind him, he heard the door open and the guard come rushing in. Dr. Abadi held up his hand to stop the man from attacking Scorpion. "You live here because we allow you to live here!" Scorpion continued.

"Because it is in your interest for me to be here," Dr. Abadi said, signaling the guard to leave.

"Maybe after Cairo, it is not so much in our interest anymore," Scorpion said, and sat down. "Where's the Palestinian?"

"Not in Syria. Or Lebanon."

"And therefore none of our business? Hardly. Tell me about him."

"The Palestinians are a people oppressed. There is nothing else to know."

"Trained in Iran?"

"Palestinians are not the only ones trained in Iran," Dr. Abadi said, his meaning obvious. Syrian GSD and Mukhabarat officers often collaborated and trained with the Iranians. "Nor is Iran the only country sympathetic to the Resistance."

"Is he in Europe?"

"What do you care? The Palestinian is an operative. Policy is decided here," Dr. Abadi said, tapping his own chest. Just then his cell phone rang.

"As-salaam aleikum," he said into the phone, then listened. He looked at Scorpion and said nothing. Scorpion began to get a bad feeling. He was about to move when Dr. Abadi pulled a gun from beneath the desk and pointed it at him. "Ahmed!" he called out, and the guard outside the door rushed in, saw what was happening, pointed his gun at Scorpion and shouted to the two other guards.

"Who are you?" Dr. Abadi demanded.

"You know who I am. Fawzi al-Diyala of the GSD. Director Najah al-Hafez sent me, as you were told," Scorpion snapped.

Dr. Abadi shook his head. "One of my men is with al-Diyala at his apartment this minute. It seems he doesn't feel too well. Someone slipped a drug into his juice today. Are you a Jew? Mossad? BND? Who are you?" he asked.

"What do you care? Policy is decided elsewhere,"

Scorpion said, his mind racing. Someone, not al-Hafez, had tipped Abadi off. An Islamic Resistance agent inside the GSD. Of course Abadi had suspected Mossad, but of all the intelligence services in the world, why had he mentioned the German BND? Did that mean the Palestinian was in Germany? Wherever he was, Scorpion realized, it didn't look like the information was going to do him much good.

"Stupid. Whoever you are, even your jokes are stupid. Get rid of him," Dr. Abadi said, pointing the gun with a two-handed stance at Scorpion. One of the guards pressed the muzzle of his gun against Scorpion's head as a second guard started to tie his wrists with a plastic zip-tie. Once his hands were tied, they'd relax, figuring they had him, he thought, waiting till two of the guards pulled him roughly to his feet.

As they started to shove him out, he did a Brazilian back leg sweep, taking down the guard to his right, then turning close into the guard behind him, he butted him under the chin while grabbing the single-edge razor blade hidden in his hair, a trick Houdini had used in his famous paper bag escape, and used it to cut the plastic zip-tie. Then he pulled the guard he had butted into a low choke hold below the level of the desk, so Abadi couldn't see to shoot, and slashed his carotid artery with the razor.

The first guard Scorpion had taken down now aimed his gun at him. He used a Krav Maga move, blocking with the hand, stepping out of the line of fire, twisting the guard's wrist and taking the gun away, all in less than two seconds. He whirled and shot the third guard in the face, and then, still on his knees, fired through the desk, hitting Abadi in the stomach. Scorpion rolled away as Abadi fired into the desk, missing him. As the first guard started to pick up the gun, he shot him in the head.

He stood up then, as Dr. Abadi, pressing his forearm against his bleeding stomach, aimed his gun. Scorpion fired, the bullet going through Abadi's hand into his stomach. Abadi cried out as he fired, his shot going wide. Scorpion fired again at his chest, killing him.

The alarm was going off, and somewhere a woman was screaming. He only had seconds. Fortunately, Dr. Abadi had left his laptop computer on. Scorpion took out a special flash drive designed by the NSA and plugged it into the laptop's USB port. The drive's software took over the operating system with admin privileges. It grabbed Abadi's e-mail files, gathering his account properties—the names and IP addresses of his incoming POP3 and outgoing SMTP mail servers and all of the document and Internet files on the hard drive—and downloaded them onto the flash drive. When it was finished, Scorpion pulled the flash drive out of the port and took it, along with two guns, including the SR-1 Gyurza.

He knew he had to leave fast, but there was something in the way Abadi had slipped the folder into his desk drawer that made him hesitate. The drawer was locked, but it only took a moment to pick the lock and pull out the folder. It contained what looked like a scientific report in Russian, and what appeared to be a typewritten translation in English titled "Modalities of Septicemic Yersinia Pestis Distribution." The Russian paper was stamped "Степень Секретности," which meant Top Secret, the intelligence equivalent of the Holy Grail.

He could hear someone shouting outside, not far away, and knew he was out of time. Stuffing the paper in his pocket along with the flash drive, he walked out of the office. The woman and little girl stood in the hallway and stared at him, wide-eyed.

"Where's the control box for the alarm?" he asked them.

They just stared at him, but the little girl involuntarily glanced at the hall closet. Scorpion opened the door, saw the metal box on the wall and opened it. He fired a bullet into the recorder drive for the security cameras and pulled all the switches. The floodlights went off outside, followed by shouts and dogs barking, and suddenly the front door was sprayed with bullet holes from automatic fire from a pair of Type 95 automatic rifles. The little girl screamed as her mother stared down at the blood blossoming on her chest a moment before collapsing. Scorpion shoved the girl down to the floor, and as the front door swung open emptied one of his guns at the opening. Then he ran back into the office, flung Abadi's laptop at the window, shattering the glass, and leaped through the broken window and into the darkness outside.

Instead of heading for the front gate, he ran toward the back of the property. He heard one of the German shepherds growling as it raced toward him. It would jump, he thought. That's how they were trained. To go for the hand or follow their instincts and go for the throat. It was almost upon him. He needed a stick or something, but all he had was the gun and the razor blade. As the dog leaped for his throat, he grabbed it by the fur on its neck and smashed his gun down on its nose. The dog yelped and lunged again. Hell of a dog, he thought, grabbing it and smashing its nose again. This time, the dog emitted a high-pitched animal scream and backed away, panting, its tongue lolling out.

A guard was running toward him. The man stopped and went down into a shooting position as Scorpion hit the ground, rolled over and fired three times. After the first shot, the guard didn't move. Scorpion waited a moment, then climbed a tree next to the estate wall, inched over the razor wire, hung down from the branch and dropped to the other side. He picked himself up and walked away. In the distance he could hear the sound of approaching police sirens.

Scorpion spent a restless night in a room rented from an Iraqi family in the Saida Zaynab district, the gun kept close to him. There was always a chance that al-Hafez might change his mind and come after him, not to mention Hezbollah and the Islamic Resistance. By the light of a bedside lamp, he tried to make sense of the translation of the Russian paper he'd taken from Abadi's desk.

It was very technical, but appeared to be a report on secret experiments done at a lab at Vozrozhdeniya involving the use of aerosol sprays to transmit plague pathogens. He recalled that Vozrozhdeniya, once an island but now a peninsula because of a severe drop in the water level of the inland Aral Sea between Kazakhstan and Uzbekistan, had been a secret biological warfare research facility in the old Soviet Union. It was essential he get the paper to Rabinowich immediately, and hated having to wait till morning to cross the border. He had to get out of Syria.

On the morning TV news, an Al Jazeera reporter standing in front of Dr. Abadi's estate said the murders were being blamed on Israeli agents. Syria was filing a formal complaint to the United Nations, and a majority of countries in the UN were already calling for a resolution condemning Israel for assassinating Abadi.

By mid-morning Scorpion was back in Beirut, having crossed the border as a Syrian auto salesman from Aleppo. At an Internet kiosk at Beirut airport, he uploaded the encrypted contents of the flash drive and a scanned-in copy of the secret Russian paper to the International Corn website. He learned from a Rabinowich-coded post on the site that the NSA had tracked Dr. Abadi's e-mail servers. There had been frequent e-mails in a code they were working on but hadn't broken, between Abadi and an e-mail account in Hamburg, Germany, belonging to someone named Mohammad Modahami.

Scorpion caught the Air France flight from Beirut to Paris. Over the Mediterranean, he played back what had happened with Dr. Abadi in his mind. There was something Abadi had said that kept nagging at him, but he couldn't put his finger on it. At a rented computer in the business *zone de travail* at

De Gaulle Airport, during a layover for his flight to Hamburg, he Googled *Septicemic plague*.

There were three versions of the plague, he learned: Bubonic plague, thought to be the disease that caused the Black Death of the Middle Ages; Pneumonic plague; and Septicemic plague. All were caused by the same *Yersinia pestis* bacteria. In each version of the plague, the pathogen infected a different part of the body. Bubonic plague infected lymph nodes, Pneumonic the lungs, and Septicemic the blood. The Bubonic and Septicemic plagues were typically transmitted by flea bites from infected rodents. Pneumonic plague was transmitted from human to human by airborne droplets from coughing. Of the three types of plague, Septicemic was the most insidious and deadly. The incubation period was normally two to five days, during which there were no symptoms. Once the patient realized he was sick, with symptoms ranging from flu-like chills, fever, coughing, and headache, to black and purple patches under the skin, the disease was nearly a hundred percent fatal. In most cases, the same day the patient realized he was ill was the day he died.

A chill went through Scorpion. The paper from Abadi suggested that the Russians had weaponized Septicemic plague at Vozrozhdeniya during the Cold War and that somehow the Islamic Resistance now had that weapon. Rabinowich had put the intel about the missing weaponized plague together from his bits and bytes of "subtexture," or maybe from a defector or an FSB mole, and connected it to the Palestinian, and Bob Harris hadn't told him about it because they wanted independent confirmation. His conclusions were slender and based on conjecture, Scorpion realized, but the pieces fit. No wonder Harris had come all the way to Karachi! If there was such a thing as an airborne version of Septicemic plague and the Palestinian set it off in an American city, tens of millions could die. The only way to stop him was to track down this Mohammad Modahami, Dr. Abadi's contact in Germany.

Scorpion bought a disposable cell phone and dialed a local Paris number. As he did so, over the airport loudspeaker he heard the first call for his flight to Hamburg. He used the day's sign, "Liverpool," and heard the countersign, "Mary Poppins." A woman's voice—he assumed she was someone from the CIA Paris station—stated that according to the BND, and confirmed by the German Bundespolizei, no such person as Mohammad Modahami had ever existed.

CHAPTER SIX

Rome, Italy

On his second night in Rome, sitting in a restaurant on the Via della Croce near the Spanish Steps and running out of time, the Palestinian considered three problems that stood in his way, each inside the other like Russian dolls, each more difficult to solve than the one before. He thought about them as he stared out at the dark street, its cobblestones lit by streetlamps hung on the sides of the buildings and the electric signs of the shops and restaurants, aware of the pretty American college girl at the next table who kept glancing over at him before returning to the conversation with her friends.

The first problem was how to coordinate multiple attacks simultaneously and get it done without breaching security. Hidden within that was the second problem, the attack that could not be known to the others and required transporting a large object into a city ringed with security checkpoints. The third task was the hardest. How to stage an attack on a location that would undoubtedly be protected by extraordinary security and that was completely off-limits to the public?

For weeks he had been thinking about how to do it. Was it possible? the blind imam in Holland had asked him, and he had been tempted to say no. Even now he wasn't sure whether he had said yes, it could be done, out of faith or vanity that he would be the one to bring down the enemy. Phase one was nearly complete. Phase two would be far more terrible. A day that would change things far beyond September 11 in ways they couldn't imagine, a day they would never forget. Both phases presented difficulties, but this target was the greatest challenge. There were so many things that could go wrong: someone who didn't do what he was supposed to at exactly the right moment, an undercover agent betraying them, an overly zealous policeman at a checkpoint. Even the weather was a factor in a complex plan where the variability of a single degree of temperature could make a difference. He'd considered and discarded a dozen different ways of carrying it out. Sooner or later, in each of the scenarios he had come up with, he found a fatal flaw. Going over locations well before he finalized plans, learning the terrain, measuring distances as he had in Cairo, helped eliminate some possibilities, but still, the three main problems, each inside the other, remained unsolved.

He had explored the city, focusing on traffic flow and geography rather than the tourist attractions of ancient and Renaissance Rome, using a golf range finder to exactly measure distances, which would be critical. He'd spent hours at the Biblioteca Nazionale Centrale, studying municipal schematics and plans going back to ancient times. He drove out on the A91 to inspect the warehouse he had arranged to rent. It was in an industrial suburb with small factories and working-class apartment houses across from open lots, and most important, inside the A90 Ring Road that encircled the city and where there would undoubtedly be checkpoints. The business card he'd given the warehouse owners said he was the owner of a transport and material freight company in Germany. If they called to check on him, they would find that the company registration, address, phone numbers, and website were perfectly legitimate; all calls and inquiries would be promptly answered and handled by the office management company on Heidenkampsweg Street in Hamburg. He paid the warehouse owners the first three months rent in cash and they were clearly delighted. They reiterated that the discretion he'd demanded would be honored without question. The owners were two brothers from Palermo, and they assured him to *non preoccupare*. Sicilians, they told him, knew how to keep secrets.

By the time he'd gone to the restaurant near the Piazza di Spagna on the second day, he had solved two of the three problems. But the solution to the third and most difficult problem still eluded him. He looked up and caught the American college girl glancing at him. He smiled, and she smiled back. He wondered if he should have her or use her as a test for the police with explosives. With her long brown hair, she reminded him of someone, and then he remembered the young Bangladeshi woman in Queens with the haunting dark eyes. He recalled how she kept glancing not at the camera, but at him, when she made her martyr's video. Or maybe it was the video he remembered. In a way, it was more real to him than she herself was.

She was not a true *shaheedah* martyr. She liked America and her job in Manhattan, but her brother was a coward. He owed money to a Bangladeshi gang, had sworn himself to jihad and martyrdom to get the money and then backed out because of his fear, trying to use his two small children as an excuse. She was doing it to keep the Bangladeshi gang members from killing her brother and leaving his children fatherless. She would never do it for herself or for the brother, but would do it for the children, and also because the way she looked at him when she made the video made him think she was attracted to him. Her martyrdom was a gift for him, he thought, glancing now at the American girl talking and laughing with her friends. The waiter came with the Campari and soda he'd ordered and he was about to tell him to give Camparis to everyone at her table when just like that, he had the solution.

The American girl raised her wineglass toward him, her eyes crinkling at the corners, confident of herself and her looks. Instead of responding, the Palestinian stood up, tossed some money on the table, and left in a hurry, the girl never knowing how close to death she had come.

He went back to his hotel near the top of the Spanish Steps, packed and got the rented Mercedes coupe from the underground parking garage. Once on the A1 and out of Rome, he drove through the darkness on the autostrada at over a hundred miles per hour, the radio blasting music by Euro groups like Tokio Hotel and Fettes Brot. Near Florence, he called ahead and made a late reservation. By midnight he was checking into the Principe di Savoia Hotel in Milan. In the morning he went to the San Vittore prison in the center of the city.

Carmine Bartolo came into the visitors' area and sat across the glass partition from him with a swagger, despite his shackles. Although he was of medium height, he looked bigger, almost hulking. His thick hair and heavy brows made his eyes seem small and dangerous. Inside the Naples Camorra, the mafia gang that virtually ran that city, Bartolo was known as "Il Brutto" for his perpetually nasty sneer and his legendary use of a butcher's cleaver as his preferred form of intimidation. He said something in a rapid slang Italian that the Palestinian didn't understand.

"Non capisco. Parla inglese? Français? Deutsch?" the Palestinian asked.

"English," Bartolo said, pronouncing it "Eengleesee." He leaned closer toward the glass. "What are you? *Turco? Musulmano?* Muslim boy?"

"Businessman. I'm here to buy something."

"You want buy, go to Rinacente store. This is *prigione. Capisce?*" Bartolo said, glancing sideways at the guard standing by the wall to see if his humor was being properly appreciated. The guard looked away, bored. He was paid to look away and not to hear.

The Palestinian motioned Bartolo closer. "I'll pay you a hundred thousand euros cash for what I want."

Bartolo's eyes narrowed under his heavy brows. He looked like the brute killer he was, the Palestinian thought.

"Who are you?" he asked.

"Someone who can pay," the Palestinian said, and covering his mouth so a camera couldn't pick it up, whispered what he wanted.

Bartolo's eyebrows came together, forming a single ridge across his forehead, making him look almost like a Neanderthal.

"What you want for? A job, *sì*?"

"None of your business. Part of what I'm paying for is no questions."

"*Figlio di puttana!*" Bartolo said, standing up, hunching over slightly because of the shackles. "I don't *fare affare* with Turco I don't know."

"A hundred thousand. I can always try the Zaza brothers or the Nuova Famiglia," the Palestinian said quietly.

"You go Zaza, do business with those *busones*? *Me ne infischio*," Bartolo said, jerking his chin at the Palestinian in lieu of the usual obscene gesture, because of his shackles. The Palestinian beckoned him closer to the glass.

"A hundred twenty thousand cash. Half now, half on delivery."

Bartolo sat down again.

"Plus forty *per cento* what job you doing," he said.

"Twenty-five percent—and no questions."

"*Trenta*. Thirty. You talk my wife," Bartolo said. He took a small pencil stub and wrote something on a scrap of paper. He slapped the paper against the glass so the Palestinian could read the telephone number he had written on it. Then Bartolo crumpled the paper up in his hand, spit on it, chewed and swallowed it, and stood up.

"You don't pay, maybe you don't look so good. Maybe don't feel so good, Turco," Bartolo said, shuffling toward the door, his shackles clanking.

"Andiamo," the guard said, unlocking the door.

"Vaffanculo!" Bartolo cursed, shuffling out.

The Palestinian left the prison and drove the Mercedes out of town, heading for Turin. Along the way he bought two disposable cell phones and called a number in Turin from an Autogrill rest stop on the autostrada.

"Fee ay fis sinima il layla di?" he asked in Arabic. What's playing at the movie tonight?

"Piazza della Republica, Porta Palazzo Nord," a man replied, and hung up. The Palestinian used the second phone to call a number in Holland.

"Bitnazaam gawalaat?" he asked in Arabic. Do you arrange tours?

"Abu Faraj is dead. In his home in Damascus," the voice at the other end said, using the nom de guerre of Dr. Abadi. The Palestinian watched the traffic on the A4 go by. Suddenly, it seemed as if every car was a potential danger. Impossible, he told himself. They couldn't be on to him so quickly after Cairo. "Also his wife and three guards."

"Who was it?" he asked.

"We don't know. The Jews or the Americans. Pick one. Whoever, the dog got away," the voice said.

"He was good enough to get past all the guards and alarms. That house was like a fortress."

"*Khalli baalak*," the voice said. Be careful. "Whoever it was is very dangerous. He also took a folder and may have accessed his computer. Is there anything on it of you?"

"*Wala haaga.*" Nothing, he said, his thoughts racing. This plus the near capture of Salim Kassem in Beirut meant they were after him. Even if they didn't know who or where he was, someone was getting closer.

"Are you sure?"

"Nothing," he said, remembering the long walk he had taken with Dr. Abadi in the Bekaa Valley after the 2006 July war with the Israelis. *You do not exist. It is the only way,* Dr. Abadi had said. There would be nothing of him on Abadi's computer, or anywhere for that matter. He was certain of it. He waited, and when the voice did not continue, finally said it: "Do we go on?"

"*Allahu akhbar!*" the voice said. God is great.

"*Allahu akhbar!*" the Palestinian replied and hung up. It was as they had agreed. No matter what, there would be no turning back.

Making sure he wasn't watched, he pulled out the SIM cards, placed the two cell phones and SIMs just behind his front tire, and backed the Mercedes over them. He jumped out, picked up what was left of the phones and tossed the pieces at intervals into the brush along the autostrada to Turin.

It was getting warm, the sun glittering on the Po River and on the mountains as he drove into Turin and parked in a structure near the Porta Palazzo. It was a working-class area, and he passed warehouses and cheap couscous restaurants as he walked to the piazza and waited on the sidewalk near a cluster of market stalls. Within minutes a van pulled up. Two Moroccan men jumped out and shoved him into the back. One of the Moroccans started to put a hood on his head.

"U'af!" Stop! "No hood. I want to study the area," the Palestinian said sharply in Arabic. One Moroccan looked at the other, who didn't say anything. He kept the hood in his hand. "Where are we going?" the Palestinian asked the driver.

"Across the river. Make sure no one is following," the driver said, weaving through the traffic, mostly Fiats, of course, from the big Fiat factory in the suburbs of the city, past the lush green of the Royal Gardens and the towering four-sided dome of the Mole Antonelliana, Turin's signature landmark. Designed to be a synagogue, the Mole was now Italy's National Movie Museum, and was said to be the tallest museum in the world. They drove across the bridge over the Po River, then cut illegally across the oncoming lane to a side street, turning back on the Via Bologna and recrossing to the western side of the river. After another ten minutes going back and forth on side streets to make sure no one was following, the driver pulled up to the loading dock of a small warehouse a few doors down from a garage that had been converted into a mosque. They got out and went inside the warehouse.

There were six young Moroccan and Albanian men in work clothes, two of them wearing the green coveralls of Italian sanitation workers, and two women in *hijabs*. They stood around or sat on metal chairs near a stack of crates in a corner of the warehouse. A bearded young Moroccan man sat behind a folding table in the front of the group, sipping a bottle of Orange Fanta. An older man in an embroidered *taqiyah* cap, who the Palestinian assumed was the imam, sat beside the bearded Moroccan.

"*Salaam aleikem*," the imam said.

"*Wa aleikem es-salaam*," the Palestinian replied, taking a seat and turning the chair sideways so he could see the two men at the table and the rest of the group. The bearded man put a Beretta pistol on the table.

"You are welcome, Brother," the imam continued in Arabic. "We have been instructed to assist you in all possible ways."

"Assist, yes. But in Torino we lead," the bearded man said, his hand touching the gun.

"You are GICM?" the Palestinian asked, naming the terrorist Moroccan Islamic Combatant Group responsible for a series of deadly bombings and kidnappings across northern Italy.

The bearded man nodded.

"Give me your gun," the Palestinian ordered, standing and holding out his hand. The bearded man picked up the pistol and pointed it at him.

"I give the orders here," he said.

"Do you submit to Allah? Have you said the Shahadah?" the Palestinian demanded, his eyes burning. "We are the Al-Muqawama al-Islamiyya. Do you know there is a *fatwa* against any who would lift a hand against me because of my work in our holy cause?" He stepped closer to the table and held out his hand. "Either kill me now and burn forever in *jahannam* or give me the gun, Brother."

The bearded man's eyes darted around, looking at his friends and followers. Everyone was riveted on the confrontation. One of the Moroccans from the van started to pull his gun out of a shoulder holster, then stopped halfway. From outside the warehouse came the sound of a car honking in traffic. No one moved. The bearded man's fingers tightened on the gun. The Palestinian could see specks of dust floating in the shafts of sunlight coming through the high warehouse window, and he wondered if it would be the last thing he ever saw. At last the bearded man exhaled. Without a word, he pushed the gun on the table toward the Palestinian.

"*Allahu akbar*," God is great, the Palestinian said, picking up the gun. The others started to echo "*Allahu akbar*" when the Palestinian aimed the gun and shot the bearded man in the head, the shot ringing unbelievably loud in the silence. One of the women gave out a muffled cry as the body slumped to the side of the chair.

The Palestinian turned on the group and stared at them. "Our moment of truth has come. There can be only one leader here," he said, and told them what he wanted them to do.

"Where do you want the delivery?" Francesca said, tossing her long blond hair, her dark roots showing only at the part. They were having dinner in a small exclusive restaurant in Milan, near Sempione Park.

"In Torino," the Palestinian said, and told her

the name of the street. He was eating the best Piedmontese veal *battutu* he'd ever tasted, washed down with an excellent Sagrantino wine. "Just deliver it and walk away."

"And the money?"

"Before your men go two meters, they will have the rest of the money."

"You understand with the Camorra, you don't get two chances?" she said.

"You aren't afraid to talk about the Camorra here?" he said, looking around at the well-dressed diners at nearby tables.

"Why not? I own this place." She had a rough contralto laugh. "Many others too. You are surprised to find a woman *capa*, yes? Of the Camorra, it is the custom when the husband dies or is in the *prigione*, for the wife to take over. Good custom. We hold it close," she said, touching her chest. "But you were surprised. I see it in your eyes."

"Only at how attractive you were." She was in her forties, her skin tan, with a good shape shown off by the red designer dress she wore, her breasts so perfect that only a world-class surgeon who was half in love with her could have done them.

"*Non c'è male*," she said—not bad—licking a drop of spaghetti sauce from the corner of her mouth. "Listen. You want to take me to the bed? What job is this? You tell me and this will be the best night of your life."

"Tempting. Also dangerous—in more ways than one," he said, glancing at the two bodyguards she'd come in with, now standing on either side of the front door, their suit jackets unbuttoned.

"You are not afraid. I can see you are not a man who fears. You understand, we women are curious, like cats. Arouse a woman's curiosity and you can have her."

"Any woman?"

"Any woman on earth—and in heaven too," she said, lighting a cigarette. "You want me?"

"I won't tell you. Ever."

"Maybe I don't care," she said, tossing her hair. "Maybe I want to make *chiavare* with you in the bed," she said, leaning forward so he could see the swell of her breasts.

"Maybe you'd rather have the money. Sixty thousand now as agreed."

"You see! You do understand women. Where is it?" she said, getting up.

"A package. I gave it to the maître d'."

She leaned over and kissed him, her tongue darting into his mouth, tasting of the lobster ragout from the spaghetti sauce. "Next time I fuck you so good, *caro*," she whispered. She got up and left, stopping at the maître d', who handed the package to one of her bodyguards.

When the Palestinian left the restaurant, he doubled back for nearly an hour, zigzagging through the dark city streets and autostrada exits, anticipating that Francesca would have him followed. When he thought he was clear, he drove to the Milan Central Station, where he caught the late night Red Arrow high-speed train to Rome. In the morning, he flew from Rome to Moscow.

The Camorra were dangerous enough, and what he had to do in Russia even more so, he thought on the long flight. All the while, the shadow hunting him nagged at the Palestinian, an unknown killer without a face or a name, like a nightmare from his childhood. Except he wasn't a child anymore. Now, he was the one to be feared. Looking through the airplane window at the snowcapped Alps below, he remembered an old Arab proverb his father had told him when he was a boy: "An army of sheep led by a lion will defeat an army of lions led by a sheep."

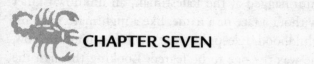

CHAPTER SEVEN

Hamburg, Germany

Scorpion first saw her on TV in the giant Saturn electronics store, her image repeated on hundreds of televisions tuned to the same German N-TV News channel like a kind of surreal electronic art exhibit, before he saw her in the flesh, standing in the middle of the street outside the large turquoise-colored mosque with a loudspeaker, demanding an end to "Islam's imprisonment of women." On the TV panel of talking head commentators, her looks were striking. Her skin was a smooth gold, her sleek black hair, cut short, a stunning contrast with her aquamarine blue eyes, a touch of mascara underlining them hinting of the Levant. She wore no head scarf, and although the credit at the bottom of the screen identified her as "Najla Kafoury," everyone addressed her only as "Najla," as if she had already achieved the one-name status that, as Harris once wryly remarked, denoted real celebrity nowadays. "You are either a one-name or a no-name," he'd said.

Now, seeing Najla Kafoury in the center of the

demonstration outside the mosque, a slim figure in a belted Burberry raincoat, she was smaller than he had expected from her TV image. Her voice rang out in perfect German through the loudspeaker as she demanded that Islamic leaders stop *"behandlung von frauen wie sklaven,"* treating women as slaves. A line of helmeted Schutzpolizei stood between her and an angry crowd of Muslims, men and women, trying to shout her down, some carrying signs that read *Feinde des Islam*, Enemy of Islam; others, *Verräter*, Traitor, and *Haretiker*, Heretic.

"The Prophet said treat women well, but the only *sura* you know is the fourth *sura*, which tells you to beat women!" she shouted.

"A good Muslim woman is obedient and does not need to be beaten," someone in the crowd shouted in Farsi.

"Das ist Europa, not sixth century Arabia. Fourteen centuries of abuse is enough! No woman should ever be beaten!" she shouted back in German.

Some in the crowd began to throw things at her, cushions, eggs, oranges. The line of Schutzpolizei started forward as she and the small band of men and women with her retreated, the TV cameramen edging forward to capture the shot.

"She got what she wanted," a man near Scorpion in the crowd commented in German to a paparazzo photographer next to him. "She'll be on *Heute* tonight," he added, referring to the nightly TV news show.

"Natürlich. Najla delivers the only thing anyone cares about—ratings," the paparazzo said, standing

on his toes to try to get the shot of her holding a hand up to protect herself. "That's *meine liebsten*," he smiled as he got the shot.

"How much is it worth?" Scorpion asked.

"Depends. A shot like this, two, three hundred euros. If I could get Najla with her top off, she'd be worth twenty thousand." The paparazzo grinned.

"She's nothing. Just good looking," the man next to him said.

"That's why she's worth every euro." The paparazzo winked, pulling his gear together.

Scorpion drifted away in the crowd that was starting to disperse as the woman and her little group left in two cars and the Schutzpolizei began waving away the rest of the gathering. He walked the landscaped perimeter of the mosque grounds, blending in with passersby who had stopped to watch the demonstration and were now hurrying home for dinner. He studied the mosque grounds for alarms and communications. Spotting a Deutsche Telekom sticker on a phone line, he guessed they were using DSL to access the Internet. They had an alarm system, but it looked like a basic dual channel alarm, and shouldn't be a problem.

A cool fog drifted in from Alster Lake as it grew dark, the streetlights glowing ghostly white. He had dinner in a nearby *gaststätte* and thought about the conversation he'd had on one of the disposable cell phones he bought in the Saturn store and afterward broke apart and dispersed into a number of trash cans.

According to the nameless male voice on the local

number he called, the NSA had traced the Moham-mad Modahami account through a series of e-mail aliases and proxy servers to the Hamburg Islamic Masjid in the Uhlenhorst district. They were still working on the code Dr. Abadi had used to contact the fictitious Modahami. The voice said nothing about the Syrian killings, so Harris had to be han-dling whatever Foggy Bottom political dustup he'd stirred up in Syria.

The voice had said, "R with M is *sameach.* Ditto for the prime confirm on the bug," which Scor-pion understood to mean that according to Rabi-nowich, the CIA had shared the information he'd retrieved from Abadi's computer with the Israeli Mossad, and that both Rabinowich and the Israelis were *sameach*—Hebrew for happy—with what they were getting. It also meant that his own information about the weaponized plague, "the bug," was con-firmation of a threat Rabinowich already had from another source, which was the information Harris, citing the Prime Directive—need to know—had withheld from him in Karachi. Scorpion knew that his operating assumption now had to be that the Palestinian got his hands on an aerosol form of Sep-ticemic plague.

The voice had asked if he was staying in a "B and B," and he said no. They meant did he want the German BND and the BPOL—the Bundespo-lizei—to raid the Islamic Masjid? Saying no would indicate to Harris that he would do it himself, he thought. A raid by the BPOL in Hamburg was the last thing they needed. After Beirut and his taking out Abadi in Damascus, it would set alarm bells off all across the Hezbollah grid. Even worse, it would let the Palestinian know exactly where they were and how close or far behind him. The Palestinian might even move up the target date, and then they'd have even less time to try to stop it.

That was always the problem when Washington got involved, he mused. They tended to overkill everything, using a cruise missile with a thousand pound warhead when what you needed was a dart. "Sure you obliterate the target," Koenig used to say, "but how much intel do you get from an obliterated target?"

He paid the check and walked back to the mosque. The streets were nearly empty now, the Alster invisible in the darkness and fog, except for the glow of streetlights along the shore. He walked the grounds around the mosque with its twin Iranian-style minarets and a light from someone working late in an office toward the back. He looked for wire connections and had to go more by touch than vision in the darkness, finding a wire connected to an outside alarm and a security camera. After peeling away the insulation from the wire with his pocketknife, he wrapped the wire with a piece of steel wool and connected it to a cell phone with two wires to an AA battery and a little capacitor he'd picked up in the Saturn store. If he called the cell phone, the current would cause the steel wool to burst into flame and short-circuit the alarm.

Scorpion scanned the silent street, looking for something out of place, a car with someone in it, a commercial van parked where it shouldn't be.

But the fog made it difficult to see anything except the hazy light from the center's second story office window. Something wasn't right. His internal antenna, honed after years in the field, was sending him a signal, but with the darkness and the fog, he couldn't see where the danger was coming from. If this were a standard RDV or a break-in, he could wait them out or reset for another time, but on this mission there was no time. It forced you to take risks that were normally unacceptable.

There was only one alarm lead, and a single security camera covering the front entrance. He disabled the alarm with his pocketknife, removed the camera's recorder and put it in his pocket. He picked the lock to the front door and then hesitated. If there was another lead that he'd missed, the alarm would go off. He held his breath as he opened the door, but nothing happened. He crept up the stairs and at the corner held a small pocket mirror angled to see who was in the lighted office. The area was open, with a number of empty desks and a bearded Iranian man with glasses working at a computer.

Scorpion tiptoed quietly down the hallway, away from the general office area, and entered the imam's office at the end of the hallway. It was dark, and he turned on the desk lamp and looked around. The fog pressed against the windows, closing him in. Nothing could be seen outside. If there was danger, he would have to rely solely on hearing it. He went through the imam's desk and turned on the computer, plugging in a USB flash drive with special NSA software that could break any OS and log him in with administrator privileges. Once in, he explored the shared directories and exchange accounts on the center's local area network.

He quickly found the fictitious Mohammad Modahami e-mail account, which apparently was only used to receive encrypted messages that NSA was still trying to break. The account never sent any e-mails or responded to those from Abadi in Damascus. It's a one-way relay cutout, he thought. They were aware of Western intelligence services surveillance and were using some low tech way of forwarding messages from Damascus to the Palestinian's contact in Europe or the United States.

He copied the contents of the Modahami files onto the flash drive and shut the computer down, then moved on to the books on the shelves, most of them religious texts in Farsi and Arabic. He went through them quickly, looking and putting them back. Every once in a while he stopped and went to the door, listening for noises from outside or down the hall. He heard nothing from the other office where the bearded Iranian was working. He could have been alone in the world. He checked for a wall safe, but found only an electronic bug behind a photograph hanging on the wall. It was of the golden-domed shrine of the Imam Reza, the so-called Shi'ite "Eighth Imam" in Iran. He used his penknife to disable the bug.

Turning off the desk light, he went to the office of the imam's assistant next door. Intel from the BND had indicated that the assistant, Parviz Mostafari, ran the Islamic Center on a day-to-day basis. Scorpion began rummaging through Mostafari's desk and shelves, pausing for a moment to look at a framed photograph on the desk of a young Iranian woman in a *hijab* and black *chador* robe with a small boy taken on a beach somewhere. Another framed photo on a bookshelf showed a bearded Iranian man he assumed was Mostafari getting some kind of certificate from an older man, most likely the imam, Ayatollah Kazimi. Then he found it.

He discovered the postcard in a copy of *Velayat-e Faqih*, the book on Islamic government by the Ayatollah Khomeini, founder of the Islamic Revolutionary government in Iran. It was an ordinary picture postcard of a canal in Amsterdam with no postmark, so it had been hand-delivered. It was written like a postcard message, but the text was a jumble of Arabic letters, not real words. It occurred to him that was how they avoided NSA electronic surveillance. They were hand-delivering coded messages by courier. He was just slipping the postcard into his pocket when the bearded Iranian man with glasses suddenly appeared in the doorway, aiming a 9mm pistol at him.

"*Wer sind sie?*" the Iranian said. Who are you?

"*Salam.* I'm a friend of Parviz Mostafari," Scorpion replied in Farsi. He knew it was his ability in Farsi as well as Arabic, Urdu, and a number of European languages that had made him uniquely qualified for this mission, and why Harris had come all the way to Karachi to see him. "We know each other from Tehran," he added.

"You're lying. You're from Tehran?" the Iranian said in Farsi, scrutinizing him.

"*Khoshbakhtam.* I've been there."

"What's your favorite coffee shop?"

"The White Tower," Scorpion said.

"The one on Jomhuriyeh Eslami?"

"*Na*," Scorpion said. The Iranian was testing him. "On Pasdaran Avenue."

"Who are you? What do you want?" the Iranian asked.

"Someone who's not supposed to be here. Why don't you call the Schutzpolizei? Go ahead," Scorpion said, nodding.

"I could shoot you now," the Iranian said, aiming the gun. "You're a thief. You broke in."

"You won't," Scorpion said, his hand in his pocket on the cell phone, ready to set off the alarm. "Both of us have things we don't want to talk to the Schutzpolizei about."

"What's your name?"

"What difference does it make? If you want, I'll give you my name and a very convincing ID. But it won't convince you. So please, make up your mind. You can shoot and learn nothing, or we can talk."

"Talk about what?" the Iranian asked.

"Let's talk about the Palestinian."

"I don't know what you are talking about. You say you're from Tehran?"

Scorpion shook his head. "Damascus. I have orders. *Inshallah*, I'm here to help you."

"What orders? Who sent you?" the Iranian demanded.

"Same as you," Scorpion said.

"That's not an answer. You speak Farsi, but you're not Iranian."

"You speak German, but you're not exactly the blond, blue-eyed type, are you?"

"You could be anyone on either side," the Iranian said. "You could be BND or CIA. You could be Hezbollah or Iranian MOIS. You are not a friend of Parviz."

"Whoever I am, we both know you are not who you appear to be either, are you?" Scorpion said, feeling for the Send key on the cell phone in his pocket. "We seem to be at an impasse."

The Iranian appeared to make up his mind. Scorpion tensed.

"Stand up and turn around. I'm going to tie you up," the man said.

Scorpion got up, and as he started to take his hand out of his pocket and turn his back to the Iranian, pressed the cell phone. A loud alarm went off outside.

"*Scheisse!*" the Iranian said. He looked sharply at Scorpion. "Did you meet Mostafari in Venice?" he asked abruptly.

Scorpion's mind raced. "I've never been there. I've heard the art is interesting," he said. Venice was the CIA's emergency password. The Iranian was a mole, he thought, the alarm blaring.

"I like the Veronese paintings in the Doge's Palace," the Iranian said, completing the sequence. "Are you the Scorpion?"

"Who are you?" Scorpion said.

"Call me Ahmad. Ahmad Harandi. I've heard whispers of you. It's an honor. *Kol ha kavod*," Harandi said in Hebrew. A Mossad mole, Scorpion thought.

"How much time do we have?"

"Less than two minutes. We have to go," Harandi

said. They ran out and down the stairs. "Whatever is happening isn't happening here in Hamburg," Harandi added as they headed for the back exit. "This is just a cutout to relay information from Damascus.

"I know," Scorpion said when they reached the back door and paused. "The Palestinian's contact is in Amsterdam, isn't it?"

"No one knows for sure except the imam's assistant, Mostafari. He's the one who's really running things here. I'm not sure how much the imam knows."

"Who's the contact in Amsterdam?"

"His cover name is Ali. I overheard Mostafari say it once."

"What's Ali's last name?"

"I don't know. Mostafari doesn't trust me. He doesn't trust anyone."

Outside, they could hear the wail of an approaching Schutzpolizei car siren.

"What else about Amsterdam?" Scorpion asked.

"Very little. I only went once," Harandi said. "They sent me as a courier to pick up a package in my car. I left it at a coffeehouse drop in the Jordaan district and kept watch. An Arab, a very small man, *ein zwerg*—how do you say, a dwarf—came out with the package. I tried to follow, but lost him near the train station."

"Where? What street?"

"Haarlemmerstraat. You have to go now," Harandi said, opening the door.

"What will you tell them?"

"An intruder. You got away."

"*Khodchafez*. You know, we broke all the rules, you and I," Scorpion said.

"Maybe our bosses would've preferred it if we killed each other," Harandi said as he started to close the door.

"Maybe," Scorpion whispered back as he stepped into the darkness outside. He crossed the open area of the grounds staying close to the bushes. All at once, the sound of the alarm stopped, leaving his ears ringing.

The night pressed close, wrapping him in anonymity as he walked back to where he had parked his rented BMW. The streets were empty except for the occasional passing car, headlights carving cylinders of smoky light in the fog. Suddenly, he was face-to-face with a young couple, and they startled each other, abruptly appearing, like ghosts.

"*Entschuldigen sie*," he muttered as they passed.

He turned a corner and waited, listening for footsteps coming from behind, but there was nothing. After a moment he walked on. The streetlights were pale globes of light and the sounds of cars were muted as they passed. Once, he thought he spotted a shadow behind him, but it was impossible to see for certain in the fog. He got in the BMW and drove carefully out of the city, across the Elbe River and down the E22 toward Bremen.

Once out of Hamburg, the fog lifted and the visibility on the autobahn made for faster driving. With luck, he would be in Amsterdam before two in the morning, he thought, checking the headlights behind him in the rearview mirror. By the time he was forty kilometers outside Bremen, he knew he was being followed. An A4 Audi had been with him since before he'd crossed the Elbe into Wilhelmsburg.

Up ahead he saw the blue sign and crossed knife and fork of a Rasthof service area. He signaled and moved over carefully to make sure that whoever was tailing him stayed with him. He exited the autobahn, parked, and went to the *gaststätte*, its neon sign and lighted windows a pool of light in the dark parking area. In the reflection of the headlights of traffic on the autobahn in the restaurant window, he saw the Audi pull into the parking area.

He went into the restaurant and out the side exit, then waited in the shadow of a corner of the outside toilet cabin. In a few minutes he heard the sound of a woman's high heels on the pavement. An overhead light above the toilet door cast the shadow of someone approaching the *frauen toilette*. As she reached the restroom door, he stepped out and, with a hammerlock, twisted her wrist out and leveraged it behind her back so she was completely immobilized. She cried out in pain as he twisted her around, and he found himself staring into the frightened yet stunning face of the female TV journalist, Najla Kafoury.

"Why are you following me?" he demanded.

"Bitte, sie verletzen mich," she said.

"I'll hurt you a lot more if you don't do exactly as I say."

"Bitte, let me go. I won't run," she said, looking at him with those strange aquamarine eyes.

"It's a waste," he said, looking around to see if anyone was taking an interest. Someone, possibly a truck driver, was leaving the *gaststätte*, but hadn't seen them. "Using that wonderful tone of sincerity in your voice on such an obvious lie."

"I'm not lying," she said.

"Of course you are. You're scared. It's to be expected," he said, forcing her toward the BMW.

"Don't do this. I just want a story. *Bitte*, please," her voice soft and, despite her fear, with an undercurrent of sexiness. He applied a touch of pressure to her arm and she gasped at the pain.

"Get in or I'll break it," he said.

"What about my car?"

"Get in," he said again, opening the door and shoving her in. He went around the other side, got in and drove out of the parking area and back onto the autobahn.

"I'm a journalist," she said. "On television. N-TV 24 *Nachrichten*."

"I know who you are."

"I'm supposed to check in. I'll be missed," she said.

"See, that works better. More believable, but you're still lying."

"I have to call. They're waiting," she said.

"No one's waiting."

For the first time she really looked at him, at his shadowed profile lit only by the dashboard light. "What makes you so sure?"

"No crew. No links. No satellite van. You followed me from the mosque on your own." He held out his hand. "Give me your cell phone—and don't be cute. Any kind of a struggle at these speeds and we could both be killed."

She found the cell phone in her handbag and handed it to him. He shut it off and slipped it into his pocket. He drove at high speed, truck lights flashing by in the darkness as he passed them. Neither of them spoke till they were well past Bremen, nearing Oldenburg.

"What are you going to do with me?" she asked finally.

"That depends on what's waiting for us in Amsterdam," he said.

CHAPTER EIGHT

Volgograd, Russia

Borya Khmelnitsky, aka Gospodin Kolbasa, or Mr. Sausage, was laughing as he poured them both another glass of Dovgan vodka, the only kind of Russian vodka he said wasn't made out of piss. They were sitting at a window table of the Avgust restaurant on the Embankment overlooking the Volga River, where, though it was April, an occasional ice floe still floated by. It was said that Khmelnitsky got the nickname Kolbasa because of what he had done to a rival from the Tsentraly mafia gang at a sausage factory, like Sweeney Todd, feeding him to them at a so-called peace gathering.

"This guy, this Yuri guy, did it because his wife, she wasn't happy with her neck, okay?" Khmelnitsky laughed. He was a big man. He wore a black leather jacket over a flashy Hawaiian-type shirt, the unofficial uniform of the Ekaterinburg Uralmash mafia. "She has, how you call it, neck like rooster, okay? So she wants operation to fix neck, make pretty like swan. Also Moskva. All the time she wants to go to Moscow; live better life. This is like Chekhov.

"So this guy, Yuri, is big shot in MOD, Federal Security Service for Atomics, *da*? We do deal for three kilos Cesium-137, make beautiful dirty bomb. Comes out with big truck and with MOD security team and two troop trucks from Twelfth Main Directorate of GUMO, Ministry of Defense. All official, *da*? They leave Ozersk. Is closed city. Secret place. No one can enter. Officially, doesn't exist, Ozersk. People call city 'Mayak,' but is Ozersk. In Soviet times, say 'Ozersk' and you be in Lubyanka Prison, if they don't kill you on the way."

"Is that where the aerosol spray came from?" the Palestinian asked. "Ozersk? They moved it there from Vozrozhdeniya?"

Khmelnitsky looked at him sharply, and for a moment the Palestinian could see how dangerous he was. This was the first time he was meeting the man since they had done the deal for the aerosol apparatus with the three canisters of liquid pathogen culture three months earlier. All at once, Khmelnitsky grinned, showing his crooked satyr's teeth.

"Who can say? When Soviet times end, many things disappear. Even people," looking hard at the Palestinian, then smiling suddenly with his crooked teeth like they were best pals again. "So like I am telling, this guy Yuri and his MOD trucks, they go through five checkpoints, scan with dosimeter, alpha radiation detector, no problem. Everything fixed, you understand," he said, making the universal sign for money, rubbing his thumb on his fingertips. "They drive through taiga, forests, villages, like army convoy right to middle of Ekaterinburg. Right down middle of Malysheva Street. I see him,

Yuri. I say *'bakapor.'*" Dumbass. "'What you doing?'

"He say, 'We do business.'

"I say, 'You crazy *mudak*. You want do business in middle of street?'

"He say, *'Chto zahuy.'*" What the fuck?

"So we go to Plotinka, big dam. Is like park, in center Ekaterinburg. We talk out in open away from everyone. See everything. No bugs, no FSB. I say, 'Where is my Cesium-137?'

"He say, 'Fuck that cesium *govno* shit. We do better deal. More money.'"

"What was in the truck?" the Palestinian asked.

"Two steel drums. Between is steel drums of water and big sheet lead. Heavy *sukin-sin*. Inside, you never believe. I never believe. No one believe."

"So it was all there? Just like that?" the Palestinian said. He'd heard the story before, although each time the details changed, except for the part about the steel drums and what was in them, which had changed everything and added a second phase to his original operation.

"We go. See for yourself. All so his *pizda* wife's neck be beautiful. Crazy, *nyet*?" Khmelnitsky said, getting up and pulling his Hawaiian shirt over the gun in his belt.

They left the restaurant and walked by a park with souvenir vendors on the tree-lined path selling Matryoshka dolls and cheap watercolor prints. They got into Khmelnitsky's Mercedes and drove past tall apartment blocks to the Central Railroad Station, with its old-fashioned clock tower, and out toward the train yard.

On a hill in the distance the Palestinian could see

an unbelievably huge statue of a woman with her upraised arm holding a sword. Someone had told him she was Mother Russia and that she was bigger than the Statue of Liberty in New York. It all had something to do with World War Two. During the Communist times, the concierge at the hotel had said, Volgograd had been called Stalingrad and was the scene of a great battle. But the Palestinian was from the Middle East, knew little of European history and believed even less. If there had ever been a battle here, unlike Gaza or Lebanon, he could see no sign of it, and in any case it didn't matter. The only thing that mattered was what was waiting for him in the railroad container car, and if he could pull it off, like World War Two itself, no one would ever forget it, he thought as they pulled into the train yard parking area and got out.

Khmelnitsky took out two railroad badges and handed him one. They pinned them on and showed them to a guard at a gate in the chicken wire fence around the railroad yard. The guard, who was sitting and reading a Russian comic book of Russian Teenage Mutant Ninja Turtles led by a *balalaika* machine-gun-toting bear, didn't bother to look at their badges. They walked into the yard and over to a section of freight, ore, and container railroad cars. Three of Khmelnitsky's men, all in Hawaiian shirts and leather jackets, were squatting near one of the freight cars, smoking and sharing vodka from a bottle.

"Is okay, *da*?" Khmelnitsky said.

"I'll let you know after I've had a look," the Palestinian said.

Khmelnitsky gestured, and one of his men got up and opened the freight car door. The car was filled with steel drums, with ALUMINUM INGOTS painted on the sides in Russian Cyrillic lettering and seals from the VOLGOGRAD ALUMINUM FACTORY.

The Palestinian climbed up and approached one of the two drums marked SPECIAL ORDER 101 in Russian and removed the top, which hadn't been welded shut yet. He turned on his handheld Geiger counter and it immediately began clicking, the needle spiking, but well within safe limits for alpha, beta, and gamma radiation levels. If it had been Cesium-137 or Plutonium-239, it would've been too radioactive to safely approach, not to mention the difficulty of handling something so radioactive, and which would burst into intense flames at the drop of a hat, like plutonium. He picked up the small beer-can-sized ingot of Uranium-235 and held it in the palm of his hand. It was a dull gray, cool and dry to the touch and very heavy for its size. That was the beauty of U-235, he thought. It was easy to work with, the radiation level safe enough so you could sleep with it under your pillow, and if it was pure enough, it would change the world. He put it back, opened the second drum and measured the second ingot.

"What you think?" Khmelnitsky said. "Uranium-235. Twenty-one kilos. High enriched. Yuri say seventy-six percent, but who knows. Not make nuclear bomb," he cautioned, "but you do nothing in Russia, I don't care *govno* shit what you do. No bomb in Russia, FSB don't care *govno* shit what you do."

The Palestinian finished his measurements

and looked up. Without converting a microscopic amount to uranium hexafluoride by mixing it with fluorine gas—tricky enough because it was poisonous—and then testing for U-235, there was no way of accurately determining the exact enrichment level, but he knew it had to be more than seventy-six percent. It was just too easy to go from seventy-six percent to over ninety. Why would you stop?

"What about the RDX?"

"Here. One hundred eighty kilos," Khmelnitsky said, taking the top off another steel drum marked SPECIAL ORDER 102.

The Palestinian moved aside a layer of aluminum pellets, there to disguise it as an aluminum shipment, and opened a wooden box still marked with the Russian Army seal and markings and filled with a white crystalline solid. He cut off a small piece with his pocketknife and took out a set of vials that he mixed it with. He would be using RDX as the powerful secondary and tertiary explosives, and exploding bridge-wire blasting caps with PETN as the primary to set it off. It was all so elegant, he thought. So perfect and easy to work with and mathematical. He liked the neatness.

He inspected the remaining steel drums and indicated to Khmelnitsky to seal them up. As Khmelnitsky's men worked, the Palestinian stood outside on the ground beside the freight car. Khmelnitsky smoked a cigarette beside him.

"Is *kharasho*, good, *da*?" Khmelnitsky said. "Fifteen million U.S. dollar. Very nice."

"We agreed ten," the Palestinian said, tensing.

He'd expected this. They had discussed it in Damascus, what to do if the Russians made trouble. This was one of the danger points.

"*Kanyeshna*." We agree. "Was ten. Now fifteen," Khmelnitsky said, squinting through the smoke from the cigarette dangling from his lips.

"Suppose I don't agree?"

"We kill you. Keep down payment." Khmelnitsky shrugged. "You die. Next one pays."

"That would be a mistake," the Palestinian said quietly. "You want a war?"

"Listen, *druk*. One time people come to Ekaterinburg for tourism; see Urals, see house where Bolshiviki kill tsar and family. *Chto zahuy!* Now people come see cemetery for Uralmash mafia. Big stones for graves with big *fatagafira* picture of mafia guy, life size, with Mercedes behind him, guy in nice suit. Some graves with laser, kill enemy after you dead. No kidding. Is big tourism. So what you do? Kill me? What I give fuck? My *fatagafira* all ready. I am still young guy. Look good forever on stone. This good business. You get bomb, fuck your enemy. Fifteen million and you, me, we stay *druks*. Get drunk. Everything *kharasho*."

The Palestinian looked at the railroad cars and the flat sky, the color of stones. A Russian at his hotel had said millions died right where he stood, although he never believed the Russians about anything, except that they knew how to die.

"After the shipment is on board the ship," he said.

"Sure." Khmelnitsky smiled. "We go, you and me, drink Dovgan vodka, go to Ukraina, Donbas oblast region. We go Donetsk city. Put on truck. First make payment. Five million U.S. dollar now. Ten million when this *govno* shit on ship."

The Palestinian nodded. He turned on his laptop and made the electronic bank transfer.

"Check your account now," he said.

"Sure thing." Khmelnitsky grinned. "I come back. Money *kharasho*, we go. If not, we kill you."

They took the Aeroflot flight to Donetsk in eastern Ukraine, a coal mining and industrial city on the Kalmius River. They flew over the vast steppes, one city and town merging into the forests, grasslands, and suburbs of another. Khmelnitsky got drunk on the flight, and every time the blond airline hostess walked by, he would slide his hand up her skirt between her legs.

"Piristan!" stop it, she'd say, pushing his hand away and almost running toward the cockpit.

"Come sit here. I give you something instead of hand," Khmelnitsky laughed, grabbing himself. "She's nice, *da*?" he said to the Palestinian. "Nice ones," molding his hands like breasts.

"What if she tells someone?" the Palestinian said. "We don't want trouble now."

"No trouble. They see this," touching his Hawaiian shirt, "they know is Uralmash. They say nothing."

The next time the hostess came down the aisle, she handed him a glass of vodka. "Compliments of the captain," she said, smiling but with frightened eyes. She let Khmelnitsky fondle her breasts as she bent over to serve the drinks, her smile like the smile on a doll's face.

"See, *druk*. I say she nice girl," Khmelnitsky smiled. "No trouble."

They landed in Donetsk and were met by four tough-looking Ukrainian men in suits with open shirts and no ties.

"Dobryaky mafia," Khmelnitsky explained as they walked toward them. "They get percents from me. You pay nothing."

The Ukrainians drove them to the railroad yard. They watched a gantry crane load the railroad container with the steel drums onto the bed of a long haul container truck. One of the Ukrainians passed money to an inspector as it was loaded and watched as he stamped and initialed the shipping manifest. Once the rig was loaded and checked through the gate, they drove Khmelnitsky and the Palestinian back to the airport, where, after a vodka toast, the two of them boarded an Aerosvit flight to Odessa. Three hours later they were having lunch at the largest of the eight commercial terminals in the Odessa port. Through the window, they could see gantry cranes loading ships along the quay.

"Dobryaky mafia same like Uralmash," Khmelnitsky said. "All time, we do business, but Ukraina truly stupid *huesos*. Best thing about whole Ukraina country is that Dobryaky is same as Verkhovna Rada—how you say, Ukraina government. Whole country is corrupt. You do business at one counter."

"Good for business," the Palestinian agreed.

"Listen, *druk*, you—me, we do *kharasho* business.

You tell me what you need: guns, bombs, drugs, women. We do business. Come through Ukraina. No problem customs, *militsiya* police, SBU. Everything taken care of."

"If this works out, why not?" the Palestinian said.

After lunch they followed the Ukrainian freight forwarder as he handled the paperwork for the port and the ship. They walked out to the berth to inspect the MV *Zaina*, a mid-size Ukrainian 26,000 ton cargo vessel flying a Belize flag of convenience. The Palestinian knew she was owned by FIMAX Shipping, a legitimate Ukrainian company, and member of FIATA, that could stand up to scrutiny by the Ukrainian SBU, the Russian FSB, or the CIA.

The paperwork took most of the day. At one point the freight forwarder—Khmelnitsky called him Mikhailo—came to them.

"The customs man, that one," glancing toward an agent behind the counter in a blue uniform, "wants another fifty thousand *hryvnia*," Mikhailo said. The Palestinian did a quick mental calculation. It was about five thousand euros.

"*Hooy tebe v zhopu!* I cut his *huesos* eyes out!" Khmelnitsky cursed. The Palestinian put a hand on his arm.

"This customs *huesos*," he said to Mikhailo, using the slang. "Is he reliable or does he always ask for more?"

"Always."

"What you want to do?" Khmelnitsky said to the Palestinian.

"Pay him now," the Palestinian said. "I'll give you

the money in the men's toilet. After the ship sails, kill him. I'll give you another thousand euros."

"I kill him," Khmelnitsky said. "But for only one euro. This is all this *huesos* is worth."

By late afternoon the big rig arrived carrying the steel drums and ingots. Before they loaded the cargo, the Palestinian inspected the steel drums marked SPECIAL ORDER for the hairs from his head he had glued from the tops to the sides. They were unbroken. They hadn't been tampered with. He used his laptop to send the authorization for the bank transfer and waited till Khmelnitsky came back after checking it out.

"Money *kharasho*. Everything *kharasho*. You see, we do *kharasho* good business," the Russian said, clapping the Palestinian on the shoulder.

"*Da svidaniya*," the Palestinian replied, shaking Khmelnitsky's hand. The Russian was smiling so broadly, he thought, you could almost forget he was called "Kolbasa."

The Palestinian walked up the gangplank onto the ship, pulling his carry-on behind him. A Turkish crewman pointed him to the bridge, where he showed his papers to a man named Chernovetsky, a bearded Ukrainian in a soiled white captain's cap. The papers identified him as a Moroccan seaman named Hassan Lababi. The captain squinted closely at the photograph on his papers then handed them back.

"New crewman takes midnight watch," Chernovetsky said in a heavily accented English.

"*Oui*, Capitaine," the Palestinian replied, using French to reinforce his Moroccan nationality.

The Palestinian went below and stowed his gear in the crew's quarters, then went out on deck. He watched the crewmen toss the hawsers and felt the shudder of the engines as the ship left its berth. The *Zaina* cleared the breakwater and began an easy pitching as it headed out into the deeper water of the Black Sea. The ship was bound through the Bosphorus and the Dardenelles for its next port, Marseilles, where the steel drums were to be unloaded. The Palestinian leaned on the rail and smoked a cigarette and watched the sun as it set behind the western hills of Odessa, the sky a vivid purple and red. As the lights of the city receded in the darkness, he smiled in the knowledge that the *Zaina* would never reach Marseilles.

CHAPTER NINE

Amsterdam, Netherlands

"Now that you have me, what are you going to do with me?" she asked. They were sitting in a brown bar just off the Prinsengracht, not far from the Anne Frank House.

"Why were you following me?" he said, poking at a *fritte mayonnaise*.

"I told you, I'm following a story," she said, putting down her *witte* beer and lighting a cigarette. It gave her a chance to study his face. It was a strong face, with dark tousled hair and shadows under gray eyes that gave nothing away. There was a scar over one of his eyes that she suspected wasn't a sports injury. His hands looked strong enough that she knew if he wanted to, he could tear her apart, and it made something shiver inside her.

"You're doing it again," he said.

"Doing what?"

"Lying when you don't have to. Whatever you were following me for, it wasn't for the TV news."

"How do you know?"

"You're Najla Kafoury, a one-name talking head

on TV. You're national in Deutschland. You don't do local breaking-and-entering stories, and nobody stakes out a mosque at night on the off chance the alarm'll go off. Why were you there and why did you follow me?"

She exhaled cigarette smoke at him and didn't say anything.

"Last chance," he said.

"Or else what? What'll you do if I don't say? Tie me up? Spank me?"

"I wish I could. Sounds like fun," he said, sipping his *pils* beer.

"What will you do?" she said, suddenly serious.

"Introduce you to people less willing to let you lie than I am. Trust me, you won't like it."

"I believe you," she said. She exhaled a stream of smoke and looked around the bar. It was dark, crowded, and noisy, and a number of football fans were arguing loudly about the upcoming match between the leading Dutch rivals, Ajax and Feyenoord. "I could make a scene."

"Not a good idea."

She looked into his gray eyes, and whatever she saw made her go cold inside.

"You're right," she said. "It wasn't a story. Islamic extremism is my enemy. You know that. You were at the demonstration, weren't you?"

He nodded.

"I thought I had seen you," she said. "There was something going on at the mosque. For weeks I'd been getting hints, e-mails, tweets, Muslims not from Hamburg coming and going. Something was about to happen. I could feel it. I was thinking maybe a *terroristischen* attack. Then tonight the alarm went off and you came out and I decided to follow. I thought you were a terrorist. When you first grabbed me, I thought you were going to kill me. Maybe you still are," she added softly.

"*Ja*—and if Ajax loses Suarez as striker?! Then what?" a red-faced Dutchman at the bar wearing the Ajax team colors, red and white, demanded loudly.

"That call I made before," Scorpion said, referring to a cell phone call he had made earlier, while they were still driving to Amsterdam. "I'm waiting to hear."

"You'll let me go?"

"I don't know. We'll have to see."

"You could let me go right now. You could let me just stand up and walk out the door and no harm. You could do it," she said, her hand resting on her handbag as if she were getting ready to leave.

"Drink your beer. Don't do anything stupid," he said.

"You're scaring me. I thought you liked me."

"Flirting too. You're putting on quite a show. Too bad we both know this isn't personal," he said. "What were you doing outside the Islamisches Masjid in the middle of the night—and please don't tell me again you were waiting for a story to drop into your lap. We're past the Girl Journalist Makes Good phase."

"I told you. They're up to something. I thought you were one of them. I'm beginning to think you really are."

"Let's go," he said, standing.

She looked up. "Where are we going?"

"To get a room," he said, grabbing her arm and pulling her close.

"Is that what this is?" she asked, looking into his eyes.

"I need to sleep. So do you. By morning we'll know more," he said, helping her into her Burberry.

Holding her by the arm, they left the bar. He hailed a taxi and told the driver to take them to the Rosseburt; the Red Light District. The driver dropped them off on a walking street with thinning groups of men and a few lingering tourists viewing the rows of red-lit windows filled with women in sexy lingerie and stockings. The windows cast a neon-red glow into the street. It was late. The night was cool and smelled of beer and hashish. Street hustlers selling drugs approached them and Scorpion shook them off.

"You already have me. How many women do you need?" Najla said as they walked by the windows where young women posed and beckoned male passersby.

"For the moment, none. You're a complication, not an asset," he said, pulling her into a sex shop. They went to the S&M section, where he picked out handcuffs, restraints, a leather gag, and a roll of duct tape.

"You are getting stranger by the minute." She looked around at the leather restraints, masks, and whips. "In case you're wondering, I'm not into this," she said.

"Well, we don't know what kind of a girl you really are, do we?" he said, paying for what he had picked out and then grabbing a taxi that took them to an inexpensive hotel near the Dam Square parking structure where he'd left the BMW. He checked them in using a Canadian passport that identified him as an engineer from Toronto named John Crane.

"Is that what I call you? Herr Crane?" she said as they stepped into the small hotel room smelling faintly of disinfectant. "Or maybe John. Like I am the prostitute and you are the john, *ja*?"

"Take off your clothes. Down to your underthings," he ordered, tossing the sex paraphernalia on the bed.

"Why?" She stood in the middle of the room, her raincoat open, looking trapped.

"Because you don't want your clothes wrinkled. You don't have a change," he said, taking off his jacket.

"You see. We play our roles. You are the john and I . . . Who am I in this little *schauspiel*? I am not Frau Crane, am I?" she said, tossing her raincoat on the chair before unzipping and taking off her dress and shoes, till she was down to panties and bra. "Now I look like one of those girls in the windows. Is this what you wanted?" she asked, striking a provocative pose.

In spite of himself, Scorpion felt his body respond. She was petite and lovely and she didn't have to pose in order to look incredibly sexy. "Turn around," he said, and pulling her hands behind her, put the handcuffs on.

"*Bitte*, you don't have to do this," she told him, turning her head.

"I can't trust you," he said. He put the leather gag

in her mouth and secured it. "And I need the sleep."

He helped her into the bed and under the covers, then took off his clothes down to his undershorts, got in next to her and turned out the light. The room was dark, except for light coming in the window from a streetlight outside. He could feel the warmth of her next to him, and it was difficult not to think about sex. It was going to be hard to fall asleep. He was about to close his eyes when he felt her moving against him. At first he wasn't sure what was happening, and then he understood and turned and looked at her. Her eyes above the gag were wide and luminous from the light reflected from the window. He removed the gag.

"Are you sure you want this?" he whispered.

"God yes. Don't you see me? Don't you have any idea what you're doing to me?"

He grabbed her face in his hand.

"Can I trust you enough to untie you?" he said.

"You don't have to untie me. I'm helpless. You can do anything you want with me," she whispered, moving her pelvis against his thigh. He touched her breasts, so smooth and silky to the touch, and felt her lips on his neck and down to his chest and belly. He pulled off his shorts and felt her mouth on him, making him crazy and rock hard, and he wasn't sure he could hold it. When he could barely stand it, she pulled away.

"Take off my panties. Do you have something?" she gasped.

"A minute," he said, and got the condom. A minute later he was inside her, going at her like he could never get enough.

"*Gott!*" she cried, and it came blindingly fast and was over.

They lay beside each other, catching their breath.

"I'm sorry it was so fast," he said.

"Next time, you will take your time," she replied, burying her lips against his neck. She kissed him, and then he felt her working her way down his body with her lips, taking him in her mouth, and for a moment he was stabbed with doubt at putting himself into such a vulnerable position with her, and then, incredibly, he was hard as a rock again.

He turned her over and came at her, this time taking his time and going on and on till she was moving her hips and moaning into the pillow, and this time when it came, she was pushing back against him as hard as he was pushing into her. He turned her around and kissed her, their tongues seeking each other, her lips so soft. Then he pulled away, because he knew he was losing control; the effect she had on him was unbelievable.

Just before falling asleep the thought came to him that with her hands tied behind her, it was as close to rape as he had ever come.

"Sit down. Don't turn on the light," Scorpion said, showing him the gun. The dwarf, Hassan Tassouni aka Ali, started for the door, but stopped when he heard Scorpion cock the hammer of the HK pistol he had bought in Germany.

"*Ik heb niet veel geld,*" the dwarf said.

"I don't speak Nederlands. Speak in English or Arabic. Turn on the table lamp, no other lights," Scorpion said.

The little man climbed up on a high stool by the small table and turned on the lamp, then sat, elbows on the table, his face in his hands. "*Godverdomme*. I knew this day would come. I should've killed myself," Tassouni said. He had a flat, squashed dwarf's face covered with a sparse reddish beard.

"Why? What did you do?" Scorpion asked. He sat on a threadbare sofa, which apart from the table and chair and a rumpled futon in the corner, was the only furniture in the apartment. The room was filled with the dwarf's artworks, jagged sculptures vaguely reminiscent of twisted human limbs made of junkyard pipes, cables, and jagged wires resembling muscles and nerve endings, painted red and overlaid with random Arabic letters in white. The walls were covered with pasted newspapers and magazine pages spray-painted with the same random Arabic letters. The walk-up apartment was cold and smelled of fish, metal, paint, and water from the nearby Lijn-baansgracht Canal. In Amsterdam's art world, Scorpion had learned, Tassouni had a small but growing reputation as a serious artist.

It had only taken him a few hours to find the dwarf. In the morning, after his normal morning workout, two hundred push-ups in four minutes, one hundred sit-ups in two minutes, twenty pull-ups by his fingers from the door lintel molding, he dressed and got coffee, water, and almond pastries from the corner café. Returning to his room, he and Najla had breakfast at a small table next to the window. The only view was of another building, and the morning light was gray, as if it might rain.

"I'm letting you go," he said. "Story's over. You're free. Go back to Germany."

She looked down at her coffee. She wore just a top and panties, her hair still bed-tousled, and he thought she was heartbreakingly beautiful and sexy.

"What if I don't want to go?" she said, still not looking up.

"I don't know where you fit in all this. I'm breaking every protocol in the business. I was planning to leave you tied up in here, because even that's better than some of the other alternatives I have to think about."

"I could help," she said softly, looking at him with those incredible aquamarine eyes.

"No." He shook his head. "Either you're mixed up in this or you aren't. If you are, you're too dangerous to have you with me. If you're not, it's too dangerous for you. Either way, you're either going back to Germany or I tie you up all day in this room till I get you vetted."

"What about last night?"

"Last night I found out just how close to losing control with you I am. It's because of last night that I'm letting you go. Go on, get out," he said in a voice he didn't recognize as his own.

She stood up, and it was all he could do not to grab her. She was close enough for him to still smell sex and the smell of her.

"You think I don't know you are some kind of policeman or spy? What if I am involved? What if you are letting an enemy go free?"

"Others will find you. It won't be me and it won't

be pleasant," he said in the thick voice that didn't seem to belong to him. It wasn't much of a choice, he thought. Even if he left her tied up, there was a good chance the *femme de chambre* would free her before he could get back.

"You really are a cold bastard, aren't you?" she said, angrily grabbing her clothes and pulling them on.

"Tell me you never exploited some poor bastard's personal tragedy for a two-minute TV network feed? We're all bastards," he said. "It's a bastard world."

Two hours later he rode a rented bicycle to an RDV with someone named Piet De Jong of the Dutch Secret Intelligence Service, the AIVD. They met on a bridge over the Herengracht Canal. The water was cool and gray, reflecting clouds that promised rain. The canal along this section of the Herengracht was lined with trees and houseboats, and the outdoor setting and passing boat traffic made it less likely a sound receiver could pick up their conversation. They stood beside each other at the railing, gazing down at their reflections in the water. De Jong took his time stuffing and lighting his pipe.

"His name is Hassan Tassouni. Moroccan. An artist. Quite a good one, according to those who are supposed to know about such things. Here's his address," De Jong said in accented English, passing him a slip of paper. "Not a bad address."

"That didn't take long," Scorpion said.

"Well, a Muslim dwarf in the Jordaan," De Jong said. "You made it easy for us."

"What else?"

"He doesn't fit the usual profile. More likely to frequent the brown bars and the *bordeels* in De Wallen than a mosque. Then perhaps eight months ago he shows on the radar at the Moroccan Islamic Center in Osdorp."

"You keep a close eye on them?"

"You know what we are dealing with in Nederland," De Jong said, puffing on his pipe. "After two months going to the mosque, he is never there again. There was something about a woman."

"Who was she?"

"A Muslim woman in *hijab*. There are a million of them." He shrugged. "Peters said you would not share."

Peters was the CIA station chief in Amsterdam. It was why he had hesitated about using Company resources to track Tassouni down. Given a day or two, he would have found the dwarf without them. As De Jong had said, finding a Muslim dwarf in the Jordaan district shouldn't be that difficult, but the time factor was burning him. Somewhere, he knew, the Palestinian was en route to whatever was about to happen, and by now he would have heard about what happened in Damascus. Every second was beginning to count.

"No," Scorpion said. "I won't share."

"It does not seem like good partners. We tell you, but you tell nothing. In Nederland we have many rules," De Jong said, his eyes searching Scorpion's face. "You do not seem a man for rules."

"Did Peters tell you that?"

"No. That is my own judgment," De Jong said. Scorpion looked at him: business suit, tall, sturdy, fair-haired; someone who did his job by the book.

"I'm not *gezellig*?" Scorpion smiled, using the word for cozy, comfortable, the Dutch ideal.

"Definitely not *gezellig*. I have the feeling you will deal with this Moroccan on your own and leave us to clean up the mess, Heer Crane," De Jong said, deliberately using Scorpion's current cover name to let him know they were aware of him. Before he left Holland, he would jettison it, he decided.

"What about his communications? Computer?"

"So far as we can tell, he doesn't have one. Either old fashioned or he doesn't want his communications tracked. And you haven't answered my question. Amsterdam is not your, how you say, *kinderbox*, for children's play."

"Peters should've explained. I don't exist. There are no rules."

"And the artist? He is a Nederland citizen."

"Stay away from him," Scorpion said, walking away, toward where he had left his bicycle.

"Our patience is not unlimited," De Jong called after him.

"Neither is mine. I don't have a lot of time," Scorpion called back as he got on the bike.

That afternoon in Osdorp near the Westhaven harbor, over a trade for cocaine with two members of the Moroccan Smitstraat street gang, Scorpion tried to find out about the dwarf's girl.

"Who was she?" he asked. They were speaking in standard Fusha Arabic.

"Some girl. I don't remember the name," the Moroccan said. His eyes were bloodshot and glassy, typical of heavy hashish use. "This is good *coca*." He held up the plastic-wrapped packet. "Listen, you want ice-o-lator hashish? They use this ice water method makes the hashish so pure, you think you die it's so good."

"About the girl?" Scorpion asked.

"Doesn't matter now," the other Moroccan said, his eyes darting around the coffee shop, filled with the smell of marijuana and hashish. It was near the overpass to the port, a bare place with Formica tables for foreign dockworkers and local gangs to stop in for a quick high. The other Moroccan was the twitchy one; the one to keep an eye on, Scorpion thought.

"Why?"

"Someone killed her. *Dood*, Brother. Pretty girl, nice, then *batoom*," he said, pointing his finger and making a sound like a gunshot.

"Who did it?"

The hashish user shrugged. "Who knows? Her family, maybe."

"They didn't want her to see the dwarf?"

"It looked stupid," the twitchy one said. "She was, you know, tall for a girl. Her with that ugly little *fatah*!"

"I saw them at the mosque," the hashish user said. "He was too old for her too. She was young. College girl. Nice, not some *shlicke* slut."

"How'd they get together?"

The twitchy one stood up. He put one of his hands in his pocket.

"*Shem et Duat!*" Go to hell! "Who cares about this *zarba*? You want to buy or not, *ya khawal*?"

"Wait! We're doing business, right?" the hashish user said.

"*Kess emmak,*" Scorpion said, insulting the twitchy one's mother. As the twitchy one started to pull a Spanish folding knife out of his pocket, Scorpion grabbed his wrist in the Krav Maga move, making him cry out in pain, and took the knife away.

"*Neem het buiten!*" the burly Dutch counterman shouted, pulling out a police club from under the counter. Take it outside! "*Nu!*" Now! The dock-workers at other tables, some Dutch, some foreign, turned to watch. The hashish user's eyes blinked rapidly. Suddenly, he stuffed the cocaine in his pocket and ran out. By the time Scorpion and the twitchy one got outside, he was running down the street.

"The *coca*'s gone. There's nothing to fight about," Scorpion said.

"Give me my knife," the twitchy one said.

Scorpion flung it across the street.

The Moroccan shouted in Arabic that Scorpion's mother had committed adultery with a thousand monkeys as he ran to retrieve his knife, but by then Scorpion was already down the block, pedaling away on his bicycle.

"Look at me," the dwarf said. "One of Allah's jokes. Bitter, a cynic. Never go to a mosque. Religion's a farce. I despise people; the ones who mock me and my art, and I hate even more the ones who feel sorry for me and pretend not to see the grotesqueness of a grown man in this ridiculous misshapen child's-size body. The only women I've ever been with are whores. So who should I love? Tell me, who should I love if not the most beautiful, most innocent, young, tall, slender, gentle, exquisite creature who ever lived?! It was my fate."

"One of Allah's ironies," Scorpion said, glancing around the apartment. He had searched it before the dwarf came home. He found nothing except a photo of Tassouni with a tall young woman wearing a *hijab* in a park, and in the trash, two torn night train tickets on successive days from the Amsterdam Central Station to Utrecht.

"She had come to an exhibit where my work was appearing. I didn't know why she was there. It is *haraam* for Muslims to make images, so of course they despise me, and yet there she was, in a *hijab* no less. But we spoke and she was so gentle and her face was like an angel. So beautiful, like Christ's mother in her perfect youthful moment of illumination. I had to have her. I had to paint her. Can you understand? It was beyond idolatry. She was more than art. She was the thing itself. The thing that art in its clumsy, self-glorified way tries to get at."

"You were obsessed."

"Obsession is a small word. She was my soul. Until I met her, I didn't believe in souls or any of that *kak*, but there she was. She talked to me. We held hands. We walked and talked in Vondelpark. I couldn't imagine what she could possibly see in me. I was too old, too small and grotesque, too ugly, not pious. It was impossible, but I didn't care. I dreamed of her. I thought of nothing but her. Her face, her smell, her touch. I had to have her. I would have done anything. Murder, anything. And then they told me what they wanted."

"Who was it?"

"Her uncle. Her father's brother. An elder in the mosque. And another. I never knew his name."

"Why you?"

"Exactly," Tassouni said, pouring them both glasses of Dutch *jenever* gin that he had gotten from the refrigerator. "*Santé!*"

"*Santé*," Scorpion toasted, and sipped the gin. The little man swallowed his in a gulp, poured himself another and downed that as well.

"I asked them. They said the mosque had been infiltrated by informers for the Dutch. They needed someone no one would ever suspect. Someone not religious or who even gave a *kak* about the Muslim community. What difference did it make?"

"You would have done anything."

"Anything. If they had told me to put on a suicide vest and kill half of Amsterdam, I would have done it."

"They promised her to you."

"Suggested. They said they would not object. For a Muslim girl, that is much."

"And she—what was her name?"

"Salima. They killed her," Tassouni said, staring into space.

"For *ikram*?" Family honor?

"I don't know. For being defiled just kissing me on the cheek once that day in the park. For knowing too much. What difference? They're coming for me now," the little man said, emptying the glass and pouring himself another.

"How do you know?"

"What do you think? They're going to kill her who was so innocent and leave me alive?"

"I can help you," Scorpion said.

"How? By bringing her back to life? That's the only way you can help me," he said.

"What did you do for them?"

"Carried messages. I would pick them up in a place and leave them in another place. I would put them behind a loose brick in an alley wall or under a specific seat in a cinema, places like that."

"Dead drops, they're called. Did you go to Utrecht?"

"So you know already. I wasn't even good at that," Tassouni said.

"Where in Utrecht?"

"Different places. Once near the university. Most were in the Kanaleneiland district."

"Muslim neighborhoods?"

"Obviously," Tassouni grimaced.

"What were they? Moroccan? Turkish? Farsi?"

"Maghrebi. You could smell the cinnamon and cumin in the streets."

"What did the messages say? Did you read any of them?" Scorpion's cell phone vibrated.

"I don't know. They were all in some kind of code," Tassouni said.

His phone vibrated again. He took it out and looked at the text message. It was from the default number and read: 000. It was in response to his Internet café query to the International Corn website on Najla Kafoury. It meant they had come up empty. They would have run checks on her through all the U.S. and foreign intelligence agencies, Interpol, the

German BND and Bundespolizei, and the response indicated they had found no alerts or evidence of criminal, intelligence, or radical Islamic connections. Too late, he thought. He had let her go.

"I have to go. You have to come with me. You're not safe here," Scorpion said, motioning with the gun.

"No, I'll stay here. You can shoot me," Tassouni said. "Do it now. Without her . . ." He looked at Scorpion. "Better to shoot."

"I can make you come."

"Then I stop talking. It's not worth it for you. A man who doesn't care if he dies can be very difficult."

"They'll kill you."

"They kill me, you kill me. What difference?"

"I have to take care of something, but I'll be back. Keep the door locked. Don't let anyone in till I return," Scorpion said, getting up. He had to find out about Najla. He had left her in the hotel room, washing her hair in the bathroom.

"Why should I trust you? I don't know you. You come in with a gun—and listen to a fool's story."

"Because I'm the only one, including you, who wants you alive."

"Then that makes two of us who are fools."

"Lock the door. If anyone comes, no matter how well you know them or what reason they give you, don't let them in. I'll be back soon," Scorpion said, opening the door.

He left the dwarf staring into his drink, and waited in the dimly lit hallway till he heard the door lock. He pulled a hair from his head and wrapped it from the doorknob to a screw he loosened in the doorjamb as a simple trap. He left his bicycle by the apartment house rack to help discourage anyone who might show up, by letting them think Tassouni had company, and caught a taxi back to the hotel. On the way, he tried calling her cell phone—he had taken the number off the phone in her purse in the morning before he got breakfast—but she wasn't using it and it went immediately to voice mail.

He thought about it in the taxi. Langley had cleared her, but he didn't buy it. Najla had earned her chops as a TV reporter, yet according to the BND and Bundespolizei, she didn't have a single questionable contact. He'd been with her. She was smart and tough and hadn't done it all on her looks. And it still didn't explain why she'd followed him after staking out the mosque in the middle of the night. Langley was missing something. Being a reporter was classic cover for an operative, he thought. He had made a mistake letting her go. The sex had colored his judgment. He had to find her again, and if he were honest with himself, wanted to see her again.

Night had fallen, the lights of the city blurred by a drizzle. He could smell the canals. Going by the Dam Square in the taxi, the Royal Palace with its cupola, the Nieuwe Kerk church and the tall pillar of the National Monument were brightly lit. They gleamed wetly in the rain. The restaurants and the brown bars were open, and despite the weather, the streets were filled with people out having a good time. Back at the hotel, he raced back up to the room. The *privé* card he had put into the card key lock was gone. When he opened the door, the room was empty.

There was no sign of Najla. He searched the room carefully. There was nothing of hers, and so far as he could see, no bugs or traps left behind. She had gone through his carry-on; the way he'd arranged the location of things, like his disposable razor and toothbrush, had all been moved. She couldn't have found out anything about him anyway. His important things—passports, money, laptop, extra cell phones, and such—were all locked in the roll-on carry-on he had taken from the BMW and put into a locker in the train station before moving the BMW to the station's car park. The room was clean and the bed was made, so the chambermaid had come in. The sexual restraints he had used to tie her up were gone. She was really gone, he thought, acknowledging that he'd been hoping she would have waited for him, although he still had no way to know whether she was just a journalist who went back to Germany or part of whatever the Islamic Resistance still had going on. With a jolt, he realized that his body physically missed the touch of her. The whole thing felt strange, and he still had to get back to the dwarf. There was something wrong, and he didn't know what it was as he went down to the lobby.

"The woman I was with, did she check out? Did she leave anything?" he asked the young man behind the desk. The man said something in Dutch to the young woman beside him, also wearing the hotel's blue jacket.

"No, *meneer*. She left earlier today, but she left no message," the young woman said.

"Was she with anyone?"

"I did not see, *meneer*," the young woman said.

"It happens, *meneer*," the young man said sympathetically, automatically assuming he was dealing with a jilted lover.

Scorpion nodded and headed out to the car park by the train station. He'd need the car and some of the things in it in case he had to evacuate Tassouni. On the drive to the dwarf's apartment, he decided there were only two options. Either Langley was right and Najla had nothing to do with the Palestinian and was heading back to her normal life in Hamburg, glad to be free and out of jeopardy, or she was somehow involved in this and was searching the city for him or the dwarf. He pulled up to the corner of the street of Tassouni's apartment building and parked the car illegally at the corner. One way or another, he wouldn't be there long.

He took his time approaching the building, scanning the parked cars and the street and the rooflines. The street was quiet except for a small party in one of the ground floor apartments, the light and sounds of voices spilling out, cobblestones glistening from the drizzle. The approach to the building looked clean, but that meant nothing. There were lights in one of the windows, but not on the third floor, where Tassouni's apartment was. He picked the front door lock and eased inside, walking carefully up the stairs to the apartment door. The hallway light was dim and there was no sound. He checked for the hair trap. It was broken. Someone had gone inside.

Scorpion took out his gun and knocked on the

door. There was no answer. He knocked again. Still nothing. He didn't think the dwarf had gone out again. His instincts were telling him it was a trap. It's just nerves, he told himself. Najla had thrown him off. Langley was right. If she'd been involved in anything, they would've found it. Except he remembered something Koenig had said once. "When you don't find anything on someone, in our line of work we call it 'deep cover.' " He looked at the doorknob, afraid to touch it. He had to get in to see Tassouni; the little man was his only lead. Except his one certainty about his adversary was that he knew how to make bombs.

He went back out to the BMW, got the roll of duct tape from the trunk and went back to Tassouni's apartment. He wrapped the tape around the doorknob and unrolled it until he was down the stairs and the hallway and well away from the apartment. Then he took a breath and pulled.

The explosion was deafening, slamming him against the wall. It rocked the building. He could smell flames and smoke as he raced back up the stairs to the shattered apartment. Two fingers of a small human hand were lying on the hallway floor. He could feel the heat of the flames coming from the door opening, what was left of the door hanging from a single hinge. He raced through the building knocking on doors, screaming, "Help! *Vier! Politie!*" Fire! Police! He heard people shouting and moving as he ran out of the building and back to the BMW. In the distance he could hear the horns of approaching fire engines.

Scorpion drove out of Amsterdam toward the

A2 highway, the windshield wipers beating steadily against the drizzle. Along the way, he stopped in Zuid-Oost, broke the cell phone he had used in Amsterdam into pieces, and dropped them in different sections of a canal near the center of town. On the E35 to Utrecht, he realized he'd have to find an Internet café and let Harris know the mission had gone off the rails. He had a sickening feeling in the pit of his stomach. He shouldn't have let Najla go. Now she was gone, the dwarf—their only lead—was dead, and worse, the opposition was onto him. The hunter had become the hunted.

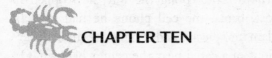

CHAPTER TEN

Straits of Messina, Mediterranean Sea

It was sometime after 0330 hours when the Palestinian decided he would have to murder the captain. He was standing the bow watch, the night clear and cool, the dark shadow of the Greek island of Milos passing off the port side. The *Zaina* was doing seventeen knots down the shipping lane through the Cyclades islands, latitude 36 degrees 44 minutes north, longitude 24 degrees 13.5 minutes east, on a heading of 193 degrees. It shouldn't have been necessary, he thought. Freighters made unscheduled stops all over the world. He was proposing just a little detour. An extra sixteen hours, approved by the owners. But the Ukrainian was pigheaded. He had gone to the captain's quarters an hour after dinner, enough time for the captain to get started on his drinking, something everyone on the ship down to the lowest AB seaman knew about.

"What you want?" Captain Chernovetsky said, looking up from his bottle of Ukrainian Tavia brandy. His eyes were bleary and a porn DVD was on his TV, the sounds of sexual groans providing a backdrop to their conversation.

"We need to make an unscheduled stop in Genoa," the Palestinian said, sitting down.

"What you say? What you talking?" Chernovetsky said, not taking it in.

"We need to stop in Genoa before Marseilles, Capitaine."

"*Pishov na khuj!* Get out my quarters!"

"It's only sixteen hours added to the schedule. We unload three containers and that's it. There's ten thousand euros for you and no questions," the Palestinian said, taking a stack of euros in cash from his backpack and putting it on the table next to the brandy. Chernovetsky stared at the money, his eyes blinking.

"What is this? You don't sit in captain's quarters. Get fuck out!"

"I have the paperwork here. I just need you to sign and go along." He took the port papers out of the backpack and put them on the table next to the money.

"Stand up, *sooka suna!* You don't sit here. Who are you?"

The Palestinian sat back and stared at him.

"I represent the owners. FIMAX Shipping. We need to make an unscheduled port stop in Genoa. Happens all the time. The ten thousand is for you. No one knows." He nudged the money closer to the captain.

"FIMAX Ukraina company. You are not Ukraina," Chernovetsky said, his voice thick with the brandy. He picked up the remote and shut the TV.

"FIMAX is Ukrainian based in Kiev, but the owners are not Ukrainian."

"How you know this?" Chernovetsky said, his voice uncertain for the first time. The Palestinian suspected it was because the captain knew the owners were Arabs, who had purchased the company six months earlier. "They send you spy on me?"

"Everyone knows about the drinking, *mon capitaine*. I am from the owners. Do this one favor and your position is secure."

"This money for do nothing? Stop in Genoa, unload containers. Inside what? Drugs? Guns? Contraband? *Pishov na khuj!* You think no one ever offer me money for smuggle before? I lose my captain ticket. Get out or I throw you off ship!"

"The owners want a stop in Genoa."

"I am captain of *Zaina*," he said, taking a swallow of the brandy. "I decide, not owners. We go Marseilles."

"No drugs, no guns, no problems, I promise. I'll make it twenty thousand euros. What's so important about Marseilles? You have a little *pétasse* whore in port? With twenty thousand you could buy a hundred women. Don't have to watch DVDs," the Palestinian said coldly.

"Get out, *sooka suna!* I throw you in irons!" Chernovetsky shouted, standing up and gesturing with his glass, spilling the brandy.

The Palestinian stood and retrieved the money and the papers from the table.

"You need a drink, Capitaine. Have another brandy. Think it over. The offer is still good," he said, and left the cabin.

He went out on the deck to wait. He didn't think Chernovetsky would try to arrest him. He would start to do it but first have another drink, and somewhere he would figure that if the owners wanted it to happen, it was better to leave it alone. Either way it didn't matter. He had already made his arrangements with the first and second officers, both of whom were Muslims. The first officer, Ademovic, was a Bosnian from Sarajevo; the second officer a Turk from Kusadasi. He had paid them five thousand apiece to make sure they would back him up. He had given the captain his chance, he thought. Now there was no choice. One way or another the *Zaina* had to make port in Genoa, where, if the deal he had made with Francesca Bartolo of the Camorra held, the contents of the containers would be through Italian customs in a few hours.

He looked forward, the horizon invisible in darkness that was complete except for the stars and the running lights of a container ship off the starboard bow, heading north, in the opposite direction, no doubt for Piraeus. The sea was running easy with one- to two-foot swells, the ship dark and silent, but for the running lights and the light on the bridge. The odds were good he could leave his post for twenty or thirty minutes without being detected. It was the perfect time.

He went to the lifeboat where he had stored a backpack with things he didn't want found. There was a complication. It was important that the captain's death not be thought of as suspicious. Otherwise they might hold the ship and the crew while they investigated, which in Italy could take Allah knew how long. He poked around in the backpack in the darkness, not wanting to show any kind of light, until he felt the pouch with the disposable latex gloves, hypodermic, and pills. He slipped the pouch into his jacket pocket and made his way aft, back to the captain's quarters. He listened at the hatch and could hear Chernovetsky snoring even through the metal door. He looked around the passageway for a final check. The only sound was the throbbing of the engine. He checked his watch; it was nearing eight bells, and realized he'd have to move quickly.

He opened the hatch as quietly as he could, closed it behind him, and turned on his key-chain pocket light. The captain was sprawled on his bunk, his snores rattling noisily at the back of his throat. He was still in his pants and undershirt, one bare foot half hanging off the bunk. The bottle of Tavia brandy on the table was nearly empty, the glass on its side, vibrating with the ship's movement. Assuming he was out cold enough not to feel the injection, he took the latex gloves and Demerol pills out of the pouch and placed them on the ledge next to the bunk. He removed the tip from the syringe, filled it with the entire ampule of liquid Demerol, and put the tip and the empty ampule back into the pouch. This was the critical moment, he thought, positioning himself so he could do the guillotine choke hold if Chernovetsky woke up.

He felt between the captain's toes for the dorsal digital vein. Chernovetsky snorted in his sleep but didn't stir. As soon as he thought he felt the vein, he jabbed the needle into the space next to the big toe and pushed the top, emptying the syringe. Chernovetsky's snore stopped in mid-snore and he started to move. The Palestinian glanced at his face. The captain's eyes were open but with consciousness just returning. Chernovetsky was about to breathe in to shout when the Palestinian grabbed the pillow and shoved it over his face, holding it down with all his strength as the captain thrashed feebly against the pressure. Half unconscious, with a rapid intravenous injection of Demerol that could cause cardiac arrest multiplied by the effects of the alcohol, the captain would be dead shortly either way.

After a minute that seemed almost endless, his arms pressing the pillow down with his weight, all movement stopped. He held the pillow over Chernovetsky's face another thirty seconds, then lifted it off and felt for the pulse in the neck. Chernovetsky was dead.

He put the syringe back into the pouch, opened the Demerol pill container, and just to be sure, wiped the container and cap clean of fingerprints with a corner of the sheet from the bunk, then pressed the captain's fingers on the container and cap. He placed the pillow under Chernovetsky's head and closed the open staring eyes, shoving two of the pills deep into Chernovetsky's mouth. Chernovetsky was still alive for about half a minute after the injection, so anything other than an exhaustive autopsy would likely conclude that he had died from a heart attack caused by the combination of Demerol and alcohol, he thought, as he put the pouch back into his pocket and quietly exited the cabin.

Back on deck, he dropped the gloves, syringe, tip, ampule, and the empty pouch one at a time over the rail into the sea. He went forward to finish his watch. The night was still dark, except for the stars and the lights of the container ship he had seen earlier, now well astern. He scanned ahead, the constellation Leo midway to zenith over the bow. He lit a cigarette and for the first time in a long time allowed himself to think about her and wonder where she was.

The steward's assistant, a Filipino everyone called Manolo, found the captain at 0830 hours when he brought him his usual breakfast of buckwheat pancakes and tea. Later that morning First Officer Edis Ademovic sent for Seaman Lababi to meet him in the officers' mess. They were alone, but Ademovic put a finger to his lips, opened the hatch and looked around the passageway to make sure no one was listening.

"Did you do this?" Ademovic said.

"I was on watch," the Palestinian said.

"So you had nothing to do with it?"

"The captain was an *ivrogne*." A drunk. "Everyone knows it. Who knows what else he took?"

"So you know there were drugs?"

"How would I know? I'm just a seaman."

"So you say."

"Are we going to Genoa?"

"You have the papers?"

"Here," the Palestinian said, handing him the bill of lading papers and authorizations. "You just have to initial at the bottom."

"I'm captain now," the Bosnian said.

"So?"

"I should get ten thousand," Ademovic said, moistening his lips with his tongue.

The Palestinian looked at him coldly. Abruptly, he smiled; a smile that had nothing to do with his eyes. "I don't have it."

Ademovic leaned close. "What can you give?"

"Seven, no more. But I'll put in a good word for you with the owners."

"Seven," Ademovic said, taking the papers and initialing them. "You leave the ship at Genoa?"

"Once the containers are off, you can find my replacement in Genoa or sail one AB short."

"Bring the money before officers' mess tonight. I have to go to the bridge," Ademovic said, getting up.

"So the *capitaine* was taking drugs?" the Palestinian asked.

"Painkillers."

"Painkillers and booze. A bad combination."

"So are you. Bring the money. After, when we get to Genoa, get off my ship," Ademovic said.

"Why are you talking this way? I had nothing to do with the *capitaine*," the Palestinian said.

"Maybe. But I am not a drunk. Not so easy to kill."

The Palestinian came close to Ademovic, forcing him to back up.

"We're on the same side, First Officer. We're just doing what the owners want us to do so they give a bonus. I did nothing, but if I were to be involved," the Palestinian whispered intently, "you would be too. You were paid. We're in this together. All we have to do is berth in Genoa. So long as we do that, I am the best friend you'll ever have in this world— or the next."

"Just remember who gives the orders."

"You are the *capitaine*, *Ilhamdulilah*, thanks be

to God," the Palestinian said as he left the officers' mess.

"Why did the first officer want to see you?" Gabir, a Tunisian seaman, whispered to him in Arabic that afternoon. They were working aft on the rust scraping and painting detail. The Palestinian wiped the sweat from his forehead and squinted in the sun as he glanced at the horizon. The ship was running northwesterly and had begun a slight roll as they headed into the tricky currents of the Straits of Messina, Mount Etna a distant smudge off the port stern.

"I was on watch when the captain died. The first officer wanted to know if I heard or saw something," the Palestinian said.

"The captain was *sakran*," meaning a drunk. "Something was bound to happen," Gabir said.

"Better he die than something happen to the ship."

Gabir looked at him. "Truly. But it is not good for a captain to die."

No, it wasn't, the Palestinian thought. He hadn't wanted to do it. That *yebnen kelp* son of a dog Ukrainian was just so stubborn. Still, Ademovic and the second officer, the Turk, Duyal Ghanem, had both been paid off. It was in Ademovic's interest to go to Genoa, especially with a dead captain, although the Palestinian knew he wouldn't be able to stop worrying until the ship passed Cap Corse at the northern tip of Corsica and he saw its heading bound for Genoa and not Marseilles.

"*Ma'alesh*," it's okay, "things happen." The Palestinian shrugged.

"Did you see anything?" Gabir whispered.

"*La*, I was on watch. Anyway, no one has suggested the captain's death was anything other than natural. He was a *sakran*. Everyone knew it. You said so yourself."

"*Inshallah*, that will be the end of it. This is becoming an unlucky ship," Gabir said, touching the silver Hand of Fatima hanging on a chain around his neck. The Palestinian went back to work. He hoped what Gabir said about an unlucky ship wasn't true. He was so close, and at that moment felt a sliver of dread that he didn't have a *haz sa'eed* good luck charm that like Gabir he could touch too. He would need the luck. Once he was ready in Europe, he would have to go back to America.

Thirty hours later the *Zaina* berthed at the terminal port in Genoa. Officers of the *polizia di stato* and gray-uniformed *guardia di finanza* came aboard to examine the captain's body in his quarters, while the dockside gantry cranes unloaded the containers marked for Genoa. As the Palestinian left the ship, he squinted in the sun, looking back at the bridge, but couldn't see the first officer. The Italian inquiry must be keeping him busy, he thought as he went down the gangplank, unnoticed by anyone. There was no sign of the Camorra on the dock or terminal building, but the containers came through the Italian *dogana* with the crates stamped and unopened in a record six hours.

Less than a half hour later Moroccan seaman Hassan Lababi no longer existed. The Palestinian, without the Moroccan passport and seaman's card he'd torn into pieces and flushed down a toilet in the terminal building, was now using an Algerian passport and Italian resident card that identified him as Mejdan Bonatello, a nod to the fact that many Algerians had Italian surnames dating from World War Two. He got into the first of two big Mercedes armored trucks bearing the logo of BANCA POPOLARE DI MILANO, into which the crates containing the uranium had been loaded. The other crates from Volgograd were loaded into the second truck: As he boarded the first truck, the Moroccan who had driven the van that picked him up that first day in Torino handed him an armored truck guard's uniform and a gun.

CHAPTER ELEVEN

Utrecht, Netherlands

It took Scorpion a critical day and a half that he could ill-afford to set up the Moroccan. By then he'd gotten the bad news from Harris. He'd spent the night in the BMW parked near a mosque in the Kanaleneiland neighborhood. It was a long shot, but now that the dwarf was dead, it was the only lead he had. There were at least a dozen mosques, *masjids*, and Islamic community centers in Utrecht. Any one of them might have been associated with the dead drops Tassouni had used.

Scorpion knew that while most Westerners, including many Dutch, tended to lump Muslims together, there was a lot of hostility between the different immigrant communities and they almost never mixed. Turks, for example, wouldn't be caught dead in a Moroccan mosque, and vice versa. The dwarf had said the neighborhood of most of the drops was Maghrebi, North African, and that you could smell the cinnamon and cumin. That meant Moroccan, so he'd parked the BMW near a Moroccan mosque in Kanaleneiland that had a reputation for radicalism.

His target was the night security guard, whom he glimpsed once an hour on his rounds checking outside during the night, and otherwise as a shadow at a back window. He was a small man with a Vandyke beard, wearing an FC Utrecht football T-shirt under a worn leather jacket. If this mosque had a link to the Islamic Resistance in Damascus—a hell of a big if, Scorpion admitted to himself—the night guard wouldn't be just anyone. He'd be a fanatic, prepared for a martyr's death to protect whatever operational information they had. And you couldn't just take him out. If this mosque were a link to the Palestinian, taking anyone out would set off an alarm that could trigger exactly what he was trying to prevent before he could get to it. The only way to do it was to flip the guard; what Koenig in his vaguely Catholic way used to call "conversion" or "getting the Joe to see the light." And he only had a day to do it.

In the morning, when the mosque finally opened and the night shift was over, he tailed the Moroccan as he bicycled back to his apartment. He lived in an area of identical, anonymous apartment buildings, reminiscent of Eastern Europe. The Moroccan's was dotted with TV satellite dishes, one for nearly every apartment. As he studied the building from the BMW, Scorpion made a call to a private detective agency in Amsterdam he'd found on the Internet. He gave the detective on the line the security guard's description and address and, using a South African ID, hired him at a double rate to get all the information he could on the guard within eight hours.

Having earlier torn up and flushed the Crane passport and driver's license down a public toilet at the Utrecht railroad station, his latest passport identified him as Damon McDonald, a lawyer from Johannesburg. Being an attorney, like being a journalist, was a good catchall profession, providing an instant cover explanation for poking into other people's private affairs.

"You understand this is a legal matter," he told the detective. "No one must know about your inquiry, especially the subject. No talking to neighbors, coworkers, anything like that. Strictly computer lookup and distance surveillance."

"We understand," the man replied. "In such cases, we typically act as a Belastingdienst tax agent, or sometimes we wear the uniform and go as the gas meter reader. It is quickly done. There are no questions and everything is normal."

"I also want surveillance photographs. Wife, children, mistress, anyone he talks to. Anyone. Again, it must be long distance. He must not see or know anything or I pay nothing. Also, copies of identity papers and anything the government has on file, and a copy of a utility bill, something that shows residence. And no reports, nothing. You tell me everything verbally and give me all your notes and photographs when we meet and then forget it. You hand me the photographs personally along with the memory drive and I pay in cash."

"It is understood, *meneer*."

Scorpion drove to a nondescript business hotel

near the Utrecht Central Station and caught a few hours of sleep. Later, he rented a furnished two-bedroom apartment near the Nieuwegracht Canal for a week and checked out De Rode Brug, the local red light street, prostitutes sitting in the windows of a line of houseboats tethered along the canal bank. The women seemed tired and ordinary. He didn't see what he was looking for and it was past time that he needed to get on the Internet so he headed to the university. After stopping a few students and asking around, he found a combination Laundromat/Internet café near the campus.

He sat at a laptop facing the wall, surrounded by students doing laundry, drinking coffee and chatting, checking Facebook and playing video games on the Internet, the hum of the washing machines and dryers drowning out the conversations and noises from the video games. Even before he logged onto the International Corn Association site, he went looking for a beautiful woman online. There were two problems. Utrecht didn't have any high quality escort services, so he would have to get a woman from Amsterdam, and there was no way of knowing what type of woman the Moroccan might be attracted to. He guessed that a beautiful Dutch blonde might be something the working-class Moroccan might have fantasized about without ever having had a chance at one.

He found a knockout-looking twenty-two-year-old blonde named Anika on an escort service website and booked her online for an entire day in Utrecht. He texted to set it up, and texting back, she assured him the photograph of her on the site was only about six months old. He arranged to meet her at the Grand Hotel Karel in the center of Utrecht, then logged onto the International Corn Association site, where he got the message mentioning the code word *Venice* and a coded Amsterdam phone number. There was no indication what had broken loose, but he assumed that Peters, the CIA's Netherlands station chief, would know.

Following the emergency procedure, he left the BMW where he'd parked it in a structure near the train station and rented a Kawasaki motorcycle for easy street parking and in case he had to make a getaway through traffic. The fact that they were trying to reach him with a Venice code meant it wasn't about Amsterdam or the dwarf or the girl. Something urgent had happened or was about to blow up in their faces. As always, he cleaned the temp files and rebooted before leaving the Internet café computer, to make sure he left no trail.

Scorpion got to the RDV, one of the pubs on the Oudegracht Canal's lower embankment, an hour ahead of time, and it was a good thing he did because when Peters arrived—he assumed the American in a tweed jacket and wearing glasses sitting at a canalside table was the Netherlands station chief—he was dirty. Watching from a table next to a tree at a café on the upper level on the other side of the canal, Scorpion spotted an Arab in a windbreaker on the street above the canal spending a long time leaning against a railing and reading a newspaper. Another Arab, a big one in a raincoat, even though it wasn't raining, had climbed into the back of a dry cleaner's van parked nearby a half hour earlier and hadn't come out, and on Scorpion's side of the canal, still another Arab spent a lot of time glancing over at Peters and talking on his cell phone. Worse, Peters didn't seem to realize he was covered. The American sat at the table, nursing a beer and glancing at his watch.

Langley rules were that if a contact at an RDV was dirty, you aborted and rescheduled. But Langley rules weren't meant for a Venice alert and when time was running out on a mission. Finally, forty minutes after the set time, Peters realized Scorpion wasn't coming. The American got up and went up the stairs to the street level beside the canal. Scorpion tossed some euro coins on the table, went back to where he'd left the motorcycle parked perpendicularly between two cars and drove across the bridge over the canal. He waited till Peters got into an Audi parked nearby and started down the one-way street toward Domplein Square. The Audi was followed by the dry cleaner's van, two cars behind, and just ahead of the Audi a Mercedes was driven by the Arab with the windbreaker. Scorpion, trailing this caravan on the Kawasaki, could see that Peters was boxed in, and he apparently didn't know it. It was a complete screw-up. The only good thing was that in his motorcycle helmet and sunglasses, he would be hard to recognize, he thought, gauging the traffic as he got ready to make his move.

When the traffic light ahead turned yellow, Scorpion hit the accelerator. He drove between lanes of traffic, past the van, and moving alongside the Audi, signaled with a circular motion for Peters to roll down his window. Scorpion glanced at his side mirror. He had their attention, all right, but for the moment they were waiting to see what happened. He didn't see any guns. He stopped with the rest of the traffic as the light turned red, his motorcycle beside the Audi.

"Get out of the car," he shouted at Peters.

"Have you been to Venice?" Peters asked.

"Climb on in back of me," Scorpion said, watching the van in the mirror. It looked like the back door was opening.

"What about my car? I can't just leave it."

"Get out of the fucking car!" Scorpion shouted. The big Arab had gotten out of the back of the van and started toward them. Peters fumbled, then opened the door and climbed onto the motorcycle behind Scorpion. The second he felt Peters's weight on the bike, he put it into gear, turning in front of the Audi just as the light changed green.

Scorpion drove up onto the sidewalk, heading back in the opposite direction of the one-way traffic, moving slowly enough to dodge pedestrians and not looking at the van, so the Arabs wouldn't get a glimpse of his face as he passed it going the other way. The big Arab had changed direction and was running on foot through the honking traffic, shouting after them as Scorpion swerved back into the street against the traffic. He cut a car off, accelerating fast as he drove between the lanes, then cut across the next bridge over the canal to the other side, his tires skidding on the pavement as he twisted and turned. He drove down side streets, doubling back again and again to make sure they weren't being followed.

"What about the car? They'll trace it back to me," Peters said loudly over the roar of the motorcycle.

"Get a new car. They already know who you are. Why the hell do you think they were there?"

"This isn't how we do things," Peters said. "I'm going to write you up and put it in your 201."

"Would you like me to tell you where you can stick my 201?"

"You can't talk to me like that," Peters said, and Scorpion felt the man stiffen behind him on the bike.

"I just did. Now do us both a favor and shut up," Scorpion shouted back over his shoulder. He swerved suddenly, making Peters hang on, then drove past the hospital and into the green open spaces of Wilhelmina Park. He parked the motorcycle in the lot between two cars and waited till they walked across the grass to a pond in a big open area, checking around to make sure no one was paying attention to them or could hear them.

"You're crazy, you know that?" Peters began. "You left behind a mess in Amsterdam we're still cleaning up and—" The station chief stopped when he caught a glimpse of the icy look in Scorpion's gray eyes.

"You came dirty to a Special Access Crit RDV, you stupid son of a bitch. Tell me about Venice, or your career and this conversation are both over," Scorpion said.

Neither man spoke for a while. They could hear the sound of two Dutch students chatting as they bicycled past on the bike path. They waited till the bicycles were well away.

"Listen," Peters said, handing Scorpion an iPod with an earpiece.

Scorpion turned it on and immediately recognized Dave Rabinowich's voice.

"Wait, let me turn this damn thing on—oh yeah," Rabinowich began. *"Eight years ago a floater from the Motherland,"* meaning an occasional source from Russia, *"gave us a song and dance about how the old Soviet bio warfare lab on Vozrozhdeniya Island had created a form of the Yersinia pestis plague bacteria that could be disseminated via an aerosol spray. We followed up with the usual suspects but were never able to confirm. NRO satellite intel indicated that whatever facility was on the island had been closed and the whole thing got filed away in the 'things we should worry about if we didn't have so many other worse things to worry about file.' Then last year, a sleeper—and that's all I'm gonna say about that—woke us up with the news that while the facility in Uzbekistan may have gone the way of the dodo, fun and games in biology hadn't and certain parties unknown in the FSU were looking for a buyer. But that's not the bad news."*

Rabinowich's voice got lower and more confidential, and Scorpion involuntarily looked around the park to see if anyone was watching, but there was no one except a few small children and their mothers heading toward the playground area.

"Our sleepy amigo," Rabinowich continued, *"dropped a bombshell that even woke up the assholes who run this place. It seems our vodka-loving friends*

had a version of the bacillus that was not only airborne transmittable, but resistant to virtually every antibiotic known, including every member of the streptomycin, gentamicin, chloramphenicol, and tetracycline families. Now we were nervous, but again we couldn't confirm until Damascus. Kudos to you for that one. I finally got our old buddy Bob to okay me telling you. You need to know what you're up against. Oh—and I know you'll do it anyway, but I'm supposed to remind you to delete this as soon as you've heard it."

So that was what Harris hadn't wanted to tell him in Karachi, Scorpion thought as he deleted the iPod file. It wasn't just the Budawi assassination that had the DCIA's drawers in a knot. It was the possibility that Hezbollah had been the buyer the Russian sleeper was talking about. No wonder Harris had come all the way to Karachi to rope him in. Except, he thought, there was something wrong. This was background data. It explained a lot, including the urgency, but it wasn't an operational emergency. It would never have been the reason for a Venice signal. He handed the iPod back to Peters, who slipped it hurriedly into his pocket as though it were contaminated.

"Harris risked the operation for this meeting," Scorpion said. "We probably have Hezbollah agents combing the city right this second looking for both of us. What is it you haven't told me?"

"We received a Special Access CRITIC from Harris. He was in Tallinn," Peters said.

Again Russia, Scorpion thought grimly. Since the end of the Cold War, Tallinn had become spy central for trading information outside Moscow, so like the bioweapon, it undoubtedly involved the Russians.

"What was he doing in Estonia?"

"To meet with Checkmate."

"Ivanov himself." Scorpion whistled silently. Checkmate was the code name for Vladimir Ivanov, head of the FSB's Counterintelligence Directorate and a legendary spymaster. "What brought that about?"

"Rabinowich found something. An NSA thread. Some MOD colonel from some shithole called Mayak got a promotion to Moscow. Two weeks later Checkmate picks him up and takes him to Adult's World."

"So why Venice?" Scorpion asked, his thoughts racing. MOD was the Russian internal security agency for atomic weapons. Although he wasn't sure if Peters had connected the dots, Mayak was the Russian cover name for the city of Ozersk. The whole oblast around the city of Ekaterinburg in Russia was filled with atomic labs and atomic weapons facilities and stockpiles, but Ozersk was the bull's-eye, the dead center of the Russian atomic universe. "Adult's World" was CIA-speak for Lubyanka, FSB headquarters in Moscow, so-called with a touch of spook humor because it stood across the way from a famous Moscow toy store called "Children's World." If Ivanov had arrested this MOD colonel from Ozersk, it could mean there was a serious security breach. They wouldn't have interrupted his operation unless there was a connection. "Come on, Peters. What does Harris want to tell me?"

"Checkmate told him they're missing twenty-one kilos of highly enriched U-235."

"Jesus," Scorpion said, realizing he'd stopped breathing. "How highly?"

"They don't know exactly. Checkmate said seventy-six percent. Harris said to tell you that Rabinowich said it could be more."

"Rabinowich is right. The Russians know exactly. If Checkmate admitted to seventy-six percent and was willing to talk to Harris in Tallinn, it could definitely be more. Christ! Anything else?"

"Harris said one more thing to pass along from Rabinowich."

"Yeah?"

"He said the Russians are all over Ekaterinburg and he's getting 'subtexture' from Volgograd. Also, he thinks someone took a couple of hundred kilos of RDX from GUMO."

Scorpion took a deep breath. It was a cool, sunny day. The trees near the edge of the pond were reflected in the water, and a fountain in the center sprayed up water that caught the sunlight in a rainbow. So much beauty, he thought, and then it hit him. This wasn't terrorism; it was total war.

"Any more good news?" he asked.

"Yeah," Peters said. "Rabinowich said to tell you to hurry."

CHAPTER TWELVE

Westerpark, Amsterdam, Netherlands

Zeedorf, the detective from Amsterdam, was a big man with a round belly. He and Scorpion met in a café near the Dom Tower, the fourteenth century church tower that dominated the picturesque center of Utrecht. The café smelled of Pilsener beer and cigarette smoke and was nearly empty. They sat at a table in a back corner so they could both watch the door.

"His name is Abdelhakim Ouaddane, age thirty-four. I have his address and telephone along with photographs for you here," Zeedorf said, tapping the pocket of his surprisingly expensive sport jacket. "Also a copy of his *identiteitsbewijs*—identity card— his SOFI tax form, and a utility bill from REMU, the gas company. He has a wife and two children, both boys, ages six and three, also living with him. He completed VMBO technical high school, average grades, after which he worked as an auto mechanic at a Peugeot dealership in Hoograven. He lost his job there four years ago. It is not clear why. There seems to have been a problem, but we haven't had time to find out more. For the past several years, as you know, he has been the night security guard at the Masjid al Islamia Ibrahim Mosque in Kanale-neiland. Two years ago he applied for a gun license as a hunter under the Wet Wapens en Munitie law, but it was denied. We are not sure why. He has never been arrested or had trouble with the police. He pays his bills, keeps to himself, although he has been heard to express strong anti-Israel comments and to deny the Holocaust, but that is hardly unusual among Muslims." Zeedorf shrugged.

"Here is his contact information along with photographs of him, his wife, and children, as you asked," he said, taking an envelope out of his jacket pocket and sliding it over to Scorpion.

"What about vices? Gambling? Drugs? Women? Boys?"

"Women. Once every few weeks or so he goes to De Rode Brug, you know, the houseboat women. Other than that, nothing. Except, he stops every day before going to work at a coffee shop on Beneluxlaan."

"Hashish?"

"Coffee and a little hashish. Nothing more. He is a quiet one. He reads."

"What does he read?"

"Islamic religious books mostly."

"Do you know any of the titles?"

"Does it matter? If you like, I can find out. We only had a limited amount of time," Zeedorf wheezed, a note of apology combined with frustration in his voice.

"Any friends at the coffee shop?" Scorpion asked.

"No one. I watched him sit alone for nearly an hour. He smokes; he reads his Islamic books; he has a coffee and leaves. That's all."

"Do you have the name and address of the shop?"

"It's in the envelope."

"What time is he usually there?"

"He'll be there in two hours. We don't know about Friday. His schedule may change for the Friday prayer. Is there anything else, *meneer*?"

"You've done well for such short notice," Scorpion said, passing him the cash on the table. Zeedorf scooped up the money and pocketed it in his jacket with a surprisingly quick and graceful move for such a big man.

"Can I be of any further service, *meneer*?" he wheezed.

"Yes. Do the same thing for the imam at the mosque where he works. I want everything you can get by midday tomorrow. And keep even farther away from the target. Keep it very long distance. Talk to no one," Scorpion added, getting up. He left the big Dutchman finishing his beer and ordering an almond pastry to go with it.

Later, he met Anika, the call girl from Amsterdam at the hotel bar. She was blond and very pretty in a short red dress that had the businessmen in the bar glancing sideways at her, no matter who they were with, to check her out. The bar was dark, intimate, located in a medieval arched vault on a lower level in a spaciously landscaped hotel popular with expense account types. When Scorpion nodded to her and she came over to his table, most of the businessmen realized she was a high-paid prostitute, and there were knowing leers and whispers as she sat down.

"Do I look like my picture?" she asked. Her English was accented but not bad.

"You're very pretty. You attract a lot of attention," he said, glancing at the businessmen at the bar who kept looking over at them.

She shrugged. "I'm used to it. I drove from Amsterdam. It's eight hundred euros for six hours, a thousand for the night. Do you want to go to your room now or have a drink first?"

"Let's talk," he said, motioning the waitress over.

"I'll have a *jenever, zeer koud*," very cold, she told the waitress.

"The same," he said.

"So what business do you do?" she asked as the waitress left.

"Is that what most men want to talk about? Their work?"

"Most men want to talk about themselves. Usually business. Sometimes they try to impress me—with their cars, their houses, *elegante* restaurants. If you get to know them, they'll talk about their jobs, their wives and kids. They talk about their kids and then they want to fuck you. Don't get me started on men."

"What about you? What do you like?"

"I like money. You pay me well, I will make you very happy."

"Don't," he said.

"Don't what?"

"The whore talk," he said. "We don't need it."

She sat up, momentarily less sure of herself. She

watched him carefully as though not sure what he might do next. The waitress brought the drinks and left.

"*Santé!*" she toasted and drank.

"*Santé*," he said, taking a sip and leaning closer. "It isn't me you need to make happy. I'll need you for a few days, maybe a week. I'll pay you fifteen hundred a day. Cash. If it's a full week, ten thousand. Up front. I'll pay you as soon as we leave here. But for someone else, not me."

She looked at him suspiciously.

"What is this? Is this some kind of *zwendel*? I don't do this."

"This man," he said, sliding the photograph of the night security guard, Ouaddane, toward her. "You need to make him fall in love with you. Can you do it?"

"He looks like an Arab," she said, frowning as she picked up the photograph.

"He is. Can you do it?"

"Sometimes men fall in love with me. Given how we meet, it seems strange to me. Sometimes I think it has nothing to do with me. I'm not in the love business," she said.

"Make him want you enough to come with you and I'll pay you the ten thousand even if you don't work a full week."

"What is this for?" She took a pair of glasses out of her handbag to look at Ouaddane's photograph, then put them back in her bag. "Is he rich? He doesn't look rich."

"He's poor. It's not about that."

She looked sharply at Scorpion.

"You don't kill him? I don't want any part of anything like this."

"If I wanted him dead, I wouldn't need you. He works as a security guard in a place where I need information. That's all. You take care of him; I get the information; I take care of you. Everyone is happy."

"That's all, just information? Nobody gets hurt?" she said, looking at him from behind her drink.

"Nobody gets hurt. Not this man, not you. Come, let's walk," he said, standing up. As they walked out together, his hand lightly touching her waist, he was conscious that the eyes of every man in the bar were on them. They walked outside the hotel to the landscaped garden lawns. Night was falling. Lights were lit along the path, giving the hotel with its Dutch farmhouse architecture the quiet feel of being out in the country instead of in the center of the city. It was getting cold, and she pulled a pashmina shawl out of her handbag. He put it around her shoulders and handed her a wad of euros as they walked around the grounds.

"There's three thousand to start for two days, plus three hundred for expenses," he said.

"What do you want me to do?"

"You're booked for the night here in the hotel. Tomorrow, you move to an apartment by the Nieuwegracht Canal. I'll show you in the morning. For how long depends on how well you get him to like you. And get some clothes. I want you to look like a student at the university. Pretty, nice short skirt or tight jeans, but not a *hoer*. Understood?"

She stopped walking. "You don't like me, do

you?" she said, her face in the shadow cast by an outdoor lamppost.

"I like you fine. Actually, you and I are in the same business. We both lie to men to get something out of them, and we both have our own set of rules. The only difference is what we sell. But I don't want Abdelhakim—that's his name, Abdelhakim Ouaddane—to want to fuck you. I want him to fall in love with you. You're not just bait, you're a reason."

"I see," she said, and resumed walking. "What am I studying at the university?"

"Islamic culture."

She made a face. "I don't know anything about it."

"Learn. Buy a book. Every afternoon he goes to a coffee shop. Tomorrow, you make contact there and get him to come with you to the apartment. That's all you have to do. Get him into bed. Then I'll take over and you leave."

"No violence? No trouble?"

"It's business, that's all. Once I meet with him, I'll call you on your cell and let you know what we need to do and for how long."

"What about you?" she said, stopping.

"What about me?"

"Do you want to go upstairs?" she said, coming close. "I don't mind. It's already paid."

He felt the urge to grab her. Whore or not, she was sexy as hell and she had shown sparks of something even more interesting. He was tempted, but time was running out. He had to get back to Amsterdam and there was still a lot to do. Worse, he couldn't afford to let anyone get close to him now.

"Maybe later. I have things to do. Believe me, it's better for both of us if I don't right now," he said, letting go of her and moving away into the shadows.

He drove back to Amsterdam and had dinner at a brown bar near the railway station. He felt a tinge when he thought of Anika, but it was too dangerous. They'd already set a trap for him once, and she was antsy enough as it was. Let somebody put the screws to her and she would sell him out in a heartbeat. He glanced around the bar, but no one was paying attention to him. The place was noisy with tourists and young backpackers, and he sat in a corner over an Oranjeboom beer and tried to put the pieces together, because it didn't add up.

At an Internet café, he had transferred money from the Credit Suisse numbered account to a secured account in Luxembourg. He would handle the rest of the banking in the morning. He also sent a coded message for Rabinowich asking if he had come up with anything on who had been funding Dr. Abadi and the Al-Muqawama al-Islamiyya in Damascus. If there were twenty-one kilos of highly enriched U-235 missing, it must've cost somebody millions. Who had that kind of money? Also, he was no expert and wondered if twenty-one kilos was enough to make a nuclear bomb. If it wasn't, then what was it for? What the hell was going on?

And then there was the RDX military explosive. A couple hundred kilos of RDX would be difficult to smuggle anywhere, particularly past Homeland Security in the United States. Plus there was the logistics problem. How the hell would you move all that from Russia and where was it going? And worst of all, they still hadn't fed him any information on his target, the Palestinian. Who was he? Where did he come from? How did he operate so far under the radar that not a single intelligence agency had been able to come up with anything on him in all this time? It was as if the Palestinian had never been born, but suddenly materialized as a fully grown trained terrorist. He was beginning to get a sense of his enemy, and he didn't like it. Whoever the Palestinian was, he was very good, and Scorpion knew that unless he could make Utrecht work, they were dead in the water.

After dinner he got up, went outside and caught a taxi, telling the driver to take him to a nightclub where he would find Serbians. Lots of Serbians.

"You want sex club?" the taxi driver asked.

"Do they have Serbian girls?"

"Sure. Serbian, Ukrainian, Asian, even Nederland girls," the driver joked.

"I want Serbian—and don't take me to the place that pays you the biggest commission."

"You Serbian?"

"Just take me to a Serbian club," Scorpion said. He didn't give a damn about Serbians or their girls, but much of the organized crime in Amsterdam had been taken over by Nas Stvar, the Serbian mafia, and right now what he needed was a forger. The taxi dropped him off at a neon-lit club in Pijp near the old Heineken brewery. Inside, the club was dark, neon red light casting shadows, and he had to fend off a half-dozen women who wanted him to buy them champagne. A twenty euro note to the bartender got him a conversation with a sweaty Serbian in a black sweater with a two-day beard stubble who called himself Javor and kept looking around as if they were being watched.

"You want identity, I got all kinds. Credit cards, American Express, Visa Black, whatever you want," Javor said.

"I want a blank Nederland passport and identity card. Official stamps. I'll put in the name and information."

"Better I do it. You do it, it won't pass," Javor said.

"Maybe I don't trust you."

"Nobody trust nobody. That's the best way."

"Good," Scorpion said. "All right, we do it now, but I watch you while you do it. I hear the standard is two hundred. You do the job and forget you ever saw me and I'll pay you double, but we do it right now."

"Double? Why didn't you say before? I thought you was a *smeerlap flikker* son of bitch," Javor said, getting up.

Scorpion followed him out of the club. The night had turned cold and a wind had come up, the overhead tram wires at the corner swaying. They got into the Serb's car and drove to a small print shop in Westerpark, near the Houthaven port. The Serb unlocked the door and Scorpion followed him into the back. Scorpion handed him the Xerox copy of Ouaddane's identity card and told Javor to use that information for the new card and passport.

"I'll need a beard," Scorpion said.

"What kind?"

"A Vandyke, like this." Scorpion indicated on his face. Javor nodded, rummaged around in a box and came up with a paste-on beard. He put it on Scorpion, who looked in the mirror, asked for a scissors, and holding up the picture of Ouaddane, trimmed the beard to match the photograph. Javor perched Scorpion on a stool and took his photograph, then used the computer to transfer the image to the new identity card and passport in Ouaddane's name.

"Give me the chip," Scorpion said, holding out his hand.

"What?"

"The camera memory chip. Give it to me."

Javor opened the camera and handed Scorpion the chip, who put it in his pocket, then took off the beard. When the new Dutch identity card and passport were complete, Javor handed them to Scorpion, who studied them both carefully and put them in his pocket.

"It's good, the *identiteitsbewijs*, yes? Fool this guy's own mother," Javor said.

"Now the computer. Delete the files and then empty the Deleted Files folder."

Scorpion watched him do it. When he was satisfied, he gave Javor the money, then took out his gun and pointed it at the Serb. Javor's eyes narrowed and he held out the money.

"Take it back. I don't want," he said.

"The only way to be sure you'll keep this to yourself is to kill you," Scorpion said.

"Please, *meneer*. This is my business. If I am talking, people don't come to me. Someone would kill me before this. I don't even know your name. Take money back."

"Keep the money," Scorpion said, putting away the gun. "Just remember. This never happened. You never saw me. You don't know the name on the card or passport."

"I swear," Javor said.

"Don't bother," Scorpion said as he opened the shop door. "If you lie, you're dead anyway."

He walked the dark streets to the Metro station, checking his reflection in store windows and waiting at corners to make sure he wasn't followed. He took the Metro to Central Station and slept for a few hours in a nearby hotel. He woke up suddenly in the middle of the night, short of breath and staring blindly into the darkness. They were hanging by a thread, he thought. The entire operation had come down to a night security guard and a whore. He got up and drank some water from the bathroom sink and fell back into a fitful sleep.

In the morning, he put on the fake beard and went to the ABN-Amro bank in the business district and opened an account for Ouaddane, using the fake ID and the papers supplied by Zeedorf. He got rid of the beard in a FEBO restaurant bathroom, then went to an Internet café and transferred the money from the account in Luxembourg to Ouaddane's new account. He finished by getting cash at the Credit Suisse branch near the Van Gogh Museum and caught the next train back to Utrecht, where he picked up the motorcycle from the parking lot.

He met Anika for lunch at a pub by the Oudegracht Canal. This time she wore tight jeans that were more than sexy enough and a Disturbia THIS AIN'T NO DISCO T-shirt. With her blond hair pulled back and without the heavy makeup, she looked like a fresh-faced college student. They sat inside at a back table, Scorpion facing the front of the restaurant.

"Why are we sitting inside?" she asked.

"We can't be seen together."

"We were seen together last night."

"Last night I was just a john. Twice is a relationship."

"What's wrong with relationships?" she said, provocatively licking the mayonnaise off her *pomme fritte* with the tip of her tongue, then smiling.

"They complicate things. Besides, this is business, isn't it?"

"Speaking of which, you never told me. What is your business?"

"I'm a lawyer. I'm on a case."

"Not a very *ethische*, how do you say it?"

"Ethical?"

"Yes, not a very ethical one."

"I've got plenty of company."

"So now what do we do?" she said suggestively, touching her lip with the tip of her tongue.

"We rent you an inexpensive car. The kind a university student would drive. Then we go to the apartment so you know where it is and you can get used to it, so you can act like you live there. Did you buy a book?"

She showed him a large textbook on Islam and its role in the contemporary world.

"Did you read any of it?"

"Very little. It's stupid," she said. "The whole thing is stupid."

"You won't tell him that?"

"I'll tell him it's *interessant*, so *interessant*, but I need someone to explain things to me and I'll lean forward and let my breasts touch his arm."

"That should do it." Scorpion smiled. "It would do it for me, but I'm easy."

"No," she said, studying his gray eyes. "You aren't."

After they rented the car, he showed her the apartment and gave her a key. He watched her drive off in the rented Renault Clio, then headed to the camera shop he'd found on the Internet in nearby Nieuwegein and got the minicamera and recorder and tools. He installed the camera behind a wall in the apartment. He set it so it could shoot Anika's bedroom through a hole in a print of a windmill hanging on the wall. Afterward there was nothing to do but sit in a chair in the other bedroom and think of all the things that could go wrong.

He awoke with a start. He must've fallen asleep, he realized. The room had grown dim. Shadows from the window stretched across the floor. He heard the sound of the key turning in the front door lock. It must have been what woke him up.

"*Here zijn we. Dit is mijn appartement,*" he heard Anika say as the door opened.

CHAPTER THIRTEEN

Turin, Italy

They drove the Autostrada dei Fiori along the coast between the hills and the sea. Past Voltri the A10 narrowed, the road running parallel to the railroad tracks across the green slope of the hills. The Palestinian wore an armored car guard's uniform. He sat next to the Moroccan from the van, who was driving.

"Once we get past Savona, we take the A6 to Torino," the Moroccan said in Darija, the Moroccan form of Arabic. "We haven't eaten. Maybe we could stop at an Autogrill?"

"Speak Fusha," meaning standard Arabic, the Palestinian said. "What's your name?"

"Mourad. Mourad Ran—"

"First names only!" the Palestinian said, cutting him off. "Call me Mejdan. We don't stop for anything. Armored bank trucks should never stop for anything anyway. It might be a robbery."

"Mejdan is an Algerian name," Mourad said, not looking at him.

"Many Algerians have Italian names. It's good cover for Italia."

The truck slowed as they climbed the hills above Cogoleto. Looking down, the Palestinian could see the buildings of the town stacked below on the hill-side, and below that the sea. He checked the side mirror. Behind them the second armored truck had fallen back. He glanced at Mourad.

"The bearded one, the one I killed? You were his friend?"

"Cousin," Mourad said, not looking at him. The engine labored as the truck climbed higher into the hills. The Palestinian hesitated, his hand resting on his leg near his armored truck guard's pistol. If the Moroccan considered it a matter of *ikram*—honor—it would be best to kill him as soon as possible. The truck went into a tunnel in the hill, and he thought inside a tunnel would be a good place to do it, but it would make everything more difficult. He decided to wait. They came out into the sunlight on the other side.

"You came to work with us," the Palestinian said. "You're still here. So either you stayed to try to kill me or because you believe in jihad. Which is it?"

"*Mos zibbi*," Mourad said, using the Arabic vulgarity to tell the Palestinian what part of him to suck. "What do you think?"

"I think you are a martyr. One of Allah's chosen. But there can be only one *capo*. Adil did not accept this. I had to kill him."

"He was of much pride," Mourad muttered. "I told him his mouth would get him killed."

Past Savona, they headed north on the A6 toward Torino. He told Mourad to idle the truck by the side of the road till the second armored truck caught up. When it lumbered into view and stopped behind them, they started up again through the pass in the mountains. Just before Priero they had to slow for a police roadblock.

"What's this?" the Palestinian asked.

"I don't know. It wasn't here when we came through this morning," Mourad said nervously.

"Call the other truck. Tell them if the *polizia* stop us and try to look inside either truck, we kill them and get out of here. Understood?"

Mourad nodded, pulled out his cell phone and told the other truck. The Palestinian took the safety off the gun, but kept it below the window level, so it could not be seen. Mourad pulled a gun from beneath the dashboard. A policeman stood beside the barrier, looking at each car as it stopped and then waited until he waved them toward the barrier. Behind the policeman were two police cars.

"Is he *carabiniere*?"

"No, *guardia*, Polizia di Stato," Mourad said.

The Palestinian felt a slight lessening of tension. The Carabinieri were the best of the Italian forces, and a roadblock here might have meant a security alert. It was why he purchased the armored trucks and had them painted with the BANCA POPOLARE DI MILANO logo. In theory, that should get them through. Police didn't like to stop armored trucks, which were presumably carrying a lot of money; nobody wanted the responsibility of something being splashed all over the evening news. Still, he could feel the sweat breaking all over his body as they approached the barrier. A handgun wasn't sufficient, he told himself. He needed something that would take out the policemen from both cars, plus any bystanders who got in the way. From now on, anywhere they went, they would be better armed, he decided.

They stopped next to the barrier. The policemen looked at the Palestinian through the window's bulletproof glass, and for a moment their eyes met and the Palestinian was glad he was wearing an armored truck guard's uniform. Neither of them smiled. The policeman looked at Mourad, and his eyes ran over both armored trucks, engines idling at the barrier. After a long moment he waved them on.

As the truck rumbled past the barrier, the Palestinian saw a car, smashed at an angle and overturned in the ditch beside the road. It was just an accident, he told himself, but he didn't relax or speak till they drove into Turin and to the warehouse they had taken him to the previous week. He was glad to see they had followed his orders and put up a sign over the door, COMPAGNIA BOLOGNA PARTES DI CAMIONS ALL'INGROSSO, a truck parts company, to help explain the comings and goings of people and trucks at the warehouse. Although he couldn't see it, he knew there was a security camera hidden behind the sign and other cameras at the corners of the roof. Mourad honked the horn twice and then twice again, and the loading door opened and they drove inside, followed by the second truck.

By evening the Palestinian had organized the teams and set up the workshops, labs, and dormitory spaces. He set up a separate closed-off space to work on the uranium. They unloaded and stored the steel drums, sheathing, explosives, and other materials from the armored trucks and then he called a meeting in the lunch area, two rows of metal tables set next to a small kitchen that smelled of lamb fat and cumin. He counted ten of them, eight young men and two women wearing black *hijabs*. There were supposed to be fourteen.

"Where are the missing four?" he asked Mourad in Fusha Arabic.

"I will find out," Mourad said.

"This is unacceptable. Our biggest danger is security," he told them, putting a Beretta 9mm handgun on the table in front of him. "All of you are *shaheedin* volunteers for martyrdom, but none of you knows what the operation is. You will not be told your assignment until the last moment. Keep any thoughts, any guesses, to yourself.

"If you have any suspicion about someone, anything at all, you must tell me at once," he said, picking up the Beretta. "If I believe there is any danger, that person dies. From this moment none of you will leave here alone. You will always be with another, and each time, who that person is will change so there can be no plotting among you. You may plot, but as the Sura says, *'waAllahu khayru almakireena.'* Allah is the best of plotters. As for the four who are missing, bring them here and keep them under guard. I'll deal with them later tonight."

* * *

That evening, after working on the uranium, he met Francesca Bartolo at her restaurant in Milan. She ordered Negronis and an antipasto for both of them.

"So there was no trouble with the *dogana*?" she said. The Customs.

"It was good," he said. "The Camorra should run Italy."

"*Bene*," she laughed. "We would do a better job than this *coglione* government we have now." She leaned forward, beckoning him closer. She was wearing a low-cut grape-colored designer dress that enabled her to show off her designer cleavage. "Listen, *caro*, where is the second sixty thousand?"

"Where's the remaining item I requested?"

"There's been a problem," she said, biting off the tip of a strip of *nervetti* meat like a guillotine. "It's not so simple."

"Meaning you want more money."

She smiled. "I like you, *caro*. You are understanding me very good. A real man understands what a woman wants without her even having to say a word."

"A real man doesn't let a woman take advantage of him," he said, crumpling his napkin and putting it on the table as if ready to leave. She put her hand on his.

"Don't leave," she said. She was smiling, but her eyes checked behind him to see that her bodyguards were in place near the door. "I want to go back with you to your hotel. But *primo*, business is, how we say, business."

"What would Carmine '*il brutto*' do if someone was trying to shake him down for more money?"

She frowned. "He does not like that name."

"What would he do?"

"His first impulse would be to kill them. *Per fortuna*, most of the time he talks with me first or half of Italy would be dead. This matter is difficult. That's why you came to us."

"How much?"

"You see! I knew I liked you," she said, putting her hand under the table and running it as far up his thigh as she could reach. "Double, *caro*. One hundred and twenty thousand more and you tell me what it's for."

"I don't have that kind of cash."

"But you can get it."

"A bank. That's the job," he said.

"Which one?" she asked, giving his thigh a squeeze before withdrawing her hand.

"Does it matter?"

She thought for a moment. "Not really. Do you have sixty thousand now?"

He nodded and pushed a messenger bag toward her under the table with his foot. She bent down, opened the bag, glanced in and closed it. She patted her mouth with her napkin and put it down.

"Let's go to the hotel now," she said.

"When do I get my item?"

"A few days. I'll let you know."

"When I get it, we'll celebrate," he said, getting up and heading for the door.

An hour later he parked the car near the warehouse in Torino and went inside. Mourad, his friend Jamal, and two other Moroccans were holding guns on four young men, one of them still a teenager, sitting on the floor in the warehouse office. The Palestinian came in and sat on the desk, facing them.

"Where were you?" he said in Arabic to the first, a thin bearded Moroccan in a Windbreaker.

"My wife. She doesn't know what I'm doing, just that it's something to do with the mosque, but she doesn't want me to be here. She says I need to be at home. We argued, the baby was crying, she said she would call the *polizia* if I left. I didn't know what to do," he said, rubbing his face with his hand.

"And you? You were ordered to be here and yet you weren't here. Where were you?" he said to a curly-haired young Moroccan in a black Settlefish Band T-shirt.

"We were at the movies. Driss and me," indicating the faintly cross-eyed long-haired teenage boy squatting next to him. "*E chi se ne frega?*" he sneered—What's it to you?—looking around to see if his arrogance was being appreciated by the others.

"Why didn't you come?"

"We figured finish the movie and then we come," the curly-haired man said.

"Good movie?" the Palestinian asked.

"Pretty good. Lots of action. Explosions. When that guy was on fire, that was *hajib*." He grinned, looking at the boy, Driss, for confirmation.

"That's good," the Palestinian said, and fired the Beretta into the curly-haired man's head, the sound of the shot reverberating in the office. As the body toppled over, he aimed at the teenager.

"*La!*" Don't, the teenager cried out, holding his hand protectively in front of his forehead. The Palestinian fired again, the bullet tearing through the teenager's hand and into his face, killing him. When he was lying on the floor, the Palestinian fired again into his head, just to make sure.

"What about you?" the Palestinian asked the last man, a sanitation worker in his thirties still in uniform, his face shadowed with resignation like a stain on a statue.

"The *capo* at work. He makes us work late. Just the Moroccans. You shouldn't kill me," he said.

"Why not?"

"Not before I kill Italians," he said, looking into the Palestinian's eyes.

"*Maashi*," the Palestinian said. Okay. "You," he said to the bearded Moroccan. "You go home. Don't come back. Say nothing. Not to your wife, not to anyone, even yourself. Here." He reached into his pocket and handed him a fifty euro note. "Buy her something. Take her to someplace *halal* for dinner. But if she ever mentions the *polizia* again, come and tell me."

The man nodded and left. The Palestinian ordered the others to pick up the two bodies and cram them into a refrigeration locker at the back of the warehouse, motioning to Mourad and the sanitation worker, whose name was Hicham, to stay behind. He told them they would be his lieutenants and would lead the others, who would be broken up into teams, with each team not knowing what the others were working on.

"They will be talking about this," Hicham said, indicating the bodies.

"I want them to," the Palestinian said.

He felt the buzz of a text message on the cell phone

in his pocket. It was his emergency phone. Only one person in the world had the number and it was never to be used unless it was absolutely critical. He read the screen message, decoding the text with growing anger and disbelief. The message threatened the entire operation; everything he had worked for all this time. Either the world had turned upside down or it was a death trap.

He had no choice. He would have to leave Italy at once.

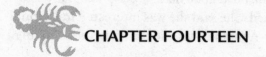

CHAPTER FOURTEEN

Kanaleneiland, Utrecht, Netherlands

"Do you like her?" Scorpion said in Arabic.

Abdelhakim stared at him from the chair, his eyes burning. He had tried to make a break for the apartment door, and Scorpion had to use the Kimura shoulder lock on him, taking him down and pushing the wrist till the pain was so intense the Moroccan had agreed to sit still in the chair. The woman, Anika, had gotten dressed and left. As she did, her hands were shaking and Scorpion had to whisper to her that there would be another thousand euros for her if she would just wait somewhere nearby for his cell phone call.

"I need you to listen," Scorpion told the Moroccan.

"I don't want to hear what you say. I am willing to die. *Allahu akbar*, God is great," Abdelhakim said. He looked small and defiant in the chair, still in his undershirt.

"I'm from Damascus. Your help is needed."

"If my help is needed, Imam Ali will tell me."

"She's pretty, isn't she?" indicating the door where Anika had gone out.

"She lied. She said she was interested in Islamic culture," Abdelhakim said sullenly, not looking at him.

"Does not the *hadith* of the Prophet, *sallallahou alayhi wasallam*, peace be upon him, say that a woman's witness is only half that of a man? What she did was for you. Now you must do something."

"Why should I?"

Before you sink the harpoon, you have to lead him into it, Koenig used to say. *First surprise him with what you know. Then make the Joe come to you, so that when it comes, it's right between the eyes and he absolutely understands the implication.* The threat had to be something he feared more than death, because if he was a true acolyte and death was an option, he'd take it.

"How important is the imam to you, Brother? If you had to choose between your wife and two boys or Imam Ali, which would you choose?"

"What are you saying? Why would I have to choose?" Abdelhakim asked, and Scorpion could see by the look in his eyes that Abdelhakim was shocked that he knew about his family. "*Inshallah*, I would die before I betrayed the imam."

"You already have. You are a *kafir* traitor. Everyone will know it."

"*Kol ayre wle*," Abdelhakim hissed at him. "Allah knows I am no traitor."

"Yes, you are. Here's the proof," Scorpion said, tossing the bank ATM card onto the table next to Abdelhakim, whose eyes darted to look at it, though he wouldn't pick it up.

"What's that?"

"Your account at the ABN-Amro bank in Amsterdam."

"I don't have an account there."

"Look at the card. It's in your name. You have twenty thousand euros in your account. Go ahead, pick up the card. It's your money."

"You're crazy! Where would I get twenty thousand euros?"

"It was transferred to your ABNA account from the Israeli Bank Hapoalim in Luxembourg."

"Israeli!" Abdelhakim gasped. "What have I to do with the Israelis?"

"You see the problem," Scorpion said. "Such bank transfers are easily traced. Everyone will know you're a traitor, even the imam. It's not just you, it's your family, the *ummah*, all will be condemned." *Make him feel it*, Koenig would say. *Before you throw him a lifeline, twist the hook. You have to make sure the poor bastard understands what he's about to lose.* "If Hezbollah learns you are an Israeli agent, you will die. Your wife and sons will die. The imam and our cause will be in great danger. We cannot allow this. How many will die because of you? And do you know the worst of all, Brother?"

Abdelhakim looked at him, numbly shaking his head, his eyes vacant as he stared into the abyss.

"The worst is that you, a 'good Muslim,' will have dealt a terrible blow to the Palestinian cause, because truly, I have just come from Al-Muqawama al-Islamiyya in Damascus and I must get something out of the imam's office before the CIA or the AIVD can get to it. Unless you help me, we are lost."

"I don't understand." He blinked. "You need to get into the imam's office?"

"If you let me in tonight at midnight, no one will ever know about you or the Israelis or that I was there. You will keep the twenty thousand and you'll be paid another ten thousand. As for the woman, if you don't want her," Scorpion snapped his fingers, "she's gone. If you choose to forgive her for her female lie, you can have her whenever you want and your wife will never see this." He turned on the camera and held it so the Moroccan could see the video and hear the sounds of the two of them having sex, Anika moving and groaning beneath him. "*Inshallah*, you will save the imam and yourself and your family."

Abdelhakim began fumbling in his pocket and pulled out a crumpled cigarette. His hand was shaking as he straightened it and he looked at Scorpion before lighting it. Scorpion sat back and waited. *You have to let them feel the trap*, Koenig said. *They have to touch the bars and the sides of the cage, so they really understand there's no other way out.* Come on, he thought. Take the carrot. It's the only rational choice, pick it up, you *humar*: thinking if it didn't work, he'd have to kill the Moroccan.

"Just this one night and no more?" Abdelhakim said, picking up the bank card and staring at it as though he had never seen one before.

"Just tonight. Nothing will be disturbed or taken. No one will ever know."

"And I get to keep the thirty thousand?" he said, and Scorpion smiled inwardly. Get greedy, he thought. The greedier the better.

Abdelhakim tapped the card thoughtfully, then put it in his wallet. Scorpion let out the breath he'd been holding.

"Do you like the woman? She's very pretty."

"I never touched such a woman. So beautiful," Abdelhakim said softly.

"She likes you; she told me."

"And my wife never knows?"

"I'll give you the chip from the camera before I leave tonight."

"I have to go to work," he said, getting up and putting on his shirt and windbreaker, then hesitated. "And it's good for the Muslim *ummah*?"

"*Ilhamdulilah*, it is a good thing you'll have done, Brother. Come," Scorpion said, walking him to the apartment door.

Scorpion watched the mosque through night vision goggles from the BMW parked down the block. The night was cool and the wind had come up, blowing dust and scraps of paper in the street. The greatest danger was when Abdelhakim had second thoughts; something that Koenig cautioned was inevitable once the Joe was out of the immediate confrontation. Scorpion could only hope that greed and sex and the threat of public humiliation would outweigh his old loyalty. "Most people," Koenig had said, "would rather be a traitor than be thought of as a traitor."

If Abdelhakim did have second thoughts, it could go either of two ways. Either he would tell someone and there would be militants lying in wait for him at the mosque, or it could come days, months, or even years later, when Abdelhakim put a bullet through his own head. The only way to know was to watch the mosque and wait, so there would be no surprises and he could try to figure out what the hell was happening, because nothing made any sense after what Professor Groesbeck had told him over beers at a brown bar near the university earlier that evening.

Rabinowich had responded to his Web question with a code that turned out to be Groesbeck's cell phone number. The bar was noisy and crowded with students, some of whom were still carrying books from late classes. Groesbeck wasn't what he had expected—an older academic along the lines of Rabinowich, someone whose brilliant sarcasm could fall like a guillotine on an unsuspecting undergraduate. But the professor was young, in his thirties, dark-haired, and with an eye for female students.

"Did Rabinowich tell you anything about me?" Scorpion asked him.

"He said don't bother asking you anything because anything you told me would be a lie, including hello and good-bye," Groesbeck said in English, with only a slight accent, meanwhile checking out a statuesque blonde in a yellow tank top and tight jeans at the bar. "Of course, that told me exactly who you are, not that it matters."

"He said you were on the IAEA inspection teams in Iran and North Korea."

"Mmm . . . she's something, *ja*?" Groesbeck said, and for a moment the two men contemplated the blonde's chest.

"Healthy girl," Scorpion said.

"Lovely. So you want to know how to make a

nuclear bomb? It's easy. All you need is enough Uranium-235. Just slap it together and—*pop!*" he illustrated by splaying his fingers open like an explosion.

"Why not plutonium?"

"Nasty to work with, Pu-239. The radiation will kill you, and it'll start fires at ordinary room temperature unless you have an extensive, dry—because ordinary water makes it worse—inert gas facility. U-235, on the other hand, is beautiful stuff. You can work it, shape it, you don't need an elaborate facility, and the radioactivity is so mild, you could put it under your pillow and sleep on it."

"So how much U-235 do I need to make a bomb?"

"Depends," Groesbeck said, putting down his beer and trying to make eye contact with the blonde.

"I have top security clearance. I'm sure Dave told you," Scorpion said.

"It isn't security. It's just not a simple number. It varies depending on how pure the U-235 is. For an ordinary nuclear reactor, all you need is four or five percent purity. For a weapon to go supercritical, much more. For the Hiroshima bomb, they used 64.1 kilos, about 141 pounds, of ninety-plus percent pure U-235, and the bomb was so inefficient that only one percent, perhaps one pound or so, went supercritical. The other ninety-nine percent of the uranium in the Hiroshima bomb was wasted."

"How about a terrorist with twenty-one kilos at seventy-six percent?"

"I already told you." Groesbeck shrugged. "It depends."

"On what?"

"Many factors. The shape and fit when the pieces of uranium are pushed together. The temperature. The density when fission starts to expand the uranium. What kind of a reflector around the U-235 is used to bounce the neutrons back into the uranium. What kind of emitter you use to start the reaction. Of course, the big problem is how do you slam the separate pieces of uranium together."

Groesbeck leaned closer. "The simplest way, the way I would do it if I were a small group instead of a government, is the gun mechanism. As you know, the basic principle of all explosives is that explosive force is directed perpendicular to the surface of the explosive material. By shaping the material you can aim the force of the explosion like a gun. Using a small regular explosive, just shoot one piece of U-235 into another, like a bullet into a cylinder made from the second piece of U-235, and have the impact start the neutron emitter. The whole thing should take less than a second or the bomb won't work."

"Maybe I'm wrong but it doesn't seem like twenty-one kilos would be enough?"

"At seventy-six percent, extremely unlikely." Groesbeck shook his head and motioned having a drink at the blonde, who signaled back *Why not?* "Unless you have a very sophisticated device, I would say fifty kilos of ninety-plus percent pure U-235 would be the minimum."

"I get the feeling you don't believe the seventy-six percent figure."

"Seems unlikely. It's not that hard to go from seventy-six to over ninety percent. Why would you stop? Of course, there is another possibility, I'm sure you thought of."

"You mean, what if there's more? The thought had crossed my mind."

"Suppose your imaginary terrorist already has, say, another thirty or so kilos of almost pure U-235 sitting somewhere to add to the twenty-one, which is maybe already ninety-plus. Then, my friend, I would definitely worry. Actually, I would worry more about your terrorist selling it to someone who does have the resources to do something with it, like the Iranians. Listen, I have a colleague I absolutely have to speak to," Groesbeck said, getting up and going over to the blonde at the bar. Which now left Scorpion sitting in a car in Utrecht in the middle of the night with the pieces to a puzzle that didn't fit. What in hell did the Palestinian want with the twenty-one kilos of U-235, which probably cost millions, if it wouldn't make a bomb?

He had other concerns too. His only lead to the Palestinian had suddenly become what Groesbeck would have called a "supercritical" red zone. According to the detective, Zeedorf, whom he had called on his cell phone from the BMW after meeting with Groesbeck, the imam of the Kanaleneiland mosque hadn't been seen in over a month.

"The imam's name is Ali el Alechaoui, age seventy-four," the Dutch detective had said. "He is an immigrant from Rabat, Morocco; a widower, with three grown sons and sixteen grandchildren. The only address listed for him is the mosque. He receives a disability pension from the government."

"What's his disability?"

"He's blind, despite which, he has written a book. A commentary . . ." Zeedorf paused, and Scorpion waited while he consulted his notes. ". . . on the *Hadith* of Sahih Bukhari, which is, I gather, some sort of Muslim religious text. I have a copy of his *identiteitsbewijs* card if you wish. One interesting thing."

"What's that?"

"He regularly led services at the mosque, but for the past five or six weeks he seems to have dropped out of sight. I have been unable to get any information from our sources with either the Utrecht or the KLPD National police as to whether the imam is or was under surveillance. Although he has not been seen, no one has filed a missing person report. Of course, he may be traveling or ill. I have not had a chance to check the hospitals."

"Anything else?"

Zeedorf hesitated, and Scorpion sensed he was debating with himself before he said it.

"What is it?" Scorpion asked, prodding the detective.

"Nothing definite, but something curious."

"What?"

"We can't confirm it, but apparently it's not just the imam—one of his sons and a number of his grandsons also seem to have recently dropped out of sight, not even appearing for Friday prayers."

Scorpion arranged payment and ended the call, his mind racing. They were going operational. Whatever happened, he had to get into the imam's office in the mosque.

He studied the building and the dark street, where nothing moved but bits of trash stirred by the wind. It was after midnight, and for the past few hours there had been no one coming or going to the mosque. The only sign of life was the silhouette of Abdelhakim occasionally appearing in a window, ghostly green in the night vision goggles. Scorpion got out of the BMW. He wore his motorcycle helmet with the visor down to prevent security cameras from identifying him and carried all the gear he would need in a backpack. He went to the front and side doors and, keeping out of the line of sight, disconnected the security cameras, then knocked on the side door to the mosque.

After a moment Abdelhakim opened the door and gaped at him till Scorpion flipped the helmet visor up and said, "It's me." He checked for internal cameras and spotted them in the usual places, near ceilings and in the *musalla* prayer area on the wall to the right of the *qiblah* wall that in every mosque faces Mecca.

"No one must ever know I was here. Where's the recorder for the cameras?" Scorpion asked, looking around. There were no wires, so it was an RF setup.

"Come, I'll show you," Abdelhakim stammered. He led Scorpion to a panel in the wall that he removed. Scorpion set the replay on the recorder to essentially have the last five minutes recorded over with nothing happening.

"They won't know something was erased?" the little Moroccan asked nervously.

"Not unless you tell them. If anyone ever does ask,

tell them there was a brief electrical surge outage and you think the recorder reset itself. Where's the imam's office?"

Abdelhakim led him to a small room at the back of the building. He was about to turn on the light and Scorpion stopped him and turned on his flashlight instead. The room was sparse, with a few bookcases, a desk, a low bronze table with cushions on the floor to serve food, and a battered metal teapot for making Moroccan mint tea. There were no computers in the room, and then Scorpion remembered that the imam was blind. He was chilled by the terrible thought that he had gone to all this effort and had come up empty.

"Where does the imam keep important papers?" he asked.

Abdelhakim, watching from the doorway, just shrugged.

"What about computers?"

"In the office. I'll show you," he said.

"La." No. "I'll find it. You go back to your usual post. Pretend I'm not here. I'll be gone soon."

"Then I get the extra ten thousand euros?" Abdelhakim asked.

"That's right," Scorpion said, thinking, I've got you, *ibn hamar.* The little Moroccan was hooked, all right. He'd be able to turn the Joe over to Peters, or whomever Peters's replacement would be, to run for as long as they wanted. As a center for the Al-Muqawama al-Islamiyya, Utrecht was compromised from here on out. But that didn't get him any closer to the Palestinian, he thought as his eyes ranged over the walls and ceiling. He went over to the bookcases and looked behind them, but there was nothing. There were no pictures on the walls. The imam is blind, he reminded himself.

He quartered the room with the beam from the flashlight. There had to be something. The imam had written a commentary on Bukhari, considered by many Muslims as the most authentic collection of the *Hadith* or sayings of the Prophet Muhammad, and second only to the *Qu'ran* itself in holiness. It was inconceivable that Imam Ali would be such a highly regarded religious authority and not be either at the center of things or at the least had given the Palestinian his spiritual blessing. And the imam had disappeared, which meant they had gone operational. There had to be something in the office, he thought while staring at a rug on the floor under the desk. It was the only rug in the room, he realized, and it was not where people might walk on it or sit or pray, but under the desk.

Scorpion moved the desk, lifted the rug up and saw the panel in the floor. He sat down beside it, pulling his backpack next to him, the flashlight in his mouth, and opening the panel, saw a high security floor safe. It was the type that had a three-inch thick solid steel body, a spoke locking handle, and two locks—a combination lock and a key lock—and you would need both in order to open it. Normally, it wasn't that hard to crack a safe. You either used explosive on the lock or drilled a hole next to the lock—or at the back of the safe if the door had a hardened cobalt plate to prevent drilling—inserted a flexible fiberoptic bore lens to see the changes in the lock mechanism as you turned the combination or digital dial, and that was that. But he couldn't do that. He had to open the safe in such a way that no one would ever know it had been touched.

You couldn't just do it the way it was done in the movies. That was nonsense. You couldn't sandpaper your fingers and either feel or hear the tumblers click when you reached the right number. Safe manufacturers had long ago put in safeguards, such as false tumbler notches or lock wheels made of lightweight nylon, to frustrate hearing or feeling the tumblers click. As for the kind of autodialers that opened a safe in seconds in the James Bond movies, in reality, autodialers needed to be model-specific, could require hours to cycle through all the thousands of number combinations, and because of that were only practicable for three-number safe combinations, not for the six-plus number combination likely on a high security safe.

For such assignments, the CIA used an audio "soft drill" like the one Scorpion pulled out of his backpack and placed next to the lock after pulling on latex surgical gloves. The soft drill used sound waves, like a sonogram, to probe and detect the contact points as he slowly turned the dial. The LED display indicated where to "park the wheels"—there was one wheel inside the lock for each number; a six-number combination required six wheels—as a starting point, and a computer chip in the drill graphed the convergent points and displayed the six-number combination on the LED. There was a sound and Scorpion looked up, his hand on his gun. He saw Abdelhakim's silhouette in the doorway.

"What is it?" he asked.

"What are you doing?" the Moroccan asked nervously. "How much longer is this going to take?"

"Get away from the door, I'll let you know," Scorpion said, waiting till Abdelhakim's shadow was gone from the doorway. The little Moroccan was antsy. Scorpion wanted to keep him alive if possible. Now that he was turned, they could run him for years, but if he got too antsy, there might be no choice.

He dialed the combination, then used a master key, tapping the key lock with the tapper tool to jump the tumblers. He turned the key and the locking handle and opened the safe.

It was filled with papers. He turned on the desk light and began to go through them one at a time, placing each one facedown on the rug so that when he was done he'd be able to put them back sorted in the original order. From time to time he took a photograph of a page with his cell phone camera. Sandwiched between two pages of an inventory of mosque supplies, he found a picture postcard of sailboats on the Aussenalster Lake in Hamburg with what appeared to be the same jumbled Arabic lettering code as on the postcard in the Ayatollah Khomeini book in Germany. He took a photograph of both sides of the postcard and put it back in the same position between the pages. Then he saw them and knew he had hit the jackpot: incorporation papers and stock certificates for a number of different companies.

One was a Netherlands property company. A second was Gelderland Sporting en Vuurwapens, BV, a Dutch sporting goods and firearms company. Two were of companies incorporated in Luxembourg: Utrecht Matériel Agricole, Sàrl, a farm equipment company; and Bukhari Nederland-Maroc Société de Financement, S.A., which looked like a holding company. They were all of interest, but the one that jumped out at him was FIMAX Shipping, headquartered in Kiev in the Ukraine. According to the papers, FIMAX was owned by the Bukhari Nederland-Maroc holding company and had as assets offices in Kiev and Odessa and two cargo ships, the MV *Donetsk* and the MV *Zaina*, both convenience-flagged in Belize.

Scorpion's mind was racing as he snapped photographs of the documents as fast as he could. They had planned it beautifully, like a big engineering project or a beautiful, complex work of art. Because of Luxembourg's secrecy laws, investigating companies headquartered there was next to impossible, even when international treaties were invoked. Farm equipment was a perfect cover for fertilizer for explosives. The sporting goods company could buy and sell as many guns and other weapons as they wanted. As for the Ukrainian shipping company, if you wanted to move something for which the logistics were almost impossible, like nuclear material or weapons from Russia, given the corruption in Russia and the Ukraine, a legitimate shipping company was perfect cover. He was so occupied, thinking and snapping photos under the lamplight, he didn't hear Abdelhakim come in.

"You have to stop. Someone's coming," the Moroccan said from the doorway.

"Get rid of them," Scorpion said, taking out the HK pistol.

"What if I can't?" he hissed.

"Who is allowed to come into the imam's office?"

"Only the imam and his sons," Abdelhakim whispered, and ran toward the door. Scorpion grabbed the papers, making sure they were in the original order. He was about to put them back into the safe when he saw it: a contract in English between Baselux Pharma, Ltd., a Swiss-based pharmaceutical company, and the Bukhari Nederland-Maroc holding company. It was for the Swiss company's entire yearly output of an experimental gram negative antibiotic, Ceftomyacole. Scorpion remembered Rabinowich on the iPod talking about the plague bacillus: "resistant to virtually every antibiotic known." It was a holocaust they were planning—only the Islamic Resistance was planning to survive.

Scorpion heard the front door open and Abdelhakim speaking to someone. He was out of time. He stuffed the contract into his pocket, put the rest of the papers back into the safe and locked it. He had just managed to turn off the desk light and grab his backpack when he heard voices coming toward him. He was trapped.

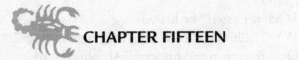

CHAPTER FIFTEEN

Papendorp, Utrecht, Netherlands

The *musalla* prayer hall was dark. Scorpion crept into it on all fours, feeling his way across the carpeted space to the *minbar*, the wooden pulpit where the imam would give the sermon at Friday services. He heard Abdelhakim talking with someone, and the lights came on just as he climbed the stairs of the *minbar* and crouched hidden behind the podium.

"What's happened? Where is the imam?" he heard Abdelhakim say in Arabic.

"Never mind. Go keep watch," a man answered. Probably one of the imam's sons, Scorpion thought. "We'll talk in here. Keep the lights out," the same man said to someone else, not Abdelhakim. They were standing in the middle of the empty *musalla*, their voices barely audible from where Scorpion was hiding.

"What about the guard?" a second man said in Fusha Arabic.

"What about him?"

"He saw my face." His words riveted Scorpion—

and there was something about this man's voice, but he couldn't place it.

"He's loyal, a good Muslim."

"Good Muslims can be turned. Show me the . . ." The words were lost as the voices moved toward the imam's office, then the light in there came on.

He knew if he was to get out, this was his chance. But who didn't want his face to be seen? The Palestinian! Was it possible? That voice! It could be the same one he'd heard on Harris's cell phone in Karachi. *It's him!* a voice screamed in his head.

He'd been given a chance in a million. It wasn't the perfect time or place, but he had to take him out now, Scorpion decided, carefully opening his backpack and screwing the silencer onto his 9mm pistol. But he couldn't do it from the *minbar*. He had to assume that both the imam's son and the Palestinian were armed, and if they started shooting, he had little doubt what the little guard, Abdelhakim, would do with his gun. Three against one in a static position wouldn't work. He had to move.

Scorpion crept down the steps and just started toward the imam's office door when the lights came on in the *musalla*. Abdelhakim, who had just turned them on, loudly cried out, "*Saadni!* Help! Intruder!" and reached for his gun, his eyes filled with hatred. A tall bearded man with a turban—he had to be the imam's son, Scorpion thought—filled the doorway of the imam's office and aimed his gun at Scorpion, caught in the open in the middle of the *musalla*, while a figure behind the imam's son ran out another door.

Scorpion whirled and fired at the imam's son, who cried out in pain as he flattened himself behind a narrow wooden post. After faking to one side as Abdelhakim fired, the bullet missing, Scorpion jumped out on the other side and shot the Moroccan in the head, the distinctive thunk of his silencer the only sound. Then he turned back to the imam's son, whom he'd shot in the belly. As the wounded man struggled to raise his gun, Scorpion shot him again, this time hitting him in the neck. The imam's son dropped to his knees, blood gurgling from his throat as he toppled over.

Scorpion went over and kicked the gun away from his hand. The imam's son lay on the carpet choking on his own blood, his eyes dimming as he watched Scorpion pick up his gun and put it in his jacket and run to the mosque door. He opened it just in time to see a black Fiat with its lights out race down the street, its tires screeching as it made the turn at the corner.

Scorpion ran out to where he had left the BMW and jumped in. He hadn't seen the man's face or anything more than a moving figure behind the imam's son, but it had to be the Palestinian, he told himself as he put the BMW into gear and roared after the Fiat. There was still a lot to do at the mosque, but the Palestinian took precedence over everything he thought as he turned the corner and caught a glimpse what might have been the Fiat heading toward the roundabout.

Scorpion drove the dark streets past stores and apartment houses. The Fiat had gone around a corner, and when he turned at the same corner, the Fiat was gone. Unsure which way to go, after a moment he headed for the roundabout. Just as he entered it, he saw a black car that could have been the Fiat, only now with its lights on, coming out of the roundabout and heading toward the canal. It was moving fast, and Scorpion edged the BMW to over 130 kilometers per hour in the narrow streets, hitting the brakes as he swerved through the roundabout and raced after the Fiat as it skidded around a corner. He was starting to gain on the other car as he slid into the corner, barely missing a parked van as the Fiat made another turn and raced down the broad boulevard that led to the suspension bridge over the canal, its single pylon and wires gleaming in the lights on the bridge.

Gunning the BMW, he pulled close enough to the Fiat to see the back of the Palestinian's head above the headrest. Scorpion picked up his pistol and held it ready as he started to pull into the lane next to the Fiat when he saw a car coming from the other direction in his lane. He hit the brakes and swerved back behind the Fiat, the BMW's tires skidding all over the road, the car swinging wildly left and right as he fought for control, losing precious feet behind the Fiat. The two cars raced across the bridge at over a hundred miles per hour, the Fiat skidding as they came onto the Papendorp side of the canal. It had shut its lights again and was hard to see as it raced past flat farmland beside the canal. In the distance on the far side of the fields, Scorpion could see the dark rectangular shadows of office buildings in industrial parks and the distinctive oval silhouette of the Daimler building.

The light turned red at an intersection. Scorpion gunned the engine again, planning to race through it, when he caught a glimpse of a small car filled with teenagers entering the intersection. He saw their eyes going wide, their mouths open in screams he could almost hear as he hit his brakes, throwing the BMW into a violent skid that flung it sideways at an angle to avoid the collision. The car bounded up on the curb and slid into the soft earth of the field, and kicking up dirt as it came to a sudden stop. When he looked up, Scorpion could just see the shadow of the Fiat far ahead, heading for the industrial park buildings. Stepping on the gas, he drove back to the intersection, driving around the stalled car, the teenagers cursing him in Dutch as he headed down the street toward the buildings where he'd caught a glimpse of the Fiat driving into a parking garage next to an office building.

Scorpion drove carefully into the garage; the Palestinian had to know he was close behind him. Because it was night, the structure was empty except for a few cars, none of them a Fiat. He drove slowly, his eyes darting in all directions. The garage interior was dimly lit, except for an overhead light over each lane. It wasn't till the third level, his nerves screaming at every turn, that he spotted the Fiat parked in an empty row facing the wall. Only a few other cars were parked on this level.

Scorpion stopped the BMW well away from the Fiat and got out. Using his car as a shield, he quartered the area. The Palestinian had proven himself an efficient killer. He had to be hiding somewhere nearby, and barring a miracle, would get the first shot. Scorpion was beginning to get a feel for his adversary, and realized if the Palestinian shot first, it would probably be the only shot. And he had to be careful about approaching the Fiat too. The Palestinian certainly knew how to make a bomb. He listened intently. Except for the sound of his breathing, the structure was silent. Glancing toward the Fiat through the windows of the BMW, it looked clear. He had no choice. He would have to approach it. After putting a fresh clip into his pistol, he stood up.

Moving along the garage wall, he glanced up and behind as well as ahead. The parking structure was silent except for the ticking of the Fiat engine as it cooled. He approached the Fiat, taking one last 360-turn, and aimed at the car windows, ready to fire. The Fiat was empty, the keys in the ignition. He got down on the concrete floor, but there was nothing underneath the Fiat. He could feel the heat from the engine as he walked around it, but his hand hesitated at the door.

Leaving the keys, he thought, meant that the Palestinian wanted him to open the car and turn it on. He was backing away from the car when he heard a car start up on one of the lower levels. He just had time to run to the outer rail and see a dark sedan, he couldn't tell what make, race out of the garage and head toward the moving lights of cars on the A2 motorway. The Palestinian had broken into and jumped another car.

By the time Scorpion got back to the BMW and drove out, the other car was gone.

* * *

In the early morning darkness the mosque looked just as he had left it. The only shot anyone would have likely heard was Abdelhakim's one shot, and it didn't appear to have roused the neighborhood. Still, Scorpion hung back, studying the mosque and approaching carefully. Once inside, he found both bodies still lying on the carpets in the *musalla*. He knew that returning to the mosque was pushing his luck, but he didn't have a choice. He needed to delay the discovery of the bodies to give him time to get away. More important, he needed to get back inside the imam's office. Something in there had been so important that it brought the Palestinian to the surface. He had to find out what it was.

He went back into the imam's office, where he spent another half hour going through, photographing, and carefully putting back everything in the safe, including the contract with the Swiss drug company. He downloaded the contents of the computers in the assistant's office onto his plug-in drive. It was useful, but he was stymied. Whatever was so urgent that it had brought the Palestinian to Utrecht, he hadn't seen it. He was about to take care of the bodies, which he'd rolled into prayer rugs, when something made him go back to the imam's office for one last look.

He moved the flashlight slowly around the room and was struck by how sparse the room seemed, reeking of poverty; almost a repudiation of the wealth in companies and assets hidden in the safe. The flashlight beam moved along the bookcases and stopped when he realized he was staring at a copy of the imam's book on the *Hadith* of Bukhari. He opened the book and began flipping through the pages, not knowing what he was looking for. Then, on a page in the middle of the book, he saw it: a penciled-in drawing of a Muslim warrior with a sword in the margin of a paragraph commenting on a *hadith* from volume 4, chapter 3, of the *Sahih Bukhari*:

It seemed he had seen it before, but he couldn't recall where. There was something vaguely archeological about the simplistic drawing and its markings in the circle of the flashlight beam. The paragraph of commentary written by the imam stated that the text of the *hadith* was in reality a secret prophecy of the Prophet. Scorpion read the original text of the *hadith* in Arabic: "The creation of these stars is for three purposes, as decoration of the sky, as missiles to hit the devils, and as signs to guide travelers." *As signs to guide travelers!*

He looked at the drawing again and all at once realized what he was looking at. It was the constellation Orion. He strained to remember the name of Orion in Arabic. Like a gift, an old memory from childhood came bobbing to the surface. He recalled a night in the desert spent gazing up at the stars that filled the sky from horizon to horizon. It was not long after the *Mutayr* had saved him after his father was killed. He was standing with Sheikh Zaid, who was pointing out the constellations. The stars were out of reach, yet so close you could almost touch them, and there were so many he could see the sheikh's face in their glow.

"Do you see there, little *dhimmi*, the belt, the sheath, and the arm of the warrior raised with the sword?"

"What is it called?"

"That is al Jabbar, the Giant," Sheikh Zaid had said.

He had to get this to Langley at once, he thought. He took photos of the cover, title page, and the drawing and replaced them where he had found them. Then he found the keys to the imam's son's Mercedes parked in front of the mosque in the dead man's pocket, carried the bodies out and dumped them into the trunk. He drove the Mercedes a few blocks away and left it parked on a side street, the keys in the ignition. With luck, a local gang member would steal it before realizing what was in the trunk.

Returning to the mosque, Scorpion reconnected the outside security cameras. Making sure he wasn't seen, he was soon driving the A2 to Schiphol Airport outside Amsterdam. It was all there right in front of them, taken from the words of the *hadith*, he thought as he drove. "Missiles to hit the devils" and "signs to guide travelers."

He checked into a hotel near the airport and, using his laptop, uploaded to the mission website the encrypted photos and intel he had collected, the image of the Swiss drug contract, his thoughts on the Bukhari *hadith* and the constellation al Jabbar. Then he requested immediate information on the mosque's companies and on the whereabouts of the two Ukrainian ships, the *Donetsk* and the *Zaina*.

Just before he fell asleep, Scorpion tried to convince himself he wasn't a total failure because he hadn't caught even a glimpse of the Palestinian's face. He thought too about pimping the woman, Anika, and dropping her into the little Moroccan's life like a tornado, destroying it completely. It left him wondering if, somewhere in the moral calculus of the universe, the lives of those who could die if he didn't get to the Palestinian in time outweighed what he was doing to save them. And then he fell asleep and dreamed that he was driving the A2 at night, only every car's driver was a man with no face, and when he looked in the rearview mirror, he had no face either.

His cell phone rang a few minutes before six in the morning. On the other end, a voice that could've been Rabinowich, though he wouldn't swear to it, said: "Remember kindergarten? Four left Mombasa two days ago, bound for Marseilles. Last was supposed to be in Marseilles, but they have no record of her. We're still checking," and he hung up.

Scorpion got up and looked out the window, trying to clear his head. He felt like he had barely slept. It was before dawn, the light a shadowy gray and the window wet with a fine drizzle.

By "kindergarten" Rabinowich meant the first days of learning codes during CST training. "Four" was the fourth letter of the alphabet, D, for the ship, *Donetsk*, and the "last" letter of the alphabet was Z for the *Zaina*. There were red flags all over this. Mombasa in Kenya was a known smuggling port for al-Qaida terrorists based in Somalia. Both ships were headed for Marseilles. He called the concierge, who checked and told him there wasn't a flight from Amsterdam to Marseilles till late in the day, but if he hurried he could just catch the Thalys train from the Schiphol Airport station to Paris, and from there connect to the high-speed TGV train that could get him from Paris to Marseilles in three hours.

Within forty minutes Scorpion was boarding the Thalys train to Paris, ordering a *café américain* and a croissant from the bar on the train. He had arranged with the concierge for the hotel to return his rented BMW at the airport. He sat by a window and watched as the train sped past the suburbs and *polders* of Holland, his face and hair still wet from the drizzle. Al Jabbar, the Giant, was some kind of key to the code the Al-Muqawama al-Islamiyya was using. But there were still so many loose ends. If the *Zaina* wasn't in Marseilles, where the hell was she? And then there was what Groesbeck had said, that twenty-one kilos of U-235 was nowhere near enough. And that the mosque holding company had made a deal to buy up the entire inventory of a new antibiotic. All loose ends, except that it was obvious that Al-Muqawama al-Islamiyya had gone operational and the clock was ticking down.

The Thalys train arrived mid-morning at the Gare du Nord. It was still drizzling in Paris, and he had to run to grab a taxi and race to the Gare de Lyon. He barely managed to catch the TGV, the French ultra-high-speed train to Marseilles, with only minutes to spare. He was still breathing hard as he entered the first class carriage, and it was with a sense of anticlimax, almost inevitability, that he spotted the final loose end. Sitting in a table seat by the window, looking very beautiful but not at all happy to see him, was Najla Kafoury.

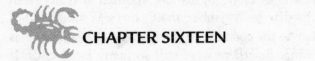

CHAPTER SIXTEEN

Le TGV, Paris-Marseilles, France

"And what am I to call you today, Herr Cr—"

"McDonald. Damon McDonald," Scorpion said, interrupting her. They were sitting across from each other over glasses of Bordeaux in the TGV first class carriage. Through the window next to them the green fields and trees and clusters of tiled houses of the French countryside flew by, punctuated by flashes of telephone poles. The only sound was the murmur of conversation and the steady hum of the train on the tracks. The electronic readout above the door at the end of the car indicated that they were traveling at 296 kilometers per hour.

"Umm, what happened to poor Herr Crane and his strange sexual habits?" Najla said, glancing at the window as a village train station flashed by in a second.

"Don't know. Seems you ran away before we

could find out. Speaking of which, where did you go after I left you?"

"Back to Germany."

"No, you didn't. And you're doing it again."

"Doing what?"

"Lying when you don't have to. Not that I hold it against you, but it slows things down," he said.

"What makes you so sure? I could've gone back."

"You weren't on N-TV. If you were back, they would've said something."

She shrugged. "I'm not that important."

"Now I know you're lying. You are many things, but modest isn't one of them."

"You say I lie, but you don't care. Why?" Najla asked, brushing away a lock of hair that had fallen over her forehead. She had taken off her Burberry and wore a simple white blouse and gray slacks. On anyone else it would have looked like a day at the office, but on her it was Fashion Week in Paris, and there wasn't anyone in the carriage, male or female, who didn't steal a glance at her.

"Professional courtesy. We're both in the lying business." He grinned. "So where did you go?"

"I talked to women in the Amsterdam sex trade to look for leads."

"Is that part of your TV reporter training?"

"You'd be surprised what a girl has to do to get on these days. So, does Herr McDonald share Herr Crane's dirty little urges to tie women up, have sex, and then leave them?"

"Which bothers you more? That I tied you up or that I let you go?"

"Don't flatter yourself, *liebling*. You're attractive, but not that attractive."

"I went back, you know. To the hotel, but you were gone."

"If I had known, I might have waited."

"Why? Do you like men who abduct you and tie you up so much?"

"Let's just say you did it with a certain charm." She smiled enigmatically. "So why are you going to Marseilles?"

"For the same reason you are—and please," he said, holding up his hand, "spare me the one about how you're being on this train is a coincidence. And don't waste my time with the latest installment of Intrepid Najla, Girl Reporter on a Mission."

"Why bother? You wouldn't believe me," she said, glancing again at the landscape whizzing by. Another TGV flashed by their train in the opposite direction with a roar and was gone in seconds.

"Why should I? The only true thing you ever told me was your name, and I already knew that."

"More than I know about you," she said, looking into his eyes.

"*Touché*. Being in France is improving your dialogue," he said, and grinned. "What led you to Marseilles?"

"A source."

"A male source?"

"Now you sound jealous, *liebling*," she said, dipping her little finger into the wine and licking the wine from her finger with her lips. "What difference does it make?"

"Actually, none at all."

"Did I tempt you with what I did just now?" she asked.

"Yes, you did, you little sexpot! But it doesn't matter because I know you're lying."

"How do you know?"

"You opened your mouth."

At that, she laughed loud enough to make everyone near them look at her.

"*Shh!*" he said, grinning as he held his finger to his lips. "We have to stop. Even if it is fun."

"You are a rare one, Herr McDonald. *Prost.*" She raised her glass and took a sip.

"*Zum wohl.* What happened to your job on television?"

"I am *auf anweisung* . . . how do you say, on assignment. I told them I will be returning soon." She sipped her wine. "So, are you going to tie me up again?"

"Not so long as you stay right next to me. It's no longer a question of whether you're an agent. The only question is for whom."

"So we're partners?"

"Or enemies."

"How will we know which?"

"We won't. Not till the chips are down."

"Like most relationships between men and women," she said. "So what are we doing in Marseilles?"

"What did your 'mysterious' source tell you?" he asked, signaling the attendant with the snack cart for more wine and a couple of croissants.

"Only that the Islamisch network in Nederland was going to send someone to Marseilles. Truly, why are you going to Marseilles?"

"I'm looking for a ship."

"Good. You know more than I."

"If I do—and you're actually telling the truth—it's the first time, on both accounts," he said, reaching for money to pay the cart attendant.

CHAPTER SEVENTEEN

Marseilles, France

The sun was shining as the TGV glided into the train station in Marseilles. They took a taxi to the port. Not the old Vieux Port, with its fish market and pizza vans and tourists gazing out at the bay and the islands, including the notorious Chateau d'If of Count of Monte Cristo fame, but the Nouveau Port, the enormous modern harbor complex, one of the largest in Europe, north of the Vieux Port. While on the TGV, Scorpion had spent a half hour on his cell phone to work his way from department to department to set up an appointment with the director for Black Sea shipping operations at the port. The guard at the entrance to the port directed the taxi to a large concrete office building a block from the quai. A sign on the building read: PORT DE MARSEILLE FOS—DIRECTION DES OPERATIONS ET TERMINAUX.

As they walked inside, Najla asked: "Who am I supposed to be on this expedition? Your assistant?"

"My mistress," Scorpion said, pushing the door open.

"You know, I'm not sure I like you," she said as

he gave his name to the security guard at the desk.

"It's not a job requirement, not even for mistresses," he replied, picking up a *Paris Match* to read while they waited in the small lobby. After a few minutes a young man came and guided them to a second floor office. A dark-haired Frenchman in shirtsleeves and tie behind the desk gestured for them to sit.

"Je suis Fabien Bartini, le directeur de la mer noire et oriental—expédition européenne. Et vous êtes le mandataire pour la compagnie de FIMAX, n'est ce-pas, monsieur?" he said.

"I'm an attorney representing their interests," Scorpion said in English, handing Bartini a business card. "I'm trying to locate the MV *Zaina*."

"And this beautiful mademoiselle is . . . ?" Bartini said.

"Ma amie, my girlfriend," Scorpion translated for Najla's benefit.

"He wishes," Najla said.

"Alors . . ." the Frenchman said, looking at Najla.

"About the *Zaina*, Monsieur le Directeur? I understood she was due to be in Marseilles yesterday but never arrived. Where is she?" Scorpion asked.

Bartini checked his computer for a moment. "She's on her way. She made an unscheduled stop in Genoa. She's due to berth at 2245 hours tonight. If you wish, I can arrange a pass."

"Why did the ship go to Genoa?"

"There was a death on the *Zaina*," he said, looking at the computer screen. "The *capitaine*."

"The captain. Isn't that unusual?"

"Yes, but people die at sea. It happens." Bartini shrugged.

"Is there any evidence of foul play?"

"I have no idea. One can contact the Italian authorities."

"Why couldn't they unload the body in Marseilles?"

"I do not know, monsieur. Hmm, *c'est intéressant,*" he said, peering at the screen.

"What is?"

"One sees that they unloaded three TEU containers from the ship in Genoa."

"Unusual because the stop was unscheduled?"

"To unload such a small number of containers is unusual," Bartini said.

"Any idea what the cargo was?"

"One does not know, monsieur. For such matters you must contact the freight forwarders. In any case, the *Zaina* will be here in . . ." He checked his watch. ". . . seven hours, and you can talk to the ship's *officiers* yourself. And with that . . ." He stood up to let them know it was time to leave. "*Bien sur,*" he said to Najla. "You, mademoiselle, are welcome to stay as long as you wish."

"One is tempted, monsieur. There's something about Frenchmen," Najla said as she and Scorpion stood.

"What about the *Donetsk*? Where is she?" Scorpion asked.

Bartini tapped on the keyboard and checked his computer screen.

"At the moment, the Suez Canal. She'll be here

in two and a half days. Do you want the pass?" he asked.

"If you please," Scorpion said, and waited till Bartini scribbled something on a pad and handed it to him.

As they left, he said: "If you come again, bring your *jolie amie*."

"It would be my pleasure," Najla said, extending her hand for Bartini to kiss, which he did.

They took a taxi outside the port gate to the Corniche Kennedy to check into a hotel for the night.

"A single room?" Najla said as Scorpion handed a credit card to the front desk clerk.

"After Amsterdam, I didn't think it was an issue," he said.

"Are you going to tie me up again?"

At that, the desk clerk glanced up at them, a smirk on his face.

"Only if you want me to," he said, signing the check-in slip. He sent her up to the room to freshen up while he intended to go to the hotel's business center to log on to the Internet.

"Suppose I go away again?" she said.

"You won't."

"What makes you so sure?"

"Because you're watching me as much as I'm watching you," he said, walking away.

Scorpion got on the Internet at the business center, but there was little new from Langley. CIA and NSA cryptographers were using the al Jabbar lead as a key to crack the code and said they should have something for him soon. They were investigating the cover companies and the Swiss drug company he had sent them, but despite the pressure from Washington, the Luxembourg authorities as well as the Swiss, as expected, were dragging their heels. Peters had been recalled from Amsterdam. For the time being only the security guard was listed as missing from the Utrecht mosque, and Accounting was balking at paying for Anika, the Amsterdam call girl, as "Miscellaneous Operational Expenses." He logged out with the feeling that Langley was just wasting his time. Rabinowich still hadn't told him the one thing he needed to know: who the Palestinian was, or at least something that would help identify him.

He bought a new cell phone in the hotel lobby shop and made a call to an ex-DGSE agent, Didier Zardane, whom he had worked with on the Paris piece of the Saudi coup operation, and who, he'd heard, was semiretired to a *mas* he was renovating near Aix-en-Provence. Didier picked up the call on the first ring and expressed no surprise at hearing from a Monsieur McDonald he had never met. They arranged to meet over dinner in Marseilles at a restaurant Didier suggested. It was near the Cours Julien, which Didier called by its local name, the Cours Ju.

The restaurant by the Cours Ju was small and dark and smelled wonderfully of garlic and bouillabaisse. It was off the square, in the artsy quarter crowded with bars and cafés, south of the Canebière, Marseilles's main street. Scorpion, as was usual, was early. He sat with Najla over drinks of pastis. While they waited, he picked out three ways to exit the restaurant in an emergency and was confident there were no other agents staking them out, although the middle-aged Corsican whose glance had fallen on him and Najla and moved away as soon as he saw Scorpion was aware of him, was almost certainly of the milieu, as the underworld was known in Marseilles.

Didier came in, spotted Scorpion and immediately came over and without preamble sat at their table. He was tall, thin, with graying, wavy hair, wearing an Armani black leather jacket. In a flowered shirt, he could have passed for the man in the Tommy Bahama ads. Scorpion remembered him as the one who had fingered Gerard as an FSB double agent.

"*Qui est-elle?*" Didier said, meaning Najla.

"We're not sure. I'm holding her close," Scorpion replied in French.

"She could be opposition?"

He shrugged. "Langley says no, but one never knows."

"You could terminate the *chatte*," Didier said, deliberately using the vulgarity. "Or have you grown *sentimental*?"

"Am I part of this conversation?" Najla asked in English.

"Very much so, mademoiselle," Didier said.

"For smuggling arms, drugs, and such, who is running things at Marseille Fos?" Scorpion asked in English.

"La CGT," Didier said, pronouncing it "say-jay-tay." Scorpion chuckled at the joke. The Confederation Generale du Travail was the national union that represented the dockworkers.

"*Pas mal*," Scorpion said. "They must miss you in Paris."

"Paris can *va te faire foutre*," Didier replied, indicating what Paris could do to themselves. "They're all like Americans now. All they know are computers and stupidity."

"Back to my question, who in the milieu could get it through the port? Is it still les Corses?" meaning the Corsican mafia.

"You know la Brise de Mer? The Sea Breeze," Didier translated for Najla.

"Sounds like the name of a boat," she said.

"It's the name of a bar in Bastia in Corsica," Didier explained. "It's where the gang started."

"Who's the *vrai monsieur*?" Scorpion asked, using the Corsican slang for a gang boss.

"Cargiaca. Albertini Cargiaca is the *paceri*," Didier whispered, motioning them closer. "As the title indicates, the one who can enforce the peace. What is this about?"

"Suppose I wanted to move something big through the port. Something *très difficile*, *très dangereux*. Could la Brise de Mer do it."

"Sure. But as you say, it is *très difficile*. The *douanes* of Marseille Fos are good."

"What about Genoa?"

Didier smiled. "Much easier. The Camorra di Napoli run the Genoa docks."

"I'm sorry you can't stay for dinner," Scorpion said, sliding an envelope stuffed with a thousand in hundred euro notes under a napkin that he pushed toward Didier, who pocketed it and stood up.

"*Bon appetit*. They make the true bouillabaisse

here. You should try it," Didier said. He was about to leave when he stopped and added in French, "What about your *petite amie*? For a fee, I'll take care of it."

"It's good to see you again, *mon vieux copain*," Scorpion said, and watched him go. As soon as Didier left the restaurant, Scorpion got up and grabbed a waiter, whispered something to him and slipped him some money. He came back and sat down again.

"What was that about?" Najla said.

"Just being careful. In our business, it's important. But of course you know that." He smiled. "Shall we try the bouillabaisse?" he said, signaling to the waiter.

As promised, the bouillabaisse was very good. It was done Marseilles style, with the fish and shellfish presented on a separate platter from the broth, which was served in a bowl with floating slices of baguette spread with rouille.

"This ship you asked him about—where's it from?"

"Ukraine. How's the bouillabaisse?"

"Delicious, and you're changing the subject. What's your interest in this Ukrainian ship?"

"Did you find it curious about the captain dying?"

"I was wondering about that too. You think someone killed him? Why?"

"Maybe he didn't do what they wanted. Or maybe he demanded more money than they wanted to pay."

"Maybe someone wanted to go to Genoa, where it would be easier to get something dangerous through customs. Something you could ship in three containers. That good-looking Frenchman at the port thought that was very odd."

"You just like him because he kissed your hand."

"With his looks, he didn't have to. You could learn from him. It'd be interesting to see the autopsy report on that captain, wouldn't it?"

"Very."

She put down her fork and looked at him. "You're a kind of policeman, aren't you?"

"No, not a policeman."

"Or a CIA spy," she said. "'The Spy Who Loved Me.' Except you don't, do you? Love me."

"That wouldn't be a good idea, would it?" he said.

"Because you don't know if I'm on your side, whichever side that is?"

"We need to finish up," he said, putting his napkin on the table.

"Are we going to Genoa?" she asked, not looking at him.

"We'll see," he said, getting up and speaking for a moment with the waiter he had spoken to earlier. He came back, tossed some money on the table, and grabbed Najla's hand.

"Come on. We have to go," he said.

"What is it?" she asked, getting up.

"Didier. I had the waiter check outside from time to time while we were eating. He's sitting in a car down the street."

"What does he want?"

"He smells money. He's decided to try to cut himself in," Scorpion said, guiding her toward the back of the restaurant. As they walked into the narrow kitchen with three workers talking and noisily handling pots, a man in a soiled white apron shouted at them:

"Attention, monsieur! Il est interdit! You may not come back here."

Scorpion handed him a twenty euro note, and pulling Najla after him, was headed for the back door when he paused for a moment in front of a small TV mounted on a shelf. A chic well-tanned woman was broadcasting the *Dix-neuf—Vingt Journal Télévisé* nightly news.

"I thought you wanted to go," Najla said.

"Wait a minute," he said, and then the woman on TV said something that stopped him cold. Suddenly all the loose ends came together and he knew exactly where the Palestinian intended to strike and when.

 **CHAPTER EIGHTEEN**

Marseilles, France

He shouldn't have gone back to the hotel. He hadn't wanted to, but Najla insisted in the taxi after they'd gotten away from the restaurant.

"Where are we going? Genoa?" she asked.

"Rome," Scorpion said. He checked flights on his cell phone and booked reservations for the two of them on an Air France flight from Marseilles Provence Airport to Fiumicino for that evening.

"Why Rome?"

"Don't you know?" he asked, his eyes searching her face in the intermittent flashes of light from passing headlights.

"We haven't even unpacked and now you want to leave. Why?"

"Because the story you want is in Rome."

"Where did that come from?"

"You'll figure it out. *C'est à quelle distance de l'aéroport?*" he asked the taxi driver. How far to the airport?

"Ten kilometers, monsieur," the driver said.

"What about my clothes and things?" she said.

"We'll buy new ones in Rome."

"That's what you think. I have to freshen up. Besides, I'm doing you a favor. You have no idea what those clothes cost. Turn around. Take us to the Pullman Hotel," she told the driver.

"*Ne prêtez aucune attention*," he told the driver. Pay no attention. "Keep going." He didn't want to tell her that the hotel was a red zone. Didier was ex-DGSE and it wouldn't take him long to track their hotel down, and that was only half his problem. If anyone from the Utrecht network learned that they had made inquiries about the *Zaina*, or if they found the bodies and got to Anika, or just put two and two together and figured out where he would go next, it wouldn't take Al-Muqawama al-Islamiyya long to look for foreigners in Marseilles, a city teeming with Muslims working at every hotel. Even more urgently, he had to connect with Langley without Najla or anyone else looking over his shoulder.

She grabbed his wrist. "I'm tired of this. Either you take me to the hotel now or so help me I'll scream 'rape' at the top of my lungs the second we get to the airport."

"Forget it," he said, pulling his wrist away. "I'll drop you at the hotel and go to Rome myself."

"I know where you're going. I can book a flight too. What is it with you? Just five minutes and we'll go, I swear."

Suddenly, he realized that he had to go back to the hotel. He'd checked in his laptop at the desk and hadn't wiped the disk. That was the problem when you weren't traveling alone. It was hard finding the privacy to do the things you didn't want anyone to see. You cut corners; you made mistakes.

"Five minutes and that's it," he said to her. Then to the driver, "We changed our mind. *Allez à l'hôtel.*" The driver signaled and made the turn back to the city.

"What is your problem?" she asked him. "What's wrong with going back to the hotel?"

"Didier. How long do you think it will take him to check out the hotels in Marseilles and find us?"

"You realize you're paranoid, don't you?" she said.

"You're not the first person to say that to me."

"Then maybe it's true."

"You'd have to ask them, only you can't."

"Why not?" she said as the taxi turned onto the Corniche Kennedy. The street was lined with buildings and hotels fronting the bay.

"They're all dead."

"You don't trust anyone, do you? Especially me."

"I don't know anything about you."

"Nor I you. As if you are really South African, *scheisse.*"

"Where were you born?"

"Lebanon. My parents brought me to Germany when I was a baby."

"Where'd you go to school?"

"What is this?" she snapped. "You know me. I hate the Islamists! You saw me at the demonstration."

"In my business we call that 'deep cover.' Five minutes," he told her as the taxi pulled up to the hotel. She went up to the room as he retrieved his laptop from the front desk clerk.

"Are there any messages?" he asked.

"No, monsieur," the clerk said, not looking at him.

"Check again," Scorpion said.

The clerk checked the room box and the computer and shook his head, still not looking at him.

"Has anyone asked about us, anyone suspicious, maybe more than one? *N'ayez pas peur.*" Don't be afraid. He slipped the clerk a fifty euro bill. The man glanced around and nodded once, almost imperceptibly. *Merde*, Scorpion thought in French as he headed for the elevator. It only took a few seconds to kill someone; Najla was in the room alone.

Their room was on the next to top floor. He took the elevator up to the top floor and walked downstairs to his floor. He took out his gun, put the silencer on, cracked the stairwell door a fraction of an inch and peered out at the corridor. It was empty. Stepping out, he walked silently to the door and, careful to stay out of sight range of the peephole, listened. The room was silent; there were no sounds of her moving around. He went to the room next door, listened and then knocked.

"*Service d'étage, madame,*" he called softly. There was no answer. He slid a credit card between the door lock and the frame, opened the lock and stepped inside. The room was dark and empty. He closed the door behind him, walked to the balcony door, opened it and stepped outside. The night was cool and clear, the lights from the hotel windows reflected in squares of light on the water of the bay. The balcony of his and Najla's room was empty, and glancing over, there was just enough curtain to give him cover. There was about two feet of space between the rails of the two balconies, where he could fall three stories to the concrete yard below. The key, he knew, was not to make a sound.

Scorpion climbed onto the rail, the gun in his left hand and his right pressed against the side of the building for balance. He stepped over the gap to the rail of his balcony, sliding his hand forward as he balanced between the two balconies, then, still on top of the rail, he knelt and while balancing precariously, almost losing it, felt for the balcony floor with one foot until he touched it. Once on the balcony, he took a deep breath, transferring the gun to his right hand and peering into the room for an instant through the glass door, then ducking back.

He'd seen two men inside, one a Corsican, by the look of him, the other a black African. The Corsican was positioned, gun raised, against the wall next to the door of his room. The African was holding Najla in the middle of the room, his hand over her mouth, a knife pressed to her throat.

Scorpion knew he would only get one shot, and he needed them alive to find out who sent them. When he was ready, he stepped into the middle of the balcony in a two-handed firing position, aimed and fired, the bullet tearing a hole at the center of a spiderweb of cracked glass and hitting the gunman by the door in the shoulder. With the gun still pointed at him, he tapped the balcony door.

"Ouvrez la porte!" Open the door, he said, aiming at the gunman, who tried to aim his own gun at him, realized he couldn't with his injured shoulder and indicated the African holding Najla.

"We'll kill the *pute*," the gunman said in French.

"Open the door or the next bullet's in your head," Scorpion answered, also in French.

The wounded gunman came over, unlocked the balcony door with his good hand and slid it open. Scorpion took his gun away, shoved him back into the room and stepped inside.

"Put down the gun or I'll cut her *pétasse* throat," the African with the knife said, his hand still over her mouth. Najla's eyes were wide and she looked desperately at Scorpion, who turned and aimed at the forehead of the man holding her.

"*Va t'enculer!* I don't give a shit what you do. You and your *mec*," he said, indicating the gunman, "will both be dead before her windpipe's cut. Don't be an asshole. I want to pay you money."

"What are you saying?" the African asked.

"Is the man who paid you tall, thin, with a black leather *blouson*?"

"Go *faire foutre* yourself! What's it to you?" the man with the knife said.

"How much did he pay you?"

"Four hundred. Two hundred each," the gunman said, and sat suddenly on the floor. "I'm shot, you *salaud*. It hurts."

"I'll give you five hundred each," Scorpion said, lowering his gun and taking out the money, putting it on a table. "Go get a towel," he told Najla as the African with the knife let go of her and came to the table for the money. As he started to pick up the money, Scorpion pressed the muzzle of the gun onto the top of his hand, stopping him.

"You're from West Afrique?" he asked the African.

"Sénégalaise. What of it?"

"And you? Corsican?" Scorpion asked the gunman, who nodded. "But not of La Brise?"

"How do you know we're not?"

"Because if you were of la Brise de Mer, you'd be getting paid from someone taking his orders from Cargiaca instead of my old *copain*, Didier," he said, moving the muzzle so the man could pick up the money. Najla came out of the bathroom with a towel that she applied as a compress to the gunman's shoulder wound.

"Cargiaca's not running la Brise. He's in Provence, counting his money and mistresses," the gunman said. "These days, it's Jacky, if he survives le Belge." The Belgian.

"Jacky?" Najla asked.

"Jacky *le chat*. They call him the cat because he's survived eight assassination attempts. But after last week, who knows?" the gunman said, pressing the towel to his shoulder. "Three of his men were killed in their auto while waiting at a traffic light right on the Canebière. The *Journal Télévisé* said it was riddled with hundreds of bullets."

"Are they still running heroin through the container terminals?" Scorpion asked.

"Not so much," the Senegalese said. "My brother works in the container terminal, the *salaud*. They pay him plenty to look the other way. The containers are mostly for *le cocaïne* and *le vert*."

"*Le vert?*" Najla asked.

"Marijuana," Scorpion translated.

"*Oui, le cannabis*," the Senegalese nodded. "For the heroin, these days they mostly recruit mules by taking a member of someone's family hostage and cutting off one finger or ear at a time till the mule brings it from Athens to Marseilles. It's a good business, but because of the fighting between the Belge and Jacky *le chat*, dangerous."

"So if I wanted to smuggle something big through Marseille Fos, say big guns, missiles, there's a good chance it would be hijacked?" Scorpion asked.

"You want to do that, *mec*, you tell us. We have plenty of *copains*; we'll do that for you," the gunman said. So Didier had lied all the way, Scorpion thought. About Cargiaca and about the *douanes* at the port making it tough on la Brise's smuggling. The reason the Palestinian didn't want to bring the U-235 through Marseilles was the likelihood of it being hijacked.

"About my old *copain*, Didier, the *salaud* in the black *blouson*. What did he want you to do with us?"

"He wanted us to take you both out in the country. He said he would call and tell us where. What happened, *mec*? He double-cross you on a job?" the Senegalese asked.

"*C'est ça.*" That's it. "You want another thousand?"

"I don't know. You shot me, you *salaud*," the gunman said.

"You shouldn't play with guns. They're dangerous," Scorpion said. "When he calls, tell him you've got us."

The gunman's cell phone rang then, startling them. *A thousand euros*, Scorpion mouthed, indicating with his gun that the gunman should answer.

"*Oui*," the gunman said, then listened. "We have

them," he said, looking at Scorpion. He listened some more, said "*d'accord,*" and hung up. "Now what?" he said to Scorpion.

"He has a place near Aix. He said to meet you somewhere near there, *oui*?"

The gunman nodded. "It seems you know this *fils de putain.*"

"I gave him a thousand euros tonight," Scorpion said. "If you take it from him, as far as I'm concerned it's yours."

"Why? You don't want the money?"

"A business expense. It's not good to let people think they can get away with *merde*. It leaves a bad impression."

"Anything else?" the gunman said, getting up and throwing the bloody, wadded-up towel on the floor.

"One thing. We never want to see either of you again."

Later, in the taxi to the airport, Najla broke the silence.

"I'm sorry. I didn't understand. The next time you say we're not going back to the hotel, believe me, I'll listen." She hesitated. "Thank you." She looked into his eyes, which was all she could see in his face, hidden in shadow. Scorpion didn't say anything. "God, you are a stone cold *scheisser*!" she said, pushing him away.

"None of that had to happen. We can't afford this. We only have seven days," he said.

"What happens in seven days?"

"Nothing, if you do what I tell you."

"I will. I swear," she said. The taxi made a turn, causing her to lean. She let it bring her close enough to brush against him.

By the time they got to the airport, they had thirty minutes to catch the late night flight to Rome. They checked the luggage and were going through the passport control in separate lines, Najla in the EU queue, and Scorpion, with his South African passport, in the non-EU queue. He had just gotten through when he saw the immigration officer, a woman, signal, and two armed soldiers approach Najla. She turned to look at him as they led her away. He had to decide quickly whether to stay or go. The plane was already boarding.

After a moment's hesitation he jogged to the gate. He had no choice. The mission was entering the critical phase. Settling into his seat, he made a call with his cell phone to set up a follow-up call with Langley from Rome. There was a lot to talk about, including why the French DGSE intelligence—he was sure they had something to do with it—had taken Najla into custody.

The jet lifted high over the lights of Marseilles and made the turn over the dark Mediterranean toward Italy. Now that there was a good chance he might never see Najla again, he allowed himself to think of her sexually, the warmth of her body next to his in the bed in Amsterdam, the stunning contrast of her aquamarine blue eyes against her golden skin and dark hair. He was more attracted to her than he had been to any woman in a long time. It had taken all his willpower not to grab her, and when she'd brushed against him, she knew what she was doing to him, and he knew she wanted it too. But there had always been the chance that she was an enemy, and if it came to it, what if he had to kill her? In a way, going to Rome alone simplified things.

He looked out the window at the lights strung along the coastline of the Côte d'Azur below in the darkness. Somewhere in Italy, the Palestinian was getting ready. Out of habit, Scorpion glanced at his watch. It was after midnight. He had six days.

CHAPTER NINETEEN

New York, United States

The danger point was the U.S. Customs and Border booth at JFK Airport. If the border agent detained him, the Palestinian knew they would fail. This was something they had known from the beginning. The key to security for the entire operation was also its fatal flaw. He was the only one who knew all the pieces. The strategy provided perfect security so long as he was operational, but without him there was no operation. And he'd already had one close call too many, barely getting away in Utrecht.

He was traveling as a businessman, dressed in slacks and a jacket, no tie, with business cards and papers from his freight company in Hamburg, which they could contact and that would pass a superficial background check. His German passport was bulletproof, he told himself. Nothing Muslim about it, and the name he was using and RFID chip embedded in the front cover were in the German Auswärtiges Amt database.

As for Liz, she was female, good-looking, and British, which already lowered her profile, since Americans tended to trust the English, not realizing that some of the most radical jihadis in Europe were in the UK. He hadn't wanted to bring her, but it was too dangerous to leave her behind in Italy because she was still seething over Francesca, though she denied it. Women were always a complication, but he needed her for Rome, his throat going dry as he stepped up to the non-U.S. citizens booth in the crowded terminal hall and handed the border agent his passport and a filled-in U.S. Customs and Border Protection form. If they were to stop him, it would happen here.

The U.S. agent checked his face against the passport photo, looked up his preboarding screened data: name, digital fingerprint, and photograph against the Watch list on his computer. He checked the arrival form again.

"You here for business or pleasure, Mr. Groener?"

"Business," the Palestinian said in English in his German persona accent, which hovered halfway over the Channel, somewhere between Hamburg and the BBC, sweat breaking out between his shoulder blades.

"What business are you in?"

"Material handling. Trucking. My card," the Palestinian said, taking out one of his business cards, which the agent waved away.

"You came from Rome via Paris?"

"Yes, we do business with DHL and also with American companies throughout Europe," he said, finding it hard to talk or swallow, his mouth was so dry.

"How long do you plan to be in the United States?"

"Just a few days," attempting a smile. The agent didn't smile back. The agent checked his computer screen again. The two men waited.

"Welcome to the United States," the agent said after a long moment, and stamped his passport.

Liz was waiting for him at the luggage carousel, and together they stood in line for a taxi that took them to a midtown hotel near Grand Central Station. They barely spoke in the taxi. At one point she started to say something and he glanced significantly at the driver. Heeding that warning, she made meaningless conversation about the cool weather as he looked out the window at the row houses along the Van Wyck Expressway, not seeing them because all he could think of was the critical pieces of the operation he had left behind in Turin and Rome, and whether by coming to America and bringing her he had jeopardized the whole thing. They checked into the hotel in separate rooms, and once his luggage was delivered, he went down two floors to her room and she let him in.

"Why the bloody hell couldn't we be together, you bastard. I had to fend off some palmy Belgian asshole who thought my tits were the business class bloody hors d'oeuvres," she began, and never finished because he kissed her and started pulling off her clothes.

He had first met Liz two years ago in Mykonos. She was topless on the beach, with her mini-breasts and leggy post-Oxonian body, and within an hour they were going at it like rabbits in his room overlooking the port and the sea. Afterward, the two of them sharing a cigarette, she told him about joining the Oxford Movement for Palestinian Justice, her eyes gleaming with conviction, and he had alerted Utrecht to see what they could do about recruiting her. He visited her several times in London, a budding *shaheedah* she-wolf in Sloane Ranger guise, all boho short skirts and Hermès scarves and meetings to ban Israeli professors from British universities. He went shopping with her on Beauchamp Place, and at night they kept her flatmates awake while they went at it nonstop, as if Knightsbridge was Mykonos North, till one of the other girls wanted to join in. Then Liz's jealousy flared up.

Looking for him, she had arrived in Turin the night before the move to Rome, making a big entrance at the warehouse, only to learn he wasn't there. Mourad, whom he had left in charge, wouldn't tell her where he was. In fact he was in Milan, in Francesca's suite at the Savoia Hotel, making the final payment after the delivery in Turin that morning.

"So, what more can I do for you, *caro*?" Francesca had whispered, kissing him after he had given her the money.

"Let's say I need to get rid of something."

"Disposal," she said, nibbling on his ear, "is a Camorra specialty."

"I think," he said, his arm around her waist, "we should continue this conversation in the bedroom."

When he got back to Turin, Liz found a long

dark hair on his shirt and smelled Francesca, sniffing at him like a cat and letting him know about it till he slapped her in the face and explained it to her. She got up and started to leave and he showed her the gun. He called Jamal in then and had him show her the bodies in the refrigeration locker, and when Jamal brought her back, she was quieter. Afterward they made love and she cried and told him she still loved him and how much she hated the Israelis. But he knew he couldn't trust her, and decided to take her with him to New York after the migration from Turin to Rome in a big rig with COMPAGNIA BOLOGNA PARTES DI CAMIONS ALL'INGROSSO on the sides and the rest of the team making the trip down the autostrada in separate vans and cars.

Now, their first stop after leaving the hotel in midtown was at the office he had rented in the Sunset Park section of Brooklyn. They went there to pick up the package he had FedExed from Calexico. From Brooklyn, they took the subway to the 169th Street station in Jamaica, Queens, exiting on Hillside Avenue. The street was lined with small East Asian stores and curry restaurants with signs in Bangla and English. They walked a few blocks to the apartment he had rented six months earlier at the same time he set up the office in Brooklyn. He unlocked the door and turned on the air-conditioner units. The apartment was almost completely bare of furniture, except for a large freezer and, in the bedroom, a few shopping bags of supplies. He gave Liz the address where the girl lived with her brother and told her to wait for him there.

"I want to stay," she said.

"It's dangerous," he said. "Once I start making it, it could explode any second. This mixture, HMTD, is the most volatile thing you can imagine. The slightest jar, ordinary room temperature, anything can set it off."

"I want to be part of this," she said, putting her hand on his shoulder, looking at him like a soldier with Palestine her flag, and the two of them kissed, her tongue darting into his mouth, a portable Mykonos.

While they waited for the apartment to cool, he put on latex gloves and took the backpack out of the FedEx box, tearing up and flushing any identifying labels from the box down the toilet. He took the spray equipment stamped APASNAST!—Danger!—in Cyrillic lettering out of the backpack and made sure it was ready. When the apartment was cold enough, Liz helped him carry the shopping bags from the other room to the bathtub along with a big mixing bowl and other implements.

"Here we go," he said, opening the first jar. He took a deep breath before pouring the liquid into the bowl. "This is a very bad explosive. I hate it."

"If it's so bad, why do you use it?"

"It's terrible to work with, but it has one enormous advantage. We don't have to take it through customs. You can make it anywhere from ordinary household ingredients: hair bleach, a food flavoring, and something you can buy at any camping or sporting goods store. It's powerful, completely legal, and the authorities never know a thing until it blows up," he said, and despite the coldness of the bathroom, which was making her shiver, he wiped a bead of sweat from his brow.

When he was done, he had about a dozen pounds of solid HMTD, which he set with a detonator connected to leads from a cell phone, before putting it in a plastic bag. He placed the bag in the backpack surrounded with pellets of dry ice to keep it cold. Then he put the spray equipment back into the backpack on a piece of canvas on top of the dry ice. He put the backpack on, turned everything off in the apartment, locked it, and they walked the four blocks to the apartment of the young Bangladeshi woman and her brother, careful not to jar the backpack and calling first to make sure the brother and sister were both home from work.

Bharati opened the door and let them in. Her brother, a small dark man with longish hair, who called the Palestinian "Bahadur" and Liz "Begum," led them toward the kitchen. The Palestinian took off the backpack and carried it like a priest with a chalice of holy wine to the kitchen, but there wasn't enough room in the refrigerator and he had them empty food out to put the backpack in.

They sat in the living room and the young woman, her large dark eyes glancing first at Liz and then at the Palestinian, served them tea. After they had sipped the tea, the brother blurted: "About the money?"

"Do you have a computer?" the Palestinian asked. The brother nodded. "Check your account."

While they waited, the Palestinian asked the

young woman if she was ready. She looked down, glancing shyly at him from under her lashes, and nodded.

"I have two children. My sister loves them. She will do what is needed," the brother said, coming back in.

The Palestinian told him to leave.

"She is my sister. I should be here," the brother said.

"In that case, I'll have to kill you," the Palestinian said, taking out a gun. The brother blanched. "We need to talk of operational matters. Afterward, the police may come to you. You can't tell them what you don't know."

The Palestinian went into a shooting stance. The brother couldn't take his eyes off the gun. After a moment he nodded and left.

The Palestinian turned to the young woman. He went over how to use the spray equipment in the backpack and showed her the photograph of the helicopter pilot, Atif Khan, on his cell phone screen. When she was sure she would be able to recognize the pilot on sight, he erased the image. He spread out an MTA map of the New York subway system they got at the hotel and went over when and how she would rendezvous with Khan. The Palestinian took a photo of her with his cell phone to show Khan.

"You understand we considered other alternatives," he told Bharati. "The simplest would have been to do it in the subway, but there was no way you could have gone through a train spraying and not attract attention. We want days for the pathogen to incubate before the authorities know what has happened."

"My brother's children, my family, will be safe?" she asked, her eyes searching his face. Liz watched her like a hawk.

"They must use the antibiotic I have given you. No other kind will work. Do not go near the refrigerator till it is time. The explosive must be kept cold, but the spray should not be frozen. If you need to, eat out. Here's money," he added, giving her cash. "You will know the exact day when you get a phone call that uses the phrase 'al Jabbar, the Giant, is high in the sky.'" He showed her how to use the cell phone for the explosive. "Remember, the explosive is only if something goes wrong. They would do things, you understand? I don't want them to hurt you."

"We have to go," Liz said, standing up.

"Will I see you again?" the young woman asked softly, not daring to look at him.

"It will be a long time before it's safe for me to be in America," he said.

On the train back to Manhattan, after they left the apartment, Liz turned on him: "What the bloody hell was that? If she could've, she'd have gobbled you up like a Cadbury."

"She wanted me to save her," he said. "Her brother got into money trouble with a local Bangladeshi gang. She's doing it to save her nieces from being without a father. She doesn't want to die."

"I could scratch her eyes out. She could barely keep her hands off you."

"I brought you with me to see her, didn't I?" he demanded over the screech of the wheels on the track. "Don't make me think you're a liability." He looked hard at her, forcing her to look away. When she looked back, her eyes were swimming. She tried to smile.

"Will she go through with it?" she asked finally.

"She's a good Muslim girl. I trust her more than some of these bullshit young men who talk jihad and killing and in the end piss themselves like children when it comes time to do something."

"I hate to admit it, but she's worth ten of the brother," Liz said.

"Yes, but she and the brother won't see it that way."

They took the train back to Grand Central, where they parted; he to meet with the helicopter pilot, while she checked out of the hotel and left for the airport. They would meet in Chicago. He took the BMT Brighton line to the Midwood section of Brooklyn, getting out at the Avenue H station and walking to the apartment house where the Pakistani helicopter pilot lived with his wife and two young boys. The Palestinian knew that, Khan, the Pakistani wasn't a true believer. Khan had a Brazilian girlfriend, and the money was for a new start for him and his girlfriend in Brazil.

They sat in the small living room after Khan told his wife to get out and bring them chai. A few minutes later she brought them green *qehwa* tea and a plate of *qalaqand* sweets and left, silent as a ghost. The Palestinian showed the photo of the young woman, Bharati, to Khan, and they went over the plan and the al Jabbar code sign. The helicopter pilot demanded more money.

"You any idea how expensive it is in Fortaleza? That's where her family's from. Once I leave here, there's no coming back, bro'," Khan said.

"You're getting half a million dollars. You'll be a king in Brazil," the Palestinian said. "But if you really aren't interested . . ." He got up to leave. Khan grabbed his arm. The Palestinian looked at him, and there was something in the look that made Khan let him go.

"Who said I'm not interested?" he protested. "I just need more."

"I got false passports for you and her. What more do you want?"

"Another two hundred thousand. That's it, I swear."

"A good Muslim doesn't swear." The Palestinian started to leave. "What you ask is impossible."

"Wait! One hundred thousand."

"I don't have it," the Palestinian said. He'd expected the Pakistani to pull something like this, and it could destroy the entire American operation. His bluff had to work. "I'll find another pilot."

"Fifty thousand. That's all! I'll fly so low she'll be able to count the fillings in people's teeth."

The Palestinian stopped. "Fifty thousand. Five now, the rest after—in Brazil."

"Fifty," Khan agreed, and they shook hands.

The Palestinian took the subway to Sunset Park. He went to the bank, got the five thousand, and FedExed it to Khan. The rest of the money didn't matter. He knew he'd never have to pay it.

That evening he caught a flight to Chicago. He met Liz on the curb outside Terminal 5 at O'Hare Airport. She had set up the Chicago part of the operation with an Afghani college student from Marquette Park. The American operation was almost finished. She would fly to London, say hello to Mum, because she wasn't talking to Daddy, then fly back to Rome to help at the warehouse; he would go to Los Angeles and join her the next day in Rome. He kissed her, and for a moment she clung to him. People pulled their wheeled luggage around them on their way to the terminal entrance.

"It's really going to happen, isn't it?" she whispered.

"*Inshallah*, yes. God willing."

"I don't like being without you," she said, pressing against him.

"I'll see you in Rome," he said, pulling away and heading over to the shuttle.

On the flight to Los Angeles he wondered whether these extra actions were worth the risk. What happened in Chicago and L.A. didn't matter. At best they were diversions. In fact, if there were any problems, he might call the FBI himself with an anonymous tip. Anything to keep them from focusing on the Bangladeshi girl and her cargo. He landed in Los Angeles before noon, and by nightfall he was back at LAX to catch the Lufthansa flight via Frankfurt to Rome.

Sitting in business class and pretending to read a *Stern* magazine over a Bloody Mary, he tried to sort out the thousand pieces that still needed to come together: the group, training, and fitting that still needed to be completed, the final arming, the forged papers. So many pieces. The biggest piece was the twenty-one kilos that weren't enough to make a bomb, and whether they could complete the circle. He couldn't be sure till he got back to Rome.

And then, whether it was the vodka or his letdown at having the American part of the operation finally in place, or the sheer femaleness of Liz, the memory of the day that had made him who he was came to him like a nightmare. His hand gripped the arm of the seat as he remembered the night lit bright by the flares and the intense heat, the sounds of soldiers, the fear that made him wet himself, and her eyes looking at him.

He finished his drink and tried to get control of himself. He pressed the button for the stewardess to bring him another. This jihad he had committed himself to was so hard, *so schwierig*, he thought in German. He checked his watch. Hamburg was nine hours ahead of Los Angeles. It was just after six in the morning there. No one would be in the management company office yet, but he could leave a message to be forwarded. He wondered if he should chance it. He was losing a full day on the flight to Europe due to the time change, and was almost certain that in less than a week he would be dead.

His hand trembling, he started to reach for the phone in the seat back in front of him and was about to call when he remembered all the security cameras at the Frankfurt airport and that all in-flight calls were monitored, and knew it was impossible. It was stupid to have even thought of it. He took a deep breath and reminded himself who he was. "You are the most important man in the world," the blind imam in Utrecht had told him.

"*Dankeschön*," he said to the stewardess when she brought him the drink. He finished it and, once more in control, his hands dead steady, tilted the seat back to try to get some sleep. He would kill the nightmare, he thought. He felt better now. He was ready to die.

 **CHAPTER TWENTY**

Castelnuovo, Italy

The safe house was a villa in the Lazio region, some twenty-five kilometers north of Rome. It was on an unmarked country road off the SS3, shaded by overhanging trees, their leaves dusty in the sunlight. The villa was surrounded by high hedges and could not be seen from the road, and the minute Scorpion turned his rented Fiat into the lane, he knew he was under surveillance. He spotted glints of sunlight reflected from camera lenses hidden in the foliage, and a man at a villa across the way, dressed in shorts and a gaudy shirt that only a tourist would wear, was taking enough time watering a row of flowers to drown the roses. As he parked the car on the grassy shoulder, he glanced in the rearview mirror and saw a Mercedes sedan parked on the side of the road near the corner behind him. If it was a trap, it was already too late; he was boxed in.

He got out of the car, and as he opened the wrought-iron entrance gate, caught the shadow of a silhouette on the roof. Sniper, he thought. They had him. He wasn't going anywhere. He walked up the flagstone path to the villa, painted a holiday pink and white, and rang the bell. A trim young woman in shorts and a U2 T-shirt opened the door.

"Signor Mangazzoni?" she said. Although she was smiling, she kept her right hand behind her, and he'd have bet serious money she was holding a gun.

"*Sono* Nicolo Mangazzoni." I am Nicolo Mangazzoni. "I'm here to see Signor Fantini," he said in his limited Italian.

"*Entri prego.* He's waiting for you in the dining room," she said, indicating the way. He walked into the dining room and found Bob Harris, looking like a Ralph Lauren ad in white slacks and a polo shirt, fiddling with a computer hookup. The dining room opened to a terrace that looked out over the trees and across the valley to the medieval town of Castelnuovo di Porto perched on the steep green hills.

"Have a drink," Harris said, gesturing at the bottle of J&B whiskey on the terrace. Scorpion went outside, mixed himself a drink with ice and soda, and came back in.

"Nice view. You feeling nervous?"

"What do you mean?" Harris said, looking annoyed at the computer.

"The SAS team crawling all over this place. Why didn't you take out an ad?"

"There's a lot going on," Harris said, raising his glass. "*Cin cin.*"

"*Vaffanculo,*" Scorpion said, putting his drink down without drinking. "Why did the DGSE detain Najla Kafoury at the Marseilles airport?"

Harris's answer was a stunner. "They didn't."

"What do you mean they didn't? Who did?"

"We're not sure."

"This is bullshit. Where is she?"

"We don't know."

"You're becoming tiresome, Bob. At the very least, these little meetings of ours always had a certain entertainment value."

"We're still checking. Marseille Provence Airport security is handled by a private security firm, Société Provence National de Valeurs Mobilières. They detained her at the request of La Piscine." He'd used the well-known term for the French foreign intelligence service, the DGSE, known in the intelligence world as the Swimming Pool because their headquarters in Paris was located next to the office of the French Swimming Federation. "They turned her over to four DGSE agents who took her away in an unmarked van, except La Piscine claims they never sent a request to hold her. Whoever took her wasn't DGSE. The van was last seen heading up the A7 toward Cavaillon. That's all anyone knows."

"So the Swimming Pool doesn't know where she is, and you guys don't know who she is. Just out of curiosity, do you have anybody working this besides me?" Scorpion asked.

"For what it's worth, what you provided from Utrecht was gold, plus your lead on al Jabbar, the constellation Orion, was the key that enabled NSA to break the code the Islamic Resistance is using. Rabinowich has a whole fancy explanation he's dying to show you, if you give a damn," Harris said. "Apparently 'al Jabbar' was a keyword for the code, only with the Arabic letters reversed and each letter used only once, so the keyword would be 'RABJL,' or whatever. The important thing is that we now know the target and when the attacks are supposed to take place."

"So do I. The Palazzo delle Finanze, site of the EU conference to consider Israel's application for permanent associate membership with the European Union. That's why I came to Rome instead of Genoa."

Harris nodded. "Exactly. Once we knew about the *Zaina* making an unscheduled stop in Genoa, we should've figured. It wasn't just the Camorra getting the containers through customs. The Palestinian didn't want to transport U-235 across any borders. You did a hell of a job," Harris said, raising his glass to Scorpion and taking a sip. "Too good."

"What happened?"

"The DNI stepped in. He says that now that we know the target cities and the date, it's a straight-forward counterterrorist op. He's given it to the Crash and Bangers," he said, referring to the Pentagon's Defense Intelligence Agency. "We're out of business."

"Are they crazy or just totally fucking insane?" Scorpion put his drink on the table. "I've been hunting the Palestinian. I've got a feel about him. Crash and Bang won't stop him."

"For once, we agree. It's Washington. The CIA and the DIA are like the Yankees versus the Red Sox. General Clayton made the case that nuclear was DIA's baby. And I haven't told you the really bad news."

Scorpion went dead still, knowing instantly what it was; the loose end that had been dangling in front of him all along. All this time he'd been telling himself there was no nuclear bomb, that like Groesbeck had said, twenty-one kilos of U-235 wasn't enough. Now he remembered something else the professor had told him: that if there were another thirty kilos of U-235, he would definitely worry.

"You're a bird of ill omen, Bob. Now that I think of it, you always were."

"We had a Russian source on the weaponized plague bacteria. We were able to get a sample to CDC. Turns out it's completely resistant to all normal antibiotics, except one that's still in development."

"Don't tell me. That Swiss drug company I sent you."

"Bingo," Harris said. "And here's the icing on the cake. Their entire supply of antibiotics for the rest of the year has been bought out by that Muslim company in Luxembourg for transshipment."

"Don't tell me," Scorpion said. "They're going to send it to Tehran. This thing's got Iranian fingerprints all over it."

"How do you know?"

"There was a photo of the Eighth Imam's shrine in the imam's office in Utrecht," Scorpion said. Harris nodded grimly.

"Speaking of Tehran," Harris continued, "an Iranian ship, the *Shiraz Se*," the Shiraz Three, Scorpion mentally translated, "sailed from Bushehr and transited the Suez Canal. She left Port Said three days ago. We have no idea where she was headed or where she is now."

"There are nuclear reactors at Bushehr," Scorpion observed.

"While the ship was in the Persian Gulf, a U.S. Navy patrol detected traces of radiation." Harris took out a cigarette and lit it. "I gave up smoking fourteen years ago. I just started again," he said, and Scorpion wondered if he was telling the truth. With Harris, you never knew.

"When were you planning on telling me?"

"We didn't know about the *Shiraz*. The DIA didn't pass it on to us. Sometimes you wonder whose side they're on. Or maybe they didn't think it had anything to do with what we were doing. Remember, your op was a sideshow on a strict 'need to know' basis. No one knew about you except you, me, Rabinowich, Rick"—he was referring to Harris's immediate boss, Richard Haley, the director of the National Clandestine Service—"the DCIA and General Brown, the President's National Security Advisor. That's not all."

"Don't stop now. You're on a roll."

"Rabinowich thinks the twenty-one kilos were at ninety-plus percent, not seventy-six. The NSA picked up a COMINT from the Russian MOD. The Russkis are really scrambling. It seems our friend Checkmate may have lied when I met him in Estonia."

"A Russian spy lying. Imagine!"

Harris took an awkward puff and exhaled, and Scorpion wondered how much of this was a show for his benefit. "I know. I keep thinking about that horrible prophetic line of Winston Churchill's, 'The terrible ifs accumulate.'"

"So who are the SAS teams for?" Scorpion asked, making a gesture that took in the paramilitary operatives around the safe house. "To protect you against Islamic Resistance or against the DIA?"

Harris grimaced. "Maybe against you. Look, don't worry, you'll be paid in full."

"You better believe I'll be paid in full," Scorpion said, going out to the terrace. He added ice to his drink and looked out over the valley and the hills. The sun cast the shadow of the sniper on the roof onto a tree in front of the villa. Harris followed him out on the terrace and stood beside him.

"The worst part is we're done. Crash and Bang's on their way to Rome. By tomorrow they'll be over it like white on rice. The Palestinian's their baby."

"They won't stop him. They don't know what he's going to do, where he is, or what he looks like."

"I know. That's why I'm here."

Harris waited, like a good salesman who knows the customer has to talk himself into it. He's good, Scorpion thought. Give him that. The son of a bitch is good. "The job's not done," Scorpion said.

"We want you to stay on it—on your own."

"Who's we?"

"Rabinowich and me."

"What about Haley?"

"He doesn't want to know. As far as he's concerned, we're done. It's DIA's baby now. Anything you do that comes back to bite us, I'll be the first to deny it. You're a rogue agent, completely on your own. The official line will be that you betrayed us."

"Completely on my own? No backup, nothing?"

"You and Rabinowich. He volunteered too."

"I should do this why?"

"Because they've declared war on us. Not just

us," Harris amended. "It's Rome, for chrissakes. It's Western Civilization, Gregory Peck and Audrey Hepburn, the Sistine Chapel, though God knows, I'm a nonbelieving Catholic who hasn't seen the inside of a church since the day as a teenager I figured out that sex with girls felt good."

"It's no good," Scorpion said finally. "Crash and Bang'll cover the palazzo, but when it comes to the Palestinian, I don't know any more than they do."

"That's why I brought this setup. Line's totally secure." Harris gestured at the computer inside. "Rabinowich wants to talk to you." They walked back in and Harris typed on keys and brought up a link to a Web cam showing the top of Rabinowich's balding head as he fiddled with something on his computer. "Hey Dave, we're here," Harris said. Rabinowich looked up, his paunchy face looking like he hadn't shaved in days.

"You've put on weight, Dave," Scorpion said.

"It's terrible," Rabinowich nodded. "I just have to look at a lettuce leaf and I pack it on. You on board?"

"I need something. This guy's a ghost. He can cross borders like he's invisible, put together a nuclear bomb with a pocketknife, and apparently he was never born or went to school or ever had his picture taken."

"I've been data mining," Rabinowich said, taking a sip of coffee from a Star Trek mug, reminding Scorpion that Rabinowich, like a lot of nerds, was a Trekkie. "I started with the assumption that our guy's good not just with explosives, but nuclear, so he probably had some kind of technical education, probably engineering."

"We know he's smart. I've thought all along he had a technical university background," Scorpion said.

"Then it hit me. Suppose the 'Palestinian' wasn't a code name. Suppose Budawi's notation was a little note to himself, that he knew something about who he was going to meet that day."

"You mean the target really is a Palestinian?"

"Say from the West Bank, Gaza, or Lebanon."

"Lebanon," Scorpion repeated, almost to himself.

"What about Lebanon?" Harris said.

"Nothing," Scorpion lied, remembering that Najla had told him she was born in Lebanon. "Doesn't prove anything. The Palestinian Diaspora is all over the world. He could've come from anywhere."

"True," Rabinowich nodded. "But based on what you dug up on the Islamic Resistance in Beirut, Damascus, Hamburg, and Utrecht, with possible links to Tehran, the Palestinian wasn't Muslim Brotherhood. He wasn't home-grown in Egypt; that means he came in and left on a foreign passport, almost certainly not from a Middle Eastern country."

"Because after the attack, the Egyptians had the same clue," Scorpion said, thinking aloud. "They would've been looking for a Middle Eastern male trying to leave Egypt who might be linked to the Brotherhood, or al-Qaida or Hezbollah."

"Exactly. The next step was to cross-check the Egyptian records on every foreign male who left Egypt, no matter how or from where—anytime during the month after the Cairo attack—against the data records of every male who went to a technical university anywhere in the world within fifteen years of the attack, most likely in Europe or the U.S., in which case it was probably on an immigrant or a student visa. Where we could match names, we did, but those were of less interest since we always figured the Palestinian used a cover name on the passport in Egypt. Instead, we matched the passport records by gender and age against the college records and saw what came up."

"That's what took so long. I take it back, Dave," Scorpion said.

"Take what back?"

"The number of times I've cursed you in my head for not doing anything. So what've you got?"

"Have you ever been to Karlsruhe? There's a very fine technical university there."

"Damn! I knew it was Germany!" Scorpion snapped.

"How?" Harris asked.

"Something Dr. Abadi said in Damascus. It kept bugging me, but I couldn't put my finger on it. At first Abadi wanted to know if I was Mossad. That was obvious. They're paranoid about the Israelis. But then he asked me if I was BND. It was a slip on his part. Just from that I should have known the Palestinian's base was in Germany." Scorpion looked down at his scotch and soda. He hadn't stated the obvious, what was out there right in front of them. Najla Kafoury was also from Germany. *There are no coincidences in this business. None,* he remembered Koenig saying once. *The minute you get near anything that even remotely looks like a coincidence, pull the rip-cord, because you are looking at something that's about to explode.*

"What about the plague?" Scorpion asked.

"It's the FBI's baby now," Rabinowich said. "They've got HRT teams on it."

"We can't do this hookup again," Harris said to Scorpion. "From now on, you don't exist." He looked around. "By tomorrow this place'll be just another summer rental."

"What are you going to do?" Rabinowich asked Scorpion.

"What I'm being paid to do," Scorpion said, getting up. "I'm going to kill the Palestinian."

CHAPTER TWENTY-ONE

Karlsruhe, Germany

Professor Reimert's house was on a tree-lined street in the Oststadt district, just east of the university campus. It was nearly eight in the evening by the time Scorpion had driven to Karlsruhe from Frankfurt Airport. Reimert's wife, Ulrike, a tall blond woman half Reimert's age, offered him cookies and coffee in the dining room.

"Tun sie mögen Dallmayr kaffee?" she said, asking him if Dallmayr coffee was okay.

"Es ist fein. Ich bin nicht ein kenner." It's fine; I'm not a connoisseur, Scorpion said.

"So what makes Rabinowich imagine I would jeopardize my position at the university to do something that is possibly illegal?" Reimert said, coming in. He was tall and thin, with long gray hair, and behind his glasses his eyes were a piercing blue.

Scorpion smiled. "He says you cheat at chess."

"Kompletter unsinn! He can't forgive how I sacrificed my knight at F6 to beat him in an interesting queens gambit declined game we once played."

"They play online," Ulrike explained. "Sometimes I think the neighbors will hear Gerhard cursing. They're incorrigible, those two." She shook her head.

"He is the cheater! I wrote a computer program to track his moves, and even when I show him, he denies them. For a time I thought a mind like his is a waste in your Amerikanisch Commerce Department till I realized that he was undoubtedly CIA. Tell him his secret is no longer safe. The next time he cheats at chess, I will publish his true identity on the Internet. As for you, you are no doubt a CIA agent as well," Reimert said, leaning forward.

"We need your help. It's important and it's urgent," Scorpion told him.

"Yes. Rabinowich said it was, how do you say *'bevorzugung' auf Englisch*?" he asked Ulrike.

"A favor."

"That's it. He asked for a favor. So why don't you go to the Bundespolizei or the Bundesnachrichtendienst? Why come to me?"

"We don't have time. And there are other reasons," Scorpion said.

"You mean you don't trust the BND."

"If I don't get your help tonight, people will die."

"Why should I, a German, trust the CIA, whom many people despise, over the German authorities?"

"This is not our business," Ulrike said, pouring the coffee.

"It is," Scorpion replied. "The reputation of the university is at stake. Believe me, you don't want the authorities involved at this stage. Please, come with me to the campus now. See with your own eyes. If I'm lying, call the Bundespolizei."

"You say this involves *terroristen*?"

"These are Muslims?" she asked.

"Most likely," Scorpion said.

"One tries to be open-minded. Many of them are good students, decent people. Still . . ." Reimert said, looking at his wife, who was looking at Scorpion in a way that gave him the impression she was comparing Scorpion to him. Reimert stood up. "As a professor, I have the right to look at student files. Therefore, I am doing nothing illegal. You won't tell me what this is about?" he asked.

"Better if you don't know."

"Better for whom?" Ulrike said, carrying the coffee cups to the kitchen.

"For everyone, especially you two. Whatever happens, don't tell anyone about this."

"You mean better for you," she said, coming back in.

"No, better for you. I know you think we Americans are all paranoid, but there are some very dangerous people out there."

"We'll go. But only because I'm curious," she said, pulling on a leather jacket and handing a windbreaker to Reimert. "It's not because I believe you. I don't. If it is not as you say, we will call the Bundespolizei."

Reimert drove them onto the campus and parked near a modernist multistory building of glass, metal, and concrete. A sign over the doorway read: FAKULTÄT FÜR PHYSIK. Despite the evening hour, there were still lights on in the building and students with backpacks walking or bicycling along the paths. They went up the stairs and down a long hallway to Reimert's office.

Ulrike turned on the light and sat down at the computer. After a few moments she turned to Scorpion. "How many students?" she asked.

"Just three," Scorpion said, handing her a slip of paper with the names.

"Ulrike was my *unterrichtassistent*," Reimert said. "Now she's an administrator. Better for her to do it. She knows the system better than I."

"Here's the first," she said, bringing up a student record. "Sermin Bayat. Here's his transcript. Emigrated from Ankara in Turkey fourteen years ago. *Diplom* in *biotechnologiewesen*, after which he did his *doktorat* at Bonn University, where, yes, he is on the faculty. Here's his address in Bonn."

"Could you call him?" Scorpion said, looking at the face in the file photograph from ten years ago.

"Why?"

"To confirm. It's standard. Tell him you're from the alumni office just verifying his address."

"If you insist," Ulrike said, clearly annoyed. She dialed a number and spoke briefly in German, said, "*Entschuldigen sie mich, bitte*," then slammed the phone down. "He wasn't so pleased. He was watching the football highlights on the television. Is that sufficient for you?" she said, looking sharply at Scorpion.

"What about the next?"

"Dieter Bockmeyer. He doesn't sound Muslim," she said, typing on the keyboard. "There it is," bringing up the file. "*Diplom* in *informationstechnik*. After graduation, went to work for Siemens in Munich, then transferred to the Siemens office back here in Karlsruhe. Secretary of the Alumni Association. Shall I call?"

"Please."

She called the number and listened for a moment. "It's asking for a message."

"No message," Scorpion said. "Try the next one."

She typed in *Bassam Hassani* and waited while the screen took longer than usual to display. When it did, except for a single line, the screen was blank.

"What is it?" Reimert asked.

"Impossible," she said, staring at the nearly empty screen. She typed another search on a wider database and the same screen came up again. "Nothing. No records, no transcript, no application file, no forwarding address. Just a single line. *Diplom* in *chemieingenieurwesen*, chemical engineering, nine years ago. It cannot be."

"It's been deleted," Scorpion said, his heart beating faster. "You don't have a photograph, anything else on this man?"

"There's nothing. I don't understand," she said, looking at Reimert.

"Nine years ago?" Reimert mused. "In chemistry. I seem to remember something." He looked at his wife. "Do you remember Keck? Bernhard Keck?"

"Must've been before my time. Or maybe when I was a freshman," she said.

"Yes." He tapped the desk with his finger. "I remember something about heat transfer. Look up Keck in the *Universitat Karlsruhe Journal für Anorganische und Allgemeine Chemie*. Now."

She typed it in and a number of links came up.

There was nothing of use in the first two, but when she clicked on the third link, it brought up a nine-year-old article in the university's chemistry journal with a photograph of a research team that had apparently come up with a breakthrough on explosive chemical heat transfers. The caption identified one of the team in the photograph as Hassani.

I've got you, you bastard! Scorpion thought. "Could you please make the photo bigger?" he asked as he intently studied the face of the man identified as Hassani in the caption. It was a young man's face, dark-haired, with dark serious eyes, good-looking enough, if he were interested and not so serious, to be able to beat women off with a stick. Nine years was a long time. It would be better if he had a more recent photograph, and then he realized that of course there was a more recent photo. "Look, could you please send the link to that file to Rabinowich? It's urgent."

"I'll do it right now," Ulrike said, typing. "There you are. It's done." She looked at Scorpion. "This is very strange. I can't understand why whoever deleted the record left the single entry about the *diplom*."

"Vanity perhaps," Reimert shrugged.

"Or credibility among his own. Whatever the reason, it's a break for us or we would never have found him," Scorpion said.

"I prefer vanity as an explanation. It's more Greek," Reimert said.

"You're a romantic, a *Sorrows of Young Werther* type," Scorpion said, smiling.

"You found him out," Ulrike laughed. "When we

first met, he presented me with a copy of that book. I wasn't sure whether he wanted to have sex with me or kill himself."

"Sex. Believe me, sex," Reimert said, kissing her cheek. "This man," meaning Hassani, "he is dangerous?"

"I know of at least six people he's already killed. I have to go. I know you may not believe me, but what you did tonight was important." He started to get up when suddenly he had an idea. "Can you access the university's exchange servers?"

"I don't know how," she said.

"May I?" he said. She got up, and he sat at the computer and logged her out. He plugged in the NSA flash drive and was shortly on the network with administrator privileges.

"How do you say 'exchange mail server' in German?" he asked.

"*Austauschcomputerbediener.* What are you looking for?" she asked.

"E-mail inquiries," he said, typing on the keyboard.

"Wouldn't whoever deleted the record have deleted any e-mails too?"

"Doesn't matter," he said, logging onto the mail server. He opened the header log files and began searching. After several minutes he found what he was looking for. Two entries to the mailbox, one incoming, one outgoing. Someone had sent an e-mail query for information on Hassani. The messages themselves were not there, but the records contained the date, time stamps, and IP addresses of the sending and receiving machines. Scorpion mentally calculated the date. Four weeks before the Budawi assassination. He used his cell phone and an RSA key to access the restricted URL of the NSA's Whois database of classified IP addresses worldwide, and there it was.

The e-mail inquiry had been sent from the Egyptian Bureau of Educational Tourism, a front organization for the Egyptian Mabahith. That was the real reason Budawi had been assassinated! If Budawi had learned the Palestinian's actual identity, it would have imperiled Hassani's entire mission. Budawi had to be eliminated. Scorpion logged off the computer and stood up.

"Did you find what you were looking for?" Ulrike asked.

"More than you know, *danke*," he said.

"Come. We'll take you back to your auto," she said, shutting down the computer and getting up. They barely spoke on the short drive back to where he had parked his car near their house.

"*Auf wiedersehen*," she said. "This has been a strange evening. I did not expect this." She looked at him oddly as he got out of the car.

"It is a disturbance to think that one of our students may be a terrorist. He was not a student of mine, but still . . ." Reimert trailed off.

"Don't ever speak of this to anyone," Scorpion said. "If anyone ever asks, even the Bundespolizei, say nothing. For your own safety, please, what you saw tonight never happened." He started to go, then turned back. "*Vielen dank*. I'll tell Rabinowich he owes you a favor."

They watched him walk back to his car, and after

a moment the car lights came on and he drove away.

Scorpion drove to the A5 autobahn to get back to Frankfurt. While on the highway he called Rabinowich on his cell phone, told him about the Budawi e-mail query, and they discussed ferreting out more information on Hassani, whom they code-named 'Hearing Aid' from the phrase 'engine ear' for 'engineer,' and most critically, they also discussed getting a more recent photograph. The odds were high that Hearing Aid had been in the U.S. at least once, probably more than once, in the last six months, which meant that Homeland Security had a photo and fingerprint on file. It would be under a different name, but hopefully, facial recognition software might find a match.

This time he didn't have to say anything; it was Rabinowich who brought up the fact that Najla was also from Germany. Scorpion didn't respond, and for a moment the only sound was that of the car speeding on the autobahn.

"I know," he said finally. They briefly discussed operational details, then Scorpion hung up. He glanced down at the speedometer. He was doing over 150 kilometers per hour. With any luck he'd reach Frankfurt in time to catch the next flight and be back in Rome that night, where somewhere, in a city preparing for the EU Conference, the Palestinian was making his final preparations.

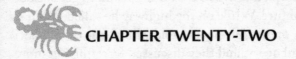

CHAPTER TWENTY-TWO

Stazione Termini, Rome, Italy

The protesters came up the Via Umbria from the direction of the Piazza della Republica. There were thousands of them, a roaring surge of street theatre sweeping past stores and cafés, crowding out traffic, waving signs and shouting demands. They were a motley collection: PCI leftists; anarchists from the Gruppo Libertario carrying signs that read, "No States, No Capital, Direct Action"; young men and women from the Green Party, their faces painted green and carrying a float that showed the Earth in a cooking pot with a sign in English declaring, "Global Warming Is Killing Earth." Skinheads threw cans of beer at shop windows, and neo-Nazis marched with posters that read, "Europe Is Not for Sale—Stop Immigration." Anti-Israel groups chanted and carried signs, many adorned with swastikas: ISRAEL = TERRORIST STATE, ISRAEL ⚡ NAZI APARTHEID, and PALESTINE WILL BE FREE FROM THE RIVER TO THE SEA.

Even though the U.S. wasn't involved in the

conference, someone had hung a store mannequin dressed like Uncle Sam from a traffic light, where it burned in effigy. Nearby, a cardboard caricature of an Israeli soldier with a long Jewish nose hung by a noose around its neck from a lamppost. Most of the signs were in English. As with most street demonstrations, the targets of the demonstrators were not the conference attendees, but the international media, some of whom were climbing on top of their SUVs to film the crowd as it surged toward the police barriers. A massive phalanx of Polizia di Stato in full riot gear, faceless in dark blue helmets with plastic visors, had lined up to block the street. Behind them were the Carabinieri wearing body armor and carrying automatic weapons. The Carabinieri had blocked off the streets approaching the Palazzo delle Finanze from any direction.

Liz and the Palestinian, going by his Algerian cover name Mejdan, had fallen in with a bunch of Oxfam demonstrators she had met at a cheap dormlike hotel near the Stazione Termini before he came back to Rome from California. The Oxfam demonstrators carried signs about hunger in Africa and Gaza, featuring photos of big-eyed, big-bellied children. Some of the Oxfamers were dressed like wraiths, black cloth draped over their heads. They wore faceless white masks with narrow holes for eyes, and carried signs that read: "Global Warming, Global Death."

The demonstrators surged toward the police lines, and one of them, a tall redheaded Italian anarchist screaming, *"Morte al governo!"* picked up a section of the metal barricade and hurled it at the *polizia*, a number of whom moved forward and smashed at him with their batons. At this, the horde of demonstrators exploded with a roar of screams and shouts, throwing rocks and cans at the police, who began pushing the demonstrators back, beating them with batons and shields. Several demonstrators went down. The police rushed them away to waiting vans. Everyone in the crowd was screaming and looking for things to throw. A long-haired Italian, his shirt torn, screamed up at a TV camera, "*Stanno uccidendo i vostri bambini!*" They are killing your children!

A group of Oxfam demonstrators were pressed forward against the barricades by skinheads behind them, and Liz's friend, Alicia, a pretty dark-haired college girl from Wales, screamed, "Don't touch me, you bastard!" as a helmeted *guardia* shoved her back with his shield.

"You are beating a woman!" Liz screamed at the *guardia*, who just looked at her with his blank face visor. The Palestinian hung back, letting the Oxfam wraiths and the skinheads surge past him toward Alicia and Liz and the *polizia*. He'd forbidden the Moroccans back at the warehouse from joining the demonstrations. They could not afford for any of them to be arrested. The main thing he had to ensure was that there were demonstrations like this when the conference started in three days.

One of the skinheads managed to grab a baton away from a *guardia* and began swinging it wildly, opening a gap in the line of police. A dozen or so protesters poured through it, shouting and shoving as a rain of rocks, shoes, and cans sailed into the ranks of the police. In response, a squad of Carabinieri moved rapidly through the police ranks. As they quickly rounded up the demonstrators who had broken through and hustled them away, enabling the police to close the gap in their line, the Palestinian pulled Liz and Alicia back and forced his way through the crowd, now retreating from the advancing police line. Alicia's Italian boyfriend, a member of the Continual Struggle student movement, dressed in a black T-shirt with the insult CHE CAZZO, You Dick, in white gothic lettering, joined them as they ducked around the corner and caught their breath.

Later, they refought the skirmish over beer and pizza at a pizzeria near the train station. Liz was still furious over how the police had beaten Alicia.

"It's unconscionable. She's a defenseless young woman. No threat to anyone, the bloody fascists. How dare they?"

"He didn't really do any damage. I managed to get out of the way," Alicia said.

"No thanks to him. The bastard wanted to hurt you. If they beat women, what's next, babies?"

"There's a way to turn it to our advantage, but it takes courage," the Palestinian said.

Cristiano, Alicia's boyfriend, said, "What are you saying?" and the others leaned closer to the Palestinian.

"A picture is worth a million words," he told them. "We need a face. A beautiful young woman's face would be perfect. That is, if you really mean what you say about the starving children in Africa and Gaza?"

Alicia looked at him sharply. "Those children break my heart."

"What are you suggesting?" Liz asked.

"We bloody you up," he said to Alicia, "and get you in front of a TV camera. You tell them it was the *polizia*."

"We'd be lying," she replied.

"Only about the details. They did rough you up, didn't they? You'd become the face of the protest. It could go viral on the Internet in an hour. You could single-handedly stop the Israelis and the EU."

"What about me?" Liz said, her eyes darting back and forth between him and Alicia. "You could bloody me."

"We need you for other things," he said, patting her arm, which she pulled away.

"Where will we get the blood?" Cristiano asked.

"From all of us."

"Won't they test it for DNA?" Liz said, looking troubled.

"That'll take days. By then the conference will be over. It'll be old news." The Palestinian shrugged. "No one will care."

They went back to the hotel after stopping off in a children's toy store in the Piazza Navona, to buy balloons they would use to hold the blood. The two young women ran around and played like children among the stuffed animals. They stopped and took "Before" photographs of Alicia outside the toy store, to post on the Web and to TV stations. Afterward, they went up to Alicia and Cristiano's dormlike hotel room. They talked about how they would do the blood the next day, then Liz and Cristiano left, leaving Alicia sitting on the bed, the Palestinian pulling on a pair of latex gloves.

"You're very brave," he said, putting a hand on her shoulder, then slapped her, and before she could even gasp, punched her in the ribs and backhanded her across the other cheek. He smacked her around a few more times, blackening her eyes, then punched her hard in the face, breaking her nose.

"I'm sorry. So sorry," he said, putting his arms around her.

"The children," she managed to say, looking up at him, tears in her eyes. He leaned forward, and as he did so, his hand cupped her breast. She looked at him questioningly as he pushed her down on the bed, his lips about to brush hers, when the door burst open and Liz rushed in.

"You bastard!" she screamed. "You just wanted to fuck her! I hate you!"

"Shut up," he said, getting up off the bed. "She agreed to it. Didn't you?" Alicia, her face starting to swell and bruise, stared wide-eyed and nodded tentatively. "So did you," he told Liz. "We're going to tell them the *polizia* beat and raped her. We're not playing here."

He grabbed Liz by the wrist. She tried to pull away, and he twisted her hand behind her back. "It had to be done. We'll meet you tomorrow for the demonstration," he told Alicia as he forced Liz out of the room. Cristiano was outside in the corridor. *"Domani. La gelosia delle donne causa molta difficoltà,"* he said to Cristiano by way of explanation, while forcing the struggling Liz toward the elevator. Tomorrow; the jealousy of women causes much trouble.

"I hate you," she said as they got in.

"Shut up or I'll hurt you before this elevator reaches the ground floor."

"Go ahead. Hit women. That's what you know how to do."

"Y'allah, the Americans and the Israelis have missiles and F-16s. All we have is our courage and our bare hands. You said you understood. This war isn't fought on a battlefield, but in the media. Bloody women and dead children—these are our weapons. I don't care about Alicia."

"Oh God, oh God, I'm damned," Liz sobbed as they left the elevator and went out to the street. A number of the backpackers outside the hotel stared at them, but hookups and lovers' quarrels were commonplace here and no one said anything.

They walked, his arm around her, toward the Stazione Termini. As they approached the red and white Metro sign, he said: "Should we go to the warehouse or the apartment?" referring to a small apartment he had rented near the Campo dei Fiori as a fallback, where he kept additional weapons and explosives.

"I want to go home," she said, tears in her eyes. "I want to go back to England."

"As soon as we do what we came here to do. You tell me, the warehouse or the apartment?"

"The apartment," Liz whispered, pressing against him. "Please, let it be like Mykonos again."

"She means nothing to me. I swear," he said, leading her to the Metro entrance.

As they started down the escalator, he could feel her trembling beside him. He would get rid of her when they got to the apartment. In the morning, he would tell Alicia and Cristiano that she'd gone back to London. The Moroccans at the warehouse would need no explanation.

When they got to the platform, he put his arms around Liz, and as he did so glanced at his watch. He could deal with her and be back at the warehouse in an hour. Then he realized he might still need her as a decoy or hostage if the authorities or whoever was hunting him from Utrecht got close.

"I'm sorry. We need to go back to the warehouse," he whispered as he held her close.

"Why?"

"I just realized. I can't trust them on their own. I need you," he said, pressing close to her.

Liz started crying again, pressing herself against him. "Oh God, I need you too," she said, her voice muffled by his shoulder and the sound of the approaching train.

The demonstration the following morning was smaller, less violent, although there was enough of a scuffle with the *polizia* for them to use Alicia. The three of them stood around her, cut their fingers and dripped the blood into the balloon. They poured the blood from the balloon over her head and face, then took videos of her lying in the street and helped her, staggering for effect, past the reporters and TV cameras on the Via Umbria. Afterward they split up, Cristiano returning to the hotel with Alicia to clean her up and keep her hidden from the press.

By the time the Palestinian and Liz got back to the warehouse, the YouTube video and Twitter photos of Alicia—the Before shots of the pretty college girl and the After shots of her with her eye blackened, nose broken, face bruised and covered in blood—had gone all over the Internet and were seen around the world. Images of Alicia were featured on the Italian RAI Uno and Canale 5 television news and on TV networks across Europe and on U.S. nightly news. There were allegations of beatings and rapes of demonstrators by the Italian *polizia* and calls for an investigation into police brutality by left wing parties in the Italian Chamber of Deputies. Angry rallies broke out in a dozen European cities, and a German journalist was nearly killed by a mob in Bologna, as more demonstrators began heading to Rome.

Watching the Italian morning TG1 news on the TV in the warehouse office where they shared a mattress on the floor, Liz said, "You were right. It's in the news. I'm so sorry, but it just kills me to see you near another woman."

"I told you, except as a symbol, she doesn't matter to me," the Palestinian told her. "But there is something else you can do for me," he added, pulling her down, his arms around her as she began to smile.

CHAPTER TWENTY-THREE

Saxa Rubra, Rome, Italy

They met in a trattoria in Trastevere on a side street near the Piazza di Santa Maria. The cobblestone street was shaded from the bright sun by a plane tree. From an outside table with his back to the wall, Scorpion could see anyone entering the narrow street from either direction. He had put a folded copy of the *Corriere della Sera* on the table as a signal that it was clear to approach.

Aldo Moretti was a short well-dressed man with round button eyes and a sharp Roman nose between them, under which a small mustache gave him the look of a somewhat cynical bird of prey. Moretti sat down, ordered a glass of the red *vino della casa*, and they nodded at each other before they drank.

The problem, Scorpion reflected, was that the bureaucrats had taken over. Rabinowich told him the DIA hadn't informed the AISE, Italy's CIA, about the missing U-235—intimating that this had come down from the DNI himself—so the Italians were treating it like a garden-variety threat, the kind that came once or twice a week and at every international conference. Security would be heavy for the conference venue, but that was normal.

"I see you as a courtesy to Signor Brooks," Moretti said, using Rabinowich's cover name. "Try the pasta here. It is not so terrible," he added, tucking his napkin in his shirt. The waiter came back with the wine and they ordered. Scorpion waited till the waiter left.

"What have you heard about the Palestinian?"

"*Solo un po'.*" Just a little. "Of course, I hear of the Budawi assassination in Cairo and that everyone is looking. You think he is here in Roma for the *conferenza*? *Metterlo qui*," put it over here, he told the waiter bringing him a plate of tortellini.

"*Grazie.*" Scorpion nodded as the waiter put down his plate of spaghetti and replaced the bread basket with a jar of *grissini* bread sticks. The Italian was sharp as a tack. He'd picked up on the mention of the Palestinian and put it all together immediately. "I know he's here. I've been tracking him across Europe all the way from Damascus."

"*È così?* And yet your DIA," glancing around to make sure he wasn't overheard, "they tell us nothing about this."

"There's a lot they are not telling you. You're right," Scorpion said, talking while eating.

"About?"

"The pasta here is good."

"What else they don't tell?"

"On orders, a lot, *molto*. Here we get onto difficult ground."

"We *italiani* have been good partnership. For the Company, the best. *Troppo buona.*"

"*D'accordo*, probably too good," Scorpion agreed. He leaned forward. "The information I have is something you need to know. My problem is that I must tell it to someone who can do something with this information, but not tell anyone else in the AISE."

"Perhaps because if everyone in the AISE knows, it gets back to your *padroni* in the DIA and CIA who do not wish to share with us."

"It is good to talk to a man who understands how such things work. It would be better if we could imagine you and I were just private citizens sharing pasta and opinions."

"Perhaps you overestimate the danger. Our security is of the best in the world."

"That's what Budawi thought. We believe there will be multiple attacks coordinated by one man in a number of cities in Europe and the U.S. Why of all of these cities do you think I'm in Rome?"

Moretti straightened. He wiped the corner of his mouth with the napkin. "I should be hearing this through official channels. Except, of course, according to you, official channels will tell us nothing, will they?"

"You know Checkmate?"

"The Russian, Ivanov? Only by reputation. He is more your problem than ours," Moretti said, taking some wine.

"Not always. Sometimes we have mutual interests."

"Is this such a time?"

"So you have heard nothing about the missing Russian U-235?"

"Russians say many things. On very rare occasions, they are even true," Moretti shrugged. "My dear Signor McDonald from South Africa, although our encounter has, how you say, American fingerprints all over it, I like your manner. You speak straight. In Italian we say '*palare fuori dai denti*,' to speak outside one's teeth. But you are asking me to take everything on faith, like a priest. This I cannot do for many reasons, one of which is if only not to lose your respect, one professional to another."

"Signor Aldo Moretti, who officially works in the Ministry of the Interior in something to do with immigration, but in fact is a deputy director in AISE," Scorpion said, at which Moretti gestured as only Italians can and mouthed *Bravo*, "a week ago a Ukrainian ship, the *Zaina*, out of Odessa, convenience flagged in Belize, made an unscheduled stop in Genoa after her captain died under unexplained circumstances. Check it out for yourself. I would be most interested in the autopsy report of what killed her captain."

"Call me Aldo," Moretti said. "And let me also speak straight, outside my teeth. You think the Palestinian killed the *capitano* and used the ship to bring highly enriched Uranium into Italy?"

Scorpion nodded. "Another curious thing," he added. "While the *Zaina* was in port, she unloaded only three containers. They went through your *dogana* inspection in less than four hours."

"That, I confess, is not *normale*. If Italy would ever be so efficient, we would be richer than America. You think the Palestinian bribed the Camorra?"

"It's been known."

"He is like your Superman, this Palestinian. If I believe what you are saying, he can do anything, *non è così?*"

"The more I learn about him, the more dangerous he becomes. There's more."

"What you tell me is already bad enough," Moretti said, motioning the waiter over and ordering *espresso* and cannoli for both of them. Scorpion shook his head no. "*Per piacere*, they make it good here. You will like. Besides, you are paying."

Scorpion motioned Moretti closer. "Five days ago an Iranian ship, the *Shiraz Se* out of Bushehr, transited the Suez Canal into the Mediterranean. No one knows what happened to her or her cargo."

"Is too much. Now you are trying to disturb me. I thought that for you and I, like Mr. Humphrey Bogart and Signor Claude Raines in the movie *Casablanca*, this would be the beginning of a beautiful friendship. But this I do not like," Moretti said, wagging his finger.

"I ask you again, *il mio amico* Aldo. Ask yourself one question: of all the cities in the world where we believe something is going to happen, why is the Palestinian in Rome? Why am I here?"

"I see," Moretti said. He took a bite of the cannoli, then put down his fork. "It's good, but you've killed my appetite. I did not know that was possible with cannoli." Moretti got up. "You give me things to do. We will talk again. *Subito*, very soon," he said, and began to walk away.

"You say something about 'in the wolf's mouth'?" Scorpion called after him.

Moretti stopped and pivoted with a small man's grace. "For good luck, *sí*. And the proper response is, '*Crepi il lupo*.' May the wolf die."

That morning, Scorpion checked the DIA's security arrangements for the conference. Thanks to Moretti, he had acquired a badge that allowed him access through all police checkpoints. He explored the Palazzo delle Finanze venue for the conference and the *polizia* lines and reviewed the security operations. The DIA had set up sharpshooters at all locations approaching the venue and on the approaches and roof of the palazzo, and together with the AISE and the police were tapping all telephone and cell phone communications in Rome. At Moretti's insistence the Italians had pushed the *polizia* barriers out another block from the venue and had doubled the police and Carabinieri presence, along with helicopters flying overhead nonstop not only at the conference site, but at all hotels and foreign embassies where delegates were staying. Police checkpoints were set up on the A90 Ring Road around the city. Two Italian F-16s were fueled and standing by on the runway at the Italian Pratica di Mare air force base outside Rome, ready to take off at a moment's notice.

Scorpion contacted Rabinowich from an Internet café off the Piazza Barberini near the Trevi Fountain. The café was loud and noisy. It was filled with tourists and people from the demonstrations, many of them young and carrying backpacks. A flat-screen TV near the front of the café showed the Italian TG1 television news. The TV announcer, a handsome man in a striped Armani suit who obviously liked his pasta, was talking again about the beautiful young Englishwoman who had been reportedly beaten by the police during the demonstrations. The screen showed side-by-side photos of her, the pretty smiling brunette before the attack and then after, with her battered face covered in blood. The images had been displayed repeatedly around the world, to the point where they had almost become iconic. There were dark allegations that the woman had not only been beaten, but raped by the *polizia*, the announcer said, lowering his voice to imply the gravity of the charge. Known only as *"la donna inglese,"* she had reportedly gone into hiding.

"What do you think?" one blond long-haired backpacker with a British accent said to his friend, watching the TV.

"Beats me," his friend, an American said. "She's pretty. That's why they're playing it up."

"Not anymore," the Brit said, and his friend laughed as they wandered away.

The TV cut to a police *assistente capo* who was shown strenuously denying that the young woman had ever been taken into police custody. He pointed to a somewhat jerky security camera video that Scorpion had seen on the news that morning in his hotel room. It showed someone in the crowd who might possibly be the young woman—it was difficult to tell from the video—being pushed back by a policeman's shield at a street barrier. Something in the video this time caught Scorpion's attention, but it was gone too fast. He needed to see it again, frame by frame.

He sat down at an open computer, called Rabinowich using his latest disposable cell phone, and hung
up the second he answered, then set up a real-time
online chat session, using slang and abbreviations he
knew Rabinowich would understand.

u 've any idea time here? 5 in f-ing am, Rabinowich
typed.

wakey, sleeping beauty ☺. *Need new HA pix*, Scorpion typed back, referring to Hearing Aid, their
code name for the Palestinian.

*u've any idea how many farangi come US in 6 mos?
12.5 f-ing million. Take time*, Rabinowich making a
joke mixing the Thai word for foreigners with the
word for an alien race with a dubious reputation on
the Deep Space Nine TV series.

ng ☹. *need pix asap. whats new?*

From amigos in P nr biergarten, and Scorpion understood that the "friends" he was referring to was
the German BND secret intelligence service; *biergarten* probably referred either to the Octoberfest
or Hitler's Beer Garden Putsch, and either way it
was Munich, so *P near Munich* had to be Pullach, a
suburb of that city where the old BND headquarters
were located.

HA fr 1st base 2 foster firebravo k Abitur, Rabinowich sent.

Scorpion took a deep breath. His first stop on this
mission, "first base," had been Beirut. It meant that
according to the BND, Hearing Aid—Hassani—
was originally from Beirut or somewhere else in
Lebanon. He had to think about *firebravo* for a
second before he realized that Rabinowich was just

using *Bravo* in military parlance for the letter B. These were World War Two German references: *fireb* plus war suggested *firebomb*, and firebombing in World War Two could refer either to Hamburg or Cologne. The *k* had to be for Cologne, spelled Köln in German. The message suggested that Hassani had come as a child from Lebanon to Cologne, where he had been raised in "foster" care and gone to school for his *Abitur*—his high school diploma.

Scorpion sat back, his heart pounding. The conclusion was inescapable and he knew it must be as obvious to Rabinowich. If she'd told him the truth, Najla Kafoury had also come as a child from Lebanon to Germany.

ditto Fräulein N, he typed.

yup. defense? Rabinowich was acknowledging the fact that both Najla and Hassani were from Lebanon was unlikely to be a coincidence. His question about defense meant he wanted Scorpion's evaluation of the security measures for the conference.

With *sol tzu,* where *sol* meant "sun," he told Rabinowich, an admirer of the ancient Chinese military genius, to recall Sun Tzu's doctrine on defense. He knew if Rabinowich thought about it, he would recall Sun Tzu's famous saying that no war was ever won with a static or passive defense.

stop HA? Rabinowich was asking whether the DIA and Italian preparations would be adequate to stop the Palestinian from accomplishing his goal.

Heavy C & B. What u think? pix? Scorpion knew Rabinowich would pick up his meaning—that though the DIA had put heavy Crash and Bang security measures in place, he did not think they would stop the Palestinian, and then he'd asked when he could expect the new photo.

innaharda, Rabinowich typed; the Arabic word for "today."

buona notte, *bambino* ☺, Scorpion joked, telling Rabinowich to go back to sleep like a baby.

f u, Rabinowich responded, and ended the session.

Scorpion logged off, and as he headed out of the café, glanced again at the TV. They were showing the arrival of the Israeli delegation to the conference. The TV reporter, an attractive woman whose eyeliner made her look like a face from an ancient Egyptian frieze, said they would be staying under heavy security at the Israeli embassy, not far from the Villa Borghese, for what could be an historic conference for Israel.

That afternoon, Scorpion waited for Moretti at a pizzeria across from Carabinieri headquarters near the wooded Villa Ada Park. Moretti was supposedly at a meeting with the local heads and station chiefs of the Polizia di Stato, the Carabinieri, the DIA, the various EU intelligence agencies, and the Israeli Mossad and AMAN, to coordinate for the EU Conference. Because it was across the street from their headquarters, Carabinieri officers would often stop in for a quick pizza and *vino*, and two of them leaning on the bar glanced over at him when the text message he'd been waiting for from Rabinowich came in.

The text read, *c pix*, and he took a deep breath. As they had arranged, he looked up Rabinowich's "Brooks" Facebook page, and there it was. Instead of his own face, Rabinowich had posted a photograph of Bassam Hassani taken less than two weeks ago for entry into the United States.

Hassani had aged well, Scorpion thought. He was no longer the geeky long-haired chemistry undergrad in the Karlsruhe University chemistry journal photograph. Along the way he had acquired expensive clothes and a new haircut. He looked smooth, confident, the kind of successful businessman who flies first class on his way to an international bankers' meeting. Rabinowich hadn't bothered to include the passport and visa information that Hassani had used to enter the United States. While Hassani would have used the cover identity while in the U.S., which would make it useful for the FBI in tracking his movements, for Scorpion it was useless. Hassani would have gotten rid of that cover identity the minute he was back in Italy.

He got up, tossed money on the table for the *conto*, and headed out toward where he had parked his rented Fiat. Moretti would have to wait. Now that he had Hassani's photograph, he needed a closer look at that video of the demonstration at the police barrier. As he walked to the car, he used the cell phone to get directions to the RAI Uno television studio that had broadcast the video. It was in the Saxa Rubra district, north of the center of Rome. He got into the Fiat and called Moretti as he headed out.

"I'm still at the meeting. Where are you going, or shouldn't I ask?" Moretti said in a hushed voice, and Scorpion could hear someone talking in the background.

"Why ask a question when you already know the answer?" Scorpion said.

"Have you heard from our mutual friend?"

"Yes."

"You will stay in touch?"

"How do you like working with the DIA?"

"Is too soon to say. In Italian we say '*metterci il cappello*,' to put the hat on the top, you understand?"

"You mean they try to run everything and then take all the credit?"

"Is good. You are beginning to think like an Italian. Where you are now?"

"Turning onto Via Flaminia."

"You go to Saxa Rubra? The *televisione*, RAI Uno? You think they see something?"

Damn, the little Italian was quick, Scorpion thought. He had to watch every word he uttered. "I'll let you know," he said.

"This is famous street, Via Flaminia. This is the road the Roman legions use when they march to Gaul."

"Are you telling me to watch out for the Barbarians?"

"Caesar was killed by his own people," Moretti said.

"I'll remember that," Scorpion said, hanging up. He drove past office buildings and apartment houses. People were out in the street, well-dressed Romans living their lives, and it hit him that in two days this could all be gone. He drove through the suburbs to the television studio, showed the badge he had gotten from Moretti to the guard at the gate, and parked. Inside, he asked to speak to the station manager. A slender dark-haired woman, of what the French called "a certain age," in a low-cut T-shirt top and a skirt too short for business, came out.

"*Il Signor Brazzani è occupato. Posso essere d'aiuto?*"

"*Forse*, it's a security matter," Scorpion said, switching to English and showing her his badge.

"What would you like?" she asked, with just a touch of suggestiveness, looking at him as if he were an especially tasty-looking piece of Amedei chocolate.

"I need to see a video you broadcast on TG Uno on *la donna inglese* at the demonstrations. But on a computer, so I can see it slow, stop it, make it bigger."

"You are not *italiano*, Signore. Can you tell me what is this about?"

"No, I can't. As you can see from the badge, it's a matter of security. If necessary, I can have a *capo della polizia* call, but that would take hours and time is critical."

She thought for a moment. "I shall have to come with you," she said, and led him down to the studio, to a glassed-in office where a number of people were working at their desks on video feeds. She walked over to a young man peering intently at the screen, tapped him on the shoulder and said something very rapidly in Italian.

"This is Bruno," she said, turning to Scorpion. "He will help us."

Bruno brought up a number of feeds on the demonstrations and *la inglese* woman. The third one, of the scuffle at the police barricade, was the one he wanted. They watched again as the demonstrators surged forward against the police barrier. The *in-*

glese woman appeared to be in the middle of demonstrators with signs that read, "Global Warming, Global Death."

"Stop!" Scorpion said. Bruno froze the image. "Who are these demonstrators?" He pointed at the signs and protesters in wraith costumes.

"*Questi sono da Oxfam. Si può dire per i costumi, come fantasmi,*" Bruno said, turning his head.

"These are from Oxfam, you can tell from the costumes," the woman translated.

"It's okay, I got the gist," Scorpion said. "Go very slowly now."

They watched intently while the video moved jerkily forward frame by frame as the young Englishwoman was pushed back at the barrier by one of the riot *polizia* with his shield.

"Stop there!" Scorpion bent and peered at the screen, at a man in the crowd behind a young woman next to the *inglese*. He wore a black T-shirt and jeans, his face in profile to the camera. "Can you focus in on him?" he asked, pointing at the man. Bruno blew up the man's profile, while Scorpion pulled out his cell phone and expanded the photograph he had downloaded from Rabinowich's Facebook page.

"That is the man," the woman said, leaning closer to look at Scorpion's cell phone screen and then at Bruno's monitor. "You are looking for this man?"

"*Come ti chiami?*" Scorpion asked her name.

"*Il mio nome è Cienna.*"

"Cienna, there is no man. This picture doesn't exist, *capisce?*" he said, closing the cell phone, and Cienna nodded. "Move it ahead slowly, *molto lentamente,*" he told Bruno, who advanced the video jerkily till Scorpion said "Stop!" again. "What do you think? Is he with *la donna inglese*?" he asked, pointing at the proximity of Hassani to the Englishwoman.

"*Difficile dire*. Could be two people in the crowd," Bruno said.

"He said is difficult to say. He is wrong. They are together," Cienna said.

"How do you know?"

"Trust me. I am a woman."

Scorpion nodded and tapped Bruno, who moved the video forward image by image, but the man turned away and then he, along with the two women, were lost in the crowd. Scorpion told Bruno to stop, his mind racing.

"You are interested in this man who does not exist?" Cienna said.

"What you've just seen is very dangerous, *capisce*? For you and everyone around you. I don't mean to alarm you, but you could be threatened. Please translate," he said.

Cienna bent over and whispered in Bruno's ear, at which Bruno turned and stared at the two of them, his eyes wide.

"Remember tell no one, not even your boss. Anyone can be killed. This never happened. I was never here, *capisce*? *Arrivederci e grazie*," Scorpion said and started to leave.

"I'll walk you out," Cienna said, and accompanied him out to the reception area. "How do I get in touch with you again?" she said, glancing around to make sure they weren't overheard.

"You can't."

"Suppose we see him again in another video?"

"It won't matter. *Ciao, bella signora,*" he said and felt her watching him as he left, his mind in a whirl. He had to talk to Rabinowich, and wondered if he should risk sharing it with Moretti. Once again there were things that made no sense on this mission. A single question churned in his mind: Why would the Palestinian risk his entire operation just to participate in a public demonstration?

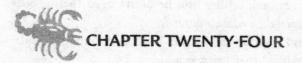

CHAPTER TWENTY-FOUR

Campo dei Fiori, Rome, Italy

The Palestinian woke in a sweat, not knowing where he was. He hadn't had the nightmare in a long time but it never seemed so real.

In the dream he was a child and they were coming for him. He was hiding in a closet, the heat unbearable, and even though it was night, the flashes of light from the window that filtered through the cracks in the closet door were intensely bright. The sound of explosions and gunfire kept coming closer, and the smell was like nothing he'd ever smelled before. He heard men crashing into the room and shooting, his mother screaming, and he wanted to scream but he was so frightened he wet his pants. They ripped the closet door open and grabbed him, and now they had the faces of boys who had taunted him at Grundschule: Aksel, his red face contorted, yelling, *"Leck mich am arsch, Türkisch schwuchtl,"* and fat Dolph, and Geert, kicking him while he was squirming on the ground, laughing at the *"Blödes arschloch"* as he tried to protect his privates where fat Dolph had grabbed his testicles and squeezed till he screamed, telling him he didn't need them, *"Sie brauchen diese nicht, mutterficker!"*

And then he was awake, his heart pounding, and he realized that Liz was gone.

They had worked late into the night, he, Mourad, Jamal, and Hicham. Earlier in the evening, he had sent the others back to Turin, either by car or by the Metro to the Stazione Termini to catch the train. After they had left with calls of *"Ma'a salaama"* and *"Allahu akhbar,"* the four of them finished packing everything into the UniMOG, filling it to the roof with just enough room left for the four of them to sit in it. They ran into a snag then. Mourad noticed that the license plates given to them by the Camorra didn't begin with the correct lettering.

"Did they do this on purpose?" he asked.

"With the Camorra, nothing is an accident," Hicham said. "They wanted us to be caught."

"Why? We could inform on them," Jamal said.

"None of us would ever live to inform if we were in prison," Hicham said. *"Il silenzio o la morte."*

"They did not want it to come back on them. *Ma'alesh,"* the Palestinian shrugged. "Just make sure the UniMOG runs when we need it."

"It's good. I checked it myself again this morning," Mourad said. "What about the license plate?"

Finally, Hicham came up with the solution. They forged white metal with the correct red letters and glued them over that portion of the license plate. It wouldn't bear close inspection, but the Palestinian thought they could get away with it on a moving vehicle while other things were going on. Although it was past three in the morning by then, they went over their roles again, rehearsed what they were to do and how to deploy and rehearsed their answers to questions that might be asked.

The Palestinian, still known to the others by his cover name, Mejdan, looked at his watch. It was almost eleven in the morning, and although he got up and walked around the warehouse to look for Liz, he knew she wasn't there.

"The woman, Liz is gone," Mourad said, looking up from making coffee in the makeshift kitchen. "Your English *sharmuta* whore will destroy everything."

"I'll take care of it," the Palestinian said.

"Why did you bring her? Just because you had to have English *koos*?" Mourad asked, using the Arabic vulgarity for the female sex organ.

"I needed Liz to get to the English demonstrators. It was part of the plan," he said. "We have one more day. Check all the cell phone batteries, but don't touch the detonators. I'll take care of the Englishwoman."

"It would have been better not to bring her," Mourad said, not looking at him.

"*Khalli baalak*," the Palestinian said. Be careful. "We will soon all of us be *shaheedin* martyrs. We should not go to Allah with words we should not have said."

He went to the hotel near the Stazione Termini, but the room was locked, and when he asked at the desk, he was told that Alicia had checked out.

"When?" he asked the desk clerk.

"*Mezz'ora*, maybe." Half an hour. The desk clerk shrugged. "Is curious. That *signorina*, she look like *la donna inglese* on the *televisione*."

"Not at all. Maybe a little, but it wasn't her. Was my *ragazza*, Liz, you know, her English friend, with her?"

"*Sì*. Also her *italiano* boyfriend with the hair long, like a girl. They all go."

"Did they say where they were going?"

"They did not say, but I think the *aeroporto*. They have all their baggages and they talk about London."

"*Grazie*," he said, and ran to the Stazione Termini. He raced through the station, hoping against hope they hadn't left yet. With relief, he saw Liz, Cristiano, and Alicia waiting on the platform of the express train to Fiumicino Airport. To avoid being recognized, Alicia had dyed her hair blond and wore large sunglasses under a Burberry bucket hat. When they saw him, the three of them started to move away, then Liz stopped.

"You didn't say goodbye," he said.

"I can't do this," she said, taking off her sunglasses. She was back to wearing a Hermès scarf and Jimmy Choos, but her eyes were glistening, he noticed. "I thought I could, but I can't."

"Children are dying."

"I know," she said miserably.

"What have you told them?" he asked, indicating Cristiano and Alicia.

"Just that we had a fight."

"Liz, nothing happened between Mejdan and me, did it?" Alicia said, looking at him.

"I'm sorry," Cristiano said in his clumsy English, patting the Palestinian on the shoulder. "Alicia want to go back to London too. She afraid the *paparazzi* find her and she will be exposed for liar."

"I understand. Can I talk to you alone?" the Palestinian asked Liz. "It's important."

She looked at her friends and nodded. He drew her to one side of the platform. Looking beyond her, he could see the train coming.

"You left your things at the apartment," he said.

"Just send them to me," she said.

"I won't have time. We can't leave evidence behind. Please, come back to the apartment with me. Just you and me, the way it was supposed to be. I need you."

"I can't help it," she said, her eyes glistening in the sunlight reflected off the rails. "I can't do it anymore."

"One last time," he pleaded. "It'll be like Mykonos. You owe me that."

"Why? Why do I owe you?"

"Because by this time tomorrow I'll probably be dead. Don't let it end like this. You can catch a later flight. I can do what I have to if I know you're away and safe." His last words were nearly lost in the sound of the train pulling in.

"Liz, we have to go," Alicia called. People were rushing to board. The cars were getting crowded and they would have to squeeze in.

"I don't know what to do," Liz said, poised between them.

"We can't let it end like this. Not us," he said, and grabbed and kissed her tightly. "Stay, just for another hour. You'll be able to remember it your entire life," he whispered. She looked back at Alicia and Cristiano.

"You go on," Liz called out to them. "I'll catch a later flight."

"You sure? You'll be all right?" Alicia asked.

"I'll be fine," Liz said, then ran over and kissed her and then Cristiano on the cheek. "'Bye, *caro*."

"*Ciao, bellissima*," Cristiano said, kissing her back on both cheeks and picking up Alicia's luggage.

They boarded the train, squeezing in to find standing room. Liz and the Palestinian waved to them and they smiled and waved back.

"Call me when you get to London," Liz called out.

As the train pulled away, the Palestinian took Liz's suitcase and pulled it behind him. She took his arm and they strolled toward the platform exit past a man in jeans and a SALVO LE BALENE! SAVE THE WHALES! T-shirt, who appeared to be looking for something in his backpack.

As they walked away, Scorpion closed the backpack, slung it on his shoulder and began to follow them.

Rabinowich didn't know. Neither did Moretti, when Scorpion had met him the previous night at a trattoria near the Piazza Navona. The night was warm and they ate outside at a sidewalk table, the lights from the piazza seeping into the street, along with shoppers and tourists walking by.

"Why would he risk it? Suppose he had been arrested by the *polizia*, that would have been the end of his operation."

Moretti shrugged. "Many things could have ended his operation. The foreign minister from Sweden—this time Sweden is head of European Union—wanted to call off the *congresso*. It was left to the Carabinieri and the intelligence agencies to decide. Only your DIA and I opposed it. The way they are talking, I think is total catastrophe; *buona notte al secchio*, good night to the bucket, as we say. Fortunately, I was able to persuade them. *Cin cin*," the little man toasted.

"*Cin cin*. What did you say?"

"I told them the truth. The threat is real. If a bomb—I say nothing of Uranium-235—is big enough, it will kill many. It can be exploded in apartment or in car parked anywhere and still kill many people and destroy *il congresso*. The only chance we have to stop and catch il Palestino is if we know his target—the Palazzo delle Finanze. To stop him there is the best chance of eliminating this threat. They agree," he said, taking a sip of his Chianti. "The real reason is not what I say, but because they do not want to cancel il Congresso Europeo and show weakness. The Swedes do not care, but the French and the German care. This *congresso* is important for Israel, and the Germans must always be sensitive to the Jews, you understand."

"It would have been a disaster if it had been cancelled. And it would have stopped nothing. As you said, he could set a nuclear bomb off in an apartment and do just as well."

"So you saw something on the *televisione*? That is why you go to RAI Uno? But what you see, you don't tell."

"You know what I saw."

"Il Palestino," Moretti said, putting down his fork.

"At the demonstration." Scorpion nodded. "I needed to see it slowly and up close to be sure. What I don't understand is why he would risk it."

"He is *fanatico*. We already know this about him."

"So you risk everything to wave a sign at people you plan to blow up? Makes no sense. But believe me, he had a reason." Scorpion shook his head through a shadow thrown by the light from the restaurant window. "He always has a reason."

"Still, he is not Signor Superman, your Palestino. He made a mistake this time. You know what he looks like, you know when he is coming and where, and now you know something more. You find *la donna inglese*, you will find your Palestino."

"That had occurred to me," Scorpion said. In fact, after leaving the television studio he went from one student hostel and cheap hotel to another, checking out places where the demonstrators tended to stay. By late afternoon a fifty euro note had convinced a desk clerk at a hotel near the Stazione Termini to admit that *la donna inglese* might be staying there with her *ragazzo*, a long-haired Italian student. From the photograph taken at the demonstration that Scorpion had printed at the Internet café, the clerk identified the other Englishwoman as a friend who sometimes came to see her. Scorpion decided to go back and stake out the hotel as soon as he left Moretti.

"You know what he looks like, don't you?"

Moretti said. "You have a photograph? Perhaps we should alert the Polizia di Stato and the Carabinieri. This becomes a simple security matter."

"Or let the DIA handle it? They won't stop him, and if you get close, he doesn't have to be near the bomb and whatever else he has planned. He just presses 'Send' on a cell phone and *arrivederci*. I have to get to him first."

"You look tired," Moretti said, studying the man across from him, Scorpion's eyes were shadowed, a two-day stubble on his face. He wore jeans and a black SAVE THE WHALE T-shirt under a jacket, presumably to blend in with the demonstrators. It wasn't a pretty-boy face, but his eyes, gray like the sea, and his look, like a wolf that never stopped moving, must attract women like crazy, Moretti thought. "What will you do when this is over?"

"Sleep. For at least a week." Scorpion grinned. "Preferably someplace where I can hear the sound of water on sand."

"You go back to America?" And when Scorpion shook his head, "You should come to Italy. Only Italians know how to live."

"Why? Do you have an apartment you want to rent?"

"No!" Moretti laughed. "But a place for you, we can always find. I have to go," he said, putting his napkin down.

"Family?"

"I have that also. Three *bambini*," he said, holding up three fingers. "No, I have a mistress. Blond, sexy," using his hands to portray her breasts, "but,

Dio mio, she is crazy! Women, when they love you, they go a little bit crazy, you know? But so *bella*," he sighed, getting up.

"You're right. Maybe I should live in Italy," Scorpion said, tossing money on the table and also getting up.

"I look forward to our next encounter, *il mio amico*. Good luck. *In bocca al lupo*," Moretti said, shaking his hand.

"And may the wolf die," Scorpion replied.

Moretti started to walk away, then turned back.

"By the way," he said, "the *capitano* of the ship *Zaina*. He died of asphyxiation, but is curious."

"In what way?"

"He had enough Demerol in the body to kill him ten times over, even without all the whiskey he drink. There are Demerol pills next to bed, but no pills in stomach. Yes, and there is an injection place with trace residue of Demerol between his toes."

"So someone shot him full of Demerol and smothered him when the injection started to wake him up," Scorpion said.

"That is also what the coroner said. He ruled it a *omicidio*. We will talk again soon. *Ciao*," Moretti said, and gestured goodbye.

Scorpion watched him walk toward the Piazza Navona and disappear into the crowd. Then he went to a Vodafone store on the Via del Corso that he knew was open late, bought two new cell phones and SIM cards, and used one to text Rabinowich.

Venice V Cross cousins hot bath pickup. nose HA. Scorpion used *Venice* to indicate that it was urgent.

He knew Rabinowich would recognize that he was talking about immediately notifying the "V Cross cousins," MI6, whose headquarters were at Vauxhall Cross in London, which Harris had once called "the worst intersection in Europe, in every conceivable way," to pick up someone who had flown into Heathrow, located on Bath Road. It was "hot" that MI6 interrogate Liz's friend, whose name he had discovered—from the hotel registry, thanks to the clerk—was Alicia Faring, and grill her because she "nose" HA: Hearing Aid. The Palestinian's girlfriend might've let something drop to Alicia, perhaps a hint about where the Palestinian was staying in Rome or where in Italy, if not Rome, he had gone after leaving Genoa.

Hoo? Rabinowich asked. Scorpion needed to use the quick and dirty Vigenère cipher they had agreed upon in Castelnuovo, employing the keyword YANKES with only one E, because Dave was a lifelong New York Yankees fan. The advantage of the Vigenère cipher was that it was impervious to frequency analysis, which made it hard to break without the keyword, and you didn't need a computer or anything fancy. You could draw the Vigenère Square anywhere and destroy it when you were finished. Scorpion did it on a piece of toilet paper in a stall of the men's room in the Vodafone store.

ylvmmsdaesry he texted to Rabinowich, to indicate Alicia Faring.

Friends in blk house looking 360 4 mrvyr, Rabinowich typed.

Scorpion assumed that the "friends" in the

black house referred to the NSA headquarters at Fort Meade. Using the Vigenère Square with the keyword YANKES, he translated *mrvyr* to mean Orion. The message meant that the NSA was monitoring all communications, 360 degrees worldwide, for any reference in any language to the constellation Orion, aka al Jabbar.

Scorpion ended the call and tore up and flushed the paper with the Vigenère Square down the toilet. He caught a taxi on the Corso and took it back to the hotel near the Stazione Termini. After slipping another twenty euros to the clerk, he camped out on the lobby couch, to all appearances just another backpacker making do.

At just past five-thirty in the morning, the sky still dark, while pretending to be asleep, his arm over his eyes to help obscure his face, he saw the attractive female friend of the Englishwoman, Alicia, from the video enter the hotel and go up in the elevator. Later that morning, as he watched from across the street, the sky bright and promising heat, he saw the three of them—the Englishwoman, Alicia, the female friend, and a boyfriend—come out of the hotel with their wheeled luggage.

He followed them to the Stazione Termini, where he was stunned to see Hassani, the Palestinian himself, come up and join them. Scorpion reached into the backpack where he kept the SIG Sauer 9mm that Harris had given him at Castelnuovo. *Do it now!* he told himself. He'd never get a better chance. At this distance it was almost impossible to miss, and if any of the others got in the way, it didn't matter. They were obviously co-conspirators. He took a deep breath to lower his heart rate as his hand closed on the gun. Then he hesitated. Even if he killed Hassani, that would still leave the bomb, with no way to find it and maybe a time mechanism or someone else to set it off. His sense of the Palestinian was that he left little to chance, always arranged a backup. He realized he couldn't do it, not yet, and let go of the 9mm in the backpack with reluctance, wondering if he wasn't making a fatal error.

The Palestinian and the woman got into a taxi outside the station. Scorpion followed in another taxi, telling the driver not to get too close, *"non troppo vicino,"* but not to lose them in the traffic on the Via Cavour. Although the Palestinian might not have recalled seeing him at the train station, if he saw him again, it would click.

Knowing he had to alter his appearance, Scorpion offered the driver an extra thirty euros to trade shirts, exchanging his SAVE THE WHALES T-shirt for a checked cotton shirt that he wore unbuttoned and outside his pants on the theory that he wanted anyone, at first glance, to look at the shirt instead of his face. The taxi ahead dropped the Palestinian and the woman off near the market stalls in the Campo dei Fiori. He told his driver to stop, and waited till he saw them head into an apartment building bordering the piazza.

He paid the driver, who was now wearing his former T-shirt and, using the canvas-topped stalls for cover, slipped through the aisles between the market stalls toward the apartment building. He

double-checked to make sure the Palestinian didn't
have someone covering his back, then studied the
building before stepping out from under the cover
of the stalls. He could see no surveillance. He tried
the building's front door. It was locked, but it only
took a few seconds with a credit card to open it and
step into the hallway, dim despite a shaft of sunlight from a window above the door. The floors
were tiled and there was a faded wallpaper mural of
the Roman countryside on the entryway wall. He
looked around, pulled his gun out of the backpack
and clicked off the safety.

There was an old narrow elevator and wooden
stairs, and after listening intently and hearing nothing, he began to quietly climb the stairs, pausing
at each landing to do a complete 360 up and down.
He stopped at each apartment and pressed his ear to
the door to listen. Nearly all of the apartments were
silent, except one where he heard a television tuned
to what sounded like an Italian game show. A smell
of chicken cacciatore came from the apartment, and
he thought whatever else the Palestinian had come
there to do, it wasn't cooking. He moved on to the
next floor.

He stood outside an apartment on the third floor,
his ear pressed to the door, when he heard a floor-
board creak just on the other side. Someone was
listening to him! He tried to make his breathing
shallow and slow, leaning slowly back toward the
doorjamb in case whoever it was fired through the
door. He considered whether he should fire first,
through the door, but it might not hit the target
and it could be some innocent person, probably old,

thinking a stranger had come to rob the apartment. Then he heard someone move inside and a sound like a slap. A woman gasped, and the gasp was cut off. The door looked solid, of heavy wood, perhaps oak, and he couldn't tell whether it had been rigged like the one in Amsterdam. It was too risky. He backed away carefully, went to the door of the next apartment and knocked softly, his gun ready to fire.

"Gli ufficio postale, signora," Scorpion said to the closed door in his best Italian. *"Gli ho una lettera per expresso per voi."* I have a special delivery letter for you. He didn't wait for a response, but tried to open the door with a credit card, and when that didn't work, used his universal key to open it. He stepped inside and closed the door behind him as softly as he could.

The foyer had the dusty silence of an empty apartment, but Scorpion moved silently from room to room, richly furnished with antiques and old paintings, just to make sure. From the living room window, he looked down and saw the canvas tops of the market stalls clustered around the statue of Giordano Bruno in the piazza. He went to the kitchen, picked up a glass and went back to the foyer. Placing the glass against the common wall with the apartment next door, he pressed his ear against the bottom of it. He heard the sound of a man talking and moving things, like he was working, but no other sounds. He had to see what was happening inside that apartment.

Scorpion opened his backpack and removed his Leatherman tool. He got a chair from the dining room and found a place high up on the wall that would allow him a good view of the other apartment and wouldn't be spotted unless someone happened to be looking for it. Then, with the Leatherman, he hand-drilled a tiny hole in the wall, making almost no noise, stopping from time to time to listen with the glass to the sounds next door. When he saw the light from the next apartment in the hole, he got a peephole scope from the backpack and fit it into the hole he'd just drilled.

Through the scope he saw the Palestinian finish rigging explosives around the woman, who was gagged with a tape across her mouth and tied to a chair in the middle of the room. She was moving in the chair, shaking her head, and he went over, slapped her in the face and said something Scorpion couldn't make out. Abruptly, the Palestinian stopped. He looked around, listening intently, a gun in his hand. Scorpion froze, his heart pounding as the Palestinian moved toward the peephole. Scorpion got ready to fire through the wall when he heard what the Palestinian had heard. Someone was coming down the hall toward one of the two apartments.

He barely had time to see the Palestinian head toward the apartment door, out of the peripheral view of the peephole scope. He got down from the chair as quickly and quietly as he could, stood beside the apartment door as the key turned in the lock. The door opened and a middle-aged woman carrying a fishnet shopping bag walked in. Scorpion grabbed her from behind, his hand tightly over her mouth.

"*Non una parola!*" Not a word, he hissed in his bad Italian into her ear as she dropped the shopping bag with a clunk that had to have alerted the Palestinian. The woman squirmed and tried to struggle against him, but he held her tight. He put his gun to her head, making sure she saw it. Her eyes were wide with fear. He gestured with the gun toward the sofa. "*Non parli,*" he whispered, putting his finger to his lips, all the while straining to hear what was happening next door.

Suddenly, he heard the other apartment door open and close, and by the time he got to the door to look out, he heard the elevator door down the hall closing. He ran back to the chair, stepped up and looked into the peephole scope. The woman was still tied up, but the Palestinian was gone.

Having no time, he knew he had to make an instantaneous choice: the life of the woman next door or his only chance at stopping the Palestinian.

Grabbing his backpack, Scorpion told the woman on the sofa, "You have to leave. *Esca della casa. Telefono per la polizia!*"

"Get out my apartment," she said in English.

He couldn't wait any longer. He ran out of the apartment and raced down the stairs, leaping down almost an entire landing. Coming to the entrance hall, he tore open the front door and was almost blinded by the bright sunlight in the crowded piazza. He saw the Palestinian point a gun at a taxi driver and haul the driver out, then get in and drive off in the taxi.

Scorpion looked around. Next to a flower stall he

saw a Vespa motor scooter chained to a lamppost. At this hour in Rome traffic, he might get through faster with the Vespa than a car. It only took a few seconds with the universal key and tapping with his Leatherman pliers to open the chain lock and the steering column lock and start the scooter. He roared off after the Palestinian as a man from one of the stalls ran after him, screaming, *"Arresto! Ladro!"*

He could see the Palestinian's taxi ahead, weaving around cars into the opposing traffic lanes and back, while he just managed to keep up on the cobblestone streets. He raced between lanes of traffic, slipping past cars by inches and going up on the sidewalk, dodging pedestrians as he raced after the taxi, trying to keep it in sight and not get it confused with other Roman taxis, all of them painted white.

Approaching a red traffic light ahead, the Palestinian suddenly looked back, stuck out his arm and fired a shot at Scorpion that tore a spiderweb hole in a car window next to him, the driver of the car staring wide-eyed at it, too stunned to move. Scorpion hunched lower over the handlebars and drove even faster, squeezing between a van and a Fiat with less than an inch to spare on either side. The Palestinian's taxi slowed at the red light, then sped up, darting into the intersection, then swerved to just miss a car. As the driver screamed and shook his fist, the taxi swerved again to avoid another car from the opposite direction and roared past the intersection.

Scorpion followed, trying to calculate which way the Palestinian was heading. He darted into the same intersection, cars screeching around him, people shouting and cursing, and then he was through and realized that the taxi was headed toward the Tiber River. He had to decide: Would the Palestinian try to go against the one-way traffic or cross over to Trastevere?

Against the traffic, he decided, based only on his sense of his adversary. Scorpion swerved up onto the sidewalk and down a stone stairway to an alley that brought him to the Tebaldi Road along the riverbank. He thrilled to see he had guessed right. He was just fifty feet or so behind the Palestinian's taxi, which was going against the one-way traffic, cars screeching to a halt and drivers gesticulating furiously. The taxi ran up onto the walkway along the Tiber, heading toward the Garibaldi Bridge. A woman walking with a little boy didn't see the taxi coming up fast behind them. At the last second she turned and screamed. The taxi cut back into a gap in the traffic, then bounced back onto the walkway, still charging at pedestrians who had to leap out of the way.

Scorpion raced on the walkway to stay with the taxi, his tires skidding as he whipped around the woman and the child who stared wide-eyed at him. The Palestinian glanced back and fired again, Scorpion swerving the Vespa to the side then back. The taxi had gone past the bridge, so the Palestinian was staying on this side of the river, Scorpion realized as they raced past Tiverina Island. Then a truck passed, blocking the view, and the Palestinian swerved back into and across the traffic lanes, heading up the Aventine hill.

Scorpion had to gear down and rev up on the incline, cutting into the opposing traffic lane to keep up. An Alfa Romeo was headed straight at him. He saw the driver blink in horror, the car's brakes screeching as Scorpion just raced past, the Alfa's bumper nearly grazing him. He could see the taxi pulling ahead as it raced around the Circus Maximus. Instead of going around, Scorpion drove past the barrier, the Vespa slowing on the green turf as he rode in a direct line across the open field to intercept the Palestinian. He got his 9mm ready to fire, holding the gun on the handlebar.

The Palestinian's taxi weaved through heavy traffic, scraping other cars and cutting into the opposite lane to get around a car in front of him before dodging back onto his side of the road. Now Scorpion could see the Coliseum ahead. The Palestinian was heading directly at a giant tour bus that was turning off the street toward the parking area for Coliseum tours. Suddenly, the Palestinian turned and slowed so he was directly across from the bus driver, who looked down at the taxi, startled. The Palestinian fired through the passenger window, hitting the driver in the head, killing him instantly. The bus lurched forward and slammed into a car, crushing it and completely blocking the street.

Jumping out of the taxi, the Palestinian ran around the bus, showed the gun to a woman in a Fiat sedan with two children in the backseat, ordered her and the screaming children out, and when they complied, drove off.

By the time Scorpion got to the bus, the street was completely blocked with cars, people, and passengers screaming and trying to get out of the bus. He crawled under the bus to the other side, but the

Fiat was nowhere to be seen. For a moment he stood there, sweating from the ride, his mouth tasting like ashes as he realized he'd made a terrible mistake. He should've killed Hassani when he'd had the chance on the train platform. Even worse, he'd lost the element of surprise, and now Hassani knew what he looked like. It was a disaster. Then he remembered the woman in the apartment.

He caught a taxi at a stand near the Coliseum and went back to the Campo dei Fiori. The taxi driver wanted to talk about the bus *incidente*, but Scorpion just kept saying, "*Non lo so*," I don't know, till the driver stopped talking.

The sun was high and hot over the market as he got out of the taxi and wondered how he would disarm the bomb. The Palestinian had likely rigged it to the apartment's front door. It struck him then that there were no *polizia*. The woman in the apartment hadn't called the police! She was still there!

He'd started toward the building when there was a tremendous explosion and a fierce rush of hot air knocked him off his feet. An orange fireball exploded out of the side of the apartment building. The roof immediately caught fire and began collapsing onto the wrecked lower floors, raining flaming debris on the canvas tops of the market stalls, which began to smoke with fire.

The piazza filled with smoke and the smell of explosive, and he could hear people screaming as he tried to clear his head, his ears ringing as he got to his feet. Most of the top three floors of the building were gone. The two women up there were certainly dead. He could hear the wailing sounds of approaching *polizia* sirens and fire engines. There was nothing to be done. He had failed completely.

Scorpion brushed himself off, and wiping the dirt off his face with his sleeve, began to walk through the debris and the burning market stalls, vendors desperately trying to save their stock.

As a final failure, he realized he'd figured out why the Palestinian had risked everything to be at the demonstration at the Palazzo delle Finanze. Only now it was too late.

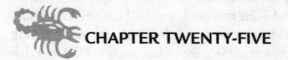

CHAPTER TWENTY-FIVE

Villa Ada, Rome, Italy/New York, United States

"Why didn't you call?" Moretti said. "We could have had a thousand Polizia di Stato. It would have been finished."

Scorpion shook his head. It was almost midnight. They were sitting at an outside table in a café in the small Piazza di Sant' Eustachio near the Pantheon. The lights from the café spilled out onto the cobblestones.

"He would've triggered the bomb with a cell phone before anyone could stop him. Even if we got him, you don't do this on your own. He has confederates. We wouldn't have stopped anything. I had no choice. I had to get him and the bomb together," Scorpion said. He could hear the bitterness in his voice.

"*E' un disastro*. Now he knows we know he's in Rome. Maybe he even knows what you look like?"

"I never got close enough." Scorpion grimaced, taking another sip of the grappa.

"Is no good," Moretti said.

"We know that," Scorpion snapped.

"I told my wife I have work, but *naturalmente* she thinks I am with my mistress. We lose the Palestinian and I am here with you and not my blond mistress. I lose twice. Is no good," Moretti said, making Scorpion smile in spite of how he felt. "What if this *figlio di gotta* changes his plan? All our preparation goes for nothing."

"He won't."

"How do you know?"

"Because he thinks it's his destiny," Scorpion said.

Moretti lit a cigarette and studied the American's face, partially in shadow from the light from the café.

"You begin to know him, don't you?"

"Maybe," Scorpion said.

"What will you do?"

"Get drunk."

"Seriously."

"Alert Langley. After what happened today, he probably sent the signal."

The next day, Scorpion got the call from Rabinowich before noon. A half hour later he was sitting next to Moretti looking at a closed-room bank of TV monitors inside Carabinieri headquarters on the Via Romania near Villa Ada Park. It was 6:00 A.M. in Washington and New York, and the FBI Hostage Rescue Teams were fully operational.

Before he sat down, Scorpion verified that his face was blurred on the TV monitor, as he'd requested. Other TV monitors showed Wade Anderson, head of the FBI task force on the Palestinian operation; Dave Rabinowich, viewed at his desk via his Web cam; a heliport by the water in what was clearly lower Manhattan; an apartment building in a run-down New York neighborhood, viewed from a camera in an apartment or on a roof across the way; a two-story building in another New York neighborhood; a subway station; and a tac ops coordination center filled with men in SWAT gear.

As soon as Scorpion sat down, Anderson said, "You're here at my request. I have a FISA warrant," and waved a sheaf of papers he picked up from his desk, the shades drawn over the office window glass behind him. "It's for two individuals whose names were supplied to us on a Special Access Critical basis by NSA and your buddy Rabinowich in Langley. I understand this was done based on information supplied by you. We've got multiple HRT teams deployed in Manhattan. Supervisory Special Agent Forrester's heading that up." A crew-cut man in a bulky SWAT outfit in one of the monitors nodded. "In fact, we're using every damned HRT in the country, so this better be right," Anderson said, glaring at the camera.

"These are people in the U.S. who received cell phone messages last night mentioning al Jabbar," Rabinowich put in. "There's also one in Chicago and another in L.A. that NSA is still running down. All the calls were made from a single cell phone in the Portonaccio district in Rome that subsequently went dead, so there's no GPS track."

"I assume that has something to do with why you are in Rome, Scorpion," Anderson said.

"The Palestinian is in Rome," Scorpion replied. Moretti looked hard at him.

"For our part, Langley's telling us to focus on New York. Correct?" Anderson asked.

"That's right," Rabinowich said.

"Well, we're not doing it just because Langley says so, but because it matches our analysis as well," Anderson growled. "But we have critical tactical decisions to make and I wanted your input, Scorpion."

"Who are the two individuals?" Scorpion asked.

"One's a woman in her twenties, named . . ." Anderson squinted at his BlackBerry. ". . . Bharati Kabir. The family's from Bangladesh; she came here when she was a kid. Lives in Queens with her brother's family and works in an insurance office in midtown Manhattan. Frankly, we have concerns. She doesn't fit the profile. The second is a Pakistani male from Brooklyn. Name is Atif Khan."

"What about the girl's brother?" Scorpion asked.

"Name's Zahid Kabir. Works in a shoestore." Anderson frowned. "We only got these last night, so we're still digging stuff up."

"This Atif Khan, what does he do?" Scorpion asked.

"You'll love this," Rabinowich said.

"He works for Prestige Helicopter Services," Anderson replied, checking the BlackBerry. "They do private tours and charters out of the Pier 6 Heliport in lower Manhattan. This Khan's a helicopter pilot."

"Christ," Scorpion muttered. "That's how he's doing it."

"You mean aerial spraying of the plague pathogen

over Manhattan from the helicopter? We thought of that," Anderson said, frowning again. "Walking and spraying through the streets or in a subway or office building would've been too obvious. They want this thing to incubate before we were alerted."

"That's not why you're here, Mister . . . uh, Scorpion," Forrester jumped in, sarcastic about the code name.

"No, it isn't," Anderson said, taking the meeting back. "Justice," indicating a man in a suit sitting next to him, "has come up with all kinds of constitutional hoops for us to jump through. These presumed terrorists—and we have concerns; as I said, the woman doesn't fit the profile—are American citizens. DOJ wants us to take them in, Mirandize them, wipe their noses for them, the usual crap."

"You'll never take them in," Scorpion said.

"Look, we don't like it either, but if we have to, we know how to do this," Forrester said, his men stirring.

"The Palestinian makes bombs," Scorpion said. "He's a graduate of a world-class technical university and he can control the blast to within a centimeter like he did in Cairo. It takes less than a second to press a button, and while I don't know whether an explosion will destroy these pathogens or distribute them to everybody in the vicinity including your men, I guarantee that he does."

One of Forrester's men came over and whispered something to him. Forrester looked at a monitor and cut in.

"The Kabir woman. She's on the move," he said. "We need to decide."

"Is she carrying anything? A suitcase, a shopping bag, anything?" Scorpion asked.

"Have a look," Forrester said, and they all looked at the monitor showing a young woman in jeans and a head scarf walking down the street from the apartment building entrance.

"What the hell is she wearing?" Anderson asked, putting on his glasses and squinting at the monitor.

"Backpack. The big kind they use for camping," one of Forrester's men said.

"She's the carrier," Scorpion said.

"So what do we do? Arrest her now before she gets on the subway?" Forrester asked.

"You've got a FISA. Probable cause is a little iffy, but I'm okay if you want to take her in," the suit next to Anderson said.

"The pilot, Khan, is on the move too, sir," another of Forrester's men said.

Another monitor showed the Pakistani, wearing a Prestige Helicopter jacket, coming out of his brick two-story house.

"Is he carrying anything?" Anderson asked.

"Just a briefcase," Forrester said.

"You can't arrest her," Scorpion said. "The second anyone gets near her, she'll detonate. Once the pathogen is out, it's out. Everyone who survives will be a carrier."

"And what's your suggestion?" Forrester said sarcastically.

"Surveillance. Lots of switch-offs. She's headed for the subway. Don't lose her, but don't keep the same agents on the same subway car with her for more than a few stops. No one looks at her; no one touches her; no one gets anywhere near her. One way or another—maybe she'll get off and grab a taxi in Manhattan—she's heading for the helicopter unless we do something stupid that forces her to do something she doesn't want to do."

"What happens when she gets to the heliport?" the suit next to Anderson asked.

"The heliport is built out into the East River," Forrester said. "There's a building next to the landing pad. We could grab her or take her out there."

"You need your two best snipers," Scorpion said. "I mean the best. Guys from Delta or SEALs; guys who won't miss. There's a building next to the landing pad, and the monitor shows skyscrapers nearby. They'll have two or three seconds as she approaches the helicopter."

"We need a decision, sir. She's approaching the subway," one of Forrester's men said. On the monitor, they saw the woman approach the subway entrance surrounded by other commuters.

"Morning rush. Lots of people," Rabinowich observed.

"Stand by," Forrester's man said into his phone mike.

"Do the surveillance on both, the girl and the pilot," Anderson said. "No one spooks them, goddammit. Switch off tails, lots of distance, like Scorpion said. It'll buy us some time while we decide."

"What if we lose them?" Forrester put in.

"We know where they're going," Scorpion said.

Anderson looked directly at the monitor that showed Scorpion's face as an oval blur.

"I want to be clear. You're suggesting we terminate both of them on the helicopter pad? Is that right?"

"A bullet in the head. Both at the same time. It has to be instantaneous and you can't miss. They have to die before they realize something's happened, so it has to be a clean head shot," Scorpion said.

"Who the hell is this guy?" the suit asked, glaring at the camera. "Have you ever heard of the United States Constitution? The presumption of innocence? If the media and the ACLU get hold of this, they'll crucify us. We can't just kill them!"

"Not even terrorists in the act?" Rabinowich chimed in.

"We don't know that! You said yourself," the suit turned to Anderson, "she doesn't fit the profile."

"Don't you get it? Tens of millions of people could die," Rabinowich said. "There's no vaccine for this thing. No antibiotic or other medication in the world that'll stop it. Once she starts spraying, we've got a helluva bigger problem than the ACLU. We have no choice."

"You're assuming they're terrorists," the suit replied, "or even if they are, that they've got this spray. That's all it is, an assumption. What if you got the wrong people? What if she's going backpacking with her boyfriend? You're basing this all on two words in a single phone intercept."

"In my business, that's usually all we have," Scorpion said.

"If you're wrong, it could be a career killer. You realize that, don't you?" The suit turned to Anderson. "You could be indicted. You need to kick this upstairs."

"Careers versus the lives of millions of Americans including your wives and kids," Rabinowich put in. "That's not a hard decision."

Anderson looked at the monitors. "They'll want deniability, upstairs," he said. "That's what they pay me for. The buck stops here." He looked directly at the TV camera. "Scorpion, are you sure about this—what is it—something about the constellation Orion in Arabic?"

"I've chased this guy across the Middle East and Europe. With all due respect, you have no idea who you are dealing with," Scorpion replied.

Anderson looked at Forrester on his monitor. "Who are your best snipers?"

"Sadlock. Him and Pesco. For the record, both were SEAL snipers," Forrester added, glaring at Scorpion's blurred image on the monitor. "We'll have my HRT squad close for backup."

"Get 'em in position at the heliport," Anderson said. "Tell them to make sure it's a head kill shot."

Forrester held up his hand, listening to his earpiece.

"The Kabir woman. She just got off the train at Grand Central."

"Don't lose her," Anderson said.

"Switching to Grand Central security feed," Forrester said.

They waited long seconds till one of the monitors showed crowds of people hurrying in all directions past a subway security camera.

"There she is," someone said, and Scorpion saw the woman with the backpack nearly submerged in a sea of people moving toward the subway stairs, before she moved out of the camera's range. A few minutes later Forrester reported that she had exited the station and was out on the street. One of Forrester's technicians put it on a live feed.

"She just got into a yellow cab. Heading west on Forty-second," the FBI tail on the scene said.

"Air, you got her?" Forrester asked.

"We got her," a voice said, nearly drowned out by the sound of a helicopter rotor. On another monitor, they were able to watch the taxi from the helicopter camera as it made its way through traffic back toward the East Side and down the FDR Drive. As the taxi approached the Brooklyn Bridge, Forrester told Air to peel off so as not to spook the woman. One of Forrester's men tapped his shoulder and said something.

"Sniper teams are in position," Forrester said. "They have their orders. As soon as they see her on the helipad, they take out her and the pilot." Forrester and his men were no longer on the monitor, although they were still on audio. Scorpion assumed he and his men were moving into position.

"What about the bomb and the spray afterward?" Anderson asked.

"We're in the basement of a building on South Street. We'll be on the scene with the robot within forty-five seconds. Anything else?"

"Yeah, don't screw it up," Anderson growled.

"The pilot, Khan, has boarded the helicopter," a technician said, and another monitor showed the Prestige helicopter on the pad, the sun glittering on the East River behind it. The helicopter's rotor began to turn.

"She's out of the taxi. Still wearing the backpack,"

a voice said as everyone tensed and leaned toward the TV monitors. The seconds seemed to creep by slowly. Scorpion and Moretti looked at each other.

Suddenly she was in view, a young woman with a head scarf walking toward the helicopter. The pilot looked like he was leaning over to say something to her. Do it now! Scorpion thought. What are they waiting for?

She was almost at the helicopter when suddenly she collapsed, the downdraft from the helicopter's rotor blowing her head scarf across her face. Forrester and his men ran out onto the helicopter pad, their Kriss Super V carbines at the ready, gear bouncing on their hips. One of them pulled the lifeless body of the pilot, part of his head torn away and bloody, out of the helicopter. Another peeled the backpack off the woman and carried it gingerly away from the helicopter, its rotor slowing down and stopping.

Moretti turned to Scorpion, his face grim.

"He's going to destroy Rome, isn't he?" Moretti asked.

"He's smart and absolutely committed. We'll only have a few seconds to stop him," Scorpion said. He thought about the two dead women in Campo dei Fiori, the beat-up Englishwoman, Alicia, the bus driver at the Coliseum. And now the dead helicopter pilot and the Bangladeshi woman. Hassani didn't mind how many people died. Maybe he even liked it.

"You'll be there tomorrow?" Moretti asked.

Scorpion nodded.

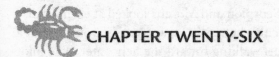

CHAPTER TWENTY-SIX

Palazzo delle Finanze, Rome, Italy

The delegates to the European Union Conference began arriving at ten in the morning. Flags hung from the window balconies of the Palazzo delle Finanze and the sounds of a military band could be heard from the building's interior courtyard as the limousines rolled up. It was already hot, and the sun-bleached sky promised even greater heat later in the day. The *polizia* had banned traffic in the area and set up barricades on streets leading to the palazzo from every direction.

Scorpion, using a pair of binoculars, watched undercover agents checking out the demonstrators at the barriers. DIA sharpshooters were on the roof of the palazzo and two Italian military helicopters circled overhead. He was positioned on an elevated stand occupied by cameramen from various European TV networks inside the barricades near the entrance on Via 20 Settembre. If he was right—he admitted to himself it was a hell of a big if—the Palestinian and his crew would be coming toward that entrance from Via Quintino Sella. It was the most logical route, and if challenged at the *polizia* barrier at the Via Flavia intersection, they could still break through and detonate close to ground zero.

Earlier that morning, around six, he'd introduced himself to the DIA sharpshooters on the roof, one a former Delta and the other three ex-Navy SEALs. They shared a few war stories about EOD explosives training at the "Point" in North Carolina, in particular about a certain well-endowed female bartender named Melissa in Elizabeth City known to one and all, and they gave him a red armband to wear on his left arm as a way to make sure, as they put it, that if they shot him, he'd know they'd meant to.

Through the binoculars, he could see the crowds at the barriers, numbering in the thousands, many carrying signs with the now-famous photograph of *la donna inglese*, blood streaming down her face, and screaming "Fascism!" and "Israeli Nazis!" The Palestinian would not be among them, Scorpion knew. But they were his catalyst; he had risked everything to join them, because without them, his plan wouldn't have worked. Scorpion had referred to it last night on his cell phone conversation with Rabinowich, making the call from the Metro station not far from the bottom of the Spanish Steps, chancing the voice call because they had run out of time.

"Helluva mess at the Coliseum and the Campo dei Fiori. Someone trying to kill the tourist trade in Rome?" Rabinowich observed.

"Anybody say anything?" Scorpion asked over the echoes of people going by in the train station.

"Not a word from our Italian friend. He sees it like you do with respect to our C and B *amigos*. You two getting married?" Rabinowich joked, indicating that Moretti hadn't spoken to anyone in the AISE or to the DIA or the Italian *polizia* about Scorpion's possible involvement in the death of the bus driver or the explosion in Campo dei Fiori, which the Italian police were saying on TV was caused by a faulty gas line in the old building.

"First I'd have to divorce you."

"No Hearing Aid?" Rabinowich was asking whether Hearing Aid got away. When Scorpion didn't answer, he added, "Do you know moo?" asking Scorpion if he had an idea about how the Palestinian planned to do it, his method of operation.

"I think so," Scorpion said, his voice barely audible over the sound of a train coming into the station.

"But you're not sharing with any of our friends?"

"Uh-uh."

"Because it's like horseshoes. He only has to get close. So it has to be you."

"You shouldn't always be the smartest kid in the class, *amigo*. You'll never get promoted," Scorpion said, and ended the call. The good thing was that, at least for now, Rabinowich was on the same page: the Italians and the DIA couldn't stop the Palestinian. Moretti hadn't said anything about what happened at the Coliseum and the Campo dei Fiori for the same reason. As Rabinowich had pointed out, the Palestinian only needed to get close; if it started going south, he could detonate at any time. Scorpion was the only one who knew what Hassani looked like and what his plan was. He was the only one with a chance of stopping him.

He watched the demonstrators through the binoculars and on the TV monitors on the camera stand. People began to surge forward and fists and rocks were thrown at a number of the police barriers. There was a breach at a barrier on the Via Voltumo and a platoon of riot police with shields moved forward, clubs extended like the swords of Roman legionnaires. He watched on one of the monitors as a reporter from France 3 News shouted rapidly into his microphone as the demonstrators began throwing things at police at the Via Umbria barrier. Someone from the crowd tossed a Molotov cocktail in a high perfect arc that crashed against a police car, and the car burst into flames. More rocks and Molotov cocktails were thrown and things began to get out of control. A woman screamed and people were trampled as some demonstrators surged toward the *polizia*, while others tried to fall back. A troop of helmeted Carabinieri moved toward the demonstrators, pushing them back, marching over people who had fallen in the streets.

Scorpion focused his binoculars on the barrier on the Via Quintino Sella. The *polizia* were being swarmed as they tried to push the crowd back, and suddenly he saw what he had been looking for without knowing exactly what it would be until he saw it. A dark blue Mercedes UniMOG truck with the red stripe and insignia of the Carabinieri approached the barrier, and he knew, with a certainty he couldn't explain, that it was the Palestinian. That's how he had planned to do it, with a Carabinieri truck. That's why he'd risked everything to ensure that there would be violent demonstrations.

The *polizia* moved the metal barrier aside and waved the UniMOG through. Scorpion watched it make its way toward the front of the palazzo. It pulled into the parking area right next to the building, where it had no need to be for riot control purposes. He caught a glimpse through the binoculars of the Palestinian's face. He was sitting next to the driver, dressed as a Carabinieri officer, and a moment later Scorpion had ripped off the binoculars and was down from the platform, sprinting toward the UniMOG before it came to a stop.

He came at it from the street side as two men in Carabinieri uniforms got out of the back of the UniMOG. He was running hard, less than thirty meters away, Harris's SIG Sauer in his hand, when one of the two spotted him. As the man started to unsling his Beretta assault rifle, Scorpion dropped to one knee and fired, hitting him in the chest. The second man turned, his rifle coming up toward Scorpion when he was dropped—by what, it wasn't clear, till the sound of the shot echoed and Scorpion saw that he had been hit in the top of the head. It was one of the sharpshooters on the roof, who must have spotted his red armband and understood what was happening. The driver of the UniMOG, looking Moroccan despite his peaked Carabinieri cap, turned toward Scorpion, who fired three shots in quick succession through the UniMOG door and window, killing him.

Scorpion could hear screaming and people running. Someone on a police loudspeaker shouted, *"Non si muova! Posi la pistola!"* Don't move! Put down the gun! He couldn't see the Palestinian, who had gotten out of the truck on the other side, and then he saw him running toward the building entrance. Hassani's Carabinieri cap had fallen off and he was frantically opening his cell phone. The cell phone trigger would kill them all, Scorpion's mind screamed.

Stopping in a two-hand stance, Scorpion barely had time to aim and fire at Hassani, who was leaping to the side. The shot missed, but another shot that came from the roof ricocheted off the pavement within an inch of Hassani's foot. Hassani looked up, suddenly aware of the sharpshooters. He dodged under a window balcony overhang that screened him from above, but as he did so, crashed into an elderly diplomat, who cried out as he was slammed against an aide who had been guiding him to the entrance. The contact jarred Hassani, who dropped his cell phone. Scorpion dove for it as Hassani bent to pick it up and grabbed it.

He and Scorpion collided, and Hassani smashed at Scorpion's face with his forearm. Scorpion parried and grabbed Hassani's arm, his leg going under the arm, the two of them grappling desperately. Scorpion completed a Brazilian arm bar by putting his other leg around Hassani's neck and pressing down with both legs to try to dislocate the parried arm's elbow. Hassani screamed and let go of the cell phone. Scorpion had to release the arm bar to grope for the cell phone, managed to grab it just as Hassani smashed Scorpion's head against the ground with his free hand, momentarily stunning him. Before Scorpion could respond, Hassani was up, quick as a cat, and running toward the entrance, staying close to the building so he was screened from the sharp-shooters above. A *polizia* guard by the entrance was fumbling at his holster for his gun. Hassani shot him and ran into the palazzo.

Scorpion got up from the ground, the cell phone in his hand, more than twenty *polizia* running toward him and pulling their guns, since so far as they could see he had attacked a *carabiniere*. He had to make an instantaneous decision: disarm the bomb in the UniMOG or go after Hassani. The main threat was the bomb, but what if Hassani had another cell phone and could dial it in before he could deal with the *polizia* and disarm the bomb?

"*Arresto! Non si muova!*" one of the *polizia* shouted at him, snapping into a shooting position.

"*È una bomba nel camion!*" There's a bomb in the truck, Scorpion shouted over his shoulder as he ducked and ran into the palazzo.

He entered into a long neo-Renaissance style hallway with an ornate marble stairway. The hallway and stairs were empty, though he could hear people shouting. Hassani was nowhere to be seen. Then he heard the shots on the second floor and ran for the stairway. He was halfway up the stairs when the *polizia* came in and started shooting at him, the bullets chipping pieces of marble from the stairs. Still running, Scorpion held up his badge toward them and yelled at the top of his lungs: "*Sono Americano; Agenzia della Difesa!*"

He raced along the second floor hallway. There was a body lying near a door, then a woman's scream and shots farther down the hall. He ran toward the sound of shooting. He dove into a large conference room with a roll, snapping into a kneeling position firing stance as a shot cut through the air above him where he would have been had he come running in. The room was filled with delegates and aides standing in a frightened group at the side of a big mahogany conference table. Hassani was in a firing stance, his gun aimed at Scorpion, whose 9mm was aimed directly at Hassani. It was a Mexican standoff.

"Get out or I'll start killing them," Hassani said in English.

"*Elif air ab tizak, Bassam,*" Scorpion said, letting him know he knew his name and using the classic Arabic curse involving what a thousand penises would do to him. Then he dove to the side as he fired. Hassani moved at the same instant, the bullet missing him as he grabbed a blond woman and fired back, the bullet ripping through the table next to Scorpion.

There were sounds of automatic firing in the hallway, presumably from the *polizia*. Hassani shot a man standing near a doorway to another room and ran through it, pulling the blonde with him by her hair. Scorpion raced after him, but Hassani, beside the door, tripped him as he ran through the doorway, sending him flying. Scorpion's hand banged against a chair, knocking the gun out of his hand. The blonde woman tried to pull away. Hassani shot her, then whirled to point the gun at Scorpion, who parried it with the back of his hand, going into the Krav Maga move, twisting Hassani's wrist to take the gun away. Hassani countered with a Sambo counterwrist move combined with the start of a leg sweep to take Scorpion down, which Scorpion countered with a pullback heel kick to Hassani's kidney as they grappled for the gun. Scorpion tried to point the gun at him, but another wristlock combined with a Sambo sidekick enabled Hassani to twist the gun away from him.

The Iranians had gotten their training from the Russians, Scorpion realized, which told him the style of countermoves he could expect. As Hassani turned the gun in his hand and aimed, Scorpion grabbed a laptop computer from a table nearby and smashed the edge of it into Hassani's wrist, knocking the gun out of his hand, then smashing it into the side of his neck, knocking Hassani sideways. Scorpion combined it with a leg sweep that took him down.

He jumped on top of Hassani then, smashed the edge of the laptop down into Hassani's face, breaking his nose and knocking out teeth. Hassani's mouth was bleeding, but he managed to grab the side of the laptop and twist it, putting his left leg behind Scorpion's neck then bringing his right leg up to the front of Scorpion's neck in a Sambo leg chokehold.

Unable to breathe, Scorpion knew he had to do something quickly or he'd be unconscious in about ten seconds. He tried to countertwist the laptop while hammering his fist into Hassani's groin. Hassani screamed but was strong enough to hold on with his leg chokehold. Scorpion felt himself starting to black out. He groped with his hand, at first missing, then grabbed Hassani's testicles and squeezed, ripping at them as hard as he could. An unearthly animal scream came from Hassani and suddenly the chokehold was broken. As Scorpion pulled back, gasping for air, Hassani somehow managed to roll away and stagger to his feet, bent over in agony.

"*Khara Yahud!*" he gasped, calling Scorpion a dirty Jew and groaning in pain as he picked up a wooden chair. Scorpion realized that Hassani assumed Scorpion was what he most feared: Israeli Mossad.

"*Ana min Amreeka, ibn el metanaka,*" Scorpion said as Hassani smashed the chair at him. I'm an American, you son of a bitch. He tried to block the chair with his forearms, but it knocked him back. He stumbled on a ripple in the carpet and fell backward, his head banging against the side of a marble fireplace. The world began to tilt. Dazed, Scorpion managed to roll to the side as Hassani lifted the chair and smashed it onto the marble fireplace base, cracking it. He ripped away one of the wooden legs. Using it as a club, Hassani pounded down at Scorpion's head. Scorpion tried to block him, grunting as each blow stunned his arms with agonizing pain. He knew he couldn't use his arms much longer.

Hassani dropped down on top of Scorpion and jabbed the chair leg at his eyes. Scorpion just managed to parry it and grab Hassani's wrist, holding on to try to go into a Kimura. Hassani, face contorted in agony and rage, understood what Scorpion was trying to do and put his hand around Scorpion's back, his knuckle digging into Scorpion's kidney. Gasping in pain, Scorpion countered by going into the Brazilian move, sitting up as best he could, sliding his right arm to the side and around the back of Hassani's neck and into a guillotine chokehold that he secured with his left hand grabbing his right and squeezing Hassani's neck. He completed the move by crossing his feet around Hassani's torso and pressing down with his crossed feet while pulling up with his arms, tightening the choke.

Hassani struggled furiously, his left hand pounding at Scorpion's face and banging his head against the marble as Scorpion tightened the chokehold on his neck with every fiber of his strength. For a second Scorpion almost blacked out, and then he felt Hassani weaken. Hassani punched him in the eye, but it was weak, almost a push, and then Scorpion felt Hassani go slack. Tightening his grip with his last bit of strength, he hung on, counting to thirty, and then let go, utterly exhausted.

Putting his fingers to Hassani's neck, he checked for a pulse. There was none. He'd thought he would feel some sense of triumph, but he was so exhausted he could feel nothing.

He rolled over, his legs still around Hassani, then got up and went through Hassani's pockets, finding another cell phone, a contact number on the screen. It had been damn close, he thought. His hands shaking, he just had time to remove the SIM chips from both cell phones so they couldn't be used, when a heavily armed squad of real Carabinieri came into the room and placed him under arrest.

Late that night, his face and clothes still stained with Hassani's blood, Scorpion was taken in handcuffs from his jail cell and put into a windowless police van. When the van stopped, they led him out to a piazza bordered by a large multistory building, lit ghostly white by floodlights. The area was surrounded by armed Carabinieri, their hands on their guns as the *polizia* led him toward the building.

"What place is this?" he asked one of the policemen.

"Il Palazzo Chigi," the *guardia* replied. "That is the Colonna of Marcus Aurelius," he said, pointing to a marble column in the center of the piazza. They led him past the towering column, into the palazzo building and up to the Italian prime minister's office.

"*Buona sera!* The man of the hour, lo Scorpione," said a tanned middle-aged man in shirtsleeves and tie, seated behind the desk. Moretti and Bob Harris and another man in a dark suit, who looked like an aide to the prime minister, were also in the room.

"Take the handcuffs off him," Moretti said in Italian to the two policemen who had come in with Scorpion. One of the *guardia* fumbled for a moment and then unlocked the cuffs. Moretti gestured for them to go, and they both immediately left the large ornate room.

"Please, sit," the prime minister said, gesturing to Scorpion. "You like cigar? It is Cubano." He nodded to his aide, who held out an open box of expensive cigars from the prime minister's desk.

"*Grazie,*" Scorpion said, picking out one of them. He waited while the aide lit it for him. "Didn't know you were in Rome, Bob." Seeing Harris gave him a bad feeling. All through this mission, there had been the thought in the back of his mind that, as always, Harris was dealing from the bottom of the deck, and that he would be the one to pay the tab.

"I was in London coordinating with MI6, the AISE," Harris said, gesturing to Moretti, "and some of the other services, when I heard what happened. I want you to know, the DNI is very pleased. He's approved your bonus. He's convinced keeping you under deep cover on the Palestinian op was his idea and is citing this success as a result of cooperation between the DIA, NSA, and CIA that he implemented."

"In Italy, it is the same. The big fish takes the credit," Moretti said.

"As it should be," the prime minister said. "But we in this room know the truth. This man," pointing at Scorpion, "saved many lives—and the honor of the Italian nation. I am curious. How did you know that the Palestino was coming in a truck disguised as a *camion di Carabinieri*?"

"You had to look at it from Hassani's point of view," Scorpion said. "His problem was how to get past the barriers of the *polizia* in order to attack the conference. When I recognized him on the TV with *la donna inglese*, I couldn't figure out why he would risk his entire operation just to attend a street demonstration. And then it hit me. He needed a symbol, like a female victim of the *polizia*, to ensure that there would be violent demonstrations the day of the conference, so the *polizia* at the barricades wouldn't question the necessity of a Carabinieri truck coming through with reinforcements."

"Why didn't you give us the photograph and let the AISE and the Carabinieri try to find him?" the aide asked.

"It would have alerted him. He could have detonated the bomb remotely anytime. We had to get him and the bomb together," Scorpion said.

"Generale Lombardi of the Carabinieri and I came to the same conclusion," Moretti put in. "The only place where both the Palestino and the bomb would be at the same time was at the Congresso."

"A dangerous strategy," the prime minister said, looking at Moretti.

"Ours is a dangerous business, Prime Minister," Harris said. "Happily, there's more good news. Thanks to the lead on the English girl—Welsh, actually—and you won't be surprised to learn that the photograph of her covered with blood and beaten by the Italian police was a fake."

"Of course. This I knew all the time," the prime minister snapped.

"We were able to round up most of the Islamic Resistance network. The young woman was a pawn. She didn't know she was being used by the Palestinian."

"She lied about the beatings. We must investigate. Arturo, make a note," the prime minister said to his aide.

"Of course, Prime Minister," Harris said. "You'll have to work that out with the British, although you may want to wait till after Scotland Yard is done. She is cooperating with them. She gave them the lead that her girlfriend—English, named Liz—was Hassani's girlfriend, and that before they came to Rome, Liz and Hassani had been staying with jihadis in Turin. After that, it was just a matter of tracking down all the foreigners and Muslim jihadi types who had been in Turin at that time, with I must say a great deal of help from the AISE and the Carabinieri." He gestured to include the prime minister and Moretti. "Also, the NSA, tracking down all the cell phone messages with the phrase 'al Jabbar.'

"We now know that in Europe, in addition to Rome, there were four additional attacks planned: London, Brussels, Paris, and Madrid. Thanks to the leads from Turin, we were able to stop three of the four. The only one who slipped through the net and wasn't picked up in time was a young Tunisian student in Madrid, who managed to detonate his suicide vest at a bus stop—prematurely, we think—killing two and injuring a young girl."

"What about America?" the prime minister asked.

"There were three attacks planned," Harris replied. "We stopped two, the big one, the bioweapon attack in New York and one in Chicago; a Pakistani college student who was planning to blow up a train. There were three deaths: the Bangladeshi woman and a Pakistani helicopter pilot in New York, and an incident in Los Angeles. So far we've been able to angle the media so the public has been reassured that they were all under surveillance and that the major threat was stopped. Nothing about the bio threat has been given to the press."

"So many attacks. This time we were lucky," the prime minister said.

"We were good," Harris said.

"Thanks to lo Scorpione. Tell him," the prime minister gestured at Moretti, "what we found in the *camion di Carabinieri.*"

"One hundred and sixty-five kilos of RDX, plus

more than twelve hundred kilos of fertilizer and diesel fuel and three kilos of Cesium-137," Moretti said.

"A dirty bomb. It would have been a total disaster," the prime minister said, shaking his head.

"What are you talking about? What about the uranium?" Scorpion asked.

"What uranium?" the prime minister said, looking at Scorpion and Harris.

"The twenty-one kilos of highly enriched U-235 missing from Russia. That uranium!"

"There was nothing in the *camion*," Moretti said. "Only the cesium. That would have been bad enough. Cesium-137 has a half-life of thirty years and it bonds with everything—walls, paint, metal, dirt, trees, air. Much of Rome might have been made uninhabitable."

"The uranium was a false alarm," Harris said. "It may have been disinformation from the Russians."

"This is bullshit!" Scorpion said, standing up. He stubbed the cigar out in an ashtray on the prime minister's desk, a sickening feeling in the pit of his stomach. "Where's Dave Rabinowich? Get him on the line now."

"Take it easy," Harris said, glancing over at the prime minister. "Remember where you are."

"Get Rabinowich now," Scorpion said through clenched teeth. Two Italian agents stepped into the room, their hands inside their suit jackets, but the prime minister waved them off, indicating that they should leave.

"Dave's been reassigned," Harris said, standing up. "He's not on this operation anymore. Neither are you. This case is closed. Prime Minister, I'm afraid we've taken up enough of your time."

"Where's Dave?" Scorpion said, not moving.

"He's on vacation. Hawaii, I think. He said he'd be incommunicado. No e-mails, no cell phones. His fat ass is probably in a beach chair right now, ogling girls in bikinis," Harris said, walking to the door.

The prime minister stood up and extended his hand for Scorpion to shake. "*Arrivederci*, Scorpione. We owe you much."

"*Prego*, but this is *merda*," Scorpion said again, shaking the prime minister's hand but looking at Moretti.

"You should clean your face. It still has dried blood on it, *il mio amico*," Moretti said, his eyes sympathetic. "There is a restroom down the hall."

Harris was waiting for Scorpion in the hallway outside the office.

"What the hell did you think you were doing in there? You don't work for the Italians, you work for us. Although maybe not anymore," he said.

"What was *I* doing?" Scorpion snapped. "How about twenty-one kilos of bullshit from Ozersk that supposedly doesn't exist? Or an Iranian ship from Bushehr that disappeared into thin air? Did I imagine that too or did I hear it from you, you son of a bitch? And now all of a sudden Rabinowich has disappeared too? This isn't an intelligence operation, it's the Bermuda Triangle."

"Keep your voice down," Harris said. "You know the rules. You tell the runner just what he needs to know. That's all."

"Yeah, but what you tell him is supposed to be

good," Scorpion said. "So what operation was I on, Bob, old buddy?"

"Your job was to terminate the Palestinian. You did it. He's dead. You saved Rome—and a lot of other people too. You've been paid in full plus the bonus. Case closed," Harris said, adjusting his suit jacket cuffs as he headed for the elevator. The door opened and Harris stepped in. Scorpion watched him from the hallway. "You coming?" Harris said.

"With you? That's always a mistake," Scorpion said.

The two men watched the elevator door close between them, then Scorpion walked to the men's room and washed his hands and face in the basin. Not looking, he sensed Moretti come in. Scorpion wiped his face with a hand towel and looked at himself in the mirror. He'd had so many identities, the man who looked back at him was almost a stranger, face bruised and needing a shave, his gray eyes catching the overhead light like a cat's eyes.

"Are you all right?"

"No," Scorpion said. "There's something very wrong. *Buona notte* to that bucket of yours."

"I know. There were traces of radiation from uranium, as well as cesium, in the hold of that ship, the *Zaina*," Moretti said. "He's holding something back. What will you do?"

Scorpion looked at the two of them in the mirror: the stranger with gray eyes and the little Italian spy. There were only two possibilities, he thought. Either it was all Russian disinformation, or his operation against the Palestinian was, in CIA parlance, "window dressing," a diversion from the real operation. If that was the case, whatever the operation was, it was still running. Either way, the feeling in his stomach was like something twisting inside, saying something truly terrible was about to happen. Worse, if he stayed with it, he was completely on his own. Harris had cut him off from both Rabinowich and the Company. Anything he did could be considered treason.

"*Arrivederci, Aldo*," Scorpion said, putting his hand on Moretti's shoulder. "This isn't over."

"*Bene.* You go to Torino? The air is good there this time of year."

"Perhaps. Rome's getting a little hot for me."

"Keep in touch, *Scorpione*," Moretti said. When Scorpion left him, the Italian was peering at the mirror, snipping at his mustache and nose hairs with a pair of tiny penknife scissors.

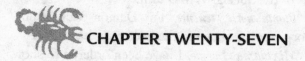# CHAPTER TWENTY-SEVEN

Torino, Italy

The warehouse was smaller than Scorpion expected. The *polizia* had roped it off as a crime scene, and at night the electric lamps in front made a hazy glow like the entrance to an underground nightclub. The street was empty, and close enough to the river that he could smell it. In this working-class neighborhood, there were few lights in any of the windows nearby. But although he couldn't see them, he knew there might be eyes watching. He stepped around the police barrier, and two *guardia* policemen detached themselves from the shadows and came toward him. He showed them the badge he had used at the Palazzo delle Finanze and they gestured toward the building. He went inside.

The interior was gloomy, a dusty space lit only by a few overhead lights. It had an abandoned, almost desolate feel. A curly-haired Carabinieri lieutenant stood in the middle of the empty space, his Beretta pointed at Scorpion.

"*Signor McDonald?*" the lieutenant asked. The

lieutenant's uniform had an insignia that showed he was of the Special WMD unit.

"*Buona notte, tenente*. I'm Damon McDonald," Scorpion said, showing the lieutenant his badge.

"*Mi chiamo Giorgio*. I have been ordered to show you everything," the lieutenant said, putting his gun back in the holster. "You speak Italian?"

"*Malissimo*, I'm afraid." Badly. "What have you found?"

"Much. Let me show you." He led Scorpion to the small warehouse office, and once they were inside, turned off the light. It took a moment for Scorpion's eyes to get accustomed to the darkness. Then he saw it. On the floor, two blood spatter patterns glowed a luminescent blue. "These were sprayed with Luminol," Giorgio said, turning the light back on. When looked at in the light, the floors were spotless. "They try to clean it up, but of course microscopic particles are always missed."

"What did they do with the bodies?"

"Come, I show you," he said, and led Scorpion to a refrigeration locker at the back of the warehouse. He turned off the overhead light and lifted the lid in the darkness. Two smudges of blue glowed in the blackness at the bottom of the locker. He turned the light back on. "You can see, there were two bodies they stuffed in the *armadio*. When the *poliziotti* come, they find one body only."

"Where's the other one?"

"*Chi sa?*" Who knows? The lieutenant shrugged. "Now I show you something *fantastico*," and he led him to a kitchen area near the office. The lieutenant opened a large duffel bag lying on the floor and pulled out a radiation protection suit and handed it to Scorpion, then took out another suit and started to put it on.

"Is this necessary?" Scorpion asked.

"I told you. Is *fantastico*." The lieutenant gestured with his hand.

Scorpion took off his jacket and shoes and put the outfit on, zipping it closed so he was completely encased head to foot, with only a plexiglass visor to see through. When they were both suited up, the lieutenant checked their air supply connections, then took out two handheld radiation detectors. He left one on top of the duffel bag and picked up the other and they walked clumsily in the suits across the warehouse to a partitioned area with a door that had been locked by a padlock someone broke off. The lieutenant opened the door and they went inside and turned on the light. The area was filled with a large worktable and electric tools, rags, empty wooden crates, and flattened cartons strewn on the floor. He motioned Scorpion closer, turned on the radiation detector and ran it over a wooden box in the corner, then pointed at the LED screen that began rapidly registering numbers.

"You see. This is *Cesio uno-tre-sette*," the lieutenant said. Cesium-137.

"How can you be sure?"

"The beta particle and gamma radiation levels and patterns are unmistakable. It's all over this area," he said, showing Scorpion on the LED as he walked around the room. "No one can use this warehouse anymore."

"Is that it?" Scorpion asked.

"No. Here is what is *fantastico*. Look." He passed the wand of the handheld detector over one side of the worktable. They watched the LED screen numbers. "You see, is alpha, not beta. The pattern is from *sette*, seven alpha emitters. Is not cesium. Can be only one thing."

"Uranium?"

"*Uranio due-tre-cinque*." Uranium-235. "The rates from Uranio-234 and 238 are different. Come. We must go out. Too long with cesium is not good," the lieutenant said, leading Scorpion outside the partitioned area.

They walked back toward the front of the warehouse and took off their protective suits. The lieutenant and he went to the kitchen and washed their hands and face in the sink. The lieutenant ran the other detector over them. The LED registered only a fraction of what it had registered inside the partitioned area.

Scorpion looked around at the shadowed interior of the warehouse.

"What will they do with this place?" he asked.

"*Non so.*" I don't know. "Maybe seal it up with concrete because of the cesium," the lieutenant said as he put away his gear.

"I have to go, *tenente. Per piacere*, put your cell phone number in my phone and I'll call you. I may need your help again," Scorpion said, handing him the cell phone. He had to think. Moretti had confirmed there had been U-235 on the *Zaina* when it berthed in Genoa. Now the lieutenant had shown that the Palestinian brought it here to Turin. What Harris had said about the twenty-one kilos from

Russia being disinformation was a lie. Whatever was running, the clock was ticking.

"*Per piacere*, call to me any hour. To do something besides technical is good for me." The lieutenant smiled.

Scorpion had a late night snack of little *tramezzini* sandwiches and Chianti at a *caffè* on the Via Po. While he ate, he went over the report from the Carabinieri antiterrorism unit that Moretti had e-mailed to him. It listed all the male members between the ages of sixteen and forty-five belonging to the small garage mosque in Torino to which all three Moroccans killed at the Palazzo delle Finanze had belonged. The report noted that more than a dozen of them, in addition to the three who were killed, had stopped coming to Friday services at the mosque during the week prior to the Rome attack, and when questioned, some of their family had indicated that they didn't know where they were. During the month before that final week, a number of them had told their families that they were doing something *speciale* for the mosque, but the imam told the *polizia* that, except for Friday services, they were rarely there.

Scorpion looked at the names and notations on some of the other males and one caught his eye. A Moroccan male named Issam Badoui, aged thirty-two, originally from Tangier. Apparently, he had been very religious and involved with the mosque until about a month ago. Suddenly, he stopped going and had not been back, not even for Friday services. He had been at work during the week before and during the Rome attack and was not considered a suspect. The *guardia* who interviewed him noted that when asked why he no longer went to services at the mosque, Badoui said that his wife "did not like him going to that *masjid*."

Scorpion heard a whirring sound and looked out the *caffè* window. A tram was going by, its windows lit like a ship in the night. He glanced at his watch. It was after midnight. This man was devout, and all of a sudden it all changed? Because his wife was worried about something that was going on at the mosque? How the hell had the Carabinieri let that remark slip by? He decided to pay Badoui a visit.

Badoui's apartment was in a run-down section of the Porta Palazzo district. The outer door to the apartment house was locked, but it only took Scorpion a second with a credit card to open it. He stepped into the entryway and using a little LED flashlight found Badoui's handwritten name and apartment number on the wall next to one of the mailboxes. Scorpion went up the narrow stairs and stood outside the door to Badoui's apartment, where he could hear a baby crying inside. He knocked on the door. There was no answer. He knocked again, harder, and when no one came, knocked again. Then he heard footsteps and the sound of the baby crying approaching the door.

"*Chi è là? Che cosa volete?*" Who's there? What do you want, a woman asked, sounding frightened.

"*È il Carabinieri. Apra il portello,*" Scorpion said. It's the Carabinieri. Open the door. He heard the woman whispering to someone and pounded on the door. The door opened suddenly and the woman stood there in a nightdress, winding a *hijab* on her head with one hand and holding the baby, still crying, with the other.

"*Già ho parlato con la polizia*," a thin, bearded man in pajama bottoms and an undershirt said, coming forward. Scorpion showed him his badge.

"I have just a few more questions. You are Issam Badoui?" Scorpion asked in Fusha Arabic.

"I have told the *polizia* everything I have to say," the man answered in Arabic.

"No, you haven't. Tell your wife to go into the next room."

"I don't know who you are, but I have nothing to say," Badoui said.

"Tell her to take the baby and go into the next room," Scorpion said, in a tone that in Arabic implied the whole issue of male-female relations and a man's ability to be master in his own house.

"Go into the bedroom and close the door, and keep the baby quiet," Badoui told the woman.

"You see what happens with that mosque. I told you this would happen," she said fiercely.

"You told me nothing! *Escoot!* Shut up! Go inside and keep the baby quiet!" he snapped.

"I told you, but you would not listen," she said, and went into the next room and closed the door behind her.

"The Carabinieri don't come in the middle of the night. Who are you?" Badoui asked.

"You know this man?" Scorpion asked, showing Badoui the photograph of the Palestinian on his cell phone. Badoui pretended not to look at it and didn't say anything. "I can see that you have seen him before."

"I don't know him. I told the *guardia*."

"You lied to the *guardia*. Don't be afraid of this man. He's dead."

"I'm not afraid. I don't know him. Now get out. I have to go to work in the morning."

"Does not the Sura, the Cow, say: 'Be steadfast in prayer; practice regular charity; and bow down your heads with those who bow down,'" Scorpion said, quoting from the Qu'ran. "Yet you haven't been to *salat* at the mosque in a month. What happened a month ago? It was this man, wasn't it?" He tapped Hassani's face on the cell phone screen.

"No, it wasn't," Badoui said in a strangled voice.

"What happened a month ago?"

"Nothing. My wife, she doesn't like that mosque."

"Why not? Should we call her in?"

"Leave her out of this," Badoui said.

"He wanted *shaheedin* to commit terrorism," Scorpion said, tapping the cell phone, "and you didn't want to. Isn't that right? He warned you to tell no one or he'd kill you. Did he threaten your family as well?"

"I don't want any part of this."

"You won't be. I promise. And I will keep my word, as is the *hadith* of the Prophet, *rasul sallahu alayhi wassalam*, peace be upon him, 'The Prophet ordered us to help others to fulfill oaths.' What did you see? Did he kill someone?"

Badoui stared at him, his eyes wide.

"You saw it, didn't you?"

Badoui nodded. "I saw him kill two men. One was only a boy. It meant nothing to him, like swatting a fly. He let me go and told me never to come back and to say nothing."

"You were afraid. I understand. This was at the warehouse, wasn't it? Did you ever go back?"

Badoui hesitated, then said, "No."

"You went back, didn't you?" Scorpion asked. Badoui didn't say anything. Scorpion took out money and counted out ten hundred-euro notes and put them on the coffee table.

"What's that?" Badoui asked.

"I want to help you, *min fadlak*, please. You have a baby. Keep the money. No one will know. In a minute I'll go and you will never see me again. What happened?"

Badoui didn't answer. He looked at the money and at Scorpion. Then he took the money. "My wife," he said. "She is a friend of the wife of Jamal, one of those who was with this man. We called the man 'Mejdan.' Jamal hadn't come home or called in days and she was worried. My wife was pestering me, as she does, talking about how maybe Jamal had a woman and was thinking of divorce. She was making me crazy, so I took an hour away from work and went to the warehouse last week. It was very strange."

"What did you see?"

"Jamal was there with Hicham, another of the group. He is a sanitation worker. They were with a woman and they had a metal coffin. I thought it was to get rid of the body of one of the men Mejdan killed."

Scorpion sat up. An aluminum coffin could be

used to transport a uranium bomb. It would be perfect to house the gun mechanism that Professor Groesbeck had described to him in Utrecht. As for the woman, even before he asked the question, he knew what Badoui would say.

"Describe the woman."

"Beautiful, like a supermodel. She was wearing a suit with a skirt. It looked expensive."

"Was she an Arab?"

"Yes. Her hair was blond, but she was an Arab. If you saw her, believe me, you would remember her." I believe you, Scorpion thought. I can't get her out of my mind. The only change was that Najla had dyed her hair blond.

"Did they say anything?"

"They were startled when they saw me. I told Jamal to call or go see his wife because my wife was driving me crazy, and they laughed. I left quickly. I don't think they wanted me there."

"No, of course," Scorpion said, getting up. "*Shokran* and don't be afraid. Mejdan is dead. He was one of those killed in Rome. I'm sure you've seen it on the television. As for my visit tonight, this conversation never happened. I was never here."

"Tell that to my wife," Badoui said, walking Scorpion to the door.

In the taxi back to his hotel Scorpion called the Carabinieri lieutenant, Giorgio. He told Giorgio what he needed and to call him when they had something.

In the morning, after working out and cleaning up, he was having breakfast in the hotel, near a window overlooking the red-tiled roofs and the imposing spire of the Mole, the city's landmark, when Giorgio called.

"*È* Giorgio. You must to come at once."

"Where are you?" Scorpion asked.

"The airport."

"I'm on my way," Scorpion said. Within an hour he was sitting with Giorgio and two of his men, looking at videos from airport security cameras on a closed circuit monitor.

"We do as you suggest," Giorgio said. "We get the videos of the woman from the German television. We take into account what you said, that she become a blond," he explained as they sped through a video, people moving in a blur till one of the Carabinieri said something and they slowed it down.

Scorpion studied the screen intently. He watched people standing in lines and going by and then saw her at the Lufthansa ticket counter, only as Badoui had said, she was a long-haired blonde, and he wasn't sure it was her. Then she turned and headed toward the security check, and as soon as he saw her face, he was certain. It was Najla.

"The video is from three nights ago," Giorgio said. "She was taking a Lufthansa flight to Frankfurt, traveling on a German passport in the name of 'Brynna Escher.'"

"Was Frankfurt the final destination?" Scorpion asked, keeping his voice calm, trying to ignore what the sight of her stirred up in him.

Giorgio shook his head. "In transit. Frankfurt to Saint Petersburg, and she wasn't alone."

"Oh?"

"She was traveling with a body. Claimed it was her brother, Pyotr. Had all the correct paperwork. They X-ray it of course. There was definitely a body inside. Have no idea who. Nobody open it. People don't like to disturb coffins."

"Did they scan it for radiation?"

"No. You think it have—" Scorpion pulled him aside, looking at the other two Carabinieri, before Giorgio could say more.

"Whatever you're thinking, stop," he whispered. "Say nothing to no one except Moretti. No one else, *capisce?*"

"You go to Saint Petersburg?" Giorgio whispered back. Scorpion nodded. "I wish I could go with you."

"*Grazie—a tutti,*" Scorpion said to all of them.

He went to the Lufthansa counter and booked the next flight via Frankfurt to Saint Petersburg. What the hell was going on? he wondered, waiting for his flight. It made no sense. He didn't need the ship, the *Shiraz Se*, to see this thing had Iranian fingerprints all over it. Someone with very deep pockets had spent a lot of money to fund the Palestinian's operation. Just the cost of the enriched uranium could have cost millions. So of all the places in the world, why would the Islamic Resistance, which, like the rest of Hezbollah, had to be funded by Iran, want to attack the Russians, their primary supplier for nuclear material, technology, and missiles? He had the sense he'd had much earlier in the mission, of being in the middle of a battle while in a fog, not knowing who or where the different opponents were or even what game they were playing. The only thing he knew was that Najla was in Saint Petersburg, and for a moment he could almost feel her body next to his, as though back in that hotel room in Amsterdam.

He was sitting in the transit lounge in Frankfurt when the text message came in. He didn't recognize the phone number it came from, but it was a scrambled text so he knew it was Rabinowich using the Vigenère code. He drew a Vigenère Square on a piece of paper he got from the lounge bartender and it didn't take long to unscramble the text. After decryption, it read in clear text: *gondolashirazsestpeteonetwoimam*. "Gondola" meant Venice, so the message was urgent. The Iranian ship, the *Shiraz Se*, was in Saint Petersburg, *stpete*, and again he wondered why on earth Iran would want to attack Russia. It was crazy. The answer had to be the last thing Rabinowich had sent, because *onetwoimam* was another matter, and it was apocalyptic.

The "one-two" or the "Twelfth Imam," was Muhammad al-Mahdi, the "Mahdi," or Messiah. According to the Shi'a Muslims, he was born in 869 AD and supposedly never died. When he comes out of hiding, he's supposed to wield the Sword of God and kill the unbelievers on Judgment Day. There were many among the top leadership in Tehran who were "Twelvers," as believers in the Twelfth Imam were called, and the Iranian government had even built special new boulevards in Tehran and in the holy city of Qom for the Mahdi to enter the city. Still, he wondered if Rabinowich had lost it, because it made no sense. Unless he was suggesting that somehow blowing up Saint Petersburg was to fulfill the prophecy.

Then it hit him. Saint Petersburg was Russia's main port. It was where the Iranian ship came in, but that didn't mean it was the final destination. What about Moscow? What would happen if they smuggled the bomb from Saint Petersburg to Moscow?

Russia was a top-down society. Always had been. If the head were decapitated, what was left might retaliate against the U.S. or Europe, unless the Russians knew it was the Iranians. They certainly wouldn't believe anything the Americans would say. It was insane, but those conditions would exactly fulfill the Twelfth Imam prophecy. And even if it didn't, there would be a free-for-all in the Ekaterinburg oblast. Whoever had guns and money could get anything they wanted, including the nuclear weapons and missiles. It would be a game changer. Except it was crazy, he thought. Even most Shi'ites didn't believe the Twelfth Imam was on his way. Except he could almost hear Rabinowich saying, "Sure, it's wacky, but remember, a lot of otherwise perfectly rational people believe Jesus is coming back any day now too."

On the airport lounge TV, the German news announcer was talking about terrorist actions in the United States. The two killed in New York. No mention of bioweapons. In Chicago, a Pakistani college student had been taken into custody. It was suspected that an explosion in Los Angeles was related to a terrorist group linked to al-Qaida. After all he had supplied, alerting the NSA to the al Jabbar code, how in hell could an explosion have happened in L.A.?

Watching the German TV news made him think with a pang of Najla, and he returned to the main question: Who was she working for? For Harris on an op that Harris didn't want him to know about, or for the Iranians? And why?

Whatever was going on, the answer was in Saint Petersburg.

 **CHAPTER TWENTY-EIGHT**

Saint Petersburg, Russia

The prisoner's hands were bound and chained to a beam from which he hung naked, like a side of beef, his toes dangling above the cell floor. His head hung loosely from his neck, the face bruised and swollen, and there were red marks on his torso where he had been beaten. The two interrogators, hefty FSB types, attached electrodes to his genitals. One of the interrogators sat down and turned a dial, and the man screamed, his body and bound feet jerking wildly until the electricity stopped and the other interrogator went over and slapped him in the face and asked him something.

Watching it through one-way, soundproof glass, Scorpion said, "We've found these methods are iffy in the way of real information, and that's even before it leaks and the media and the politicians go crazy."

Ivanov shrugged. "He's Chechen. Of the Daik-hoi *teip*. They're tough, these Chechens. To them, a beating is like how you say hello. He won't tell us anything. We think he's from a cell of SPIR, the Chechen terrorist group. This," gesturing at the

Chechen writhing and crying out as the current ravaged his privates, "is just for show so he thinks he's resisted us. Later we give him a shot. We tell him it's a truth drug, but it's really just a barbiturate. Once he's unconscious, we endoscopically insert a tiny tracking transmitter and attach it to the inside of his stomach. In the morning, when he wakes up, we let him go. He doesn't know we've done anything and we don't have to put surveillance on him or anything. The bug is GPS-based. We can track exactly where he is every second on a laptop computer. Over the course of a week or two he will lead us to his associates, and when we're ready, we pick them all up."

"I could use one of those," Scorpion said.

"*Ladno.*" Sure. "I'll see that you get it before you leave. Just don't use it on one of my people."

"Tell your people to stay the hell out of my way."

"*Izvinitye*, but you aroused our curiosity. Come," Ivanov said, leading him away from the one-way glass. They walked down a concrete corridor to a steel prison door. Ivanov tapped on the thick door glass and a guard opened it and they stepped into a tiled corridor. They climbed a steel staircase and Ivanov led him to an office with a window that looked out over the Neva River. It was a cool, gray day. Dark clouds were bundled over the buildings along the river, the water dark as the clouds. Ivanov sat down behind the desk wearing the well-tailored suit of a senior apparatchik in the New Russia. He had cold intelligent eyes behind steel-rimmed glasses, his hair iron-gray, and he looked fit for a man in his sixties.

"I'm borrowing this office while I'm in Saint Petersburg. *Pozhalsta*," please, he said, gesturing for Scorpion to sit down as an aide came in and put a bottle of vodka and two glasses on the desk. Ivanov filled both glasses to the brim. "This is Stolichnaya Elit. The best. The other Stolichnayas are *govno* shit. *Na sdarovy*," he toasted, raising his glass.

"*Budem zdorovy*," Scorpion toasted back. "I'm flattered at the attention."

This wasn't the reception he'd expected when they picked him up outside the Astoria Hotel, the black Mercedes sedan swerving to cut off the taxi he just got into, the four tough-looking types who surrounded the taxi, showing him and the driver their guns. He'd gotten into the backseat, sandwiched between two beefy men with the universal look of cops, without any idea who they were or how they'd ID'd him. At first he wasn't sure if they were FSB or Russian mafia. When he saw the grim red brick prison, he'd expected to be treated more like the poor Chechen bastard whose gonads were being used to complete an electrical circuit. It never occurred to him that Checkmate, Vladimir Ivanov himself, would have come all the way from Moscow just to see him.

"You are too modest, Scorpion. We heard about the Palestinian. My congratulations. As I told your Mr. Harris, we have an interest in this matter."

"He's not my *Gospodin* Harris."

"So. That is interesting," Ivanov said, studying him intently. "But I don't believe you as a double. That would take more than electrodes on your testicles to convince me. I understand New York, but why did the Palestinian also choose Rome?"

"The EU Conference and the Israelis. Cradle of Western civilization. The Vatican, home of Christianity. Take your pick. Maybe they don't like pasta."

"Maybe they don't. So the operation is over. Backs are slapped, champagne corks are popped, politicians and senior officials like myself who had nothing to do with it take the credit. As Voltaire says, all is for the best in this best of all possible worlds. So what is the Scorpion doing in Saint Petersburg?"

"How'd you find me?"

"You're concerned there's a mole in the Company? You wouldn't expect the truth from me on something like that?"

"I wouldn't expect the truth from you on anything," Scorpion said, suspecting Ivanov was just fishing with his talk of a mole. The only people on earth who knew he was coming to Russia were him, the Italians, and Rabinowich. It could have been Moretti or one of the Carabinieri, but he didn't think so, and he knew Dave wouldn't have betrayed him. How'd they find him?

"Can't you guess?" Ivanov teased.

It had to be something obvious, Scorpion thought. To get a Russian visa, he'd provided a photograph, and as they required a local address in Saint Petersburg, he'd made reservations at the Astoria Hotel in the center of town, so if they knew who he was, it would have been easy for them to pick him up. But how did they know who he was and what he looked like? Who could have seen him and taken a photograph without him knowing? Unbidden, an image floated up of a man in shorts and a gaudy shirt watering flowers in a rented villa. Harris! That son of a bitch! Either Harris had sold him out or the safe house in Castelnuovo wasn't safe.

"You were looking for me. You had a picture of me from Italy and you had software matching it to my visa photograph, probably matching visas from every Russian embassy and consulate in Europe. You went to a lot of trouble," Scorpion said, putting down the glass of vodka. He'd only sipped it and it had already started to go to his head. Like Ivanov himself, it was smooth as silk.

"Atlichna!" Bravo! "I wish you were a double. *Budem.*" Ivanov raised his glass to Scorpion and drank. "Except, I owe you from Arabia. You killed several of my men. By rights, I should put a bullet in your head," he said, opening a drawer and placing a gun on the desk.

"Why don't you?" Scorpion said, measuring distances and moving his foot back under him so he could spring out of the chair.

"Because I don't know why you are here in Saint Petersburg. There is also the matter of the missing twenty-one kilos of U-235."

"No one told you? Not Harris? Not your moles in the AISE and the Italian government? No one?"

Ivanov shook his head.

"It wasn't there," Scorpion said. "It was smuggled into Italy through Genoa on a Ukrainian ship, the *Zaina*, but it wasn't in the truck they were planning to blow up the Palazzo delle Finanze with. Harris says the talk about uranium was disinformation from you."

"It wasn't," Ivanov said, his eyes icy behind the steel-rimmed glasses.

"I know. There were signature traces of U-235 radiation in the hold of the *Zaina* and in a warehouse in Turin used by the Palestinian. The U-235 was brought into Italy, but it isn't there now."

"Where is it?"

For a moment neither man spoke.

Ivanov leaned forward, his arms on the desk. "You think the uranium is in Saint Petersburg? Should I be worried?"

"Yes."

Ivanov drummed his fingers on the desk. "Then I can't put a bullet in your head, can I? Maybe I should have them work you over and implant a bug in you like the Chechen?"

"You don't want to do that—and I don't think we have the time," Scorpion said, glancing at the window. The sky had grown darker. It was going to rain any minute.

"It seems for once we may be on the same side, Amerikanets," Ivanov said, taking another sip of vodka and refilling both their glasses from the bottle. "Perhaps we can help each other."

"You can help me by staying out of my way. No surveillance. I can't have something blown because someone spots one of your *mudaki* where he shouldn't be."

"What are you looking for?"

"A woman."

"Beautiful?"

"Very."

"There is no shortage of beautiful women in Saint Petersburg." Ivanov smiled wryly.

"This one's not from Saint Petersburg."

"You should let us help you find her. We could do it quickly, just as we found you."

"And the moment you do, perhaps a confederate of hers presses 'Send' on a cell phone. Then what?"

"And you are the only one who can get close to her. So we must trust you. That is not a condition I am comfortable with."

"Give me your cell number. If I need you, I'll call."

"So apart from the bug, there's nothing we can do?"

"I need a gun. I left mine in Italy to avoid problems on the plane."

"Take this. You know it?" Ivanov said, handing him the gun on the desk.

Scorpion nodded. "SR-1 Gyurza, special for the FSB. Eighteen rounds. Armor piercing," he said, pulling out the clip. "It's not loaded."

"I don't trust you that much. You are not called 'Scorpion' for nothing," Ivanov said, placing three clips of ammunition on the desk.

The coffee shop in the Vladimirsky Mall looked for all the world like a Russian Starbucks, even to the oval green sign. From behind a pillar on the second floor, Scorpion watched Prosviyenko sit down at an outer table. From a distance, Scorpion couldn't be sure, but he had to assume the reporter was wired. After twenty minutes Prosviyenko glanced at his watch, got up and started to walk to the mall exit. Scorpion waited to make sure he was alone, then bumped him from behind and said, "*Izvinitye*," and then in English as he passed, "Meet me in the men's toilet."

As soon as Prosviyenko entered the bathroom, Scorpion told him to empty his pockets and open his shirt. Scorpion remembered Koenig telling him that local reporters who knew their beats could be invaluable sources of information, but you had to be careful they didn't make you the story.

"Is this necessary?" Prosviyenko said, keeping his hands in his pockets. He was tall, fair-haired, with the jeans-and-tweed-jacket look of a young professor. A man came out of a stall and looked at the two men, then went to the basin to wash his hands.

"I need to know if you're wired."

"Suppose I don't want to open my shirt?"

"*Da svidaniya*," goodbye, Scorpion said, and started to walk out.

"You said you had a story," Prosviyenko called out.

"There's no story. I just want some information and I'm willing to pay for it. Say five thousand rubles for a few minutes, ten thousand, if it's worth my time." Scorpion wasn't sure how much local print reporters made, but it couldn't be that much.

"Ten thousand?" Prosviyenko said. He emptied his pockets and opened his shirt, letting Scorpion pat him down. The man washing his hands made a face as he watched them in the mirror, his expression suggesting he thought they were fairies, then he went out. "Do we do it here?"

"There's a pub on the third floor. Meet me," Scorpion said, and walked out. Five minutes later they were sitting opposite each other, Scorpion facing the concourse to make sure no one was paying attention to them.

"You mentioned money," Prosviyenko said after the waitress brought them bottles of Baltika beer.

"I did," Scorpion said, and reaching over to shake Prosviyenko's hand, pressed the folded-up rubles into his hand.

"What do you want to talk about?"

"I saw in the *Saint Petersburg Times* where you covered a story on corruption in the port, only you were careful not to name names."

Prosviyenko put down his bottle of Baltika. "You know what means '*zamochit*'?"

"You mean, to kill?"

"It means literally to piss on someone. Among the *blatnoi*—the criminals—it means, yes, to kill. Don't think I didn't get little anonymous phone calls even when I didn't name names. Here." He put the five thousand rubles on the table. "Take it back. You don't know who you are dealing with."

"Keep the money. I just need to ask you a question. You decide if you want to answer. You know the port?"

"Which one?"

"Ekateringofskiy Basin." There were three separate ports in the Saint Petersburg complex on the Gulf of Finland, west of the city. Scorpion had checked with the port before the FSB picked him up. The *Shiraz Se* had berthed at the Ekateringofskiy wharves and left port yesterday. With the hotel concierge's help, he'd hired a Russian temporary secretary and had her contact all the funeral homes in Saint Petersburg. There was nothing about a Pyotr Escher or a body having been brought in by anyone named Escher to any funeral home in Saint Petersburg during the past week. Nor were there any hotels or apartments for rent where a Brynna Escher had registered. He didn't tell the secretary about the name Kafoury, because he didn't want the FSB to get it. Both Najla and the coffin had disappeared as soon as she left Pulkovo Airport. The only lead he had left was the port. "Suppose I had some contraband, something serious I had to get through customs and out of the port. Who would I need to talk to?"

"Drugs? There are plenty of *fartsovchiki*. The city is full of them."

"Something bigger, more difficult. I need someone who can get things done, someone with real *blat*," meaning connections.

Prosviyenko leaned closer. "You mean the Tambov mafia? Listen, mister. This is not tourist Russia we're talking about. If you want to die, there are better ways to do it than to deal with Tambov."

"Who's the boss, the *pakhan*? Who do I need to talk to?"

"You mean Vasiliev? Everyone knows of Kiril Andreyevitch Vasiliev. You don't have to pay me for that, mister. But no one gets to see him, understand? If half the stories about him are true, believe me, you don't want to see him."

"Where would I find him or someone close to him?"

"Listen, this is crazy. What is this about?"

"I'm looking for someone. A woman who may have asked the same questions."

"You care for this woman?" Prosviyenko asked. Scorpion nodded, thinking that ironically enough, it was true. "Try the Dacha Club on the Nevsky Prospekt," he said. "Go after eleven. *Pozhalsta*, don't mention my name."

"*Spasiba*," thanks, Scorpion said, passing the additional five thousand rubles to him on the tabletop. The reporter put his hand on it and slipped it into his pocket.

"Don't thank me. Believe me, telling you about Vasiliev, I didn't do you any favors. So there's no story, just you looking for a woman who is a smuggler?"

Scorpion hesitated. "It's complicated."

"With women, what isn't?" Prosviyenko shrugged. "*Fsyevo kharoshiva!*" Good luck! "Listen, there are many beautiful women at the Dacha. Maybe you will see her, maybe someone else. Sooner or later everyone goes there."

The bar in the Astoria was leather and glass, subdued lights reflecting off drinks, expensive-looking women in designer dresses perched on stools, looking for business. One of them, a pretty blonde in her early twenties, kept looking over at Scorpion until finally he shook his head no and she shrugged and smiled as if to say, "You can't blame a girl for trying." He sent the waiter over to tell her he was buying her a drink but that he wasn't available. When the waiter told her, she raised her glass to him.

Cheers! she mouthed.

Za Vas! he mouthed back, raising his glass. He watched the rain streak the window in the gray twilight. It wasn't close enough to summer for the White Nights, when it barely got dark, but it was late enough in spring so that although it was ten in the evening, it was still light outside. He sat sipping Stolichnaya Elit over ice and tried to work it out. He badly needed to talk to Rabinowich.

In the taxi on his way to meet the secretary he had hired, he tried calling him, but the cell phone number had been disconnected. At the secretary's office he'd tried to track the transmission center from which Rabinowich's last call had originated, the one he got in Frankfurt, but the best he could do was to be told that the message had been sent from somewhere in the Middle East. Perhaps Rabinowich had gone to Egypt, where the operation started, or else Israel. If it was Israel, was the Mossad involved? That was assuming that he had gone to the Middle East instead of Hawaii, or hadn't just turned in the SIM on a disposable phone.

What was Rabinowich trying to tell him about the Twelfth Imam? If the Iranians wanted to attack through a proxy, why against Russia, Hezbollah and Iran's supplier? Unless Russia had reneged on a deal. Suppose the twenty-one kilos hadn't been stolen. What if it had been made to look stolen to cover Russia's dealings with Iran, and suppose it wasn't supposed to be twenty-one kilos of U-235 but fifty or a hundred kilos, or a plutonium plant or S-300 missiles, or God knew what, and the Russians had reneged on the deal? What then? The Iranian Revolutionary Guards were like any other strong-arm outfit. They couldn't allow themselves to be cheated. They'd have to send a message. That was a possibility, he thought. That Hassani was the diversion, Najla, the enforcer.

He started to signal the waiter for the check when it occurred to him that a bit of arm candy might be useful at the Dacha Club. He motioned to the blonde. She came over and sat down.

"I am hoping you change your mind, *milenky*, my dearest." She smiled, resting her hand on his thigh.

"What's your name?" he asked.

"Zhana. For you, I am Zhanochka. And you?"

"Damon," using his cover ID. "I'll give you five thousand rubles to come with me to the Dacha Club. We won't be leaving together. I have business there."

"Listen, Damonya, my sweetness, give me two hundred euros, I do anything you want, any place you want, any way you want," she said.

"This isn't love, Zhanochka *golubcha*. One fifty euros and you find your own way home from the Dacha," he said, taking her hand as he got up. They caught a taxi outside the hotel. It was still raining, the sky the strange tangerine-gray of the long northern twilight. Once inside the taxi, he gave her the money. She counted it and slipped it into her bra. The taxi turned onto the broad Nevsky Prospekt, the lights from the buildings reflected in the rain-slick street.

The taxi pulled up, and even in the rain there was a line of people standing outside the awning entrance to the Dacha Club. With fifty euros to the doorman and Zhanochka on his arm, they walked past the crowd waiting to get in and into the club, its sleek multistoried metal and glass interior pulsating to loud Russian rock music. Zhana began to sway to the music as she walked beside him to the bar. They pushed in between two men, one of whom was big and broad-shouldered, in an Italian leather jacket, with the look of someone in the underworld. A glance at the tattoo on his neck confirmed for Scorpion that he was of the Belaya Energia, a white supremacist gang. The man started to say something harshly, then stopped and smiled when he saw Zhana. They began talking rapidly in Russian, and she indicated Scorpion with a movement of her head.

"He wants me to go with him," she told Scorpion, nearly shouting to be heard over the noise of the crowd and the music.

"Tell him you're free to do what you want if he'll introduce me to someone," Scorpion shouted back.

The man laughed and gestured toward the tables near the bar, where there were at least a dozen good-looking women in tight low-cut dresses. "Take you pick, *druk*. No need introduce. Her I take," the man said in broken English, grabbing Zhana by the buttocks and pulling her tight against him. She tried to twist away but he held her tight. Scorpion reached over, pried the man's little finger off her and bent it back nearly to the point of breaking. With his other hand, he grabbed the man's other wrist in a Krav Maga hold so he couldn't use the knife he had pulled out, all of it done so quickly no one else noticed.

"The person I want to see is Vasiliev," Scorpion said.

The man immediately stopped. "You want see Kiril Andreyevitch?"

"*Da*," Scorpion said, letting him go. The man put the knife away and let Zhana loose. She turned and looked warily at Scorpion.

"He not see you. Is Tambov," the man said, holding the finger that Scorpion had twisted.

"Let's let him decide, *druk*. Tell him it's about a beautiful woman and a shipment in the port. We'll wait for you here."

The man whispered something to a friend with a badly scarred face, also in a leather jacket, who turned to look at Scorpion, his open shirt revealing the top of a *blatnoi* prison tattoo on his chest. Then the scar-faced man motioned to his friend and the two of them left, weaving their way through the crowd to a glass elevator. Scorpion watched them till Zhana tugged at his arm.

"We should go now, *pozhalsta*, my sweetness," she said urgently. "I give you back the money. We fuck like crazy. I don't like these *bandity*."

"You go. Keep the money," Scorpion said, kissing her cheek, his eyes on the crowd in the mirror.

"You sure? I mean it. I don't want no money. I like you," she said plaintively.

"I don't want you to get hurt. Go, *pozhalsta*," he said, giving her a little shove, never taking his eye off the crowd in the mirror.

"*Da svidaniya, golubchik*," she said, looking back at him, but this time Scorpion wasn't watching. Instead, he walked up to a striking blonde woman in a Burberry raincoat who had just come into the club. She was standing between two Middle Eastern–looking men in suits, their raincoats over their arms. He made the move as he pretended to squeeze by, deliberately bumping into her.

"Hello, Najla," he said as her eyes widened at the sight of him.

"Well, if it isn't Herr Crane," she said, just managing to recover. "Or is it Monsieur McDonald or whatever your name is these days?"

"McDonald'll do. I guess they were right. Everyone does come to the Dacha Club." He took her arm. The two men started to react, and at a nod from her they stopped. "He's an old friend," she said to them in Arabic.

"*Ismak*, who are you?" one of the men said in Arabic, with what Scorpion thought was a Farsi accent.

"*Emam mardar sag ast*," Scorpion said in Farsi. My name is your mother is a bitch. He added, "We have to talk," to Najla in English, pulling at her arm. They stood next to a glass wall sparkling with colored lights. The two men watched Scorpion with hard eyes, their hands in their jacket pockets.

"Talk about what? Marseilles?"

"Not here," he said, looking around.

"Why? Do you want to tie me up again, *liebling*?" Her dark eyes on him, and hearing her call him darling, even though he knew she meant it as little as the hooker, Zhana, sent a tiny electric spark through him.

"Maybe I should've." He peered at her. "I think I like you better as a brunette."

"So do I. It was supposed to help disguise me. It seems it didn't work." She smiled ruefully.

"You're hard to miss," he said.

"How did you find me?"

"Airport security camera in Turin."

"Of course. One always underestimates the Americans. But I should never underestimate you, should I?" she said, looking into his eyes.

"Don't play me, Najla. We need to talk—without your gorillas," he added, glancing at the two men. "Where can we go?"

"Just like a man! We find each other again, like a miracle, and all you want is to get a room."

"Or maybe a ship. You like ships, don't you? First the *Zaina*, then the *Shiraz Se*," he said, grabbing her arm. She looked stunned.

"I can't talk now," she said, trying to pull away.

"Not this time, Najla. Or is it Brynna?" Scorpion said, tightening his grip. He saw the two men start to move and he got ready for it. Najla stared at him, her eyes dark, unreadable. Then Scorpion felt a hard poke in his back.

"Go away," he said, not turning around. The poke came again.

"Vasiliev wants to see you," the scar-faced man said. His friend and another tough-looking man stood next to him.

"I'm busy," Scorpion said.

"Kiril Andreyevitch is not the kind of man you keep waiting," the scar-faced man said, showing Scorpion a gun in a shoulder holster. Scorpion looked at Najla. She leaned close, as if to kiss him.

"*Diese männer sind Iranier*," she said. These men are Iranians. "They are forcing me to go with them. We're meeting Chechens in the Summer Garden by the Coffee House in two hours. For God's sake, help me," she whispered in his ear in German. She looked into his eyes and kissed him full on the lips.

"Come," said one of the Iranians, pulling her away.

"*Mein Gott!*" she said, looking wistfully at Scorpion. "How did we land in the middle of this?"

"I'll see you," Scorpion said, watching her as she stood looking tiny between the two Iranians.

"Will you?" Najla said as the three Tambov gangsters closed around Scorpion.

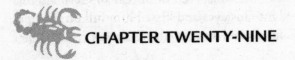

CHAPTER TWENTY-NINE

The Summer Garden, Saint Petersburg, Russia

Scorpion came up to street level from the Gostiny Dvor station. It was almost dark, a hint of light lingering on the horizon as he crossed Sadovaya Ulitsa. Although the rain had stopped, the air was wet and the street glistened under the streetlights. He caught a gypsy Lada taxi and took it through empty streets and across the bridge to the Summer Garden. The park was deserted, the wrought-iron gate dripping wet as he pushed it open. Inside, a plastic map on a post showed where the Coffee House was. The path through the overhanging trees was barely visible in the near darkness and there were a hundred places for an ambush. They had picked the perfect spot, he thought. Scorpion took out Ivanov's gun and clicked off the safety.

They would expect him to take the most direct path. Instead, he set off toward one side of the park. He would circle around and approach the Coffee House from the opposite Neva side of the park. Seeing the shadow of a figure cast by a streetlamp,

Scorpion instantly snapped into shooting position before he realized it was a Grecian statue on a pedestal beside the path. He studied the dim outlines of the trees. Realizing it was too dangerous to stay on the paved path, he stepped off and moved through the dark tangle of the trees, thick as a forest, the ground soft and carpeted with wet leaves underfoot. He thought about Najla and the feel of her lips and the closeness of her body when she kissed him at the club. Even now he still didn't know if she was playing him. Even if she was, he didn't know if he had it in him to kill her.

Vasiliev had been another surprise, he thought, pushing silently through the wet branches. They had taken him to the second floor of the club to a private elevator that required a key and a number code to enter. The elevator took them up two floors to a hallway carpeted with Persian rugs and lined with expensive oil paintings; landscapes by Levitan and portraits by Serov from the Soviet era. Two men in suits stood by a metal detector like those in an airport. He had emptied his pockets, including the gun, into a plastic tray.

"*Paspart*," one of the men said.

Scorpion handed him his McDonald passport, which the man pressed on a scanning machine. Then he went through the detector and one of the men pressed a button next to a steel door that looked like it had been designed to survive a bomb blast. They waited while someone inside checked the security camera and buzzed them in.

Scorpion walked in alone, the others taking their

places in the hallway beside the door as it closed behind him. Inside, Vasiliev sat behind a Louis XV desk in an office that could have been a library in an English manor house, if not for the bank of TV flat screens arrayed on one wall and a row of computers on a table. Vasiliev wore gold-rimmed glasses and an impeccable Armani suit. He looked like a banker, sitting with his left hand resting on the desk, until Scorpion realized that although lifelike, the hand was artificial. A tough-looking Russian with prison tattoos and a shaved head sat next to the wall behind Scorpion, holding a Beretta pistol with a silencer in his lap.

Vasiliev said something in Russian as Scorpion sat down.

"*Izvinitye*, I only speak a little Russian," Scorpion said.

"Mr. McDonald," Vasiliev said in good but heavily accented English, "you said something about moving an item through the port and a beautiful woman. It aroused my curiosity."

"It was meant to. I need to locate a shipment. The woman, I've already located."

"Ah." Vasiliev tilted his head. "Where is she?"

"Downstairs, or at least she was till your men pulled me away. What someone told me was right. Everyone comes to the Dacha Club."

"The Dacha is like the turnstile of the New Russia. Sooner or later everyone must pass through—and pay the toll," Vasiliev said. "She is beautiful, of course, this woman. Otherwise, you would hardly risk talking to me about it. Suppose I take her from you?"

"She can look out for herself," Scorpion said. "She is dangerous, even for the Tambov."

"I'm not so easy to kill," Vasiliev said, showing Scorpion his artificial hand. "Point her out," he added, gesturing at the bank of TV screens showing different interior and exterior views of the club. Scorpion looked but didn't see her or the Iranians.

"She's not there. She must have left."

"Or she doesn't exist. As for tracking a shipment, go to a freight agent. I'm a simple club owner. Why come to me?"

"Not this shipment."

"What's so special about this one? Guns? Drugs? You're wasting my time." Vasiliev said something in Russian and gestured dismissively with his good hand to the shaven-headed man, who stood up.

"Because this involves the FSB and state security," Scorpion said.

"We do business with the FSB every day. There is no problem." Vasiliev raised a finger to indicate to the shaven-headed man that he should wait a moment.

"An Iranian ship called the *Shiraz Se* just left the Ekateringofskiy port. She may have unloaded an atomic device. This is not business as usual and it involves more than the FSB."

"An atomic bomb, no less. Beautiful women who disappear. The CIA. You do weave stories, Mr. McDonald; no doubt not your real name. And how do I know this is true, instead of a rare form of insanity, baiting me this way?"

"Because you'll check me out with your contacts in the FSB and you'll kill me if I'm lying. Probably painfully," Scorpion said, standing up. He reached over, took a pen off Vasiliev's desk and wrote something on a slip of paper.

"You cannot imagine," Vasiliev said, looking at him as if memorizing his face.

"This is my cell phone number," Scorpion said, handing him the paper. "Call me when you have something. Oh, and tell your *byki* to give me back my gun. It has sentimental value. Checkmate himself gave it to me," he added as he went to the door.

"You don't seem the sentimental type."

"I'm not," Scorpion shot back as the door slid open.

Outside, coming to the edge of the line of trees, he spotted the Coffee House in a clearing next to a lake. It was a rectangular building that looked like a nobleman's summer house from the time of the tsars. The house was closed and the clearing empty; the only sound the water dripping from the trees. He saw something move near the edge of the clearing, and through the underbrush spotted the barely visible silhouette of a man hidden in the foliage, kneeling in a shooting position, rifle aimed at the clearing. Najla had been with two men, and there might well be more, he thought, studying the trees. His eyes scanned the same spot three times before he saw another man, well camouflaged and wearing night goggles, holding a pistol with a silencer. Fortunately, the man was looking at the clearing and not at him. They hadn't expected him to come from this direction. Although in this light he couldn't be sure, he thought he recognized the man with the night goggles as one of the Iranians at the club. He had to assume at least two, possibly more, in the ambush. And where was Najla? If he shot one of the gunmen, the other would take him out. He would have to take one out quietly and then try to get the other.

Scorpion put his pistol back in the holster at the small of his back. He crept forward on all fours toward the first man; silently, only his fingers and toes touching the soft ground. He could smell the wet earth. The man ahead of him was holding what looked like an AK-104, a compact version of the AK-47. The trick was how to come at him silently from behind without the man turning the rifle around.

He moved close enough to see the Iranian breathe, and then launched himself out of his crouch, the man already starting to turn around at the sound. Scorpion got him in a choke lock with his right hand while grabbing and breaking the man's trigger finger with a sudden twist with his left hand. The Iranian gasped, the sound choked off by the choke hold, as Scorpion did the Krav Maga wrist lock to twist the rifle away. The Iranian countered by smashing back with his elbow at Scorpion's head, causing him to drop the choke hold, switching into a wrist lock to force the Iranian to his knees. The man cried out in pain, "Son of a bitch!" in English.

Scorpion wondered what was going on as he stepped over the Iranian and bent his left leg at the knee, catching the man, who was struggling furiously, in a leg choke hold to his neck. Kneeling down, he applied the choke pressure with his weight through the crook of his knee.

"Are you American?" Scorpion asked. He could feel the man try to nod yes and was about to release him when he heard the soft *pfffft* of silenced shots. The man sagged, suddenly dead weight. Scorpion dived behind his body as silenced bullets thunked into the man's body and the tree he'd been hiding behind. He grabbed the AK-104 and was about to shout "Don't shoot!" when automatic weapon fire with the unmistakable staccato sound of AK-47s opened on his position from two different directions. What the hell? he wondered again as he rolled behind a tree and came to his feet, hidden behind it. It sounded like one of the shooters was moving, getting closer. He had to get out of here.

He began running in a zigzag pattern, using the trees for cover. A bullet ripped a spray of wood from a tree next to his leg as he passed it. Still running, he pointed the AK-104 back and fired an automatic three-shot burst, then leaped to the side to avoid a burst of return fire at the spot from where he'd fired. Panting, he broke out of the trees and onto a path. Knowing he couldn't stay in the open for more than a few seconds, he threw himself behind a statue of a female nude in a gap in a hedge beside the path. He rolled into a prone firing position with the AK-104, panting for breath and struggling to hold the rifle still. A shadow emerged from behind a tree and he fired a full burst at it. The shadow went down, and before it hit the ground Scorpion was up and running again. He ran out the park gate and across the street bridge over the canal, then down a side street, where he broke into a parked car and jump-started it. He drove around the block to make sure they weren't on his tail yet and abandoned the car on a street near the Metro station, leaving the rifle in the trunk.

He descended what seemed an endless escalator, looking back up behind him all the way down, his hand near his gun in the holster at the small of his back. The city of Saint Petersburg is built on swampland, and because of it, the subway is the deepest in the world—some of the stations were used as bomb shelters during World War Two, when the besieged city was called Leningrad—and it seemed forever till the escalator reached the platform, where he watched the entrance. If anyone came from the park, it was essential he get a shot off first. He waited, every nerve straining, but only an old tired-looking babushka came. At last a train pulled in. Scorpion waited till the few people who were on the platform boarded. As it pulled out again, he walked to the underground passageway to the Nevsky Prospekt station and took the long escalator back up to the street.

He walked back to his hotel and went back up to his room, washed his hands and face, looked at himself in the mirror and tried to understand what had just happened. He wondered if he'd imagined the dead Iranian saying "Son of a bitch" in English, because if he had heard it, nothing made any sense. But he knew he had, and that meant everything he thought he understood about the mission was wrong.

He went to his laptop computer and turned it on. The software Ivanov had given him and the GPS tracking were working perfectly, as though he were living in a rational universe. It was superimposed on a street map of the city. The transmitter he had slipped into Najla's Burberry pocket when he bumped into her at the club showed that she was stationary at a location in the Narvskaya area near the port complex in the western part of the city.

After changing his clothes and checking his gun, Scorpion caught a taxi outside the hotel. Najla had set him up, he decided as the taxi drove through the city, the sky already starting to lighten in the east with the predawn. He no longer had a choice. He would get to the bottom of things or he would have to kill her.

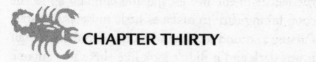 **CHAPTER THIRTY**

Narvskaya, Saint Petersburg, Russia

The warehouse was a gray building that seemed to blend into the gray dawn sky. It was near the port, with its smell of the sea and diesel fuel and machinery. There were no lights in any of the windows, only exterior lights, and Scorpion wondered if he had gotten lucky and they were all asleep. There were security alarms and cameras over the main and side doors, but they were old-fashioned single-circuit setups that shouldn't present any problems.

Keeping to the shadows across the street from the warehouse, he walked around the building. Apart from the main door and the loading dock, there was a side entrance and, in back, a fire escape that led down from the roof with no security cameras. He decided to go in that way. He looked toward the port and then down the empty street toward Prospekt Stachek, where he'd had the taxi drop him off. The drizzle had stopped and there was a thin ribbon of blue on the horizon. It was going to be a nice day. He wondered if he would live to see it.

Checking around one last time, he pulled down the ladder of the fire escape and climbed up to the roof, taking care to make as little noise as possible. Passing a second story window, he peered inside, but it was dark and it didn't look like there was anyone about. He went up on the roof and looked around 360 degrees. From up there he could see the gantry cranes of the port and the Gulf of Finland. It reminded him of Karachi, where he had started this mission. It seemed a thousand years ago. Back then, there hadn't been anyone he cared about. Now there was, and he was on his way to kill her.

Scorpion tried the metal roof door, but it was locked. He used his universal key with a tap of his gun to open it. The door was rusty and hard to move. It creaked as he forced it open, and he froze at the sound, listening intently, his gun ready. He thought he heard something but wasn't sure. He tiptoed carefully down iron stairs to an open walkway high above the main floor of the warehouse, found a steel column to hide behind and peeked down.

Most of the main floor was still in shadow, but there was a light at one end, and then someone turned on a television. A man said something and another man answered and the first man laughed. That section of the warehouse floor looked like a dormitory with a half-dozen bunks. He heard the sound of a toilet flushing. The sound gave him cover to move silently along the walkway toward an office by the far wall. Looking around one last time, he opened the office door.

The office had been converted into a kind of

bedroom, and there was no need to wake her. He could see the burning tip of a cigarette glowing in the darkness. Keeping his eyes on her, he locked the door behind him, pulled down the window shade and turned on a lamp. She was sitting up in bed in a black slip, her eyes on him.

"Have you come to kill me?" she asked.

He leaned over and slapped her across the face as hard as he could, sending the cigarette flying.

"You'll start a fire," she said.

"They say hell's a hot place. Get used to it," he replied, and sat on the bed.

"I know. I lied about the Summer Garden," she said, holding her hand to her cheek, the marks of his fingers on her skin.

"That doesn't count. I didn't believe you. It's the part about trying to have me killed that I resent."

"It's killing me. I don't know what's worse, having you dead or alive," she said, clutching at him, her eyes filling with tears.

"Stop it! Stop the play-acting, *inti sharmoota*, you whore," he said in Arabic, shoving her back against the wall. He put the muzzle of his gun against her forehead. "We're done playing. Where's the bomb?"

"It's not here," she said.

"You're lying," he said, slapping her again and pressing the muzzle of the gun against her forehead deep enough to leave an imprint. "Where's the fucking bomb?"

"I can't tell you," she cried, tears sliding down her cheeks.

"I will kill you. I don't want to, but I will," he said,

cocking the hammer. "Do you really want to kill a million people? Women, children? Is that who you really are?"

"Who I am?" she laughed, with a touch of hysteria. "Don't you understand? That's the whole point! I'm a Palestinian! Who am I? What am I? I don't belong! Don't you see? I don't belong anywhere. No family, no country, nothing! I wanted to belong to you, that's the horrible joke!" She laughed wildly. "To the enemy!"

"Keep your voice down," he said, putting his hand over her mouth. He put the gun to her head again and took his hand away. "I won't ask again. Where's the bomb?"

"You can't threaten me, *habibi, habib albi,* love of my heart," she said, touching the gun with her fingers as if to push it away. "You see, I die today no matter what. Both of us do."

Scorpion started to pull the trigger, looking into her dark shining eyes, then unable to stop himself, leaned over and kissed her, his hand to the back of her head. She kissed him back as if she knew it was the last thing she would ever do. Whatever happened, he knew he would never forget it.

"I've been wanting to do that since we met," he said.

"I know. I almost went crazy lying next to you in that room in Amsterdam." She put her hand to his cheek and looked into his eyes. "What do we do now?"

"Tell the truth. It's all we have left." He eased the hammer down and rested the gun on his thigh.

He glanced at the door. They would be coming, he knew, but for now there was time. "How did we come to this? Who are you?"

"I can't," she said, her eyes welling again with tears.

"You have to," he said.

"Let me have a cigarette," she said. He found her pack of cigarettes on the table next to her handbag and handed it to her. She lit it and inhaled deeply. "I've been Najla Kafoury for so long. My real name is Alia. When I told you I was from Lebanon, I told you the truth, *habib albi*, but not the whole truth. No one knows the whole truth, not even Allah."

"How old were you when you left Lebanon?"

"Five."

"What about your parents?"

"Dead, both of them on the same day. Do you really want to know?" looking at him while holding the cigarette, and he thought that in the brightening light creeping through the edges of the window shade, her hair covering part of the side of her face, that she had never looked so beautiful.

"This is all about Lebanon, isn't it?" he asked.

"You know about that, do you?" She smiled wryly. "You know everything and understand nothing," tapping the cigarette ash into a little dish by the bed. "You want to know who I am? That day made me who or what I am, only it wasn't what you think. Losing my parents. It was something else that happened that day. It began in the morning when Israeli tanks surrounded the camp."

"You were in the Sabra and Shatila camp in Beirut?"

"It wasn't the killing," she said. "In Lebanon, there was always killing, especially if you were a Palestinian. And it wasn't just the Israelis or the Maronites or the Druze. You had Palestinians killing Palestinians. If you disagreed with them, the PLO would kill you. We weren't citizens of Lebanon, we were refugees, even though we had lived there as long as most Lebanese. If you were a Palestinian you couldn't get a passport or even a job. Still, we lived. As a child I was happy there, playing in the narrow streets, running past the men working in makeshift shops in the street amidst the garbage and the dust. Everyone knew everyone on our street, even what you were cooking for dinner and my mother would comb my hair and call me 'Princess Alia' and tell me someday a prince would come to our little street and everyone would see I was a princess. And he would take me away and marry me. Even when the Israelis came and the PLO left, we felt we would live, but then somebody murdered Bashir Gemayel, the president of Lebanon. I didn't understand any of it, but my father, who was an educated man, even though he had no work and sometimes made money fixing auto parts, which he had taught himself to do, told us, 'You will see, they will blame the Palestinians. They will want their revenge,' and although I did not know it, he made a plan.

"The Israelis came with their tanks in the dark before dawn. That day, when the sun came, was burning hot. Maybe it's a trick of memory, but in my mind that was the hottest day in my life. The heat in our little apartment was stifling, the air so hot it felt like it was burning your skin even with every window open and a fan going, and when you breathed, you could feel it burning your lungs. I wanted to go outside and play, but my father said no one would go out to play that day. I looked out of our window at the dusty street, baking in the sun, but no one went outside. Then we heard the shooting.

"All that day we heard shooting and shouting, sometimes far away, sometimes closer. You could not make out the words they were saying, only the sounds, and I clung to my mother's skirt and would not leave her. My mother did not cook that day. We ate day-old bread and water from the sink, and Father made us fill up every bottle and basin with water, in case it stopped flowing. I don't remember that day. All I remember was the heat and the shooting and the smell of gunpowder and garbage rotting in the sun.

"My father came into the apartment—I didn't even know he had gone out—and said, 'It's the Phalange.' He started to say something else, but my mother said, 'Not in front of the children,' looking at my brother and me. I wanted to go to the window to see the Phalangists, the Christians, whoever they were, because I had never seen one, but my mother kept me away from the window and I saw nothing. But the night, I remember.

"You never saw a night like that, *habib albi*. Here in the North you have White Nights, where the sun is up most of the night in summer, but that night was no night. The air was still hot from the day, and the sky was intensely bright from the flares the Israelis shot into the sky. So many flares, trailing light like lightning floating in the sky. It was like a football stadium lit up at night. The light cast sharp shadows into the room where we huddled on the floor, now and then hearing the crack of a rifle or the firing of a machine gun, and once, a terrible scream. I must've fallen asleep, because when I woke, my parents and my older brother were asleep on the floor, and for a moment I was afraid to touch them in case they were dead.

"I crept to the window and I saw the body of a man lying in the street below. He was just lying there as though he had gone to sleep. And then my parents got up, and when my mother turned on the water in the sink, there was no water. That day was just as hot as the day before, only now we could hear the sounds of jeeps and trucks and men shouting and more shooting, much more shooting, only it was getting closer. We were thirsty and hungry, but there was no more food. My mother couldn't cook and we drank the water from the bottles and the bowls my father had us fill the day before.

"My father made my brother and me hide in the closet. He told us to huddle down next to the panel in the wall he had put in. He told us not to come out, no matter what happened. I didn't want to get into the closet. It was hot and dark, with only cracks by the side of the door that let slivers of light through. It was too hot and I refused, but my father gave me that look he sometimes did, and my brother took my hand and we went in and sat on the closet floor and my father closed the door. I could hear the guns and the men and the trucks coming closer and I held tightly onto my brother's shirt in the dark. Then I heard sounds of shooting outside. It was very loud and very close, and there was shouting and then a woman screaming '*Ibni, ibni*, my son, my son,' over and over until I thought it would never stop.

"Then I heard men coming up the stairs and loud voices and screams and they were banging on our door. My heart was pounding so hard I thought it would come out of my chest. I couldn't help myself. I peeked through the crack and saw men dressed like soldiers come into the apartment. They started smashing everything and they grabbed my father and tied his hands with those plastic ties." She looked at Scorpion. "When you tied me up like that in Amsterdam, you have no idea what you did to me," she said softly, and lit another cigarette. "Do you know why they bothered to tie his hands? Because they wanted him to watch.

"Four of them grabbed my mother. At the time, I didn't understand what they were doing. I just thought they were pushing her, but when I was older, in Germany, it came back to me and I understood, one at a time, the others holding her down and laughing, and when the last one was zipping himself up, one of them took out a knife and carved a cross on her naked chest, the cross bar right across her breasts, the cut dripping blood like Christ himself. My mother was begging and screaming, and my father was yelling, 'Don't beg, *min fadlik*, don't beg!' and then they shot her, and carved a cross on my father's chest with the same knife.

"My brother was tugging at my arm. I had to watch. I couldn't pull away from the crack by the side of the door. But he pulled me back and pushed me into the opening of the panel at the back of the closet, which led to the closet of the apartment next door. I heard them shooting in our apartment, very close and loud, and I'd never been so scared in my life. My brother just had time to follow me through the opening and close the panel as they opened the closet door and light came in.

"My brother and I stood in our neighbor, As-sayeda Sayegh's, apartment. My brother was ten and he was embarrassed because there was a big stain in front, where he had wet his pants, but he took my hand and pulled me away. I wanted to say something, but he put his fingers to my lips to stop me and we started to run. I don't know how we got out of the building. All I remember is that we ran out into our street and we saw the bodies of young men, at least twenty of them, lying along the wall, blood leaking from their heads. We ran and ran. I didn't know where we were going, hiding from the Christians as they went from street to street, and then we came to an open street and there was a crowd of people. The Christians were around them with guns and loading them into trucks. We stopped and tried to run the other way and two soldiers caught us.

"'Here's two more kids,' one of them shouted, and they pulled us by our hair and forced us to climb up into one of the trucks. There were only women and children in the trucks and some of the children were crying, but they kept loading the trucks. I was so scared I couldn't breathe. I thought they were going to take us somewhere and kill us. One woman asked, 'Where are they taking us?' and another said, 'Our men are dead, now they want us too,' and I knew I was about to die.

"When they had filled the line of trucks, they began to roll toward the gate of the camp. I wanted to ask my brother what was happening and what I should do, because he was everything to me then, but he shook his head and indicated that I should say nothing. He was sitting with his hands over his lap to cover the wet stain on his pants. The sun baked down on us. The sides of the truck were too hot to touch. The trucks moved through the dusty streets, and there were bodies on every block. If bodies were in the way, the trucks rolled over them. The bodies had begun to bloat in the sun and the stench was unbearable. I wanted to throw up, but I was so afraid I could barely breathe. We came to the entrance to the camp where I had lived all my life. I had never been outside before. There were Israeli tanks lined up outside and I thought, 'I am going to die now.' And then the thing happened that I told you about, the thing that changed who and what I am.

"Two trucks were in the front of our column. They were filled with Christian Phalangist soldiers. They stopped at the gate of the camp, and then an army jeep pulled up in front of them and a man got out. He walked in front of the trucks with all those soldiers and their guns and said to them in Arabic,

'No more killing. You have a half hour to get all your men out of the camp. It's finished.' He was a lone Israeli officer. He didn't even have a gun. And just like that, he stopped the massacre. Can you imagine? To have that power. To be able to decide life or death without even holding a gun. They could've stopped it at any time, but they chose to let it happen. They chose death. Do you understand? That's the Palestinian option. When given a choice, to choose death."

"How'd you get to Germany?" Scorpion asked.

"A German refugee organization brought my brother and me to Germany. They had to split us up. I cried and clung screaming to my brother. I didn't want to go. My new family in Germany was Lebanese. They wanted me to change my name. My brother told me to do it, that it would be safer. You see, he was already planning."

"You mean his revenge."

"No, not revenge. Power! The power of that Israeli who didn't even have to carry a gun. Even at that young age, my brother knew what he had become, what we had both become," she said, finishing her cigarette and stubbing it out.

"Why Russia? Why Saint Petersburg?"

She shrugged. "They reneged on a deal, or so I was told."

"With the Iranians?"

"You know too much. I was right to follow you in Hamburg. I knew you were dangerous."

"When you were split up, your brother was sent to Cologne?"

"How did you—" she looked at him sharply.

"His name was Bassam Hassani. Hassani was your family name in Beirut."

"Was?" she said, her breasts rising and falling rapidly with her shallow breathing.

"He was one of the terrorists killed in Rome."

She got up off the bed, went to the window and raised the shade. The sun was up and he could see the building across the street. She was a silhouette against the bright light.

"I must look a mess," she said, and went to the table and picked up her handbag. Her hands were shaking. "Did you kill him?" she asked, not looking at him.

"Yes," he said.

She screamed at the top of her lungs. It was like nothing human. Still screaming, she began tearing through her purse and then picked up her cell phone. She was so fast, she had caught Scorpion by surprise. He didn't have time to reach her before she sent the call.

He raised his gun and fired, the bullet hitting her in the head and spraying out blood and fragments of brain matter as she crumpled to the floor. He grabbed the cell phone out of her hand, opened it and pulled the SIM card out. She lay exposed on the floor, her slip hiked up on her hips, blood leaking from her head. She looked helpless, her face spotted with blood, still beautiful. They had to have heard, there was no more time, he thought. He pulled her slip down so she was covered.

Suddenly, there was shouting and the rattle of

automatic weapons down on the main floor of the warehouse. A savage firefight erupted and his ears rang with the sound of shattering glass and bullets flying everywhere. He heard bursts of firing and the pounding of feet coming closer on the walkway and toward him. He put his gun down and stood up, moving to the side, so if they shot through the door there was a chance they wouldn't hit him. He raised his hands over his head as a blast of bullets tore holes through the door.

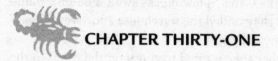 **CHAPTER THIRTY-ONE**

New York, United States

"Where was the bug?" Rabinowich asked. They were sitting in a midtown delicatessen just off Lexington Avenue. Periodically, Scorpion glanced toward the front of the deli, but he didn't expect to see any watchers. To anyone who might be looking, they were just two men having a late business lunch.

"In the gun, the SR-1 Gyurza that Checkmate gave me. It was inside the handle. After he let me go, I figured he would keep tabs on me. I checked all my clothes, but I didn't have time to take the gun apart. Then I figured either he hadn't planted one on me while I was in detention, or if they had, I was better off with the bug, because if I disabled it, he'd know and he might have his FSB *byki* pick me up again and I'd never get to Najla," her name hitting him in the pit of his stomach like a punch.

"What about the bomb?" Rabinowich said, chewing and putting down his double-decker corned beef and pastrami on rye sandwich. "Instant heart attack," he called it.

"Hidden under a load of coal on a barge on the Fontanka Canal, a few blocks away. The FSB found it after they raided the warehouse and arrested me."

"Why a barge?"

"Either they wanted to run it on the canal to the middle of town, say to the Nevsky Prospekt, to maximize the number of casualties, or if you were right about the Twelfth Imam and it being some kind of Iranian doomsday scenario, they could run it down the Neva and Svir Rivers to the Volga-Baltic Waterway and take out Moscow. Nobody inspects coal barges on the canals."

"Was the device workable?" Rabinowich asked, glancing around to make sure no one heard him.

Scorpion nodded. "He was brilliant, Hassani. Fifty-one kilos at ninety-two percent purity. Twenty-one from the *Zaina*, that we knew about, and thirty from the *Shiraz Se*. From what they said, he used the gun mechanism that Professor Groesbeck told me about. Think male-female. The conventional explosive shoots a male plug into a hollow U-235 cylinder. Hassani almost did it. Ivanov said, 'It is terrifying to think what one person on his own can do.'"

"They treat you all right?" Rabinowich asked, taking a gulp of his Guinness beer so he didn't have to look at Scorpion. In a way, it was bad form to ask. An operative picked up by a nonfriendly service was expected to be able to handle the torture. "They didn't rough you up too badly?"

"I'm a hero." Scorpion shrugged. "After I handed them the SIM from Najla's cell phone and they saw how close it had been, Ivanov told me, 'This makes us even for Arabia.' They even wanted to take me to Moscow so the Russian president himself could thank me personally, just like Italy. Now you answer a question for me. Who blew my cover so the FSB were able to pick me up? Was Harris just being a screw-up about the safe house in Castelnuovo or did he blow my cover on purpose to make sure once I'd taken the Palestinian out that I was out of the game?"

"You'll have to ask him. I really don't know," Rabinowich said, glancing up at the television over the deli counter.

Scorpion followed his glance. CNN was showing the arraignment of one of the terrorists picked up by the FBI, involved in what the announcer was calling "the recently uncovered plot."

"Fucking idiots," Rabinowich muttered. "Did anyone tell you what happened?"

"All Harris told me in Rome was that the mission was over. 'You're a hero. Now go screw yourself, you're done.'"

"He tried to get rid of me too. Then America would've just had good old Bob Harris to defend it. Think about that. Fortunately, I still have a few friends left or I'd be manning the desk on Tibet or Uruguay or something else no one gives a shit about," Rabinowich said, nibbling a bite of potato salad. "As for rounding up Hassani's recruits, the FBI almost blew it." He shook his head. "The first one was easy. The Kabir woman's brother, Zahid Kabir. Even the Keystone Kops were able to figure out he might be involved.

"Then, even though they'd been given the cell phone number of the Pakistani college student in Marquette Park in Chicago, with the al Jabbar code and everything, they just managed to grab this dude, literally as he was on his way to the El near Midway Airport, wearing a vest filled with HMTD. He was going to blow himself up when the train got to the Loop.

"But L.A. was the worst. This Iraqi guy, he'd been a doctor in Iraq but couldn't get licensed here, drove a rental truck loaded with fertilizer and diesel into the parking structure of Beit Israel Hospital. The Iraqi panics at the valet parking and leaves the truck sitting there while he runs through the reception area and disappears. The valet, a Mexican, gets suspicious, checks the back of the truck, figures it out, and completely on his own—'cause his boss is yelling at him to just park the damn truck—drives it out of the parking structure and down San Vicente Boulevard, where it blows a fifty-foot deep crater in the pavement.

"Luckily it was early in the morning or God knows how many would've been killed. As it was, there were four badly injured; no one was killed except the Mexican. There was enough explosive in the truck to bring the entire building down. Thousands killed, a major medical institution, one of the best in the country, destroyed. Jewish, of course. That's why it was the target, though you'd think someone might've figured that out. You want to hear the punch line?"

"Sure."

"This is L.A. The Mexican was an illegal. Him

and his whole family. Now he's dead, and as a reward for saving thousands of people and billions of dollars, his wife and kids are being deported back to Mexico. These idiots can't stop terrorists, but that they know how to do," he said, raising his beer in a mock toast, then drinking.

"What about the Mossad? Where were they in all this?" Scorpion asked.

"You know, you're not unintelligent. I enjoy our little chats. What makes you think they're involved?"

"For Israel, Iran is an existential issue. They've got Iran on the brain. Also, when I called the contact number in Hamburg, I was told 'M' was *sameach*. Hebrew for 'happy' about what I'd sent from Damascus, so I knew you and Harris were sharing the wealth with the Mossad. But most of all, Harandi, the guy in the Hamburg Islamic Masjid, was a Mossad sleeper, probably an Iranian Jew. Hamburg was the communications hub for Al-Muqawama al-Islamiyya, especially between Damascus and Utrecht, so Harandi was in a perfect position to misdirect Najla and her brother. Except peripherally, this was never about stopping the Palestinian. So what *is* this about, Dave?"

"No one's talking," Rabinowich said.

"I think I killed two Americans, CIA operatives, in the Summer Garden."

"I don't know anything about it," Rabinowich whispered, looking nervously around the deli. "Whatever this was, it's not just you. If you're right, it could destroy the Company. All of us."

"What were they doing there?"

"There's only one person who can answer you, and he never tells the truth."

"He will this time," Scorpion said.

The fund-raiser was a black tie affair at the Peninsula Hotel on Fifth Avenue. The heavyweight guest list included party leaders and high-powered donors, who for a minimum donation of $100,000 had been guaranteed photo ops with the guests of honor, the U.S. Vice President and the Secretary of State. Security was heavy and all guests had to go through metal detectors before they were allowed into the ballroom. For Scorpion, getting an invitation wasn't difficult. All it took was a rented tuxedo and using a credit card to open the door lock and sneak into deluxe suites on an upper floor of the hotel. In the second one he entered, he found an invitation and a wallet on the desk. He pocketed the invitation and the man's driver's license, and after pausing at the bathroom door and listening to someone in the shower, he went down in the elevator to the ballroom. He showed the invitation and the ID to the security guards, went through the metal detector and walked in.

The ballroom was starting to fill with men in black ties and women in designer gowns. Waiters circulated with drinks and hors d'oeuvres, and the laughter and backslapping had officially gotten under way. It was a high-powered crowd. The value of the women's jewelry alone could have easily financed a third-world country, and Scorpion's hardest task was to avoid having his picture taken by one of a dozen photographers circulating around the room. He ditched the stolen invitation and ID in a potted palm tree and waited, gin and tonic in hand, near the bar.

He didn't have to wait long. He had just started across the floor when someone loudly announced, "Ladies and gentlemen, the Secretary of State and the Vice President of the United States." Everyone stood and applauded loudly as the two dignitaries entered the ballroom, giving Scorpion perfect cover as he stepped next to Bob Harris. He grabbed Harris's fingers and twisted it in a painful aikido hold.

"We need to talk, Bob."

"I'm busy," Harris said, grimacing at the pain.

"Now or so help me I'll say what I have to say to the Secretary of State in front of everyone. It's still early," Scorpion said. "There might even be time for it to make the late night news."

"You might want to reconsider. You don't want to burn any bridges," Harris said, his teeth gritted, nodding and smiling through the pain at someone.

"You mean like Castelnuovo," Scorpion said, tightening his grip and forcing a gasp from Harris. "I mean it. Come now or see it on TV."

"You don't want to do that. You'll destroy everything."

"Maybe I do. I'll bring down you, the Company, this whole damned administration if I have to. What's it to be, Bob? You know as well as I do, once it's out, it's out."

"Let my hand go. It hurts."

"You have no idea how much it pleases me to hear that."

"Where can we go?"

"Your suite. Now."

They wove between tables and made their way out past the security. Neither man spoke as they walked down the carpeted hallway and then went up in the elevator to the top floor. Harris opened the door to a large suite, luxuriously furnished, with a view overlooking Fifth Avenue.

"You do the taxpayers proud," Scorpion said, looking around. "Where's your gun?"

"I don't have one."

"Tell me where it is anyway."

"Over there," Harris said, indicating his attaché case on the bureau. Keeping an eye on him, Scorpion walked over, opened the case, took out a small Glock automatic and stuck it into his jacket pocket. Watched by Harris, he went around the room, checking for bugs and cameras. "How about a drink?" Harris said, going to the wet bar.

"What have you got?"

"Let me look. They've got a Glenlivet, eighteen years old."

"Old enough to be legal; on the rocks," Scorpion said, watching Harris to make sure he didn't pull anything from under the bar. Harris handed him the drink and sat on a striped sofa. Scorpion sat in an armchair facing him. The lights of the city framed Harris in the double window behind him. "What are we drinking to?"

"How about not bringing the temple down on everyone's head, in the interest of the United States?" Harris said.

"I killed three people in Saint Petersburg. I'm not sure what to do with that."

"You've killed lots of people. It's what you do."

"Not like this. Two of them were Americans and one was a woman who never had a chance in life, not since she was five."

"Then, to the Palestinian option," Harris said, raising his glass.

"Go to hell," Scorpion said and drank.

"That's good scotch," Harris said after drinking. "So you know about the Iranian Americans? That's the trouble with using you. You're too good. You're a sword that cuts both ways. I don't know who's more dangerous—you or Congress."

"What about the Mossad?"

"So you picked up on Harandi, the Mossad's mole in Hamburg?" Harris nodded. "Clever boy."

"Stop jerking me off, Bob. What was the mission? The real mission."

"If I tell you, it never leaves this room," Harris said. "If you're not willing to do that, you can kill me, but I won't tell you. You may not believe it, but I'm a patriot too."

Scorpion shook his head wryly. "You say I'm good. You're better. The only problem is that snake oil you're peddling is starting to stink the place up. You'll have to do better."

"Tell you what. After I tell you, you decide. Do what you think is right. After all, you've got the gun."

"They were Iranian Americans in the Summer Garden, weren't they?"

"The bread crumbs were Iranian. When Checkmate investigates, as I'm sure he's doing this very minute, the trail will lead to the MOIS and the Revolutionary Guards. That was critical."

"What was the mission? The real mission? Why the bomb in Saint Petersburg?"

"About eight months ago the Treasury Department's OTFI picked up an electronic transfer from an Iranian account in Frankfurt through Moscow to a numbered account at the UBS Bank in Zurich. Fifty billion rubles, about 1.6 billion dollars. This was not government-to-government. It was a private transaction, one individual to another, but we were able to confirm that the transfer had Russian involvement at the highest level at the Kremlin. The highest level," Harris repeated.

"Hell of a bribe," Scorpion nodded.

"That's what we thought. Then came the Budawi assassination in Cairo, which sent everyone scrambling, just as I told you in Karachi. You've heard about the Russians shipping S-300 missiles and nuclear technology to Iran? Now I'll tell you something you don't know. There was a secret protocol to the agreement that in the event Iran had to stop weapons-grade uranium enrichment, either because of UN sanctions and outside pressure from the Americans and the Europeans, or because they couldn't get it to work, Russia would provide them with a plutonium reactor capable of producing weapons grade plutonium. Iran would dominate the

Middle East in unofficial partnership with the Russians. In effect, they would become OPEC, not to mention the possibility of nuclear war between Iran and Israel."

"And you know this because—of course, a high-placed Russian mole. I'm not the only double-edged sword."

"A mole in Moscow; well, we've been in that business for a long time," Harris said.

"Jesus, you combined them!" Scorpion shook his head as if to clear it. "The two missions. The one to stop the Russians and the one to stop the Palestinian."

"You have to understand," Harris said, putting his drink down. "The Russians were going to go through with the deal no matter what. Plus we had to deal with the Palestinian, a bioweapon attack that could kill millions and a nuclear terror attack, the ultimate nightmare. That's when we had the idea to combine them."

"Who's we?"

"Me, the DCIA. We kept it close."

"What about Rabinowich? Was he in on it?"

Harris didn't say anything.

"You son of a bitch," Scorpion said.

"Don't object too much, Scorpion. We're none of us virgins here," Harris said, and finished the rest of his whiskey. "All the scenarios led to war. We saw a chance to stop it and we took it."

Neither of them spoke. Scorpion looked through the window at the city lights. After a moment Harris stood up, got the Glenlivet and refreshed their drinks.

"So you diverted the Palestinian's operation to make it an attack by the Islamic Resistance, an Iranian surrogate, against Russia. That way the Russians would blame the Iranians. They would react to the attack the way we did to 9/11 and join with the West in blocking Iran from getting nuclear weapons or advanced missiles. That's why you needed the Mossad. And that's why the Palestinian showed up at the mosque in Utrecht. Because he didn't like the change in plan."

"The Israelis had the sleeper, Harandi, in place in Hamburg. He was at the communications hub for Hezbollah and Islamic Resistance. We used him to send messages between Dr. Abadi and the imam in Utrecht—by the way, we didn't know who they were; you're the one who found out; hell of a job." Harris raised his glass in salute. "That the Russians were going back on the deal, but were keeping the bribe."

"Najla said something just before she died," Scorpion said, half to himself.

"What?"

"That the Russians were reneging on a deal."

Harris nodded. "It wasn't true, but thanks to Harandi, the imam and Abadi thought it was true. We got each of them to think the other had changed the target to Saint Petersburg."

"But you still had one problem. The Palestinian."

"That's where you came in. The real danger was that the Palestinian would go rogue or run into a roadblock, and instead of following the orders he was getting from Utrecht and Hamburg, would launch an attack, say take out Rome or New York on his own. He could've been anywhere in the world. That part was true. We didn't know who he was and we didn't know about Najla Kafoury or that she was his sister and that there were two of them involved. Look, I know you're upset with me right now—"

"I'm not sure 'upset' is the word I'd use."

"You should thank me. You killed American agents, but I saved your ass. Thanks to me, officially, the men you killed in the Summer Garden in Saint Petersburg were Iranian agents. I shredded their 201s myself."

"Who were they really?"

Harris stared at his drink. "Iranian Americans. Sleepers. Patriots. Victims. They didn't know it, but it was a one-way mission. Whether it was you or Ivanov or the bomb going off, there was no way they were going to get out of Russia alive."

Scorpion took a sip of the whiskey and put his glass on a side table. "There's just one problem, Bob. The bomb was real. If I hadn't killed her, Najla would've set it off. Maybe a million people dead. Hassani was brilliant. You underestimated him."

Harris looked at him, his eyes sea-blue and utterly cold. "We didn't underestimate anybody," he said.

"You son of a bitch!" Scorpion snapped, jumping to his feet. "That's why you blew my cover in Castelnuovo and pulled me off the mission in Rome. To stop me so I couldn't prevent it from happening. You wanted the bomb to go off in Saint Petersburg! You wanted the Russians to go after the Iranians!

Let 'em kill each other! That was your wet dream, wasn't it?"

"Screw you! If you weren't the apple of the DCIA's eye right now, I'd burn you myself. Only a real attack would've convinced the Russians about the Iranians. Now we have to hope and pray that Ivanov tracking the bread crumbs back to the Islamic Resistance and the MOIS will convince them. You risked everything over a piece of Arab pussy!" Harris snapped back.

"A million dead! That doesn't matter? The end justifies the means, is that it?"

"Always."

"You know, I know why Najla and the Palestinian became who they were, but what rock did you crawl out from under?"

Harris stood up to confront Scorpion. "My job is to protect America. So is yours. If that means a lot of dead Russians, so be it. We stopped a possible world war. What you did was a betrayal. My conscience is clear. I sleep just fine."

Scorpion picked up his glass.

"I'm glad I stopped it. Thanks for the drink," he said, and started to drink, but instead threw the whiskey into Harris's face.

"That's a waste of good whiskey," Harris said, wiping the liquor from his eyes with his sleeve. "I was right about you. You're a sentimentalist. You still believe in right and wrong. You're in the wrong business."

"Change your shirt. You've got whiskey all over it," Scorpion said, and left.

Harris made his way to the bathroom. He took off his shirt and washed his face and hands in the sink. He wiped his face with a towel and went back into the living room.

Something drew him to the window. He went over and looked down at Fifth Avenue, still busy with people and traffic far below. He wondered if Scorpion would go to the DCIA. Then he thought, the DCIA was a political appointment. They came and went, but he would stay. For a moment he thought he saw Scorpion walking away from the hotel. He blinked and tried to spot him again, but Scorpion had disappeared in the crowd.

U.S., RUSSIA ISSUE JOINT STATEMENT
ON IRAN SANCTIONS
By Thomas Cohen and Jason Wilson,
Special to the *New York Times*.

MOSCOW—U.S. Secretary of State Jane Hinton and Russian Prime Minister Sergei Dimitriyov issued a joint statement on Tuesday on an agreement to impose severe new economic sanctions on Iran. The new sanctions cover a broad range of activities, including restrictions on international travel by Iranian officials and scientists and on companies doing business with Iran, a ban on the export of gasoline and other refined fuels to Iran, and strict oversight on international financial and banking transactions with Iran. Any exports to Iran involving nuclear material and technology or advanced weaponry are strictly banned under the new agreement.

These sanctions are considered a reversal of Russia's prior policy on Iran. Russia had previously opposed the imposition of stricter sanctions long advocated by the United States and its major European partners, France, Germany, and Great Britain. As Iran's principal supplier of fissionable material, nuclear technology, and military hardware, such as the advanced S-300 missile system, analysts believe that Russia's agreement will have a significant impact on the Iranian economy and on Iran's nuclear and military ambitions.

It is believed that this agreement will also affect the ability of the Iranians to make the new atomic reactors at Bushehr fully operational, since these reactors were being built under a contract with the Russians.

Among the permanent members of the UN Security Council, only China now still opposes heavier sanctions on Iran.

When asked what caused the change in the Russian policy, Prime Minister Dimitriyov stated that this was not really a change in Russia's position, which has always opposed nuclear proliferation. He added that the declaration was in response to the latest IAEA report to the UN Security Council on Iran's uranium enrichment program.

Secretary of State Hinton stated: "This breakthrough was achieved not through military action or the work of intelligence agencies, but through long, hard diplomatic efforts by both Russia and the United States. Military power and intelligence services are useful tools and they have their place, but nothing can replace the importance of the everyday work of diplomacy in resolving serious international problems."

 **GLOSSARY**

Mabahith. The Egyptian domestic intelligence service, aka Mabahith Amn al-Dawla al-Ulya, aka State Security Intelligence (SSI). The Mabahith is responsible for internal security and counterintelligence for the Egyptian government. The Mabahith should not be confused with the Mukhabarat, aka Jihaz al-Mukhabarat al-Amma, aka General Intelligence Service (GIS), which is Egypt's external intelligence service, the equivalent of the Egyptian CIA. There have been allegations that the Mabahith's primary function is to provide security for Egypt's current regime and that it has engaged in the persecution of political opponents, Islamists, Christians, Jews, and homosexuals.

CST. The CIA's Clandestine Service Training Program. While most CIA trainees go through the CIA's Professional Training Program, only those CIA employees slated for the clandestine Special Activities Division field operations go through the additional one-year CST training.

Hezbollah and the Muslim Brothers. The Muslim Brotherhood is a jihadist organization with branches or related groups in nearly all countries with significant Muslim populations. Founded in Egypt in 1928, its stated goal is the reestablishment of the Islamic caliphate under strict sharia law. The Muslim Brotherhood has been linked to acts of terrorism in Egypt and elsewhere and has ties to other Sunni jihadist organizations, such as al-Qaida. Hamas, the organization that currently rules the Gaza Strip, is a Palestinian offshoot of the Muslim Brotherhood. Although once illegal in Egypt and subject to arrest by Egyptian authorities, Brotherhood members have won seats in the Egyptian parliament. Since the overthrow of the Mubarak regime in 2011, the Muslim Brotherhood has attempted to present itself as a legitimate Egyptian political party. On the other hand, Hezbollah is an Iranian-sponsored Shi'ite paramilitary and political movement based in Lebanon. It was founded in 1982 in the aftermath of the First Israeli-Lebanon War as a resistance movement against Israel. The reason for Scorpion's initial skepticism about Hezbollah and the Muslim Brotherhood is that they are on opposite sides of the Shi'a-Sunni divide, and apart from their common hatred of Israel, are rivals, not allies. Harris, speaking for Rabinowich, suggests this may have changed; a potentially dangerous development in the Middle East.

COMINT. Acronym for Communications Intelligence; that is, intelligence derived from the interception of electronic or voice communications.

MASINT. Acronym for Measurement and Signature Intelligence; that is, intelligence derived from the analysis of technical data, such as the spectrographic analysis of the fuel exhaust of an enemy's new rocket. MASINT is sometimes referred to as the CSI of the intelligence community.

DNI. Acronym for the Director of National Intelligence. This position, established post-9/11, acts as head of the U.S. Intelligence community (IC) and reports directly to the U.S. President. Affiliated IC agencies (aka "elements") reporting to the DNI include the CIA, DIA, and other Department of Defense intelligence agencies; NSA, Department of Energy's OICI, Department of Homeland Security, FBI, DEA, Department of State's INR, and Department of Treasury's OTFI (Office of Terrorism and Financial Intelligence). The DNI's office is responsible for preparing the President's Daily Brief (PDB).

DIA. Acronym for the Defense Intelligence Agency. The DIA is the agency tasked with supplying and managing military intelligence for the U.S. Department of Defense.

Special Access Critical operation. A level above the highest security classification (Top Secret), a Special Access Program is a Top Secret operation that may be designated by the Director of the CIA (DCIA) to deal with an exceptional threat or intelligence action for which access to information on the operation is limited to as few Top Secret Clearance personnel as is absolutely necessary. "Critical" is the highest level of operational urgency.

The Farm. Camp Peary, aka Camp Swampy, is a CIA covert training facility of nearly 10,000 acres near Williamsburg, Virginia. Contrary to popular opinion and its portrayal in movies, only a portion of CIA training is actually done at the Farm (also see "The Point" below).

FSB. The Federal Security Service of the Russian Federation, aka FSB, is the primary Russian counterintelligence and domestic security service. It is the successor organization to the KGB of Cold War fame and is headquartered in the former KGB headquarters building, aka Lubyanka Prison, aka Adult's World, in Lubyanka Square in Moscow. After the fall of the Soviet Union, the KGB was dismantled. Subsequently, the FSB was reconstituted as Russia's primary domestic security agency, while the SVR, the Russian Foreign Intelligence Service, Sluzhba Vneshney Razvedk, was reconstituted from the KGB's First Chief Directorate as the Russian external intelligence service. The SVR is headquartered in the Moscow suburb of Yasenevo.

RSA. A security mechanism developed by the security division of EMC, a major data storage company. RSA is designed to prevent hackers or unauthorized persons from accessing a website by requiring the user to enter not only a password to log in, but also a randomly generated number (which changes every sixty seconds). A token key carried by the user supplies this multidigit number that provides time-synchronous authentication with software at the website. As an added security measure, intelligence services such as the CIA also provide a special pass-word to field agents to signal if they are forced to log in under duress.

Scorpion's "strange interrupted childhood in the desert of Arabia." For readers not familiar with the first novel in the series, *Scorpion*, Scorpion's (real name: Nick Curry) American parents divorced when he was an infant. His mother was killed in a car accident in California and his oilman father took the child with him when he went to explore for new oil fields in the Arabian Desert. When his father's team was killed by terrorists, the boy was rescued by Bedouin tribesmen. Afraid the Saudi and American authorities would blame them for the deaths of the Americans, they decided to raise the boy as one of the tribe. This Arabian Huck Finn–like childhood gave the boy a unique perspective, as well as language and culture skills that would make him invaluable as a CIA operative. These skills were further enhanced by his stints at Tehran University, Harvard University, and the U.S. Army Rangers and Delta Force in Afghanistan, prior to his recruitment by the CIA, which he subsequently left to become an independent agent. The theme of his life would be his sense of himself as an outsider, never quite sure where he belonged, to America and the West, or to Asia and the Middle East.

CQC. Close Quarter Combat; Delta Force and Navy SEAL martial-arts techniques distilled from a variety of disciplines, including Krav Maga, Muay Thai, Sambo, and Brazilian jiu-jitsu.

The Houdini trick. A world-famous magician and illusionist of the early twentieth century, Harry Houdini was known for his death-defying escapes from prison cells, from inside locked bank safes, from a straitjacket while dangling upside down from the top of a building, from a locked trunk tied with ropes and dropped into a frozen river, and most famously, from the Chinese Water Torture Cell. Houdini often performed these escapes wearing only a bathing suit, as a way of proving that he was not concealing any tools or other trickery. The secret to many of his escapes involved his use of lock picks or keys that he concealed in his hair or had previously swallowed and then regurgitated. He also learned to dislocate his shoulders to assist him in escaping from ropes and straitjackets. What Scorpion was referring to was one of Houdini's more mystifying yet simplest tricks, in which he escaped from inside a large sealed paper bag without tearing the paper. Houdini accomplished this by concealing a razor blade and gum arabic in his hair. Once behind the curtain, he simply cut the bag at the top, where it had been sealed, stepped out and resealed it. The committee that examined the bag after the escape typically looked for holes or tears in the paper and missed the fact that the razor blade opening had been folded over and resealed.

The Eighth Imam. Shia Muslims believe in a hereditary imamate in a line descending from Ali, the Prophet Muhammad's son-in-law and companion. Imam Reza (765-816 AD), the Eighth Imam in this line, was designated as a successor to the Caliphate by Caliph Al Mamun. However, during a military campaign to retake Baghdad from Al Mamun's rivals, Imam Reza died suddenly, leading many Shia to suspect that the caliph had poisoned Reza out of jealousy for his popularity. Reza was the only Imam of the Shi'ites to die in Iran. A shrine was established at his tomb, and eventually the city of Mashhad in northeastern Iran grew up around the shrine, which is today a major pilgrimage site for Iranian Muslims.

201 File. CIA employees and nonemployees considered "intelligence assets" have 201 files. While these files are often considered equivalent to personnel files, they are, more correctly, information profiles. Peters's threat about Scorpion's 201 file is an idle one since Scorpion is an independent agent, not an employee, and his operation was "Special Access"—at the highest security level—so that even a CIA Station Chief like Peters may not have had access to it.

NRO. The National Reconnaissance Office, a U.S. Department of Defense agency, operates the spy satellites that supply satellite data for all U.S. intelligence agencies.

FSU. Acronym for the Former Soviet Union.

Kimura shoulder lock. A Brazilian jiu-jitsu submission hold that applies pressure that can inflict
extreme pain to the shoulder joint. The lock is
typically done starting from a ground position, as
are many Brazilian holds. However, it can also be
done from other positions and there are a number
of variations in how it is applied. The basic hold involves grabbing the opponent's wrist and twisting it
away from his body, placing your other arm over the
opponent's shoulder and down, grabbing your own
wrist while holding his wrist and then shifting your
body, depending on your original position. The
submission involves applying pressure and pushing
the opponent's wrist and arm toward his back, or if
on the ground, locking his arm with your leg and
then applying pressure. The "Kimura" was named
after the *judoka* Masahiko Kimura, who used it in
a legendary match to defeat one of the founders of
Brazilian jiu-jitsu, Hélio Gracie.

**Plague, antibiotic resistant bacteria, bioweap-
ons, and new antibiotics.** Pathogens increasingly
resistant to antibiotics (due to overprescription of
antibiotics in both humans and livestock, natural
adaptation, and other causes) have become a very serious public health concern. Antibiotics are the only
treatment for many bacterial infections, including
Yersinia pestis (the plague bacteria). Certain antibiotics, such as vancomycin and polymyxin, are considered the antibiotics of last resort, despite potentially
serious side effects. However, these "last resort" an-

tibiotics are only effective on gram-positive bacteria (which can be stained with violet dye because of the nature of the bacterium's cell wall) and have limited or no effect on gram-negative bacteria (bacteria that cannot be stained). Plague is gram negative. There is no plague vaccine.

This novel hypothesizes a weaponized Septicemic plague bacteria that is resistant to all antibiotics, except one in development by a Swiss pharmaceutical company. (Few drug companies develop antibiotics. Most drug companies prefer to develop more profitable medications that require regular use, such as statins, as opposed to less profitable drugs that are typically only used once or occasionally, such as antibiotics.) Both the Swiss drug company and the antibiotic cited in this novel, Ceftomyacole, are fictional, as is the weaponized Septicemic plague. However, it is true that the Soviet Union created bioweapon facilities on what was then Vozrozhdeniya Island (today a peninsula in the inland Aral Sea between Kazakhstan and Uzbekistan), where bioweapons based on anthrax and plague pathogens were developed. There were other bioweapon facilities in Siberia. After the collapse of the Soviet Union, as suggested in this novel, Russian bioweapon facilities were primarily relocated to the Sverdlovsk oblast region.

Al Jabbar. The constellation Orion, called the "Central One" by Arabs in the pre-Islamic era, later called "al Jabbar," the Giant. Much of what we know about astronomy came from the Arabs, who during the Golden Age of Islam (the ninth to fifteenth centuries) translated early Greek texts, which would have otherwise been lost (such as the works of Ptolemy), into Arabic and then expanded upon that knowledge. This is reflected in the many astronomical and navigational terms derived from Arabic, such as zenith, nadir, azimuth (from the Arabic term, *as-samth*, meaning way or bearing), almanac (from the Arabic, *al-mnaakh*), etc., and star names, such as Algol (in the constellation Perseus), Deneb (Cygnus), Rigel (Orion), Aldebaran (Taurus), Betelgeuse (a corruption of the Arabic *baith al jawza*, or armpit of the Central One; in the constellation Orion), and Vega (Lyra). The picture of the al Jabbar constellation shown is from an original drawing commissioned by the author to his specifications for this book. All rights to this image are reserved by the author, Andrew Kaplan.

Explosives: HMTD, cell phones, and nuclear. Although a great deal of authentic information has been included in this book, some has been deliberately omitted, for reasons including public safety and national security, although such information is available elsewhere. As indicated in the story, HMTD (hexamethylene triperoxide diamine) is a powerful explosive that can readily be made from three ordinary household products, all of which are sold legally over the counter for other purposes and are widely available; the compound's main drawback is its extreme volatility, particularly to temperature. Similarly, the rigging of a cell phone to detonate an explosive is not fully described. Also, certain details about the procedure for building a nuclear bomb have been omitted, without which the probability of a successful detonation is less likely. That said, the key preventative against terrorists obtaining a working nuclear device is by preventing them from getting their hands on a large enough quantity of sufficiently pure fissionable material. If that should ever happen, the so-called "nightmare scenario" would become almost inevitable.

Vigenère Square Code. The Vigenère Square was invented by Blaise de Vigenère, a sixteenth century French diplomat. Although old fashioned, Scorpion uses it as an expedient because it's a quick way to create a code that's difficult to break and that can be composed anywhere with just a pen and paper. The Vigenère Square was designed to foil the ability of code-breakers to break a code based on frequency analysis, which up to that time had been the Achilles' heel of secret codes. Medieval cryptanalysts were often able to break codes that substituted numbers, symbols, or letters of the alphabet for other letters based on the frequency that letters appear in a given language. For example, in English, the letter e is the most common letter, then t, and so on. Also, certain letters may appear as doubles or in combinations, such as qu, ee, ou, th, whereas certain other letters, such as ii, virtually never appear as doubles. The most famous example of breaking codes with frequency analysis was in the case of Mary, Queen of Scots, whose doom was sealed when her secret letters, written in code, were deciphered in this way.

The Vigenère Square limits the ability to decipher code in this way because a different row of the square is used to encrypt each letter, so that the letter a, for instance, can be encoded in one place in the message as D, in another place as a *Q*, and so on. The square consists of a plain text alphabet at the top and letters shifted one place over in each row, as shown below (there are numerous representations of the Vigenère Square from various sources on the Web; the example below was created by the author, Andrew Kaplan).

Plain Text	a	b	c	d	e	f	g	h	i	j	k	l	m	n	o	p	q	r	s	t	u	v	w	x	y	z
1	B	C	D	E	F	G	H	I	J	K	L	M	N	O	P	Q	R	S	T	U	V	W	X	Y	Z	A
2	C	D	E	F	G	H	I	J	K	L	M	N	O	P	Q	R	S	T	U	V	W	X	Y	Z	A	B
3	D	E	F	G	H	I	J	K	L	M	N	O	P	Q	R	S	T	U	V	W	X	Y	Z	A	B	C
4	E	F	G	H	I	J	K	L	M	N	O	P	Q	R	S	T	U	V	W	X	Y	Z	A	B	C	D
5	F	G	H	I	J	K	L	M	N	O	P	Q	R	S	T	U	V	W	X	Y	Z	A	B	C	D	E
6	G	H	I	J	K	L	M	N	O	P	Q	R	S	T	U	V	W	X	Y	Z	A	B	C	D	E	F
7	H	I	J	K	L	M	N	O	P	Q	R	S	T	U	V	W	X	Y	Z	A	B	C	D	E	F	G
8	I	J	K	L	M	N	O	P	Q	R	S	T	U	V	W	X	Y	Z	A	B	C	D	E	F	G	H
9	J	K	L	M	N	O	P	Q	R	S	T	U	V	W	X	Y	Z	A	B	C	D	E	F	G	H	I
10	K	L	M	N	O	P	Q	R	S	T	U	V	W	X	Y	Z	A	B	C	D	E	F	G	H	I	J
11	L	M	N	O	P	Q	R	S	T	U	V	W	X	Y	Z	A	B	C	D	E	F	G	H	I	J	K
12	M	N	O	P	Q	R	S	T	U	V	W	X	Y	Z	A	B	C	D	E	F	G	H	I	J	K	L
13	N	O	P	Q	R	S	T	U	V	W	X	Y	Z	A	B	C	D	E	F	G	H	I	J	K	L	M
14	O	P	Q	R	S	T	U	V	W	X	Y	Z	A	B	C	D	E	F	G	H	I	J	K	L	M	N
15	P	Q	R	S	T	U	V	W	X	Y	Z	A	B	C	D	E	F	G	H	I	J	K	L	M	N	O
16	Q	R	S	T	U	V	W	X	Y	Z	A	B	C	D	E	F	G	H	I	J	K	L	M	N	O	P
17	R	S	T	U	V	W	X	Y	Z	A	B	C	D	E	F	G	H	I	J	K	L	M	N	O	P	Q
18	S	T	U	V	W	X	Y	Z	A	B	C	D	E	F	G	H	I	J	K	L	M	N	O	P	Q	R
19	T	U	V	W	X	Y	Z	A	B	C	D	E	F	G	H	I	J	K	L	M	N	O	P	Q	R	S
20	U	V	W	X	Y	Z	A	B	C	D	E	F	G	H	I	J	K	L	M	N	O	P	Q	R	S	T
21	V	W	X	Y	Z	A	B	C	D	E	F	G	H	I	J	K	L	M	N	O	P	Q	R	S	T	U
22	W	X	Y	Z	A	B	C	D	E	F	G	H	I	J	K	L	M	N	O	P	Q	R	S	T	U	V
23	X	Y	Z	A	B	C	D	E	F	G	H	I	J	K	L	M	N	O	P	Q	R	S	T	U	V	W
24	Y	Z	A	B	C	D	E	F	G	H	I	J	K	L	M	N	O	P	Q	R	S	T	U	V	W	X
25	Z	A	B	C	D	E	F	G	H	I	J	K	L	M	N	O	P	Q	R	S	T	U	V	W	X	Y
26	A	B	C	D	E	F	G	H	I	J	K	L	M	N	O	P	Q	R	S	T	U	V	W	X	Y	Z

The way the square works to create a code is through the use of a keyword known only to the sender and the receiver of the code. In the example in this book, the keyword used was YANKES, for the New York Yankees baseball team without duplicate letters. To encrypt the phrase, "confirm agent," the person creating the code would spell the keyword over the message, repeated as needed. For example:

> *Keyword*: Y A N K E S Y A N K E S
> *Plain Text*: C O N F I R M A G E N T

To code the message, go to the row corresponding to the keyword letter. For example, for the plain text letter c, the keyword letter above it is Y. The person creating the code would go to row 24, the row that starts with Y. At the top of the table find the plain text letter you want to encrypt, in this case c, and the letter in row 24 that corresponds to c is *A*. For the second plain text letter of the message, o, you would use the keyword letter A, which starts in row 26, where the plain text letter o happens to correspond to O. For the third letter of the message, n, go to row 13, which starts with keyword letter N, where the plain text letter n corresponds to A, and so on. The plain text message "confirm agent" would be sent as: AOAPMJKATOL. The code is resistant to frequency analysis, and without the keyword there are billions of possible combinations, enough to slow any code breaker down.

The Black House, NSA headquarters. The National Security Agency/Central Security Service (NSA/CSS) is headquartered in the "Black House," aka the Black Building, aka the Building, so-called because of the color of the rectangular building's window glass. The building is located on the grounds of the Fort Meade army base in Maryland. There are also facilities in Texas, Georgia, Utah, and elsewhere. The NSA is the U.S. intelligence agency primarily responsible for COMINT (see above), cryptanalysis, computer intelligence, and security. The NSA's partner agency, the Central Security Service (CSS) is responsible for coordinating cryptanalysis and related activities between the NSA and the Department of Defense agencies also engaged in such work. For many years the U.S. government refused to acknowledge NSA's existence, leading Washington insiders to quip that the letters NSA stood for "No Such Agency."

SAIC. Special Agent in Charge; the FBI designation for the agent in charge of a local FBI office. FBI Supervisory Special Agents typically head FBI HRTs (Hostage Rescue Teams).

The Point. Also known as Harvey Point, aka Harvey Point Defense Testing Activity Facility; this is a CIA training facility near Hertford, North Carolina. As previously noted, only part of CIA training is conducted at the Farm (see above). The CIA's Directorate of Operations uses the Point for training in specialized covert operations and paramilitary skills (the so-called Black Arts), such as breaking into buildings, "snatch and grab" (recovery of friendly or hostile persons), CQB (Close Quarter Battle—fighting with weapons in close quarters), EOD (Explosive Ordnance Disposal) and AET (Applied Explosive Techniques), etc. Other organizations, such as the DIA , the ATF (Bureau of Alcohol, Tobacco, Firearms and Explosives), the FBI, the U.S. Navy SEALs, and the U.S. Army's Delta Force sometimes do specialized covert training at the Point.

Sabra and Shatila massacre. The massacre of Palestinian and Lebanese civilians at the Sabra and Shatila refugee camps in West Beirut in September 1982 was carried out by the Lebanese Forces Christian Phalangist militia following the assassination of the Christian Phalangist leader and president-elect of Lebanon, Bashir Gemayel. The number of persons killed, as with much about this event, has been disputed, with estimates ranging from 328 to 3,500 dead. Although the actual killing was carried out by Lebanese Christians, many in the international community placed much of the blame for the massacre on Israel. It was claimed that the Israeli leadership and the Israeli Defense Force, whose soldiers surrounded the camps after the expulsion of the Palestine Liberation Organization (PLO) from Lebanon, should have foreseen what the Phalangists would do when the Israelis allowed them into the camps after Gemayel's assassination, and that once the massacre started, the Israelis were slow to act to stop the killing. Within Israel, massive street demonstrations demanding an inquiry led to the creation of the Kahan Commission, whose report concluded that while no Israelis participated in the massacre, Israel bore an indirect responsibility for not acting sooner to end the massacre. The report placed "personal responsibility" on Ariel Sharon, who was forced to resign as Minister of Defense.

In August 1983, Israeli Prime Minister Menahem Begin retired from political life. The story of the brother and sister and the account of the massacre from a child's point of view was part of the author's conception of this novel from the very beginning.

 **ACKNOWLEDGMENTS**

No work exists in a vacuum. This book would not have seen the light of day were it not for the exceptional efforts of my agent, Dominick Abel, the best I've ever known, and my editor, David Highfill, who went the extra mile. Thank you both for your belief in this book and in me. I must also acknowledge my wife, Anne, and son, Justin, without whose help, support, and honest criticism the outcome would not have been nearly as positive. Thank you all.